To Peter,

I hope you

enjoy the Story!

THE
IMMORTAL
GAME

JOANNAH MILEY

Second Story Publishing

Second Story Publishing
secondstorypublishing.com

Contact the author at joannahmiley.com

Publisher's Note: This is a work of fiction. Names, characters, places, and incidents are a product of the author's imagination. Locales and public names are sometimes used for atmospheric purposes. Any resemblance to actual people, living or dead, or to businesses, companies, events, institutions, or locales is completely coincidental.

Cover Design by Pintado
Developmental Editing by Drew Cherry
Copy Editing by Virginia Herrick, Kestrel's Way Editorial Services
Book Layout ©2013 BookDesignTemplates.com

Ordering Information:
Special discounts are available on quantity purchases by schools, libraries, associations, and others. For details, contact the publisher at the web address listed above.

The Immortal Game/ Joannah Miley. -- 1st ed.
ISBN 978-0-9860555-2-2 (pbk.)

For Fran and Hope

How did I get so lucky?

"Every pawn is a potential queen."

—James Mason

ONE

"DO YOU PLAY?" the barista asked as Ruby approached the espresso counter at the back of the bookstore.

"Huh?" Ruby blinked. Her mind was still stuck on the organic chemistry chapter she had been reading at her table by the window.

The barista nodded her mass of dark spiral curls in the direction of the chess table to the right of the counter.

Usually a crowd hovered around the board, but tonight there were only a few stragglers watching Ash play a man Ruby didn't recognize. It had been three days since the Rogue terrorist attack killed a dozen people and knocked out both the landlines and the cell towers throughout the Northwest.

The war, which was safely across the world for over a decade, had unexpectedly blown up on the outskirts of Portland and most people were still holed up at home.

"Do you play?" the barista repeated as if picking up the thread of a casual conversation.

"Sure." Ruby shrugged. She scanned the chalkboard menu with the words *Athenaeum Books: Used and Rare* drawn in swooping green letters across the top.

"You should play Ash," the barista said as she opened a bag of coffee beans. "You've been here for hours. Take a break from studying." The whole beans clinked in rapid-fire succession against the plastic sides of the coffee grinder, nearly drowning out the tail end of her words.

The rich aroma reminded Ruby of lazy Sunday mornings playing with her father. Chess had been his favorite game, one of the few he liked to play between his long trips away. She pictured his wide smile poised over the rim of his coffee cup and the way sunlight turned his brown eyes, the same color as hers, a golden shade of honey.

She stole a furtive glance at the chess table. Ash's opponent flashed a peace sign as he rose to leave with his friends, but Ash was busy putting the man's captured white marble pieces back on the board and didn't notice.

Ruby didn't think Ash was a student. She only knew his name because of the constant chatter of the college girls who fawned over him and because of his reputation for being unbeatable. She winced when she saw the back of his left hand. It was a livid shade of red and the skin was puckered along a deep maroon furrow that ran from pinky to wrist at a diagonal.

"Sage, you want to play?" he asked without looking up from the board.

"No. I don't want to play," the barista said. "I'm helping a customer." She sounded annoyed, like she'd been asked too many times already.

Ash's turquoise eyes darted up to Ruby and she felt herself stiffen. His white T-shirt set off his dark complexion. A loose tangle of black curls framed his angular face. "Do you want to play?" he asked.

"I ... I can't," she stammered at the unexpected invitation. There was usually a line of people waiting to play him. "I have to study."

"A quick game," he said to one of them, although Ruby couldn't tell who he was talking to. His injured hand came up to rub his temple. "I'm leaving soon anyway."

"Of course you are. Your mistress is high maintenance." Sage flipped the coffee grinder's switch and filled the air with a loud whirring. Ash glanced at the night-darkened windows that made up the front wall of the room.

Ruby looked that way too, but all she saw were the red and orange lights of Inferno Wood Fire Pizza blazing from across the street. No cars passed by. No one came or went through the restaurant's large wooden doors.

Sage turned to Ruby when the grinder finished. "What can I get you?"

"Vanilla latte, please," she said, ignoring the odd exchange between the barista and the chess master.

"Like I said, you should play him." Sage reached for a plain white mug. "I'll throw in an Ambrosia Bar. You're in here enough. We'll call it customer appreciation."

Ash sat back in his chair with his ankles crossed and his long legs stretched out to the side of the table. His injured hand rested in a loose fist on his thigh. The chess board was set up for the next game.

Ruby hadn't seriously considered playing. It had been so long.

She looked at her table across the room near the window. The top was covered with books. The organic chemistry chapter sat open and she had a week's worth of reading to do for western civ.

The bombing had not kept her from going to class or from following her strict studying schedule. If the war was ramping up, she needed to be even more focused. She knew she should go home and study, but the quiet there was stifling.

She glanced back to Ash, looking at her. Waiting.

Ruby moved a white pawn out.

Ash matched it.

She moved another, sacrificing it to offer a King's Gambit.

He accepted and took her piece.

"How did you get so good?" she asked.

"Instinct." His voice was deep and a little husky. His attention remained on the worn black and white marble chessboard between them.

She moved a bishop, deliberately leaving her king open.

Ash brought out his queen. "Check," he said, sounding tired, or irritated, or both.

She took a sip of her latte, but quickly put it back down. She felt too warm already. She moved her king to safety and picked at the brown Ambrosia Bar next to her. "Who taught you to play?"

His eyes met hers but he didn't answer. She knew that serious chess was played in silence, but not usually a friendly game in a coffee shop, and definitely not when she played her father.

She glanced at his injured hand and saw that it wasn't as bad as she had originally thought. The skin was a light pink. The gash wasn't too deep, but there was no doubt that he should have gotten stitches.

"I used to play with my dad," she said, pulling her eyes away from the injury. "Before he was killed in the war."

Ash's good hand stopped with his knight pinched between his fingers. "The war, huh?"

She wasn't sure why she said it. She hadn't told anyone here, not at Athenaeum, not in the study group, not in any of her classes. She kept to herself mostly. A pre-med major—and the three-point-five GPA she needed for medical school—was a stretch for her, she knew that. When it came to research or writing, the A's came easy. When it came to math or molecules, there was work to be done and redone.

Ruby glanced across the room. Low lamps hung over the empty tables. Floor-to-ceiling bookshelves lined three walls of the rectangular room. Horizontal stacks of books lay on top of the crowded vertical rows and she could smell the aged paper under the strong aroma of fresh-brewed espresso.

"Was he Army?" Ash asked, still holding the black marble horse poised over the board.

She shook her head. "He was a doctor. With Medics for Mercy."

He set the knight down but he held Ruby's stare. "How?"

How? "You mean ... how did he die?"

Ash's face was steady.

"It was a roadside bomb," she said, matter-of-fact. "He was treating wounded civilians when a second charge went off. His entire team was killed."

"He's a hero," Ash said.

"He was brave. I know that." The word *hero* always left her cold, and still fatherless, no matter how well-meaning the sentiment. She broke away from his gaze and moved her knight, letting the familiarity of the game take over. "He died helping people," she said after a long pause. Her father had told her helping people was what really mattered in the world.

Ash didn't say anything more and Ruby was happy with the silence.

He took her bishop with a lowly pawn. In the next few moves he took her queen as well. He sat deep in his chair and put the fingers of his wounded hand to his lips as if contemplating his next move. As if planning the impending win.

Ruby's eyes lingered at his mouth, then went to the long gash on his hand, and from there to a simple black ring on his fourth finger. The ring was pitted and old looking. A smile passed over her lips as she pictured the women swarming around him. She thought of Sage's irritation about his "high maintenance" girlfriend. *Not a girlfriend*, she realized, *a wife*.

Ash was looking at her. She dropped the smile and nodded at his hand. "What happened?"

He cocked his head to one side as if confused. He looked to where she had motioned. "It's nothing." He leaned forward and put the injured hand below the tabletop. His attention returned to the game.

"It will heal faster if you—"

"Your move," he said without looking up.

Her head pulled back in surprise at his abruptness. She moved her bishop and checked the position of her knights. She looked across the table at the same time Ash looked up, dark eyebrows coming down low over blazing blue eyes.

She grinned. "Checkmate."

ॐ

Athenaeum was quiet when Ruby walked in the next morning, too early for book buyers, too early for most coffee drinkers. Sage smiled at her from a table she was wiping near the door. "What happened last night?" she asked. "He's been going over your game for hours." She motioned to the back where Ash sat alone, moving both white and black pieces on the board.

"Nothing," Ruby said. She swept a golden-brown tangle of windblown hair behind her ear and unzipped her rain jacket. "I mean ... I beat him, that's all."

"You beat him?" Sage's smile fell. She glanced at Ash and then back to Ruby. "How ...?" She shook her head. "Never mind." She slung the dishcloth over her shoulder and walked behind the counter.

"Can I have a latte?" Ruby asked. "And an Ambrosia Bar." She walked to a table and hoisted her heavy messenger bag onto its wooden top. Ash and his chess game had interrupted her study schedule. She had organic at eight and then western civ. She knew from Greek mythology the previous semester that Dr. Garcia loved to give pop quizzes; catching up on the reading was her first priority.

She turned to pay for her breakfast but stopped short when she saw Ash striding toward her through the deserted coffeehouse.

"Where did you learn that?" he said. There was no preamble. No *Hi* or *Good morning* or even an acknowledgment an entire night had gone by since their game.

"I ..." She trailed off, rattled by his demeanor. She shook her head and narrowed her eyes. "I don't know what you mean."

"How did you *beat* me?"

Heat rose into her cheeks despite the chilly autumn morning. "Hey, don't blame me if you have a problem with your game."

He reared back as if she had stabbed him with a knife, then scowled. "We need to play again."

He turned toward the back corner of the room clearly expecting her to follow.

"I can't. I have reading to do."

Ash turned toward her again and she stepped back at the fiery look in his eyes. He didn't say anything more and turned again to the chessboard.

"Really, *I can't.*" She threaded through the eclectic mix of mismatched chairs and tables toward the counter.

"I want you to walk me through what you did." It was like he hadn't heard her.

She took the coffee and Ambrosia Bar from Sage—who watched their conversation as if it were a volley in a tennis match—and walked back to her table.

Ash followed.

She took out her history text, sat down and crossed her arms, daring him to push further. "I told you," she said. "I have reading to do."

He pulled out a chair across from her. "I'll wait."

Her eyes shot to his face.

"What?"

He wasn't smiling, just staring.

She exhaled in a huff, flipped open the text, and searched for her page.

He sat back and crossed his arms over his chest. Dark circles shadowed his lower lids but his eyes were unwavering.

She did her best to ignore him and take in the finer points of the Battle of Hastings, but Ash's presence was distracting. When she glanced up, his determined look had not faltered. He seriously planned to wait her out.

She dropped her book flat onto the table with a loud thud and leaned forward. "I really can't concentrate on William the Conqueror and all of his..." She blinked. "... *conquering*, with you staring at me."

He sat forward too. A glimmer of recognition lit his hard eyes. Was he getting the hint after all?

"William? Of Normandy?" he asked.

She looked at the page, to a picture of a general astride his horse leading a regiment into battle. The caption read: "William the Conqueror leads the Norman army against King Harold II and the Saxons." She was about to nod, but Ash was already speaking.

"Now that was a battle." A smile turned up the corners of his mouth. "None of this dropping bombs from planes or shooting from inside armored tanks. It was man against man. Harold and his Saxons had the better position on the hill. Their shields overlapped and they held a steady front line, but they were tired from riding across the country."

She stared at him, but his eyes slid past her.

"William and the Normans were rested. And eager. They led with archers and followed with the infantry. Swords clashed with axes and thudded against shields. The shouts of the men were deafening." Ash's nostrils flared. "The cavalry at the rear held their horses back and waited for the signal from Will, who was at the center of everything."

Will? she wondered. *Will of Normandy?*

"The archers were soon whittled down and the cavalry descended. Early on there were rumors Will had been killed. His men faltered." Ash paused for effect. His eyes were on her. "He rode the ranks without his helmet, risking himself, and spurred the troops on. Will was new to battle." Ash smiled, his white teeth lined up like soldiers. "But he was a good leader of men.

"When Will realized the armies were well-matched, he called his men back. Harold took it for a retreat." Ash shook his head. "Harold was too cocky. He'd beaten his own brother's army just weeks before. Harold's troops followed Will's withdrawing men in an unorganized show of force. When Will turned his feigning soldiers onto Harold's broken ranks it was the beginning of the end, right there."

Ruby glanced at the picture in the book. It was like any other scene of a general in battle. William was in uniform with the troops around him, suspended forever in the moment before they met their fate: death or glory.

"And do you know what helped to start it all?" Ash asked. "Do you know that Halley's Comet helped William the Conqueror win the crown of England?"

All she managed was a small shake of her head. She was trying to take it all in; Ash's knowledge of the battle, his understanding of troop movements ... *Halley's Comet?*

"The comet was a bad omen," he said. "It gave Harold reason to worry and it gave William a reason to build his ships!" He laughed, a deep sound that resonated somewhere in her chest.

"It did turn out to be an unlucky day for Harold. In the evening there was a lull in the fighting. Harold heard the whiz of an arrow and looked up." Ash *tsk*ed and shook his head, but still smiled. "Got him right in the eye."

Ruby's face dropped. Anger filled the empty stunned space in her mind. "You think that's funny? All that killing." She thought of the bombs at the telephone exchanges and the cell towers, all those people dead. She thought of her father. She thought of the wound on Ash's hand. He had acted like it wasn't there the night before. Her eyes darted to the edge of the table but his hands were below the surface. She couldn't see if he had bothered to put a bandage on it or not. It might get infected.

"I have to go," she said as she packed up the book and wrapped the half-eaten Ambrosia Bar in a napkin.

"What about our game?" He moved his chair out as if to stop her.

"I don't have time."

His nostrils flared again, this time in anger rather than excitement. His jaw clenched. His eyes darted around as if he'd lost something that should be right in front of him.

She wondered what might come next. He acted like a man who could easily start punching a wall. The outline of muscle beneath his T-shirt told her that he had the strength to do some damage.

Instead his hand came up and rubbed at the dark stubble along his jaw.

What she saw made her stomach lurch. She stopped worrying about his temper and stared at his hand sliding back and forth.

Had it been *that* hand? The left? She knew it had. It had the same ring, dark and pitted, old looking. But where was the wound? It was gone.

There was nothing but a faint shiny line where the gash had been.

TWO

A COOL BREEZE rustled the gold and crimson leaves in the trees that lined the campus walkway and Ruby caught the woody scents of autumn. She unwrapped her half eaten Ambrosia Bar and ate it in two big bites as she walked. The chewy brown outside was the perfect contrast to the gooey golden filling and she was disappointed when it was gone. She consoled herself with a sip of her latte but it tasted flat and ordinary in comparison.

Extra police and security guards had patrolled the quads and the corridors since the telephone bombings, but the grip of panic had loosened as days went by without another attack. Now the wide concrete path became busier the closer Ruby got to the science quad.

Mendeleev Hall buzzed with people comparing stories of the bombing. Ruby picked up her graded exam from the pile at the front of the room and found her seat in the stadium-style lecture hall.

She put the quiz facedown on the desk and watched Dr. Reed, in his signature tartan sport coat, take a thick pile of papers out of his briefcase and ready himself for the lecture. She drummed her pencil on the tabletop and told herself that this grade wasn't *that* important. It was just a quiz, a preface to the weightier exam at the end of the week. But she knew she needed a ninety. She needed at least a three-point-five GPA.

She took a deep breath.

In a fit of courage she flipped the paper over and looked for the red number she knew would be neatly written in the upper left hand corner. Her face fell. She blinked. *Seventy?* She checked for her name at the top of the paper. This couldn't be *her* test. She must have picked up the wrong one. But it was hers.

She looked down at the questions, then at her answers. She had studied for days. How could she *not* know this stuff?

There was little time to dwell. Dr. Reed's tartan coat now hung from the back of a chair near the front of the room and his shirtsleeves were rolled up to his elbows. He wrote a series of molecules on the whiteboard. Ruby folded her quiz in half and jammed it between the pages of her textbook. She opened her notes and scrawled the complex shapes of the molecules as fast as she could.

After the lecture Mark caught her eye as she flexed her cramped right hand. He slipped out of the space between the desktop and the molded plastic chair and waved. "Hey, Ruby, wait up."

"How'd you do?" he asked as he pulled out his copy of the quiz in the crowded hall. "I got a ninety-five."

She had met Mark at her study group. His hair was gelled into a frenzy of short blond spikes and he had a painful looking pimple by his right ear. He rubbed the back of his neck and scanned his paper. "I can't believe I missed one. What did you get for number six?"

"I'd have to look," she said, avoiding eye contact. They passed the microbiology lab and she caught a sharp whiff of ripe bacteria, a cross between sweaty socks and moist cheese.

"I forgot to finish balancing my equation," he said. "Too many hydrogens in my product. I'll need to be careful on the exam Friday. Are you coming to the study group?"

"Yeah, of course. Why wouldn't I?" She glanced at him, wondering if maybe she wasn't invited.

"You want to get a coffee or something before?" he said, a little too quickly.

"Nah." She looked down at the glossy grey- and brown-flecked floor. "I'll probably just study."

"Yeah." He cleared his throat and nodded. "Me too."

Mark had asked her to coffee before, and to the movies, and to a party once, but her focus was school. It had to be. Her father's legacy was her driving force. She would be a doctor. She would dedicate her life to helping people in war-torn countries. Helping people was what mattered.

∽◉∾

Dr. Garcia's rendition of the Battle of Hastings was drier than Ash's, all dates and locations. He mentioned that William the Conqueror rode through the fighting without his helmet to reassure his troops he hadn't been killed.

Ruby wondered if Ash was a chess master *and* a history buff. Maybe he was a genius.

She thought about the wound, or the lack of a wound, on his hand. Had there been a big open gash there? Yesterday? *Last night?* Of course there had. She hadn't just imagined it.

In the end Dr. Garcia confirmed everything Ash said— even the part about Halley's Comet, when Ruby asked about it. It wasn't the fact that Ash knew minor details about a war that happened a thousand years ago that struck her as odd. It was *how* he knew them. Like he'd been there.

Dr. Garcia asked if there were more questions and Ruby had plenty, but none that he could answer.

❧

After class Ruby walked to Athenaeum, two blocks off campus. She started directly for the chess table in the back. She'd play Ash again, but this time *she'd* get some answers.

Halfway there she stopped short. The chess board was set up but the seats were empty. She scanned the coffeehouse.

Athenaeum was more crowded than it had been in days. The room was once again filled with the familiar chatter of students in late afternoon, sipping coffee and eating Ambrosia Bars. Sage moved around the room, shelving books. She held one up in a gesture of hello. Ruby responded with a weak little wave. A tall man with close-cropped platinum blond hair read poetry from a black journal to a group of people near the window. She thought his name was Langston.

But there was no Ash.

It seemed like he had always been there before. But had he? She didn't know. She studied at Athenaeum most days, but she hadn't paid attention.

She wanted a coffee and an Ambrosia Bar, but instead of ordering she sat in a chair that faced the wood-framed glass door. She could hear Langston reading a poem over the din of the room. He was reciting something about love denied when a much closer voice broke in.

"I got to play him last week," a woman said to her friends at the table next to Ruby.

Ruby looked at them from the corner of her eye.

The woman who had spoken had dark hair and sipped her coffee without making eye contact with the other two women at her table. Her deliberate casualness only exaggerated the comment. "He's totally brilliant," she added as an after-thought.

"And *hot*," another one said.

Ruby heard honest-to-goodness giggles from all three of them.

She took out her chemistry notes and tried to focus. She'd spent too much energy on Ash already and not nearly enough on what was important.

"I know a girl who knows a girl who dated him," said another of the women, a petite blond.

Ruby's eyes widened at the intrusion into her thoughts. She leaned toward them, unable to help herself. "Ash's married, you know?"

The three women's heads swiveled in unison to stare at her. Ruby opened her mouth to elaborate, but it was Sage, shelving a book nearby, who spoke instead.

"Ash? Married?" She laughed, as if it were the most ridiculous idea she'd heard. "No. Not Ash."

"But he has a wedding ring." Ruby turned to face the barista. "And he had to leave here last night. To go to his wife. You said she was 'high maintenance.'"

Sage laughed harder and shook her head. Her black curls bounced on the collar of her white shirt. Her amethyst earrings swayed with the rhythm. "That's an entirely different sort of problem."

Ruby watched Sage's brown skirt swish as she walked back to her piles of books at the counter. The poet stopped reading and looked up from across the room. Ruby saw him make eye contact with Sage. She waved him away but she was still laughing.

There was no time to make sense of it all before Ruby realized that the three women were still looking at her.

The blond smirked. "Wrong much?"

Ruby looked down at the scuffed wooden floor. The tips of her ears burned. Where had her line of logic gone wrong? The ring, the …

The front door opened in a rush. The force of it rustled the papers hanging on a nearby bulletin board. Her head popped up and her heart thudded as she saw Ash striding toward her, tall and lithe.

He wore jeans and a black T-shirt, cowboy boots and dark sunglasses. She couldn't see his eyes, but he didn't waver from

"When can we play?" he asked. His voice was less forceful than before.

"Are you dense?" she asked. "I told you: I have to study. I'm not going to play you again."

He pulled the dark shades off his eyes and jabbed them at her. "I want a rematch."

She sucked in her breath at what she saw. His right eye was swollen shut with a gash that split the eyebrow. His other hand, the one with the ring, still lay on the table. She glanced down. The skin was smooth and unblemished. The scar was completely gone now. She dropped her own hand down on top of his, a reflex. "My god. Are you okay?"

He started, as if her touch had given him a shock. He looked at her hand resting on his. His one good eye darted back up to hers. The eye was glassy, feverish.

Quickly, or maybe slowly, the rest of the world faded. Sounds were muted and distant. Her only coherent perceptions were through their touching hands and their locked eyes. Everything on the periphery was a blur. She felt a jumbled wave of energy come off him, but it soon smoothed out and lengthened to a steady beat that could have been a pulse at rest. Time stretched out. It was just them in a frozen moment—

"What did you do to yourself, Ash?" The poet, Langston, stood next to the table with a hand on Ash's shoulder.

Startled, Ruby began to pull away. Her fingers trailed along Ash's hand. A chill shot up her arm. Her heart beat a steady rhythm. She felt calm and rooted, and oddly at peace.

"It's nothing," Ash said. He held Ruby's stare for another moment. His brow creased as if he might ask a question. Instead he put the glasses back on and got up from the table.

⁂

The next morning Ruby lay in bed with the empty house all around her. After her father died, she could have slept in the master bedroom, or in what had always been the nanny's room, but she chose to stay in the room she had been in since the day she was born.

The dollhouse her father built for her when she was three stood in the corner, with its happy family of five busy around the kitchen. Above the dollhouse were three shelves of polished rocks, each with a display tag naming the specimen. The rocks were a collection Ruby started in third grade but had abandoned by middle school.

She looked at the pictures on her nightstand. There was one of her father with his sandy blond hair, wearing khaki pants and a field jacket. She couldn't remember what country he had been in at the time. There were low scrub trees and a pale blue sky in the background.

The picture of Ruby's mother was in the back. Her mother had brown hair, like Ruby's, and she stood in the same room Ruby lay in now, but with a long-forgotten collection of stuffed animals in the background. She held an infant Ruby in her arms and smiled at the camera. A drunk driver had killed her soon after it was taken.

Ruby rolled over and tried to tempt herself out of bed with thoughts of coffee and Ambrosia Bars, of Athenaeum … and Ash.

No. Not today. She needed to concentrate.

She made drip coffee and ate takeout leftovers in the little yellow kitchen. Early sunlight filtered through the white lace curtains at the back door, making a filigreed pattern on the faded linoleum.

She studied for chemistry at the kitchen table and rode her bike to class. Thankfully, Dr. Reed reviewed for the exam in organic, and Ruby was ready when Dr. Garcia finally popped the quiz in western civ. She smiled as she wrote her answers about the Battle of Hastings and thought of how Ash helped her study for the test.

Mark offered a ride to the study group later that day but she thought biking would clear her mind and sharpen her focus. She headed out toward northeast Portland and rode down Fremont.

She was so much more agile and unrestricted on her bike than she would have been in a car and so much faster than she could have been on foot. She blew by long lines of traffic and paced herself so that she never had to stop for a red light. Dried leaves crackled under her tires. She got that feeling: like she was flying, like she could ride forever.

The stresses of school slid off her like oil off water. She floated on the top of it all, able to see it at a distance. Her grades: they *had* to be better. Medical School: applications were due in a few months. The war: she needed to help where she could.

Ash came into her mind too, sudden and unbidden. She pictured him sitting across from her, wanting to play chess. An emotion, huge and unnamed, caught in her throat. She began to push the image away, but then she pulled it back.

She tried to remember that feeling, her hand on his, and the way he looked at her. The way his eyes connected with hers. Yes, he was cute—*hot* one of the women at Athenaeum said. But there was more there, something that drew her in. A sense that—

She shook her head and pedaled faster. Who cared how Ash knew so much? Or why he always seemed to have just come from a bar fight? Or even why his hand healed too quickly? Who cared that he made her feel that way?

She rushed on into the clear autumn afternoon and let every thought slide past her mind like the ground that flew past her spinning tires.

ঔৡ৹

Ruby's normal route to the study group was blocked by several road closures. An officer redirecting traffic at one told her it was part of anti-terrorist maneuvers. "We'll keep them guessing," he said with a reassuring wink.

She turned down one residential street after another, looking for a main thoroughfare. The world here was silent, almost eerie. She didn't know this part of town well. In the end she doubled back to Fremont and ended up close to where she had started.

Her stomach growled. She stopped in front of a coffeehouse and leaned the frame of her bike against her hip.

For the first time since the bombing she wished she had cell service. She could have called Mark to accept the ride he had offered earlier, or at least warn him that the roads were closed.

The traffic on Fremont was backing up further and further with new cars trying to enter the crowded roadway at every intersection. This was the only thoroughfare open in this part of town. It would be too dangerous to ride in that kind of gridlock.

She looked up at the coffeehouse's minimalistic steel awnings and two walls of glass that came together in a sharp point at the corner. Her stomach growled again.

Inside, sleek wooden tables were spaced out on a grey concrete floor that reflected the sun coming in through the large windows. The menu board was written in stark neon marker. The earthy smell of coffee and the shriek of frothing milk made the austere coffeehouse feel familiar.

Ruby ordered a latte and a sandwich. She smiled awkwardly at the barista—a woman with purple hair and a face full of piercings—when her credit card was denied. She realized she forgot to pay the credit card bill and she hadn't transferred money from her trust account into checking either. She paid for her food with a fistful of crumpled bills she scrounged from the bottom of her bag.

"Iced vanilla latte?" called the barista, though Ruby was the only one waiting. The cool plastic cup felt refreshing under her warm palm. She took a long sip and savored the chilly sweetness.

She scanned the coffeehouse for a place to sit. A couple talked quietly in the middle of the room. Two teenage girls had their heads close together as they looked at a magazine near the back. A man sat alone by the wall-sized windows. His head was turned to the side, looking out. Her eye lingered, moved on, then shot back to him again. In slow motion her mind took in the curly black hair, the faded jeans, the dark sunglasses.

It was Ash.

THREE

RUBY'S HEART WAS FIXED, stuck on one long beat. Ash's head swung slowly from looking out the window to looking at her. Her feet felt like lead weights. The cool plastic coffee cup vibrated in her hand. She managed a deep breath. She commanded her feet to move.

The dark shades he wore the day before still hid his eyes but she felt him staring at her as she walked. Under the table his foot pushed out the chair across from him.

She sat, still numb, and stared at him. "Ash, what are you doing here?" Her voice was less forceful than she wanted.

"You didn't come to Athenaeum this morning."

"No. I had …" She paused. "other things to do."

He was quiet.

She didn't know what to say.

Finally he leaned forward as though he were about to whisper a secret. "How did you beat me?"

"What?" She felt her eyes get wide. "This is still about a chess game?"

She saw her reflection in the dark lenses of his glasses. Her hair fell around her face from a loose ponytail. Her cheeks were tinged pink. "Can you take those off please?" She would rather look at his black eye than at her own reflection.

He sat back and looked to the street again.

She was ready to stand up and walk away in frustration when he took the glasses off, folded the arms, and placed them on the table without looking at her.

Her eyes ranged over his profile. He seemed to be something out of classical art. His features were angular and strong, almost sculpted.

"How'd you win with no queen?" he said. "How did you win with so few pieces?"

"Why won't you look at me?" she demanded.

He closed his eyes and sighed, a gesture that seemed unnatural for him. His shoulders dropped as though his body was yielding to some unspoken, unhappy thought.

When he turned he looked her in the eye. Her lips tightened and she understood. Yesterday he wore the glasses to hide the black eye, the cut. Today he wore the glasses to hide the fact that there was no black eye, no cut. Today his eye was as perfect as the rest of him.

She shook her head in disbelief. "How ..."

"... did you beat me?" His voice was forceful but not loud.

She looked into his eyes and saw his determination. She didn't want to play this game anymore. "It's just a game I know," she said. "I memorized it when I was a kid."

"A *book* game?" he said, almost under his breath.

"I guess. It's been played before. That's what that means, right? It's not *novel*." She dusted off the term her father used for the moment a chess game went "out of book," the moment the first original move of the game was played. She pictured her father playing and laughing in the front room of their house.

"My father loved chess. I was never any good so he taught me this one game. His favorite. We played it over and over." She smiled at the memory. "I always got to win."

Ash stared at her in disbelief.

"It's famous actually," she said. "I mean, if you're into that kind of thing. Two guys played it, in the 1800s. I think they were French, or maybe German. Dad said you could beat most people with it—"

Ash stiffened. "I'm not most people."

Her eyes shot to his. He was dead serious.

"How did your eye—"

"I want to know about the game." He cut her off. "The *moves*. You gave away so much material." His eyes narrowed. "It ... You ... seemed so ordinary."

Ruby flinched at the insult, intended or not.

She knew "material" meant pieces in the chess world. Her father told her losing your most valuable material was the key to winning the game. "People see you gambit a pawn on your first few moves and they assume you're an unskilled player."

Ash's nostrils flared.

"By the time you're giving up a bishop and both your rooks they're convinced you don't know what you're doing."

His fists tightened on the table in front of her.

"You sacrifice your queen and they think they've got you." She paused, knowing that he knew what came next. She shrugged, feeling smug now. "Then you checkmate them with a few minor pieces. They don't expect it. It's called The Immortal Game—"

"A diversion tactic," he said on top of her words, like it was a cheap trick pulled out of a felt hat.

She bristled. "It's a good game of chess. Like William the Conqueror and Harold II. I faked. You fell for it." She took another sip of the cold vanilla coffee and relished its sweetness.

He stared at her. She wondered if he would storm out, still having a tantrum about losing one chess game. To her shock he laughed. The sound was deep and true. It startled her. She felt warm, despite having cooled down from her ride.

"When were you born?"

"Huh?" She scrunched up her nose at the sudden change in topic.

"Your sign?" he insisted.

She thought it must be a joke. Wasn't that a bad pickup line from the '70s? But he continued to look at her like he'd asked her to explain away the mysteries of the universe and she was being deliberately vague.

"December," she said. "Sagittarius. Why?"

"Fire sign." He nodded, but he didn't answer her question.

"What do you mean?" she crossed her arms. The smug feeling of recounting her chess win was gone. "What are you talking about?"

"Where did you grow up? Your father was killed; what about your mother?"

"I grew up here. My mom died in a car accident when I was a baby. Why are you asking me all these ..."

"Siblings? How many? Where are they?"

"None, nowhere." She pulled back at the unexpected interrogation.

He searched her eyes. "Yoga? Meditation? You're so ..." He gritted his teeth. "*Calm.*"

Ruby thought of her life, her intense studying schedule, the laundry everywhere around her house. She ordered dinner out most nights for lack of fresh food and clean dishes. She didn't *feel* calm.

"How about you answer a few of my questions instead?" she said. "How do you know so much about the Battle of Hastings?" She paused for only a split second. "The truth this time?"

He stared at her.

"Why is your eye healed? And your hand? Why are you in this coffeehouse? Why do you care so much that I beat you?"

"You can tell a lot about a person by how they play chess." He leaned forward in his chair. "Are they guarded and cautious? Or are they bold and stupid?" He picked up the sunglasses on the table between them and fiddled with the folding arms. "Maybe they're greedy, and all they want is material. You ..." He swallowed, his Adam's apple working.

"What about me?"

He shook his head. "I'm not sure about you."

She swallowed too and looked to the tabletop, to the window, to the cars outside, and then back to him. "Do you just play chess all day?" she asked, realizing that she never saw him do anything else. "Don't you go to school, or have a job, or a girlfriend ... or something?" She came up short at the implication of her last question.

"Me?" His head reared back.

"I mean ..." She tried to backpedal.

"Just chess," he said, as if it was normal.

"I have to go. I have a study group." She began to stand.

"Sage is the only ambitious one of us," he said, as though she weren't about to leave.

"Sage?" she asked, confused at the connection. Her messenger bag dangled in midair.

"Langston worked once. He was an EMT for a little while, but ..." He paused. "It didn't work out." He put the glasses down and looked out the window again.

"Langston?" she asked. "The poet who reads at Athenaeum?" She remembered the shared look between Langston and Sage when Ruby thought Ash was married and Sage had laughed.

"We don't need money," he said absently. His eyes shot to her from the side. "I mean ... We have money. Our family does. We don't have to work."

She lowered her bag back down to the floor and sat again. "I didn't know you were related." She thought of Langston's white-blond hair and Sage's unusual grey eyes. "You don't really look alike."

"Half-siblings. Different mothers." He twisted the dark metal ring on his healed hand. "My family's pretty … complicated."

She thought that most families were pretty complicated, though her family wasn't complicated at all. It was only her. She picked at the plastic wrap of her uneaten sandwich.

"My father wasn't always faithful," he said. "Actually, he wasn't even *usually* faithful." He laughed, but it was a humorless sound that soon turned into a long low groan. He slowly doubled over and his hands went up to cradle his head. His long fingers tightened and pulled at his dark curls.

"What is it?" She looked all around his face and head, not sure what was wrong.

His breath came out in a whoosh. "Give me your hand." He reached across the table and grabbed for her.

She clasped his warm hands between both of hers. "What—" She started to say, but the electric sizzle of energy that came off of him took her breath away. She tried to pull away from the frantic sensation but he held her tight. The buzzing slowly quieted and the wild pulsing faded. A tranquil feeling filled her. It mixed with the subtle rush of excitement of his skin on hers.

His shoulders relaxed. His breathing slowed. He kept his eyes closed. "Calm." He nodded.

When he looked at her his blue eyes were rimmed in red and the sockets were surrounded by dark circles. It had all happened in a minute.

"I get headaches," he said. "They're sudden. It's gone now."

A small smile flitted across his lips and Ruby felt like her chest might explode. Self-conscious and confused she let his hand slide out of hers.

"I better go," she said. It was midafternoon and she was sure the study group had long started.

"You want to go do something?" he said, and she saw a lightness come into his shaded eyes.

"Huh?"

"There's something I want to show you."

Recognition dawned on her. So he was *that* guy. He wanted to *"show"* her something. How gullible did he think she was? She knew about guys, though she hadn't dated much.

"Listen," she sighed. "I have a lot of studying to do."

"You say that a lot." He leaned back again and crossed his arms.

"I say what?"

"That you have to study."

"Well, I do. I have plans," she said. "And they require work."

"What?" he shrugged. "What plans?" His head was cocked to the side, looking at her, daring her.

"Well…" She picked up her coffee cup and rattled the latte-colored ice at the bottom. The familiar architecture of her future flowed naturally from her. "Medical school. Double residency in emergency medicine and surgery. A contract with Medics for Mercy."

At this point people usually nodded and congratulated her on her ambitious future. Instead Ash shrugged again. "What about having a little fun?"

A rush went through her. "I …"

He stood and reached for her hand. "Do you drive?"

FOUR

THE LITTLE BLUE TRUCK'S doors squeaked. An ancient crack ran along the windshield's lower edge and rips in the plastic seats let yellow foam show through. The truck had been Ruby's father's. Ruby and the nannies that cared for her when she was young had what they needed in the city, but when her father was home between trips to war-torn countries he liked to go camping. She could almost smell the faint woody scent of campfire in the worn carpet.

She distracted herself from these memories by watching Ash fold himself into the small space next to her. His head brushed the ceiling. His knees jutted up in the gap between him and the dashboard, which was also beginning to crack, she realized.

There was a loud screech from the engine as she started it. She quickly threw it into gear to silence the loose belt, but Ash didn't notice the sound. The dark circles and the redness in his eyes from the headache were gone. Now there was nothing but eager excitement there.

There were no roadblocks or traffic as Ash directed her to drive out of the city and up into the mountains. Ruby felt the electricity of his body close to hers in the tight cab of the truck. Butterflies fluttered in her chest and her head felt like it was floating above her body. Twice she misheard his directions and they had to turn around.

"What's this?" Ash touched the ID tag that hung by a lanyard from the rearview mirror.

"My dad's," she said. "His first Medics for Mercy ID."

Ash turned the badge over and looked at the picture. She glanced too. She saw how young her father was then, not much older than Ash, mid-twenties.

"You have his eyes," he said and glanced from the picture to her.

She squinted out the side window, embarrassed he noticed anything about her. The tall evergreens created an impenetrable wall on either side of the road. "Where are we going?" she asked.

He flashed a playful look from beneath dark eyelashes, but he didn't say anything.

Her heart sped up, first at that look he gave her, then at the idea of being alone here with him. She realized she was breaking some pretty basic rules by going off with a man she hardly knew. But if Ash was preparing to do away with her, he hadn't planned very well. She thought of the purpled-haired barista and the couple in the coffeehouse who smiled at them when they left.

In the end it was a matter of artless intuition. Ash simply felt safe.

Cool mountain air flowed into the cab windows as they followed the twisty road. The truck strained up the unrelenting hills and the conversation, like the mountain, didn't flag.

She told him about her father's work with Medics for Mercy and how she wanted to make him proud, how she changed her major from history to premed after he was killed, and how she wouldn't let his death be in vain.

"But you love history?" he asked.

"History doesn't really help people. Not like knowing how to heal someone does." It was her mantra. It was what she told herself when she switched majors. What she told herself when she read through the history department's course offerings every term and chose only one class as an elective, though choosing felt impossible.

"Those who don't remember their history are doomed to repeat it," he quoted the famous line.

"I think we're doomed to repeat it anyway," she said. "At least from what I've seen. People have always been at war. I think they always will be. Humans can't seem to figure out how to simply love each other."

He scoffed and looked out the window. "So that's it then." He sounded annoyed. "You don't think of the present? Only the future?"

She shrugged. "I have goals."

"You could die tomorrow. Or today," he countered. "Life is short."

No one knew that better than she did. "That's why I have to make my life count."

"You're not," he shot back. "You're wasting it."

She blinked at the green trees and tried to make sense of what he said. "I'm making the future count," she finally said, stating the obvious.

He shook his head. "All you really have is right now, Ruby. This moment. You better look around and enjoy it before it's gone."

"I don't see it that way," she said.

"But that's the way it is." There was no humor in his voice, no apology over giving her unsolicited, and unwanted, advice.

There was silence for the first time since they got in the truck. She thought of the chemistry test the next morning. She shouldn't be here now. She should be at the study group, or home, or at the library; anywhere but here, driving into the mountains with a stranger for who-knew-what. She sat up straighter in the driver's seat and glanced in the rearview mirror, but there was only the receding forest to see.

"I thought all you did was play chess," she said, annoyed that he had called her out. "What could be out here?"

Instead of answering he pointed ahead of them. "Make a left up there."

She turned off the main highway and onto a narrow dirt road. Thick trees ran outside the windows and branches scraped at the already useless paint of the truck as it crept along, bobbing in and out of craters on the old complaining shocks.

Ash peered ahead. "We're close." They passed over a set of railroad tracks. "Pull over up there."

She parked in the weeds beyond the rails and turned the truck off. The clamor of its old engine and the rattle of its loose body were replaced by birdsong and a soft breeze coming in through the open windows. The silence made it seem like they were even more alone. She glanced at him, looking for a clue as to what could be here, but he was already out of the truck, motioning for her to follow.

The mountains were textured by the spikey tips of evergreens and the scent of pine and fern filled the clear autumn air. Ash walked toward the railroad tracks that led into the forest on either side of the road.

"This way," he said, walking down the tracks to the left.

She walked there too, slowly, second-guessing her decision to come here with him. Clumps of wildflowers grew up through the wooden railroad ties and she saw the tracks running straight ahead into an infinity point in the distance.

"Where are we going?" she asked, still several feet from him.

"It's up here." He held out his hand to her.

A pleasant shiver ran through her at the thought of touching him again, but she hesitated. What did he want to show her?

"Why should I trust you?"

He shrugged. His eyes were steady on hers. "You'll have to trust yourself."

She felt like she couldn't breathe as she fought between reason and instinct. His hand was still stretched out to her.

When she took it, a current ran up her arm and all the way into her chest. Her muscles relaxed and breathing came easy.

The smell of creosote drifted up from the timbers beneath their feet. Soon trees gave way to an empty space and then there was nothing but the tracks held up by wooden supports suspended over a gorge with a stream far below. Boulders littered the streambed and they looked like pebbles. Her hand became sweaty against Ash's.

At half span he stopped and turned to her. His eyes were bright. "This is it."

She felt her heart pulse through her body. She looked around, trying hard not to look down, trying not to see that between the ties was sheer nothing.

"What?"

He let go of her hand and she tottered without him to hold onto. She watched him bend to the defunct railroad tracks and pull out a large black bundle, a duffel bag that had been secured beneath the ties.

He didn't look at her but began to unpack the bag near her feet. First he took out a metal ring with several large carabiners attached, then a rope as thick as her arm and covered in shiny black material. He held part of the rope up to her. "Ever been?"

She shook her head, still confused. "Ever been what?"

"Good." He smiled a lopsided, knowing grin. "You'll never forget your first time."

She felt her cheeks get warm. "My first what?"

"Your first jump."

Ruby's eyes darted around, below Ash, down to the riverbed. "What?" she whispered.

"Your first bungee. You'll never forget it." He pulled foot after foot of the black cord from the bag.

"I can't bungee jump." Her eyes searched the empty space around them. The cool breeze chilled the sweat gathering on her brow.

He stopped untangling the cord and looked at her again. "Why not?"

Her eyebrows shot up. "I've never even thought about it."

"Don't worry." He laughed. "You don't have to think."

He couldn't possibly expect her to really jump off a bridge, could he? Wasn't it what her father always warned her about? *Don't jump off a bridge because a cute guy tells you to.*

"The first time's the best." He stood up and began to untangle the cord he held in his hands. "You're lucky you live now."

Her wide eyes met his. "What do you mean?"

He looked down at the rope as he let loop after loop fall below the level of the bridge and hang down into the empty void beneath them. "I mean we're lucky. That we live now. You know? A hundred years ago there was no such thing as bungee jumping."

He secured the other end of the cord to the railroad tracks with metal carabiners and locked them in place by spinning a case up around their openings. He stood. "You're first," he said.

She swallowed. Her mind raced. She looked down into the gorge. The river below was a thin line of green and white water. "Is it safe?" she asked, breathless.

"Usually," he said.

Her face fell and she looked into his eyes. He wasn't going to lie to her now. He wasn't going to tell her it was safe when maybe it wasn't.

"I'll go first if you want," he said.

She felt like her heart might burst with fear and excitement. *Why do such a thing?* a voice said in her head. *You could be killed.*

Or maybe I'll live, she countered.

She shook her head and chased the voices away. Ash's words came back to her: *All you have is right now. This minute.* The words filled her with certainty.

"No …" She looked down into the gorge. Her eyes snapped back up. She took a breath, though she doubted any oxygen was getting to her brain. "I'll go first."

He nodded.

Her heart pounded loud in her ears.

Ash bent back to his bag and pulled out a set of red straps connected together. He untangled them, adjusted the buckles, and bent down to her feet. "Here, step into the harness."

She hesitated and looked down at him, trying to focus on him, and not the abyss beyond. She shook her head. "I'm not very brave."

He sat on his heels and looked up at her. "It's okay to be afraid, but you can't let fear stop you."

Her legs shook as she stepped into the harness. He pulled the straps up along her calves and thighs and sent chills over her already tingling body.

He stood up close to her. When the metal buckle was just above her hips he cinched it tight and pulled her close to him. She looked up into his glowing, smiling face, only inches from her own. He paused. She thought he might kiss her. She wanted him to. But he only looked back to the harness and finished adjusting the straps.

Her disappointment was soon replaced by raging nerves as he bent to attach the black bungee cord through yet another strap, with more carabiners, around her ankles.

"Okay." He stood and looked at her. "You're ready."

She bit her bottom lip hard enough to draw blood. Her heart pounded as she turned toward the edge, determined to not look down. He was behind her. She could feel his breath on her neck, raising goose bumps.

He breathed out a single word. "Jump."

And she did.

The free fall was terror, exhilaration, and freedom, all at once. The boulders at the bottom of the gorge rushed up at her. The mountain before her was unchanging as she accelerated down and down at breakneck speed. Her thudding heart felt like it would break free from her body with each beat.

It went on until she was sure that the bungee had snapped and that she was plummeting to her death. But when the stretchy cord caught, it threw her back up into space. At the top she felt her body pause, floating, for a split second, and then free falling once more.

Each bounce was a little shorter than the last until finally they were just little rebounds and she was hanging upside down by her feet with the white-water spray reaching up to splash her from below. It was then that she heard herself screaming, loud, above the sound of the rushing water beneath her.

She heard Ash too, distant, from the railroad bridge so far above. "Whoo!"

Her screams turned into frenzied laughter. She tried to do a sit-up to look at Ash, but he was busying himself with something on the tracks. She couldn't hold the position.

She relaxed and looked at the banks of the river from her upside-down vantage point. Fear, or adrenaline, or both, had sharpened her senses. She could see every needle on every pine tree, every drop of water coming up off the river. She smelled the pine, not just the needles, not just that Christmasy smell, but the trees themselves, the bark, the xylem, the phloem, the earth itself.

Each hair on her skin stood on end, stiff in the breeze that skimmed her body. A slight metallic taste had replaced the moisture in her mouth.

A rope slid past her. "Grab it," Ash yelled down to her, "I'll pull you up." She reached for the nylon rope, solid, not stretchy, and soon she was upright again. Ash pulled her with a strong steady rhythm.

"Incredible!" She beamed as he pulled her over the side of the bridge and back onto the railroad tracks, which now felt as steady and stable as any flat ground.

He smiled at her, his eyes a luminescent blue. She stared back, wanting to kiss him more now than she had before. He pointed to her hips, and she felt her already flushed face become hot. Then she realized that he was waiting for her to take the harness off so he could have a turn.

He deftly adjusted the harness and the bungee to his size and weight. He winked at her and turned to the abyss. There was no scream from him, only the sound of a single breath leaving his lungs as he pushed off into nothing.

He fell gracefully away from her and then flew back up on his own rebounds. She remembered that feeling in the core of her being. Terror and joy and relief. Relief that it wasn't the day she would die.

She smiled and screamed for him.

☙

The thin fabric of Ruby's curtains did little to keep out the bright morning sunshine. She pulled her pillow over her head and then pushed it away again, caught in a half-conscious battle between wanting darkness and needing oxygen.

She thought of the day before, bungee jumping, and grinned into her pillow. She tried to picture Ash and found it almost too easy. Too easy to see the exact way sunlight lit up the crest of his dark curls, too easy to see how his bright eyes stood out against the backdrop of the blue sky, too easy to see how his red lips flattened into a wide smile.

She thought of the sensation of his hand on hers, the way the conversation flowed, and the disappointment of watching him walk away from her in the muted twilight when he suggested they go to Athenaeum and she said that she needed to study—really, this time.

Then a dark, half-remembered dream floated into her thoughts. Someone warning her away from something. Something she wanted. Something she *needed*. She winced and tried to think of Ash again, hoping to regain the feel of him. Instead doubt crowded in and blotted out everything else.

What is he doing even talking to me?

She thought of the women who swarmed around him at Athenaeum, hoping he would notice them, though he never seemed to. *What is he playing at?*

Her hold on the blankets slackened. She hadn't made it to the study group and she had found it nearly impossible to concentrate on chemistry after a day of bungee jumping.

She *had* to do well on the test.

Her eyes flew open. She glanced to the alarm clock, suspiciously silent in the bright morning light. Seven-fifty! She hadn't set it? A flash of a memory shot through her: brushing her teeth, getting ready for bed, and thinking of *him*.

Dr. Reed did not admit latecomers to exams.

"Stupid!" She said to no one. She glanced at the pictures of her mother and her father on her nightstand. Their chance to make a difference in the world was gone. Ruby couldn't throw hers away. She gave her muddled head a quick shake. She looked at the clock again: seven-fifty-one. Nine minutes.

She threw off the covers and grabbed a pair of crumpled jeans from the lavender-colored carpet. She pulled the jeans up over the boy shorts she had slept in, grabbed a shirt from one of the many piles, and sniffed at the green fabric—clean enough. She pulled it on over the cami-tank she was already wearing as she ran down the stairs.

Her messenger bag sat by the door, still fully packed, evidence of her neglect. She grabbed it and looked at her bike, but ran out the front door instead.

The sidewalk near campus was nearly empty, allowing her the room she needed to run and reminding her of how late she truly was. As she approached Hawthorne she paused. In one direction was campus, the test, her future. In the other was Athenaeum. She wanted a coffee, an Ambrosia Bar, and...

She shook her head and ran on.

She sprinted across campus and saw the last stragglers arrive in the science quad. Once the door to Dr. Reed's classroom closed that would be it. She would get a zero on the exam. She could not recover from that.

The thought propelled her even faster. She ran into the large glass entranceway of Mendeleev Hall and down the long corridor. She got a whiff of the microbiology lab and caught a glimpse of a tartan jacket sleeve as it pulled the door to the chemistry lecture hall closed.

"Wait!" she shouted.

Luckily, thankfully, blessedly, he did. She ran into the room, out of breath, and took the heavy test packet from him as she passed. She sat in the first open seat she came to, half-blind with adrenaline.

She placed the exam facedown and waited for the signal to begin. Someone a few seats over leaned in close to her. She glanced up and saw that it was Mark. He had a look on his face that was somewhere between relief and bewilderment.

"Where were you yesterday?" he whispered.

"Uh ..." she huffed, still out of breath. "Sorry ... There were road blocks and ... I ran into a friend." She busied herself with taking pencils out of her bag. "I hope you guys didn't wait for me."

"You should have been there. Sarah had a bunch of old *tests.*" Mark said the last word with the same inflection a prospector would have when finally striking gold. "Even last year's."

"The questions will be different," she shot back, hoping it wasn't as big a deal as he was making it out to be.

"No. But the same ideas." He still leaned toward her, but his eyes were on Dr. Reed, who now stood at the podium in the front of the room.

Ruby closed her eyes and blew out a long breath. She would fail. She would fail this test because—

"Begin," Dr. Reed interrupted her self-castigations.

The sound of a hundred test packets being turned over filled the room. Ruby blinked and turned hers over just a beat behind everyone else.

She read the first question: "Draw all isomers of 1,2-dichlorocyclobutane."

She couldn't think. She didn't know where to begin. Her heart was still pumping hard from running.

She glanced over to Mark, who was writing furiously, already moving on to the second question. She squeezed her hand painfully around her pencil and tried to dissect the complicated chemical name down into its more manageable parts. She tried to picture the molecule in her mind.

Instead she saw Ash.

At first she pushed his image away, more frustrated than ever, but she found that if she concentrated she could feel the sensation of touching him.

Her muscles relaxed.

Her breathing slowed.

Her heart became steady.

She put her pencil to the paper.

FIVE

RUBY WALKED DOWN THE SIDEWALK in a daze, distracted by the exam she had just taken, distracted by the thought that—maybe—she had done well. She remembered how easily Ash had come to her mind during the test and how calm and focused she felt. The questions seemed obvious after that and their answers easy. She wanted to celebrate, but she kept her emotions in check. She couldn't assume anything.

Ash was more and more of an enigma to her. She still had all those unanswered questions about his healed injuries and the Battle of Hastings, though his knowledge of the battle no longer seemed so odd. Of course he could have learned about it in books.

She knew she should ride the wave of clarity and go home to study for other classes but her feet headed toward Athenae-um instead.

When she walked in she only glanced in the direction of the chess table. Ash was there, playing a pretty blond with legs long enough to match his. He might have looked up, but she pretended not to notice. She didn't want him to think she made too much of the afternoon they had spent together.

Sage was at the espresso counter with Langston, the tall poet—Ash and Sage's brother.

A sudden darkness came over her, followed by an unexpected shiver of fear. Maybe it was the exam. Maybe she hadn't done as well as she imagined. She shook her head and tried to chase the feeling away, but it lingered.

Sage looked up when Ruby reached the counter. Langston was leaning with one elbow on the glass top. A woman in a short denim skirt rested against the curve of his bent body.

"Rubes," he said, as if he knew her, though no one had ever called her that before.

Sage held a tattered book with a single gold word stamped on the stained yellow cover: Myths. "Look at the illustrations," she said as if Langston hadn't spoken. "Hand-drawn lithographs." She opened the book to a picture of a young woman with long flowing hair standing in a field of wild flowers. The woman held a large bouquet against her body with one arm. It would have been an idyllic scene if it weren't for the black robed figure coming up out of the ground pulling her down as if he would drag her into the earth with him.

"Hades and Persephone," Sage offered.

"Yeah, I think I remember that one," Ruby said, thinking back to her mythology class from the previous term. "He's the god of the dead. Right? He kidnapped Persephone and took

her to the Underworld to make her his queen. Or something."
She paused, not sure if she had the story right. She had skimmed most of the reading in that class.

"Or something," Langston said sarcastically.

Sage shot him a dark look. "Ruby, this is Langston."

He stood up to his full height. He was at least six-and-a-half feet tall. Ruby felt the strain in her neck as she looked at his classic sharp features, platinum-blond hair, and sky blue eyes that were a foot above hers. He wore white pants and a green polo shirt. The smell of his cologne was subtle, but out of place in the Athenaeum, with grungy college kids sitting at most of the tables and the heavy smell of coffee in the air. He wasn't a typical coffeehouse poet. He might have been more at home at a country club with a stem of champagne in his hand.

"A pleasure." He winked. She took his hand to shake it but almost pulled away when he turned it over, bowed, and brought her hand up to his warm lips to kiss the back.

She smiled awkwardly at the antiquated gesture and glanced at the dark-haired woman standing there. She wore thick eyeliner and a heavy metal T-shirt with the denim skirt that barely managed to cover her backside. No one introduced the woman. Ruby smiled at her, but she didn't smile back.

"I was about to read my latest poem: 'The Immediacy of *Lust*.'" He drew out the last word and glanced at the woman in the denim skirt. He held up a black journal with an ivy leaf sticking out like a bookmark.

"What can I get you, Ruby?" Sage asked, ignoring Langston.

"Double latte, please," she said, glad Sage had changed the subject. "And ..." she peered into the glassed-in case of Ambrosia Bars, brown and plain looking, "*that* Ambrosia Bar." She pointed to a fat one with golden filling oozing out the side.

Sage measured out the coffee and looked at Ruby. "You okay? You look tired."

Ruby nodded. She didn't want to talk about the exam. It turned out she wouldn't have to.

Ash was suddenly there, standing next to her, close enough that she could feel heat coming off his body. She glanced at him and noted in an instant the broken-in jeans, the blue Henley shirt, the black cowboy boots. His hair was unruly. Part rodeo, part grunge. *Very un-country club.* A giddiness rose in her chest. She tried to swallow it down.

"Hey," he said, in that low husky voice that made her stomach flutter.

She looked at the chess table. The blond woman he had been playing reached for her bag, glanced in their direction with a scowl, and turned to leave.

"She beat you?" Ruby asked.

"What?" His eyebrows came together in a V. "No." He searched her face and shrugged. "It was a draw."

Her eyes widened. Jealousy rose up, not at the woman's beauty, but that maybe she could beat him too. "Really?"

"No." He shook his head. "No way."

Ruby laughed despite her lingering doubts about the exam.

Ash smiled and the room brightened, dark clouds lifting. Sage handed Ruby the latte and the Ambrosia Bar, but her grey eyes were on Ash.

"Thanks." Ruby took the plate and the mug. Sage ignored her when she tried to pay.

Ash followed her to a table and sat in a chair across from her. He rested one boot on the opposite knee. "No more tests, right?" He raised both eyebrows in a quick flash and smiled. "Let's go do something."

"Ash …" She started. She wanted to tell him that she couldn't. That *really* it was time for her to study; there was *always* another test. But now that he was sitting across from her, she didn't seem to have the words for any of it.

"It's Friday," he said. "We have all weekend."

"I … I …" she stammered. *We?*

෧෧෬

Ruby stood at the bottom of the sixty-foot cliff with the briny smell of the ocean all around. Seagulls cawed overhead. She watched Ash pull himself up with ease as he reached from one impossibly small crevice to another on the sheer rock face.

An orange rope flecked with blue was tied loosely around a belt loop on his jeans, trailing down behind him. She bit at the inside of her cheek as she watched. She had never been rock climbing before but she knew a rope tied to your jeans would do you no good if you fell. Ash had insisted that he would be safe free-climbing. "I know every hold on this rock," he had assured her, but still her knees felt weak.

He told her that when it was her turn to climb he would attach one end of the rope to the harness she was wearing. The other end would run through an anchor that he would set at the top, and then run back down to a belay device on his harness. If she fell, the rope would catch her.

She turned to the empty beach behind her, unable to watch. The rock was half a mile down an unassuming trail they had accessed from the coastal highway. "Just a place I know," he had said, as he directed her to drive the little blue truck toward the Pacific.

She glanced to his boots lying at the base of the rock, thrown together with her worn sneakers. They had changed them out for rock climbing shoes. A chalk bag hung from each of their waists in the back.

She dug her feet into the sand and watched Ash disappear over the top of the dome-shaped rock, gone to find a place to set the anchor and attach the rope. He climbed down with the same surefooted ease he had climbed up, as steady as if he were on a ladder.

"Okay, you're ready," he said after he made a knot that looked like two figure eights, one eight lying inside the other, and slipped a loop of rope into a metal device on the harness he wore. Now they were tied together, connected by this rope that she would rely on for her life. His eyes were the same bright blue she recognized from the railroad bridge when they bungeed off it.

She looked up the rock face and tried to see what she had gotten herself into.

"Good," he said. "Plan ahead. It's a lot like chess in that way. You can't just know your next move. You have to know the one after, and the one after that."

She mapped out the first ten or fifteen feet in her mind and reached into the chalk bag hanging off her waist. The fine white powder was silky on her skin. It dried the sweat that was already slick on her fingertips.

She placed her right foot at knee level, in a small crack, then reached up to a knob of rock above her head and pulled up. The muscles in her shoulders and forearms tensed. She placed her left foot into a wide fissure. The gripping surface of her climbing shoes gave her traction. She placed her left hand and then moved up with the right.

She looked up and sighted her next move. She stepped high onto a small ledge, then reached far to the right and braced herself by pushing her hand against a crevice. She moved up, slow and steady, not looking back, not looking down, focused in the moment. The rock was rough under her chalked fingertips. She could feel blisters forming.

She was near the top when she placed her foot on an outcropping and felt a slight give. She had already committed to the move. A hot wave coursed through her when the rock broke away. She heard the hollow sound the broken piece made as it bounced down the rock face to the beach below.

Her leg dangled into empty space. Her arms held, though. She was able to look down to search for another foothold. She saw that the brown sandy ground had lost its texture at this distance. Ash, strong and steady when he was next to her, now looked small and unreachable.

Her pulse thrummed through her. A fall would kill her. She tried to remember the rope, thick and secure; her harness, adjusted to fit her exactly; Ash holding the other end of the line.

Reason could not reach her. Her arms felt weak. Her other leg, the only thing holding her lower body up, began to shake.

From the ground she heard Ash's voice. "You can do this," he called. "Trust your instincts."

Her eyes searched the rock in front of her: dark, grey, and menacing. Her foot scrambled up and down until it found purchase on a hold that felt tiny and tentative.

She held her body flat against the rock and let her muscles rest. She closed her eyes, took a deep breath, and leaned back slightly. The moves she had originally intended were just above her. She pulled her left foot up, relying on the unknown footing, and reached with her right hand. In one smooth motion she pulled herself back onto her chosen route.

At the top she could not see her next moves. They were beyond the edge of the domed rock. She felt around and found a well where her two fingertips fit. She hauled herself up in one last push of effort.

Exhausted, she lay flat on top of the cool rock. Her limbs were shaky and tired. Her heart pounded and her shirt was wet with sweat. She rolled onto her back and laughed at the grey sky. Slowly she stood. Her legs wobbled. She looked out to the beach, with its high bluff and deep green forest on one side, and the steel blue ocean on the other.

She closed her eyes and breathed in, filling herself with clean sea air. Her lungs were not big enough for the breath she wanted to take. She wanted to breathe in the world. She would consume it. Make it part of her. Devour it whole.

They walked up the path to Ruby's front door to wait for dinner to be delivered from the Thai restaurant around the corner. The sun was low behind the craftsman houses of her neighborhood and the lone fir tree in her front yard cast a long shadow across the mossy grass. She felt pleasantly wrung out from rock climbing and in the comfortable silence she found the opening she was waiting for.

"Ash …" she hesitated. "Did you know I was going to stop at that coffeehouse on Fremont yesterday?" It sounded insane, but it was as if he had been expecting her.

He laughed, but it was shallow, not his usual deep gut laugh. "How would I know that?"

"I don't know." She ran her hand through her hair and tucked it behind her ear. "It was an odd coincidence."

"I was there when you came in," he said simply. His face was turned away from hers, looking at the college rental next to her house.

"Oh," she said, still thinking that it was *too* coincidental. He hadn't even bought anything, she realized. He had just been sitting there. But what was she suggesting? That he had somehow appeared there right before she went in?

Her key shook in her hand as she slid it into the lock of her wooden front door. Once inside she realized how empty and quiet she was used to the house being. Ash filled the room the same way he filled the cab of the little truck, with his height, and his voice, and his presence. Her limbs felt lighter than normal, like her movements were exaggerated and overly deliberate.

The front door opened at the base of a long set of stairs. To the right was the TV room. To the left was what her father had always called the front room. She went left out of habit.

Ruby's mother had bought most of the furniture in the house when she and Ruby's father first moved in as a young couple. The wood-and-jacquard couch, the hand-hooked Oriental rug, and even the subtly patterned drapes had all been her mother's choices. Ruby's father had never bothered to redecorate after she died.

Pictures from the major events of Ruby's life marched up the wall along the staircase. One of Ruby's early nannies had started the photo collection. Her father had kept up with it over the years and Ruby had added pictures of her parents to the mix.

Dirt swirled around her father in his most recent photo. The wind had been created by helicopter blades carrying out the last of the wounded, he had told her. He was smiling in the picture, tired and satisfied, frozen forever in the past.

Ruby's stomach clenched. Another entire day of studying wasted.

"What's wrong?" Ash asked, though she hadn't said anything.

"Nothing. Do you want a beer?" she said, dusting off the seldom-used role of host.

The kitchen was at the back of the house, through the front room. She cringed when she got there. Several cardboard containers sat on the counter. Thai noodles stuck out of one.

She collected the containers in a lopsided stack and put the used forks in the sink. Ash was only a few steps behind her.

She turned to gauge his reaction but he didn't seem to notice the overly ripe scent that reminded her garbage day had come and gone again, and he wasn't looking around at the dirty glasses by the edge of the sink, or at the day-old coffee in the coffeemaker. He was looking at her.

She glanced at the hollow at the base of his throat and then briefly at his lips. She reached for the fridge handle and cast around for something to talk about. "What's the number thirty-seven?" she asked, thinking of how he had ordered by number off the Thai menu without even glancing at it.

"We'll find out." His voice was soft. He leaned against the counter, absurdly gorgeous in her faded little kitchen.

"You don't care?"

"I like to be surprised," he said.

Her hands were sweaty against the refrigerator handle. She turned and grabbed the sole beer from the door, glad that she actually had one. She opened the bottle and handed it to him.

The TV room was connected to the kitchen on the far end, completing the downstairs of the house in a small loop. "We can wait for our food in here," she said as she walked through and sat on the brown leather couch. She rubbed gently at the blister that had formed on her thumb from rock climbing.

Ash sat too, not right next to her, but close.

Her eyes darted around the room, unsure of what to do in her own house. She stood again and went to the line of CDs on the wall-sized entertainment center across the room. She had grown up listening to her father's favorites: big band music and old bluesy jazz. She spoke without turning. "What do you like to listen to?"

"Surprise me," he said from right behind her.

Her eyes shot up to a small stone statue her father had brought back from a trip.

Ash rested his hand on her hip. She chose a CD without looking at it and turned around to put it in the player.

She expected him to step back.

He didn't.

She found herself facing his blue Henley, inches from her. The top buttons were open and she could see the steady beat of his pulse at the base of his neck. He smelled of ozone and sweat, not unpleasant, but masculine, with something clean and subtle beneath that. She looked up at his face which was shockingly coming down toward hers.

His soft, warm lips brushed hers and his hot breath sent a chill across her skin. She gasped and saw him smile at the sound. When he pressed his lips into hers the energy she felt between them was there, mixed with a deep stirring of desire.

His lips parted and his tongue grazed hers in an electrifying rush. He brought his hand up to touch her hair and the back of her head and he pulled her in gently for a deeper kiss.

Her hands came up to his sides. She felt his heat through the fabric of his shirt and the well-defined muscles beneath. She moved closer and pressed into him, her breast against his hard chest.

His free arm wound around her waist and pulled her even closer, their stomachs flat against one another's. Her shirt came up slightly. She felt his bare fingers on her skin.

Her eyes snapped open. She pulled away. "What are you doing?" she breathed.

He followed her and kissed her again, as if he hadn't heard.

"Wait," she said.

He stopped then. His eyes were a soft blue, not bright and intense like on the bridge or at the rock, but shaded and deep. She looked away. She wanted this. Why was she stopping? "I need you," he whispered and followed her movements. He tried to kiss her again but she turned her head.

She looked at his arms, wrapped around her, then to his face. She shook her head. She couldn't let him distract her. She had already wasted two days with him and she was only getting further behind.

She caught their reflection in the large plate glass window to her left. She saw how ridiculous they were. It wasn't that she was ugly. She was *cute*. That's what people said. But she wasn't beautiful. She wasn't the type to be seen with a guy like Ash.

She realized then that he probably took all the girls bungee jumping and rock climbing. He probably always ordered strange things off foreign menus. She was sure he kissed them all like this, and stared into their eyes the way he was looking at her now. He probably told them all that he "needed them."

His arms were slack around her. He seemed to be waiting for her to come to her senses and kiss him again. She was pretty sure he wasn't used to women rejecting him.

Her mind went back to the picture of her dad in the staircase, the one taken on the battlefield with helicopter blades and a war swirling around him. She might have done well on today's chemistry exam but she would definitely fail the next one if she didn't start to focus.

She pulled away. "I can't."

He stepped in, closing the gap, and looked into her eyes. Whatever he saw there made him kiss her again, a tender kiss that pulled a soft sound from deep inside her. The excitement of their energy flowed through her. She fought the deep stirring in her body that ached for her to kiss him back.

"I can't," she said, louder, breaking contact.

He searched her eyes. "Don't you feel it?"

She glanced away from him, to the line of CDs. "Feel what?" But she knew.

He looked at her for a long time. "You don't—"

She cut him off. "I think you should leave."

He winced and she felt something massive and hollow fill her chest. He took her hands in his.

She tried to fight the energy that came from him.

He looked down at her hands and stroked her fingers, soothing the tender blisters and sending shivers through her. He pressed her palm flat against the middle of his chest and covered his hand with hers. His dark ring pressed into her skin on the back of her hand.

"You don't feel *that*?" he asked. His eyes locked with hers.

A sound tried to escape her when she felt the calm of him intensify—and beneath that his steady heartbeat—but she kept it in check.

"I don't feel anything," she lied.

A look of confusion passed over his features, but it was gone in an instant. He dropped her hand and moved past her. He strode out the front door, almost running over the delivery guy from the Thai restaurant.

ও৬৩

The number thirty-seven turned out to be a whole fish, with the head still attached, in what looked like chili sauce. Ruby put it in the refrigerator with the Pad Thai and spring rolls. Her appetite had left with Ash.

She took the picture of her dad, the one from the stairway, and propped it up against a pile of books next to her notes at the kitchen table. She looked to the picture often, but she still had a hard time focusing.

As she lay in bed that night, she touched her lips with the tips of her fingers and tried to remember the feel of Ash's lips there; the warmth, the pressure, the taste.

He "needed" her. That's what he had said.

She rolled over and pulled the covers over her head. It took a long time for sleep to find her. When it did she dreamed of falling, and falling, and falling, and then being caught by the bungee cord at her feet and thrown back up into the air. When Ash pulled her back to earth, he kissed her and she felt like she was falling again, but this time her feet were on the ground.

In the dream, the sun on her skin was warm and Ash's arms were strong around her. He tightened his grip and she laughed, but the embrace soon became too much, too tight, crushing. She pulled her head back to look at him. He smiled but the grin was too large and his eyes were the wrong blue. She tried to get away but he gripped her tighter, pulling her against his body.

Then it was Langston holding her, his features impossibly sharp, sharper than any human's. His teeth were jagged points. His breath was hot and fetid on her skin. She pushed on his chest, desperate to get away, but he held her tight. His eyes widened and he grinned at her fear.

"Ruby," he whispered. "Do not veer from your dreams. Ash is a perilous man."

She stopped struggling, "No. Ash is—"

"Death and destruction," the Langston monster hissed. "He will ruin us all."

His smile faded and she was glad that his lips now covered most of those sharp yellow teeth. His face melted away and became a tangle of snakes pouring out at her. She felt their dry scaly skin and their muscles undulating beneath.

She tried to scream, but Langston held her too tight for her to get a breath. She beat at his arms. Each was a snake around her waist.

She woke with a start and tore at the sheets twisted around her. She was breathing hard.

The dream faded. She tried to hold on to it: Langston crushing the breath out of her and telling her Ash was dangerous—*perilous*—but it was like trying to hold water in cupped hands and the dreamed slipped out of her grasp. Soon it was gone and she was left with the fear without the how or why of it.

Then she heard the knocking.

Her already-racing heart sped. The sound was distant, from somewhere downstairs. She sat still and listened. The light of the streetlamp outside her window came in through the gaps in her curtains.

Thud, thud ... thud.

It sounded like someone was dropping something heavy. There was no rhythm to it. She got out of bed and walked to the top of the stairs. She peered down the long flight and waited.

Thud … Thud … Thud.

She went down a few steps.

Thud, thud.

Someone was out there knocking something against the front door. She plucked up her courage and hurried down the stairs. She looked through the peephole but saw only blackness. Had the streetlight gone out? To her right she saw that light still streamed in through the front window.

Thud. Thud.

Her head jerked back as the door shook from whatever was banging on the other side. She looked through the peephole again. The blackness had texture to it. It wasn't that the street was dark; there was something in the way, something black, and—

She sucked in a breath. She grasped the door handle with her left hand, and placed her right on the bolt lock ready to turn it. She looked through the peephole again.

"Hello?" She said more softly than she intended. The blackness on the other side of the door moved. She heard a quiet moan.

She swallowed, turned the deadbolt, and swung the door wide.

Ash's body crashed to the floor without the door to lean on.

She seized at the sight of him lying there. Facedown on the hardwood floor. Covered in blood.

SIX

WHEN RUBY'S BODY REMEMBERED how to work, she fell to her knees and hovered over him. "Ash," she started, tentative, and began to roll him over. He moaned. Her father said to never move a patient until you've assessed their injuries.

She scanned his back and legs in the dim light from the streetlamp. There were no cuts. Nothing was obviously broken. There was just the blood. She had to roll him over. What would she tell 911 if she didn't know what was wrong?

She pulled again, on his far shoulder, and tried to roll him toward her, but he was heavier than she imagined. "Ash," she whispered, "can you hear me?"

Another small moan escaped him, but no more.

She gripped his shoulder, this time from a wider stance above him and with better leverage. When he began to roll she got her first glimpse of the wound and dropped him in surprise. He made no sound. That, combined with the red raggedness of what she glimpsed, made her wonder if he was already dead. She sucked up her fear, bent again and pulled him over in one tremendous movement, grunting with the effort.

When he was flat on his back she crouched over him. She could see deep inside his body: maroon muscle, bright red blood, and something pink and spongy too. White jagged bones. Ribs, she realized, stood out in contrast, broken and splintered. She looked away, her stomach roiling from the metallic smell of blood, but something caught her eye. In the middle of the train wreck of his chest she saw something small, black, and hard looking. Metal?

She began to shake.

Ash was going to die.

Her hand came up to her mouth. It too was covered in blood. She lost the tentative grip on her senses and propelled herself backward, socks slipping on the wooden floor, until her back rested against the wainscoting.

She watched his chest rise and fall and with it was a low gurgling noise. His breathing was shallow and uneven. He was alive. But for how long? Would he die right now? Right here? In the front room?

She clambered to her feet and ran to the kitchen. She grabbed the yellow phone from its cradle. The receiver shook in her trembling hands as she placed it next to her ear. But there was nothing. The phone exchanges! The bombing! She dropped the phone and let it swing from its curly cord.

Her messenger bag was on the table. She threw the top flap open and rummaged through it with bloody hands. She seized on her cell phone and whispered, "Please." But all she saw was the all too familiar notice: *No Service.*

A sharp cry escaped her. She clamped her mouth shut and thought of her father. What would he do? The metal piece was deep inside Ash's chest. Should she try to remove it? Her father had told her stories, but she was no doctor, and she had no tools.

She went back to him and sat by his head. His face, the face that so often crept into her thoughts, was now streaked with blood. There was a long cut on his check. The blood there had dried. It was an older wound, probably by a couple of days.

Her eyes snapped wide.

It hadn't been there before. It hadn't been there when he left, when she *made him leave*, a few hours ago. This cut was new.

Flashes of memory ran through her mind; the long gash on the back of his hand, the black eye with the cut eyebrow. He healed too quickly.

And then she knew.

The cut on his face wasn't days old. Only hours. A tingle traveled across her scalp and down into her shoulders. Her eyes went to the wound in his chest. Could he heal from that too? No, she didn't think so. No one could recover from that, not without surgery. It would kill him, and probably soon.

She tried not to breathe in the heavy smell of Ash's blood as she looked inside him again, at the metal there. Her head pulled back in surprise. The metal moved. Not with the rhythm of his breath, up and down and irregular, but closer to her. She could see more of it now, not much, but a little. Part of it seemed peeled, like a banana. A bullet? She looked to Ash's face again.

His eye twitched and then his lip. "Ruby," he said, a labored pant. Her ears pricked at the first word he had said, her name. He was breathless, and there was that odd gurgling noise. With an effort he added, "Close—the—door."

"What—"

"Close it," he said with more force than she thought could come from his wrecked body.

She looked back outside. The light reflected off the dark empty street. Her thoughts were frozen between reason, she should run for help, and her acute awareness that he was asking something important of her. Would he be in trouble somehow if she got help?

"Please," he whispered.

She nodded slowly, but the movement felt disconnected from her body. She maneuvered his feet carefully and closed the door, blocking the light outside. She turned on the table lamp next to the couch and went back to him.

She watched as the cut on his face got smaller. She surveyed the wound in intervals and watched the bullet in his chest move closer to the surface. After a time she lost sight of it and peered in to get a better look. Her attention was yanked away by a sharp pain in her knee.

"My god," she whispered to the dim room. She picked up the peeled metal that had been inside Ash. Her eyes darted back to the wound. His body had driven it out.

She put a blanket over him, careful not to cover the wound, and pushed back to the wall. She propped herself up against the cool white-painted wood and watched him.

Her mind drifted, full of dark images. Ash injured. Ash *shot*. And something even darker than that. Oppressive warnings. And snakes.

She jerked, sometime later, and hit her head against the wall. There had been a sound. She scrambled to Ash and leaned over his face.

The wound on his cheek was gone. The dried blood flaked away. The gurgling had stopped and his breath had fallen into an even but shallow rhythm. His eyes opened and then fluttered closed.

She gasped. The blue she expected was gone. They were bright red.

He moaned.

"Ash." she croaked. "Tell me what to do."

His eyes closed again. He swallowed hard. His face contorted in pain. She put her hand on his cheek where the cut had been. His face relaxed, but frantic electricity ran off him. The connection she usually felt was there, but it was weak.

She kept her hand on him, hoping to smooth away his hurt. She didn't know why it helped, but she knew it did and was sorry she hadn't thought of it sooner. He slipped into unconsciousness again, his mind, like her, wanting to spare him from the pain.

∽⊙≀

Weak grey light came in through the curtainless windows of the front room. Ruby opened her eyes, and sat up next to

Ash. He was still unconscious but he seemed more peaceful now. Her hand rested on his shoulder and the energy that came off him was strong and smooth.

There was a pool of dark red blood surrounding him. His blue Henley was ripped and bloody. It was the same shirt he had worn when they went rock climbing, when they had ordered dinner. It was the shirt he was wearing when he kissed her.

She looked to the wound on his chest and let out a relieved breath. There was only a depression and a hideous purple bruise where the bullet wound had been. The cut on his cheek was a memory.

She shook her head. It was impossible. But she had seen it with her own eyes. An emotion, maybe relief, but stronger, welled in her. She bent and kissed his lips, feeling bold.

His eyes fluttered open. A small smile turned up the corners of his mouth.

Her body produced an odd soft sound, a combination of a laugh and a cry. She kissed him again, but he was already gone, back under a wave of unconsciousness.

In the bathroom she washed the blood from her hands and looked at her reflection in the old mirror with the silver gone from the edges. Her hair was tangled on one side. There was dried blood on her face and dark circles under her brown eyes, the same color as her father's.

Would she see herself like this often?

A rugged and lonely life on the front treating war casualties seemed less appealing this morning. Not because of seeing Ash's injuries. She was a doctor's child, and even if she had never been in an operating room, or even taken a CPR class, she had certainly heard it over the dinner table; the guts, the gore, the poor prognoses.

What made that life uncertain today was the feeling she had when Ash came, stumbling and half-dead, into her house. At that moment something inside her had broken. The part of her that thought she would never get to see him again, never get to talk to him again, never get to feel that sense of him again. It was the moment she thought she had lost him.

She looked back to the mirror, back into her brown eyes; the same as her father's. But they were different too, weren't they? Maybe they were bigger, or less honey like, or maybe they were just hers.

People leave, she reminded herself. It's what they do. Her mother and her father had both left her. And Ash would too. Not today, it seemed, but someday. Even if they were really *together*, even if they got *married*, even if they both lived a hundred years. He *would* leave. Or she would. Eventually one of them would die. And she would be alone. Again.

She shook her head and tried to clear these senseless thoughts. She hardly knew the man.

Marriage!

She snickered out loud and bit her lip hard. It was the same sore spot she had bitten before she jumped off a bridge with only Ash's encouragement pushing her over the edge.

ॐ

Ruby made scrambled eggs. Ash would need protein to rebuild cells, she reasoned. She sat on the couch in the front room, her own plate in her hands, and tried to ignore the blood on the floor, but she had no appetite at all.

Instead of eating she watched him. At first he just slept. When he twitched, there was a sound, not quite a moan, softer. His eyes opened, and then closed again. Minutes later he stared at the ceiling, either already aware of where he was or unconcerned about waking up in a strange place.

"Ruby?" he said. It was no more than a whisper.

She sat by his head and stroked his stubbly cheek. He breathed a deep satisfied sigh and her heart felt like it might break open.

When he opened his eyes again she saw that they were no longer bright red. They were still bloodshot, but the blue shone through and she felt like she was looking at him again, not Ash possessed by a demon.

"Thank you," he managed.

She laughed nervously. "For what? Exactly?"

He closed his eyes without answering.

She felt foolish. Her own emotions were too strong. "What can I do?" She tried to sound composed. "Should you eat? I made eggs."

"Ambrosia," he whispered. His eyelids flickered closed when he tried to open them.

"I made eggs," Ruby repeated, wondering if he heard her.

His throat worked up and down. "Ambrosia," he managed.

"Ambrosia?" she said, puzzled. "You want an Ambrosia Bar?"

He remained quiet, resting from the effort of speaking. She stood and searched the familiar room with her eyes.

"Will you be okay?" she asked.

He nodded, a small movement of his head.

She went to her room and pulled sweatpants and a sweat-shirt on over the boxers and T-shirt she had worn to bed. She ran back down to Ash and kneeled beside his unmoving form. The depression in his chest was hollow, and the bruise was puffy and dusk colored.

She began to stand but felt his hand on her arm in a shaky attempt to tug her back toward him. Warmth surged inside her. She kissed him and felt his lips curl up in a weak smile under hers. His eyes remained closed.

"I love you," he said, the words pushed out of his lungs like a breath, barely audible.

She jerked back and stared at him as one might look at a viper in the quiet pause after it's struck. An unexpected chill ran through her at the thought of Ash and snakes. A hiss of a word; *perilous.*

His eyes were closed though. He hadn't seen her reaction, hadn't waited for a response.

"Ambrosia," he whispered.

∽ର୧

Ruby ran to Athenaeum, only a few blocks away. Would Sage even be there? Dawn was still breaking over the city sky-line across the river.

As she approached the building her heart sank. There were no lights on inside. She peered in through the plate glass win-dows, between the words painted on the glass: Used and Rare. All she saw were chairs tipped up onto tables and rows of books quiet on their shelves.

She turned with her back to the window and let her head fall with a thud onto the glass. She gave out a little cry, as much from frustration as from pain. She looked up to the green awning above her and wondered if she should wait until...when? Should she go to the grocery store and get some kind of muffin or something? But Sage was Ash's sister, and his request had been specific. Maybe he wanted the comfort of his family's food. It was crazy, but what wasn't at this point?

Her mind raced through her options when a pale grinning face appeared in the window to her right. She gave out a gasp of surprise before she recognized Langston.

"Let me in," she demanded, and then tempered it with, "Ash is hurt. He wants Ambrosia Bars." It sounded stupid, even as she said it, but it was true, and Langston was his brother.

Langston's smile dropped. For a moment she thought he wasn't going to let her in. She thought that he might turn his back and walk away. But he did open the door. He turned the deadbolt and left it to swing open on its own. He was in no rush.

Ruby hurried in and headed straight for the counter. She hoped the case of Ambrosia Bars was full. She would take them all, every last one.

Sage stepped out from the kitchen wearing a flour-dusted apron and holding a large baking tray on her shoulder. "Ruby. You're early."

Ruby smelled the warm Ambrosia Bars before she could see them. "I need those."

"Yeah, okay." Sage lowered the tray to the counter, but she kept her eyes on Ruby. "Just a minute."

Ruby imagined what she must look like. Had she managed to get all the blood off of her? Was her hair still a mess?

"It's Ash," Ruby said. "He's ..." *Hurt* was what she was going to say, but he was getting better. "He wants an Ambrosia Bar."

"All right." Sage let the word hang in the air. "He can come get one." Sage looked beyond her.

Ruby could feel that Langston was behind her before he even spoke. "He's *hurt*." He said it like it was an obscenity.

Sage's eyes flew back to Ruby but her voice remained calm. "Where is he?"

Ruby wasn't sure if she should tell them or not. They seemed irritated. It made her mad. Ash needed their help, even if it was just to put an Ambrosia Bar in a bag and say: *Tell him we're pulling for him.* But in truth she thought maybe *she* needed their help. Ash was getting better and she didn't know why.

Her eyes swung from Sage's look of annoyance, to Langston's look of outright hate, and back again. She got a chill and was suddenly frightened. They're siblings. But *what* are they? The thought shocked her. Could they hurt her? Would they? Did she know too much? It sounded like something from a B movie, and she didn't *know* anything.

"Take us," Sage said.

Ruby found her courage. She needed to protect Ash. "Why?"

Sage's face softened. She looked Ruby in the eye. "We want to help him."

"He wanted an Ambrosia Bar," Ruby said, as if she were negotiating the delicate handing off of information for Ambrosia Bars.

Sage smirked. "Yeah. I bet he did."

❧

The sun was higher now and the morning brighter. There was a chill in the air. Ruby directed Sage and Langston the few blocks to her house. A paper bag full of Ambrosia Bars swung from her hand. Langston's long legs walked faster than Ruby could keep up with. He looked back at her often, obviously annoyed.

On the front porch she turned on the pair and looked them each in the eye. She wanted to remind them that this was her house. Ash had come to her, not them. They looked back at her with blank stares and unrivaled boldness.

She prepared herself for the sight of Ash's limp body on the floor and opened the front door. The blood was still there, dark and puddled, but he was not.

She looked up when Langston pushed passed her and headed for the rose-colored chair that sat across from the couch. Sunlight came in through the window behind it. Ash was sitting there. His face was drawn and pale. His eyes were bloodshot and they had deep brown hollows around them.

Langston said something to Ash that Ruby couldn't quite make out. She was still taking in the fact that he was healed enough to sit up.

Sage took the bag of bars from Ruby's limp hand. She walked between Langston and Ash. "Here," she said to Ash. "This will help."

He took the bar from Sage, chewed it in one bite, and swallowed it down. He closed his eyes and groaned with satisfaction. Color came back into his cheeks and filled in the hollows beneath his eyes. When he opened them, the red was gone. He looked at Ruby. She forced a smile, stunned by the transformation.

Langston was still talking in a low and annoyed tone. Sage cleared her throat and gave him a pointed look. She turned to Ruby. "Thank you, Ruby. He's going to be fine." She turned her attention back to Ash. "It's time we get back." Her tone was flat, matter-of-fact.

Ruby's mind raced. Her eyes darted around the room, to the blood on the floor, to Langston standing near Ash, his eyes furious, to Ash bringing another of Sage's bars to his mouth.

"But …" Ruby hesitated. She searched the scene again. "I need some answers."

The three of them looked at her in surprise, as if watching Ash heal on her floor overnight, waking to want only an Ambrosia Bar, and having his brother and sister berate him instead of being worried, were the most natural things in the world.

Sage turned to her, her spiral curls swinging, and shrugged. "What questions?"

Ruby looked into her flat grey eyes and swallowed. She glanced at Ash. His cheeks were rosy. His eyes were once again a radiant blue. "Well …" She looked back to Sage, and then at Ash again.

"I'm telling her," Ash said. He looked first to Sage and then to Langston. "She has a right to know."

Ruby got a shiver. There was something. Something big. She knew it of course, but Ash was actually admitting it. There was something to be told.

"A *right?*" Sage laughed and then became stone serious. "Don't be ridiculous."

"*She* gets to know. She *must* know." Ash looked at Ruby. "I love her."

Ruby's heart rose up into her throat. She tried to swallow. She tried to breathe.

Ash looked back to his brother and sister who remained silent. "It's my mess. It's my thing. But she gets to know."

His *mess?*

Ruby opened her mouth to speak, to protest, but a darting look from Langston kept her quiet. Sage also looked at her. Ruby thought Sage liked her, but now she saw only suspicion in her odd grey eyes. She spoke to Ash but she kept her eyes on Ruby. "We had a deal. Are you going to break it over a—"

"You don't understand." Ash's voice rose. He looked to the worn rug and then at Ruby. "She quiets it. I'm not sure how. But she does."

Sage's eyes ran up and down Ruby's body, as if seeing her for the first time. "Do *you* love *him?*" She said it like she was asking Ruby if she was willing to take part in a murder.

Ruby glanced at Ash, now completely healed. She thought back to when he came stumbling into the house the night before. She thought back to when she had looked at his wound and *knew* he would die. She thought of bungee jumping and rock climbing, of living in the moment. She thought of the way Ash made her feel. Calm. Whole.

She didn't say anything. She was too confused. There were too many questions. Too many emotions. It was crazy. Wasn't it? People didn't fall in love in a matter of days.

The silence grew long. Not even Langston had something to say. Sage's arms fell limp at her sides.

"Well, do it then," Langston snarled, an unrefined sound that startled Ruby. "Just keep us out of it. See her when you have to, but don't expect us to cover for you."

"No." Ash shook his head and looked at Ruby. "She's coming too."

Langston's head whipped around to Ruby. She saw an image from something half remembered; snakes coming out at her and the word *perilous*. She jerked, aware it wasn't real but feeling like it was a sleight he could pull forth on demand.

She swallowed and found her voice. "What are you talking about? Go where? I have class and studying ..."

"Oh, shut it," Langston shouted and walked toward her. Her heart pounded faster with each of his steps, but he passed by her and walked out the front door.

Sage handed her the bag of Ambrosia Bars and then she too was outside, closing the door behind her.

Ruby looked to Ash, still sitting in the old chair. Sunlight streamed in behind him. His clothes were a mess. They hung on him, limp and bloody.

He didn't say anything.

She walked toward him and put the bag of bars on the table. She wasn't sure where to start. "Someone shot you," she said. "I have the bullet." She pulled the squashed and shredded piece of metal out of her pocket. "I thought you were going to die." Her eyes went slowly from the bullet to his face. "Why didn't you?"

He laughed, but it was a flat sound.

"What happened?" she asked.

He stood and took the bullet from her. He closed his fist around it and shoved it in his own pocket as if to dismiss it. He reached out his hand to touch her.

She pulled away. "How did you heal like that? Where do you want me to go that Sage and Langston don't?"

"Do you love me?" was his response.

She laughed. "What?"

But did she?

His face remained serious.

"Ash," she pleaded. "I don't know. We've only known each other—"

"You know." He continued to look her in the eye.

She blinked repeatedly and turned her head away. She let herself feel those feelings; the wholeness, and then the feeling that she would lose him. Her head lowered. If she said yes she'd be tied to him. Eventually she'd lose him. If she said no, she'd lose him now.

He put his hand under her chin and raised her head to look at him. His energy was steady and smooth.

She searched his eyes. "I'm not even sure I know what love means," she said.

"It means we jump together."

Her breath caught in her throat at the image. She remembered what she had said to him on the bridge. "I'm not very brave."

"It's okay to be afraid, but you can't let fear stop you." He touched her cheek with the back of his fingers. "And I can feel your strength," he whispered.

She closed her eyes, blocking out the sight of him. A deep chill ran through her shoulders and clear up into her ears, damping down her eardrums. She swallowed and opened her eyes again. "I ..." She hesitated. "I love you."

The muscles in his face relaxed, almost imperceptibly. Only a person who had studied his features well would have noticed.

He kissed her and this time she let him. It was the kiss she wanted on the bridge, the one she wouldn't allow herself to want the night before. His tongue was electric against hers. He pulled her in at the waist and her body bowed into his. She smelled the sweat and blood on his clothes, but something primal kicked in and even those scents fanned her desire for him.

"I *knew* you felt it," he said later, kissing her softly between his words.

She laughed at being caught trying to deceive them both. She shook her head and pulled away. "Ash, how ...?" She wasn't sure where to begin. "Why ...?"

His face became serious and in the next moment he answered all her questions with a single sentence, and created a thousand more.

"I'm Ares, the god of war."

SEVEN

RUBY TOOK A STEP BACK. "Ash ..." She whispered, not sure why he would take this moment to make a bizarre joke.

"I could lie," he said. "I could even make you believe it. But you have to know the truth."

She blinked, repeatedly, trying to wash away the absurdness of it. "The god of war?" She laughed, still searching his face for the punch line.

He didn't say anything. His eyes did not shift from hers. There was no smile. There was not a hint of mirth anywhere. She opened her mouth, about to plead for reason, but was interrupted by a succession of three quick knocks at the door.

Her eyes shot around the room, and then back to Ash. "Langston?" she asked, frightened.

He took her by the arm and pulled her behind him, shielding her with his body. "Who's there?" he bellowed.

"Is Ruby home?" A tentative voice came from the other side of the solid wood door.

For a split second Ruby felt relief. The voice was unsteady. It wasn't like Langston's at all. But the reprieve passed as quickly as it had come. Who then? It was still early in the morning. She stood behind Ash and looked at the back of his shirt, at the blood dried there.

"Who is it?" Ash said with more force.

"A friend," came a puzzled reply. "From school."

Her face screwed up in confusion. She had no friends. Her study group might have passed for friendship to a casual on-looker, but it was a loose collection of people held together by ambition and not much more.

The voice came again, more confident. "Is Ruby around?"

Ash turned to her. She shrugged.

"I wanted to know if she checked her organic grade yet," the voice broke in on them.

Ruby's eyes shot to the door. "Mark?" Was her voice shaking?

"Ruby? Are you okay?" he said with a nervous tenor.

"Yeah." She laughed, feeling almost hysterical. "Yeah, of course. I'm fine."

"Oh," he said, sounding relieved.

She looked to Ash again, to his torn and bloody clothes, to the blood on the floor. "Um …" She couldn't think. "It's not really a good time …" She cast her eyes around the room, looking for any excuse that didn't involve blood or bullets.

Instead Mark spoke. "Dr. Reed posted the grades."

Ash's eyebrows went up in surprise, or maybe it was disbelief that grades would mean that much to him. Or her.

"You got a ninety-eight," Mark said.

"What?" She moved deftly around the pool of Ash's blood and walked to the door. "How do you know?"

"I," he paused, possibly searching for his own excuses. "My roommate's a chemistry major. He knows the teaching assistants that did the grading. I thought we could go over the exam. You know, if you're not busy." He paused again. "I brought you a coffee."

Wasn't it illegal to ask about someone else's grades? Or unethical? Or both?

She didn't care. A *ninety-eight!* She hadn't studied, at least not enough. She'd been so distracted. She remembered the adrenaline-crazed feeling of being late for the test and then how focused she had felt when she thought of Ash.

"Ruby?" Mark said with a mixture of curiosity and concern.

"I ..." She still couldn't think. Fatigue and fear crowded in on her.

"Are you okay?" Mark asked again.

"She's fine," Ash said from behind her.

"Ruby, who is that? Should I get the police?"

"No!" she said, too fast. Her eyes widened at the thought of trying to explain any of this to the police.

She turned to Ash, looking for help. He stood in the middle of the front room in a shaft of sunlight streaming in through the window. Rust-red puffs of dust rose up off his shirt, his pants, and his skin. In an instant the blood was gone.

She felt her jaw slacken.

He held her gaze. From the corner of her eye she saw more of the dark red dust move into the air; from the chair where he had been sitting, and from the wooden floor between them.

She looked down. The powder did not move lazily into the air, but with a great force, as if it had been blown off by the very boards themselves. In a moment the dark oval was gone.

Her breath left her in a rush. Still Ash looked at her, unsmiling.

She swallowed as she saw the rusty clouds coming off her own clothes. Not from the sweatshirt and sweatpants she had put on to go to Athenaeum, but from the T-shirt beneath. She held her breath, though she felt nothing, and in an instant the cloud was gone.

"Ash?" she whispered.

But from the other side of the door came, "Ruby—"

She turned, reached for the door handle and swung it open wide.

Mark stood there with a paper coffee cup in each hand. His eyes darted from Ruby to Ash and back again.

She forced a smile. "I'm fine. I just ..." but still she had no excuse.

It didn't matter. Mark filled one in for her. "Oh ... right." His boyish face fell. His cheeks colored clear up to his blond spikes. "Sorry to interrupt."

Ruby searched his face. She thought of herself, obviously in night clothes, and Ash still wearing jeans and the ripped shirt, boots even. Did it look like she hooked up with some random guy?

"No. It's no problem." She tried to be casual, though everything felt deliberate.

"I thought we could go over the exam," Mark repeated his earlier reason for his visit.

Ruby's mind reeled. And then, with Mark standing in front of her, a reminder of her normal life before Ash, before chess games and bungee jumping, and fatal injuries that healed in the night, she felt clarity descend upon on her. With it came flashes of memory: Ash retelling battles as though he was remembering, not reciting; Ash winning at chess, not sometimes, but always; Ash in a coffeehouse she'd never been to before, waiting for her.

Not Ash, she realized. Ares, the god of war.

"You like lattes, right?" Mark stretched out one of the white cups to her. "Vanilla?"

She took the coffee in her numb hand, but she didn't invite him in.

&&

Ash still stood in the front room, in the sunlight, where she first saw the blood fly off him in a cloud. They locked eyes and he stepped toward her. She backed up, though there was little room between her and the closed front door. He stopped short, halfway to her. Confusion spread across his features. "Ruby—"

She shook her head. He took another step in her direction. She turned and ran to the kitchen. Hot coffee splashed out of the drinking hole in the lid of the cup she was holding.

"Ruby!" he shouted.

She stopped in the kitchen and turned on him. "How …?" She didn't know where to begin. "What was that?"

His hands were up in front of him like stop signs. "I'm not going to hurt you."

This hadn't occurred to her.

"Please." He paused. "I need you."

She felt her knees go weak. The cup fell from her hand. The plastic lid came off and sent sprays of creamed coffee around the room. The cloying smell of artificial vanilla filled the air. She felt Ash's arms encircle her, strong and solid. They propped her up and held her close against him.

A sob escaped her. He put his rough face next to her cheek, and whispered softly, "I've got you." And the feeling was there, the feeling of Ash, the calmness, the connectedness, the wholeness.

Her mouth was thick and hot, and when he kissed her she shuddered and cried harder. It didn't matter who he was or what it meant. She did love him, and already it hurt.

He held her tight, until her sobs quieted, until she could stand again. His steady energy flowed into her. He led her into the front room and sat with her on the couch. "Here," he handed her one of Sage's bars. "It will help."

"I wanted the coffee," she said with a weak laugh.

"Trust me." He laughed. "This is better."

She looked at the bar, suspicious now. "What is it?"

"Trust me," he repeated.

She took a bite of the Ambrosia Bar and savored the unusual taste that she could never quite place. She felt her fatigue slide away. It wasn't like coffee, she didn't feel up, but she wasn't as tired anymore either. "What is it?"

"Ambrosia," he said. "The food of the gods. Not pure, of course. That would be—" He didn't finish the thought.

"You ... You can't ..." she said. Her eyes searched a narrow space in front of her. "You can't be serious." Her emotions rode a fine wire just beneath her control, her rational mind on one side, her gut on the other. Her thoughts jumped to her father. She licked her lips and spoke in a whisper.

"Why war?"

His jaw clenched. He closed his eyes. When he opened them again he shook his head. "I didn't choose it."

He reached for her hand, motionless in her lap, but she pulled away, not ready, not yet. "I don't understand."

Gods, like everyone, feel the energy of emotions, he told her. "A happy person can bring you up. A negative person can bring you down."

Gods could direct and move that energy, but they also reacted to it, and certain energies resonated more or less with certain gods. The energy that resonated with each god wasn't a choice. It was a part of them, like dark hair or blue eyes.

He told her that he felt the pain of conflict and combat— and with it the highs of glory and triumph. The two battled inside him. He was caught between the adrenaline of the fight and the agony of war's destruction. His anger ramped up wars on Earth, and wars on Earth raged within him.

"I feel hate and prejudice. Anguish and fear. Loss and desperation." He twisted the old pitted ring he wore.

She tried to keep her eyes steady. She wanted to know. She wanted to be strong.

"But I feel the adrenaline of it, too. The ferocious raw nerve. The pure thrill of knowing *you're not dead.* The feel of being *alive.*"

She nodded. She knew that feeling. It was the euphoria of realizing the cord had caught, that she was being thrown back up into space, that she was alarmingly alive.

"I feel it all at once," he went on. "One pulls me in, the other makes me want to claw my way out."

A heat rose into her chest thinking of all of that, going on inside of him.

"Today it's quiet," he said. "Oddly so. Today I don't feel any of it." His face was serene. "*You* do that to me."

A small smile flitted across her lips. She shook her head. "Hmm?"

"Everyone has energy," he said. "We all feed off of it. We all respond to it. But *our* energy, yours and mine, it runs *together.* Like two streams meeting to form a river. That *feeling,* when I touch you, or hold you, or kiss you." He smiled. "It's harmony. And it's rare."

They talked well into the afternoon. Ash told her that Sage was really Athena, the goddess of knowledge, come to Earth in the vibrant information age. She was drawn by new technology, but she wanted to preserve old technologies too: paper and books. She knew they would soon be forgotten.

Langston was Apollo, the god of poetry, music, and healing. Ruby winced when she heard that. Those things were good and right and true. But Langston felt all wrong. Ash told her that Langston hadn't always been so callous and malcontent. He was in love with a nymph, a being that was long forbidden to them, like *all* mortals were forbidden.

"Why?" she asked, but her mind had already jumped to the obvious conclusion. *She* was forbidden.

"With mortals everything is now, in the moment. Gods have forever. What we don't do today, we can do tomorrow, or in a thousand years. Mortals only have today, and they know it. It makes them very ..." He smiled. "... seductive."

She saw the pictures of her life marching up the stairs on the other side of the front room. Her first lost tooth, an elementary Thanksgiving play, high school graduation.

Ash was the one who taught her to live in the moment, not to spend all her life living for some unknown future. And here he was, a *god. Immortal.* Do gods even have a life? Wasn't a life a finite thing?

"My father, Zeus, could never fight that seductiveness. He could never fight the immediacy of humans. Hera, my mother, was jealous. She took her anger out on the women he cheated with and their children."

Ruby remembered reading about Zeus's famed infidelity and his notorious temper in her mythology class, but what of Hera's temper? She couldn't remember.

"Sometimes Zeus didn't know about these reprisals, and sometimes he didn't care. Sometimes other gods interceded but ..." He paused. "It was a heady time for us all. We reveled in humans and their lives. We intervened where we wanted, and sat back to watch the results play out." His voice became quiet. "Chess, but with people."

Ruby remembered his assertion that you could tell a lot about a person by how they played chess. Hadn't the gods played rough?

"For thousands of years Zeus chased and bedded the women of Earth. Eventually he saw how much it hurt Hera. But he couldn't control it. Gods have desires, and ambitions, and tempers, like people, but more intense.

"In the end the only way Zeus could keep himself from the women of Earth was by separating himself from them. Eventually he forbade all the gods from interacting with mortals. He restricted us to the core of Olympus."

"Olympus?" she whispered. "In Greece?"

"No. We moved it a thousand years ago, maybe more."

Ruby laughed, but Ash didn't.

"Olympus, the true home of the gods, is not a place like a mountain. It's created and maintained by the twelve major gods of Olympus: The Olympians. We can dissolve it and recreate it at will. Olympus exists in the astral plane, above the physical world. It sits above a different Mount Olympus, northwest of what is now Seattle."

"But ..." Ruby stammered, "A collective consciousness? You imagined it and it became real?" Her eyes darted to his. "Near Seattle?"

"Zeus doesn't know Athena, Apollo, and I are on Earth," Ash said, bringing her back to the more practical and pressing facts. "We visit Olympus often and avoid suspicion. Some of the others know, but not Zeus or Hera. If Apollo tells Zeus I'm here ..." He paused. "If he tells him that I'm in love with a human ..." He exhaled a forceful breath.

"What?" she demanded.

"Zeus can be ..." he searched her eyes. "...*creative.*" A muscle near his eye twitched.

"What do you mean?"

"You've read the stories. Right?"

There were so many myths that involved Zeus and she had read them so quickly; the class had been an elective. Then she remembered something about Zeus and an eagle. Something gruesome.

"Prometheus," she said. Her face went slack. "Zeus punished him by having an eagle eat his liver out of his body every day. And because he was immortal it grew back every night."

Her next breath shuddered in her chest. This was for real. That could happen. She had seen Ash heal. She had seen his lungs, and his bones, and his skin knit together overnight. What if he were shot again today? He would heal. And again tomorrow. And the day after that. On and on forever. Immortality, she realized, could be a curse.

"We should go to Athenaeum," Ash said. "We need to find Apollo. I don't think he'll think it fair that he's kept his love a secret and that I should fall in love and refuse to do the same. I don't want to have to hide. I want you to come with me, but we need to time it right."

"Where do you want me to go?" she asked.

He looked at her like she was asking him what color the sky was. "Olympus."

She looked around the room. The blood left her head and everything seemed fuzzy. She stood, with no destination in mind, and soon found herself in the kitchen.

The spilled coffee was splayed out on the yellow wall like a Rorschach, all chaos and confusion. She grabbed a handful of paper towels from the plastic holder near the sink and rubbed at the stain furiously.

She heard Ash come up behind her, but she didn't turn.

"Ruby, what is it?"

"I'm not going to Olympus." She rubbed at the spill harder than was necessary. The towels were soaked through with the aromatic coffee. She longed for a cup, for the familiar taste and the warmth of the mug in her hand, for something to be normal.

He bent down to her and put his hand on her shoulder. She felt their connection, but she ignored it and kept scrubbing with the useless towels. "Ruby, I want you to be with me. I want to face Zeus. I want you to live on Olympus."

The softness of his voice did nothing to soften her mood. She was supposed to just take this all in as truth? Uproot her life and change everything for him? She was supposed to face the wrath of Zeus, whatever that meant, so that *he* didn't have to hide? She gritted her teeth until the muscles near her temples throbbed.

"Can't you clean up this mess like you did with the blood?" she spat. "Can't you turn it to dust?"

"Ruby calm down. It doesn't work like that."

"Well, tell me then. How does it work exactly? Because I don't understand any of this."

He let out a long sigh and ran his hand through his curly hair. "The blood is a part of me," he said. "I'm immortal because my chemical bonds are strong. Stronger than any human's. Stronger than the ones holding this house together. Stronger than the ones in the rock we climbed yesterday.

"The only thing stronger than my chemistry is my will. I can will for my molecules to fly apart, but their chemical bonds will always pull them back together.

"It's how I can disappear from this kitchen and appear a second later in a coffeehouse blocks away. It's how I can heal from a mortal wound in a night. It's why immortals never get sick, or cough, or even sneeze. Our bodies deal with anything foreign immediately."

In her mind she saw him at the coffeehouse on Fremont, waiting for her. She felt the memory of the sharp pain in her knee as she leaned on the bullet his body had rejected. Weakness and exhaustion flooded into her and she felt the sting of tears in the corners of her eyes.

"I willed for those blood molecules to dissipate," he said. "My body has already made new cells, like anyone else's would, but faster. The old molecules will join all the others in the universe." He shrugged and smiled weakly. "I'm useless with coffee."

She sank to the worn linoleum and began to sob. He sat next to her and tried to pull her hands away from her face. When she finally let him, he put his large palms on her cheeks and wiped at her tears with his thumbs. His eyes were dark and full of worry but the energy that came off of him was as smooth as water over worn stones.

"I've got you," he whispered.

EIGHT

RUBY NOTICED THE CHANGE on the street as soon
as she and Ash walked out of her house and turned toward
Athenaeum after cleaning up the coffee. Portland had been
getting back to normal after the bombing and she was used to
seeing people out, but today they were everywhere. Music
came out of open windows they passed. She recognized John
Lennon's voice streaming out of one. "Imagine all the people
…"

They rounded the corner to Hawthorne and she saw that
there was practically a party on the bigger four-lane street.
People stood in loose groups on the sidewalk, talking and
laughing. The road was full of cars honking, with passengers
waving and half-hanging out of windows.

Ash reached for her hand. He slid his silky fingers down in
between hers so that they were meshed together like fabric. A
group of four women passed. They had peace signs painted on

their cheeks in different shades of lipstick. A flag with a picture of the Earth taken from space hung out of one of the apartments above the storefronts.

What had happened? What had they missed?

She felt a tug on her hand and looked up. They stood under the green awning of Athenaeum, her second time there that day. Would Sage and Langston still be angry? Would Sage hate her now? She was pretty sure Langston already did.

Everything inside the coffee shop was familiar, but new. The Ambrosia Bars were real ambrosia, god food, and the owner was the goddess of knowledge. Ruby scanned the shelves of books. There were hundreds, maybe thousands. She saw people buying coffee from Sage all day, but had she ever seen her sell a single book? Ruby didn't think so.

Sage stood behind the counter filling an order for two women. The three of them chatted and laughed. Ruby felt relief that Sage was in a good mood, but the feeling left when she spotted Langston sitting at a table across the room. He was reading something from his black journal to a woman Ruby recognized from her genetics class. Langston's eyes darted up and caught Ruby's.

She looked away.

The two women left with their coffees. From the corner of her eye Ruby saw Langston stand and say something to the woman from genetics. She also left, with a surreptitious glance backward.

As soon as the door closed, and the four of them were alone, Langston spoke, his voice loud. "You can't be serious." He looked at Ruby, but he didn't say more.

"Just try not to make this about you." Ash's eyes bored into Langston.

Langston closed the distance of half the room in two strides and towered over Ash. "*I* won't risk it."

Their faces were inches from one another's. "*You* don't have to." Ash looked to Sage then. "The risk is mine."

"Ash ..." Ruby began, though she didn't know what she might say to keep them from fighting.

Langston laughed. "You haven't even told her."

Sage walked toward Langston. "Apollo," she glanced to Ruby.

"She knows," Ash said.

Langston sneered. "I can't believe your stupidity, Ares. A human?" His eyes rolled up. "Really?"

Ruby's cheeks burned. She thought of the odd assortment of women he paraded around with. He seemed to like humans well enough himself. She almost said so, but her fear of him held her back.

"Look," Sage said. She picked up a folded newspaper from the table next to them. She opened it to the front page. The headline was simple and bold: "Cease-fire."

Ruby's eyes flew to Sage's face.

Sage began to read. "In early morning diplomatic talks, the Allies and the Rogues have come to what many were thinking was an impossibility, a signed cease-fire. The document is effective immediately, and for the duration of peace talks ..."

Langston looked from Ruby to Ash, then to Sage, but he said nothing and turned away.

Now Ruby understood the people in the street, the music, and the honking. After more than a decade of war, there was hope of peace.

"I felt it," Ash said. "I thought it was Ruby. It *is* Ruby. This—" He took the paper from Sage and held it up to Langston, though he was still turned away from them. "—this is what she does for me. And, yes, I will risk *everything* for her."

Langston walked further away. His head was down. Ruby wasn't sure what the cease-fire meant, beyond the obvious. She didn't know what it meant to *them*.

Sage turned toward Langston. She spoke softly. "Think of Kissiae. Think of what it could mean."

Ruby saw Langston's shoulders rise up, tightening. "It could mean we all end up being the next Prometheus or the next Kronos," he said. When he turned his blue eyes were cold and icy. "Have you forgotten about the prophecy, my vision? This is proof. I will not risk all of Olympus." He looked at Ruby. "Not for her." He walked to the door and was through it in the next moment.

A group of students pushed in after he left, slapping each other on the back and laughing. Music followed them in from a car driving by on the street. Ash took Ruby's hand and led her to the chess table. The board was set up, ready for him.

"Let's play," he said.

"What vision?" Ruby asked as she stood next to the seat across from him. "What did he mean about risking Olympus?"

"Sit." Ash's voice was commanding. It startled her. "Please," he said more softly. "I want to teach you how to play. Not just moves to memorize."

Her eyes shifted to the group that had come in. They were ordering at the counter, oblivious that they had walked in on two gods arguing. Ruby sat across from Ash and absently moved a white pawn out on the far left.

"No," he said and put the pawn back. "You want to control the middle."

She sighed, frustrated that he wanted to play chess when she had a million questions running through her mind. "Ash—"

"Please," he said. "It helps me to think."

She looked at the board again. This time she tried to really *see* it. She moved out the pawn in front of her queen. It was the first move of The Immortal Game, but this time she used the opening because it seemed like the right move to make.

"Good. Trust your instincts. Now your queen and this bishop," he pointed at the white marble pieces, "can move out too."

Ruby's thoughts couldn't help but wander. She thought of Prometheus and the eagle. Kronos was familiar too. He was a Titan, she thought, maybe Zeus's father. There had been a war between the generations, but she couldn't remember the details. Had there been anything about visions or prophecies? She remembered something about oracles, gods or priests who knew about the future. She thought that maybe Apollo was an oracle, or that his priests were. *Ugh!* She cursed her lack of attention to the reading. Who could have known *that* would be the important class?

"Ash." She waited until his eyes lifted from the chess board. "You've told me this much. You have to tell me the rest. What did Langston mean?"

"They don't always come true," he said, as if it were an excuse not to say more.

"Ash, I need to know everything."

He hesitated. "Apollo's an oracle. He sees glimpses of the future, but he hasn't had a vision in a long time. The last one was before you and I met."

She licked her lips. "What vision?"

He looked at her from the side. The corners of his mouth turned down slightly. "A human. A woman who would cause a split between the gods." His voice was quiet. "Some gods would fight against her, others would fight in her favor."

A deep shiver ran through Ruby's chest.

He didn't say more but looked beyond her, out to the street. She could hear distant shouts of celebration through the glass.

"And?" she said.

"And what?" Ash looked back to her.

"What happens? Who wins?"

"Oracles only get impressions and fleeting images. They don't see everything and they don't always come true," he reminded her.

"Langston didn't see how it ends?"

"No," was his only answer, followed quickly by, "Ruby, I won't give you up because Apollo has a *feeling*. I *will* fight for you."

She felt an unexpected excitement at the thought of Ash risking himself for her. She hadn't thought she would ever want that—the guy who would defend a woman's honor, by force if necessary—but something deep within her stirred.

"Apollo's been far too willing to settle." He looked her in the eye. "I won't." Veins came to the surface along the muscles in his arms. She could feel his increased energy from across the table.

"Kissiae?" she asked. "That's Langston's nymph?"

"Yes. The ivy nymph. And there have been other gods who have loved mortal beings. It's almost impossible that there wouldn't be. There are only so many gods on Olympus."

"No one has ever questioned the rule?" she asked.

He held her gaze. The chessboard sat between them but even Ash had given up on playing. "The danger is real, Ruby. I don't defy Zeus lightly, but we have all been a slave to his lack of self-control for far too long."

He took her hand, lying on the side of the chess board. "I have been in love before," he said. "Only once. She was my beginning." He paused. "But she belonged to someone else. Losing her was more painful than any wound of the flesh, and ultimately I thought she was my end.

"That was over two thousand years ago, Ruby. I have known many women but I haven't loved another until I met you. Now that I've found you, there is no turning back for me. No matter how much it scares Apollo."

She looked to the crowd that had come in. They had put several tables together and talked noisily over one another.

"Why don't you stay here?" she said in a sudden gust of brilliance. "Why bother with Zeus at all?"

"I can't not go back," he said.

"Why is it so important that *I* go?" She glanced out the window and saw that the streets were filling up with even more people. "Tell him you've met someone. Isn't that the same thing? You get to confront him, but I don't have to be there to start some kind of a civil war?" Her mouth went dry at the thought.

"I don't want to live in two worlds. I can make him accept you."

"How ..." she said, louder than she meant to. Her eyes shot around the room, but no one looked at her. She lowered her voice, unable to believe what she was about to say. "What would a life on Olympus even mean?"

"What would it mean?" He squinted and deep furrows formed on his brow.

"How would I get there?" she asked. "What would I do there? Would we ever come back?" All of the logistics came rushing out of her, the sheer enormity of it. She thought of her father and medical school. His legacy. Her dreams. "What would I *be* there? Your *girlfriend*?"

Ash blinked and cocked his head at her. "It's *Olympus*. Everything is perfect. We'd be together. I'll *find* a way to get you there."

"But I have plans, and dreams, and a future. *Here*."

"To do what? To be a *doctor*?" There was a snide edge to his voice; disbelief that she could have such a lowly dream when what he seemed to be offering her was a life of luxury and idleness. She was Cinderella and he was the prince. But she didn't want a prince. She wanted a partner.

"Yes," she said. "To be a doctor like my father. To help people. To join Medics for Mercy and work on the front. I want you to be there with me." The thought caused a deep pang in her chest and tears threatened. She hadn't even realized how alone she felt. Now that she had Ash, she didn't want to be without him. "We can still be together."

"Ruby, there won't be any front. Do you understand what's happening?" he asked. "What *has happened?*"

Maybe she didn't.

"We stopped the war, Ruby. You and me. *We* did that."

She searched his eyes. "What do you mean?"

"*Us.* The moment you decided to love me—the moment I felt it—the war … It slipped away. I'd never felt it before. I didn't know what it meant. But now I do."

"Ash …"

"Ares," he said. "*Please.* When we're alone, you can call me Ares."

She looked into his eyes, so serious.

"Ares," she said, with a moment of hesitation. "What we have. What we *feel.*" She squeezed his hand. "It's strong." She laughed. "But world peace?"

He didn't laugh with her. "Not world peace. Not yet. But this war. This one is ending. Because of *us.*"

NINE

ASH HAD NO REACTION to the number thirty-seven, a whole fish staring up from its chili sauce, when she pulled it out of her refrigerator. Ruby ate her Thai noodles and speculated about what foods he had eaten over the centuries. She realized that in some ways their lives were too different for her to wrap her mind around.

When they finished eating he leaned against the counter in her kitchen with his thumbs hooked in the front pockets of his jeans. Ruby put the forks in the dishwasher. She could feel her pulse in her head and she wondered if he could see how nervous she was. She wanted to kiss him but she wasn't sure how. They were in love, right? Could she just lean over and kiss him? Was he *hers* in that way?

She didn't have long to wonder before he moved toward her. Her heart pumped wildly as he took the box of dishwasher soap from her hands and set it somewhere, though as far as she was concerned it ceased to exist.

He closed his eyes and softly rubbed his cheek against hers. "I love you," he whispered.

She could feel herself breathing, high in her chest, as his lips finally brushed against hers. The sweet taste of the Ambrosia Bars they had eaten for dessert was still on his lips.

At first his kisses were soft but they soon turned hungry and eager. He lifted her by the waist, as if she were as light as a feather, and sat her on the counter. She opened her legs and he leaned in between them.

Her hands tangled into his curls and grabbed at their roots. Their lips never left one another's as he trailed his fingers along her jawline and down her neck. A shudder traveled through her.

She worked at the buttons of his shirt but she quickly gave up and began to pull the fabric up his torso.

He carried her to the TV room and laid her flat on the cool leather couch. He stopped kissing her long enough to pull the shirt off over his head. Long languid muscles contracted as he moved. His chest was smooth, with a few dark hairs between his subtly defined chest muscles. When he pressed his hard body down on hers, he kissed her like she was air or water to him, like she was his sustenance.

Soon her shirt was on the floor next to his. His hands ran along her ribs and over her bra in an electric rush. His skin moved across hers like heated silk. His kisses traveled from her mouth to her throat.

Ruby may have always been the one who held back, those few times in the past. She may have always been stronger than the guy, more willing to wait. But with him she seemed to have no control. "Ash," she breathed.

"Call me Ares," he whispered, raising goose bumps on her skin with his hot breath.

"Ares, I ..."

He continued to kiss her, inching ever lower. But when she didn't say more he pulled away and looked at her. His blue eyes were bright. His face was flushed. "It's been a long time," he said. "I want it to be perfect."

"There's something ..." She licked her fevered lips and glanced away. "I'm a ..." She couldn't say the word. It would seem ridiculous to him.

His face changed. Worry replaced desire.

"I've never ..." She trailed off, still unable to look at him. "I mean. I've come close. It's just that I wanted to wait. I'm not sure what for." She looked at him from the corner of her eye, trying to catch his reaction.

He swallowed and looked at the leather couch cushions beneath her. His eyes darted around as though he were thinking. He lifted himself off of her and she immediately missed the weight of him. She felt cold and untethered.

"But I don't want to wait anymore," she said as she sat up. Her hand reached out to catch him. She wanted to pull him back down with her. "I want this. I was waiting for *you*."

He stared at the floor, not making eye contact with her. Would this be what chased him away? Her lack of *experience*?

Her heart, racing a moment ago with desire, now fluttered with anxiety.

"Ash, really …"

He looked at her then, almost as if he had forgotten she was there, like he had been thinking about something else. After a moment he said, "This is good." He reached for his shirt and pulled it on over his disheveled curls.

"What's good?" she asked. She felt like they were having two different conversations.

He looked her in the eye, unembarrassed. "You're a virgin."

She felt her hot face get hotter. Her eyes darted away. "So?"

He reached for her shirt and handed it to her. She pulled it on, feeling naked for the first time.

"Are you leaving?" she asked, trying to hide the disappointment in her voice. Had she misjudged him?

He turned, his head cocked. "Do you want me to leave?"

"No," she said quickly and then wondered if she should have lied.

"Then I'll stay," he said, like it was obvious. "I can sleep on the couch."

"I have plenty of beds," she said. "That's not really the point."

"Good." He smiled and leaned down to her. "I do prefer a bed." His lips met hers with all the passion he had shown moments before, when separate beds was the farthest thing from his mind.

"Trust me," he said when their lips parted. "Hera would want it this way."

∾ଚ୧ଡ଼

Ruby jerked her foot at the snake that was caught in her sheets as it wound around her ankles. The snake tightened its grip. She sat up in one swift pull and tried to beat the snake away in the semi-darkness. A scream was halfway up her throat when she woke with a start. Instead of screaming she breathed out a single word. "Langston …"

She blinked and looked around her bedroom, but there was nothing unusual. She glanced at the alarm clock. It was already six-thirty. She went over her Monday class schedule in her head. She hadn't done her homework for genetics, or the reading for western civ. She hadn't even recopied her chemistry notes. She pushed the covers off, but instead of going to the kitchen, where her books were, she walked to her father's old room.

From the doorway she saw Ash lying under the grey comforter. He took up most of the queen-sized bed with his sprawled out limbs. She smiled to herself. Maybe she should be thankful they weren't sleeping together. It didn't look like there was any room for her.

She tiptoed across the floorboards, over the braided cotton rug, and climbed in on the far side. She nuzzled into the small space next to him. She breathed in his sleepy scent and savored his warmth. He wore only boxer shorts. The skin of his chest and arms was smooth as they wound round her.

"Morning," he said. His hands ran along the curve of her legs and he pulled her closer to him. She felt his excitement rising against her, but she knew from a weekend of long make out sessions that he would only let them take it so far. His commitment to her virginity was maddening.

"Why do you even stay here?" she asked, glad he did. "Don't you have a home?" She knew he had an apartment, in the same building as Sage, but he never wanted to go there.

He snuggled deeper into the curve of her body. His hand slipped up inside her shirt. "I never liked that place," he said kissing her neck and her earlobes. "I never stayed there anyway."

"Where did you sleep?" she asked before she decided if she really wanted to know.

He pulled his hand flat against her stomach. "Never mind," he said. "That's over."

She rolled to face him. "Where did you go?" she asked, remembering that he had always looked tired then.

His eyes darted past her.

"I was just curious," she said. She wouldn't press him. It was his business.

"I used to go to the war," he said quickly. "I'd play chess until I couldn't stand it anymore. Then I'd go to fight."

She thought of the bullet wound in his chest and put her hand on the now healed skin there.

"I almost never got seriously injured," he said. "I already knew I loved you that night. I got upset when you told me to leave. When you said …"

Ruby shook her head against the pillow. She didn't want to hear what she had said.

"This cease-fire is surreal," he said. "I've never heard it, or felt it, or sensed it so little." He touched her face and stroked strands of hair behind her ear. "Wherever you are. That's where I want to be."

He pulled her tight again and settled his chin on the top of her head. Her cheek lay flat against his chest with the sound of his heart slow and steady in her ear. She dozed to the rhythm.

Later she woke with a start. "What time is it?" she said, trapped in Ash's arms and unable to see the clock.

"I don't know," came his mumbled response.

She pulled away and sat up. She glanced at the clock on the nightstand. "Crap ..." She threw off the blankets and ran down the hall.

She dressed in her room and ran back to Ash with her shoes in one hand. "I have to go. I'll see you later."

He sat up and the blankets fell away from his bare chest. "Where are you going?"

"Class," she said, pulling her eyes away from his body. "I'm already late for chemistry."

"Why are you going to class?"

She put one sneakered foot on the floor and began to wedge in the other foot. "If you want good grades it helps to go to class."

"But— You won't need any of that. Not on Olympus."

She left her shoe half untied and let the laces fall to the floor. "Ash, I told you. I need to honor my father's memory. There are still other wars in the world. Medics for Mercy sends help to all of them."

"Ruby, you are helping people," he said. "You have already saved lives. The peace talks are ahead of schedule."

"I know that's what you think. But *I* don't control wars. *I* haven't done anything."

"Ruby ..." He took her hand and hesitated.

She expected the same argument he had given her before: he needed her, he would fight Zeus for her, and if Apollo's visions came true then it was high time for a change on Olympus anyway.

Instead he said, "But his dream *isn't* your dream."

She blinked.

"You loved your father and you miss him." His voice was gentle. "But being a doctor won't bring him back. Healing *everyone* on Earth will not bring him back."

She sat heavily on the edge of the bed.

"You have to discover your own dream," he said. "Whether you're here or on Olympus."

She glanced away. His answers felt too easy.

"I'm late," she said. "I'll see you later."

⌾

This time there was no hesitation. Ruby flipped her test packet over and beamed down at the red ninety-eight in the corner. She thought of meeting Ash at the coffeehouse the night before the test. Had the god of war given her the power to ace her chemistry exam?

From what she was learning about gods, it didn't work that way. It wasn't him, at least not directly. It had come from within herself somewhere. Somewhere that he helped her to reach.

Dr. Reed tapped on the whiteboard to get the room's attention. "Aldehydes ..." he began.

After the lecture Mark caught up with her. His spikey hair was messier than usual. "Ruby, I ..."

"Listen Mark, about the other day ..." She realized that she had never got in touch with him about the exam.

"Yeah, who was that guy? I mean, it's none of my business, but he seemed pretty intense."

"He's just a guy I met," she said.

Mark fidgeted with one of the straps that hung down from his backpack.

"Thanks for the coffee," she finally thought to say. "And for letting me know about my grade."

"Yeah, no problem. We only have a few weeks to get ready for the final." He dropped the strap and hitched the backpack higher onto his shoulder. "The group was thinking of a Monday, Wednesday, Friday schedule. Does that work for you, or would longer weekend sessions be better?"

Cold air washed over them as she opened the door that led out to the quad, but what took Ruby's breath away was how unappealing a tight studying schedule sounded. A few weeks ago she would have thought it smart, even necessary, but today it felt stifling. That kind of commitment would leave no time to go *do something*.

"I don't know, Mark. I have other classes too," she said.

He blinked repeatedly, but she couldn't tell if it was from the low autumn sun or from lack of comprehension.

"I mean, we should study," she said quickly. "Obviously. I just can't commit to a schedule right now."

"Okaaay…" He drew the word out like he was buying time to deal with a deranged person. "The rest of the group is on board for Monday, Wednesday, Friday. We were waiting for you to vote on the format since you didn't come last time and the phones are still down."

"Thanks, but the group should probably go ahead and decide without me."

He slowed his pace. "Are you quitting?"

"No," she chuckled, mostly to get the sound of the word *quitting* out of her head. "I'm just not sure I can promise anything."

Mark stopped walking. "Are you sure? They'll give your spot to someone else. It already came up at the last meeting."

She swallowed as she pictured them sitting around criticizing her for not showing. Her mind contrasted it with the feeling of free-falling from a railroad trestle in the woods. She turned to him. "I'm sure," she said and kept walking.

ംരഉ

After the initial euphoria of the cease-fire, the country fell into a comfortable rhythm of peace. People seemed to have more patience, fewer cars honked at her on her bike, more people smiled on the street. Even the clouds seemed a lighter grey than was normal for this late in the fall. But today a misty drizzle fell outside the plate glass windows at Athenaeum.

Ruby sat with her books, like she had always done, but instead of never looking up at the life around her, she now found it difficult to concentrate at all.

She glanced at Ash often, playing chess in the corner. If he caught her eye he would raise his eyebrows at her. It was his way of asking her if she wanted to play, or if she wanted him to sit with her while she studied. She knew that he would send his opponent packing if she gave even the smallest nod of her head.

She smiled, self-conscious of the way everyone at Athenaeum looked at her now. Ash's girlfriend. "How did she get him?" She heard people whisper. It made her smile, not because she knew the answer, but because she asked herself the same question.

Ruby's foot tapped in time to the soft indie rock music that came from the radio behind the counter as she skimmed her history text. She wanted to know the basics of the Thirty Years War before she asked Ash about it. Movement caught the corner of her eye and she looked up with a start.

"Rubes," Langston said, journal in one hand, ivy leaf in the other. Her eyes flew past him, to Ash, who was already standing and coming toward them.

Langston pulled out a chair and sat across from her. He sat back in his seat and crossed his legs. "Your body will wither with all this information, you know." He said it as if they were picking up a friendly conversation. "Look at Sage. It's practically ruined her complexion."

Ruby glanced at Sage. Her skin was flawless and her lustrous curls swept her shoulders with her movements. Her grey eyes were bright as she talked to a customer about her latest literary find; some treasure she probably dug out of some basement to save from booklice or careless owners. The customer nodded a little too often for real interest.

"You have to be careful ..." Langston paused. Her eyes shot back to him. The phrase, familiar, kicked something up from the depths of her mind. He smiled. "Your skin may never recover."

"Thanks for the warning," she said, and tried to keep her voice steady. "I'll try not to overdo it."

Langston hadn't shown up at Athenaeum for days. Sage had gone to Olympus, but he hadn't been there either. Ruby bit at her lip, not sure where this conversation was going. Not sure why he was here now, talking to *her*.

"Yes." He drawled the word. "There are perils."

Then Ash was there, thankfully. He sat with them and glanced once around the crowded coffeehouse, as though he were scoping the area for enemies.

"What do you want?" There was no patience in Ash's voice.

"Just making sure Rubes understands the consequences of her choices." Langston kept his eyes level with Ash's. "But who am I to interfere with her plans. Medical school. Isn't that right?" He looked at Ruby.

She wasn't sure what to say. She and Ash were still at an impasse. She wanted him to stay on Earth with her and he wanted her to go to Olympus.

"Very good then," Langston said. "You go to medical school and save a few lives. Ash can go home and end a few thousand more. Just like normal."

Her jaw clenched.

Langston stood and left Ruby to glare at his back.

Ash leaned toward her. "Don't let him get to you." She was surprised that he was so calm. He had been worried while Langston was gone.

"He has a point." Ruby didn't make eye contact with him. She was suddenly angry at them both. "We *are* different."

"No. We're not." He ducked his head and caught her eye before she could look away. "What's wrong?" he asked.

"I don't know." She sighed and sat back against the chair. It wasn't him. She was tired. "I'm sorry. I didn't sleep much."

He studied her face. "Why not?"

"I've been having these dreams." She rubbed at her eyes. "I can never really remember them, not the details. They're just vaguely awful."

His eyes narrowed. "Can you remember anything?"

"Snakes." It was the first thing that came into her mind. She glanced at him. "And you," she laughed, nervous to admit that she had bad dreams about him. "They don't mean anything."

"What else?"

Ruby's eyes darted across the room to Langston.

Ash stood before she could say more, before she could stop him. He strode across the room to the taller god who also turned, as if he was expecting a confrontation.

Langston and Ash—Apollo and Ares—stared each other down. Customers glanced their way. The gods spoke low, barely controlling themselves in the room full of people.

Ruby suddenly worried for humanity. Would the world feel Ares's anger?

She looked at Sage, who was still standing with the customer, but now her focus was on her brothers. Her eyes darted to Ruby and back again. Ruby wondered if she should intervene, but the idea of getting between two gods seemed crazy.

Ruby approached them warily and bit her lip.

"You, of all people, should understand," Ruby heard Ash say in a low voice.

"I won't let your carnal nature break Olympus apart," Langston hissed. He turned away without looking at Ruby, and strode out the front door as if he had never come back in the first place.

Ash watched him go with his fists balled up at his sides.

⁓◉◡◉⁓

"You should let me win," Ruby said as she moved her bishop. She hadn't beaten Ash since The Immortal Game, but she was getting better.

He looked up from the chess board. "Surrender?"

"I'm just saying that if you loved me you would let me win once in a while." She smiled, trying to lighten his mood, hoping he would talk. He still hadn't said anything about the fight he had earlier with Langston.

"I don't lose. And I don't give up. Not willingly." He shook his head. "Not ever."

"That seems like a character flaw," she feigned seriousness.

He flinched. "A flaw?"

"Sure. You gotta 'know when to fold 'em,'" she quoted.

"Yeah?" He looked to the door, but it was near dark and no one had come or gone in a while.

"What did Langston say?" she asked, her anxiety overriding her patience. "What did you say?"

"He has to leave you alone," he said as he moved his knight and took her rook. "He can't invade your dreams like that. I won't tolerate—"

He grunted and doubled over. A bestial moan, like something from a dark jungle, came from deep within him.

Ruby reached for his hand. A bolt of electricity came off his skin and rushed up her arm. "Ahh!" she cried and pulled away.

He cradled his head in both his hands.

"What is it?" She stood and went to his side, hovering over him. He grunted, and moved his chair out. The chair's legs grated across the floor. Ash's face was hidden in his hands.

"What can I do?" Her hands hovered over his shoulders, afraid to touch him, afraid of that feeling. But she needed to help him. She laid her palms flat on his back and tensed her muscles in anticipation of the pain.

When she touched him he relaxed for a moment, until she felt another jolt, a sizzling that came through his shirt. She had to let go. She couldn't stand it.

He grunted again and Ruby was thankful that the few customers in the coffee shop were across the room from them. He stood and began to move away from her.

Ruby looked to Sage for help. But by the time Sage got to him he was halfway to the door. "What is it?" Sage demanded. But he kept walking, faster than her words could follow. In the next moment he was gone.

Sage and Ruby locked eyes. "What happened?" they said in unison.

Sage didn't answer, and it terrified Ruby.

Sage's voice rose to a shout, "What happened?"

"We were talking and he ..." Ruby stammered. He what? Ruby didn't know. "He got a headache, or something. Something went through him. I felt it. It stung. It burned." Her hands still tingled.

She wanted Sage to tell her that everything was fine, just a little god thing, no big deal. But Sage remained silent.

The radio announcer broke in on them, interrupting the local indie-rock station. "This is an alert," he said. "An Allied ..."

Ruby almost ignored it. She had gotten used to the bulletins on the radio, always updates about the peace process.

But the announcer paused. "Oh my God," he said, under his breath.

Ruby looked up at the radio, as if that could give her a clue as to what he might say next.

The announcer cleared his throat, and tried again. "This is an alert. An Allied soldier opened fire in a Rogue territory market full of civilians. When he was out of ammunition he detonated a suicide bomb. It happened moments ago."

Ruby's mind glazed over, unwilling, unable to believe what she heard. *One of our troops? An Ally? Blowing up markets in Rogue territory? But we're the good guys, and the peace ...*

"Hundreds are feared dead or injured," the announcer continued. "We will update you on this important development and what it means for the cease-fire and the peace talks as we get more information—"

Ruby looked at Sage, but the goddess of knowledge was staring out the glass door, staring at where the god of war had run out.

TEN

"THERE'S NOTHING I CAN DO," Sage said. She sat across from Ruby with both hands wrapped around the white ceramic of her coffee mug. "Ares will have to come back on his own."

"When?" Ruby insisted. It had been hours since the news of the suicide bombing, hours since Ash had walked out of Athenaeum with no explanation. The revelers had flown off like a murder of crows at the sound of the shattered peace. Ruby glanced around the quiet coffeehouse and out the wall of windows. The sky was a uniform grey that gave away nothing and the streets were once again empty.

"I can't know that, Ruby." Sage's voice was not unkind, but it was not sympathetic either.

"What about the dreams?" Ruby asked. "Ash seemed to blame Langston." She had been peppering Sage with questions, hoping that information might make her feel less help-less.

Sage's head cocked to the side. "What dreams?"

Ruby looked down at her now cold cup of coffee. "I don't really remember. Mostly it was a feeling." She looked up at Sage. "And snakes."

Sage's eyes shifted away. She didn't say anything.

"What is it?"

"Gods can influence dreams. Create them, even."

"What do you mean?"

"A few suggestions in a sleeping person's ear," Sage said. "The kernel of an idea. A whisper. Their subconscious will do the rest."

"A whisper?" Ruby repeated. She felt her nose wrinkle in revulsion. "Langston was in my room? While I slept?"

Sage didn't respond.

Gods could disappear in an instant and reappear anywhere they wanted. Even into someone's bedroom? What else had Langston done to her while she slept?

She glanced to the door, eager for Ash to appear there now.

He didn't, and hot anger flared in her chest. She wanted to strike out at Langston for invading her privacy and at Ash for leaving her here alone and worried.

"What's the big deal about Kronos?" she shot randomly at Sage, the only handy target for her unwieldy fury. "Langston said you would all end up being the next Prometheus or the next Kronos because of me. Was he a—"

"He was our enemy in the Great War." Sage startled her into silence. "The war between the Olympians and their parents, the Titans. We won. Zeus cast most of the Titans into the depths of Tartarus, including Kronos, his own father." Sage's tone was flat. She could have been reading from an encyclopedia.

"So?" Ruby heard the condescending annoyance in her own voice. "There are more of you. You can rise up. You can fight Zeus." Ash's words and confidence filled her.

Sage laughed, but her heart-shaped face crumpled into a look of horror. She placed her hands on the table, palms up. "Let me show you."

Ruby looked at her upturned hands and thought of the painful electricity that had come off of Ash. She thought of Langston in her room while she slept.

Sage flicked her fingers inward as if to say 'come on.' Ruby's arms felt heavy as she placed her chilled palms on Sage's warm ones.

Sage closed her fingers around Ruby's hand. A gold and amethyst ring flashed in the dim light. "Close your eyes."

Ruby glanced at the door one more time and shut her eyes.

"Now imagine the darkest, dankest portion of the Underworld," Sage said. "Not Hades: the realm of the dead. Tartarus: the realm of the *damned*."

A sensation came to Ruby through her hands. It was not like what she felt with Ash, but a slight tingle, subtle and not uncomfortable. In her mind's eyes she saw a dark cavern. Flames flickered somewhere on the periphery.

"Smell it," Sage said. "The decaying, fetid corruptness."

The smell of the anatomy room came to her. Not the chemicals that preserved the delicate tissues of life, but the smell under that. The smell of what could not be saved, of what had passed over. That smell filled the cavern around her.

"Feel it," Sage said. "The creeping damp chill that sets up in your marrow."

A cold crept into Ruby, not into her hands, or her toes, but into her bones. Into her being. She shivered, but the convulsion provided no extra heat.

"Hear it," Sage said.

First it was the sound of water dripping off rocky walls that came to Ruby, but then it was the moans she heard, distant and animalistic. It mixed in with the smell and the cold; a symphony of discomfort.

"Hunger," Sage said. "There is no food. Not in Tartarus. You're immortal and the desire to eat will tear away at your soul."

A dull hollow feeling stole into Ruby's middle and her stomach growled painfully.

"Thirst," Sage said. "The only water is from the scant rivulets that run down the dirty rocks from Hades above."

Ruby's throat tightened with the desire to drink.

"There is no companionship, though your wife and your siblings are in their own cells carved out of the rock around you. You can barely see them through the dimness, but you can hear their moans and sobs. You have not held or touched your wife in thousands of years."

Ruby felt the deep ache of infinite loneliness, the most familiar of all the sensations.

"The worst are the memories you carry with you into this place," Sage went on. "Dreams that wake you in the night, as clear as the springs of the great river Oceanus. You were the king of the gods. The lord of all. Now you languish in the bowels of hell.

"You will never forget that it was your own sons and daughters who sent you to this place. They were led by the youngest of them all; the one who looked you in the eye and made this pronouncement with a grin. The very son, who, it was prophesized, would be the undoing of you, as *you* were the undoing of your own father."

Anger, mixed with crushing desolation, filled Ruby. It was hopelessness so profound, so real, so endless, that she could not imagine ever feeling joy again, until a flicker of hope sparked on the periphery of her mind: revenge.

"Can you feel it?" Sage whispered.

Ruby didn't respond. She didn't have the energy or the will.

"Now *know*. Not think. Not feel. But *know*. That this is forever. Your cell is so permanent there isn't even a door to try to open. The only thing that can alter your state is the will of the gods who sent you to this place."

Ruby tried to swallow but her dry throat shuddered with the effort.

"And where is their will?" Sage asked. "Are they for you? Are they against you? Are they ready to show mercy after thousands of years?" She paused. "No. The worst part. The very worst, is that they've given up their will entirely."

Sage let go of Ruby's hands and the vision disappeared.

"We've forgotten how to fight," Sage said as she sat back in her chair. "And we're too afraid to try to remember."

Ruby looked around the familiar coffeehouse, glad she didn't have to feel the punishment of Kronos anymore.

"That's the power Zeus holds over us. Any one of us could become the next Kronos."

Ruby searched for something to say. She could still feel the lingering cold, the gnawing hunger, and the crushing despair. The front door swished open behind her. Her head snapped around at the sound.

Ash?

Instead Langston strode in, his cheeks pink and his hair windblown. He only looked at Sage as he approached their table. "It's chaos out there," he said.

Ruby looked to the street outside but it was still empty. Even the pizza place across the road was closed.

"The Rogues are drawing their defenses together again." He snickered. "The timing couldn't have been better. They hadn't even begun to pack in their weapons."

"What are you talking about?" Ruby stood and faced him. She was anxious for any news, but fearful of Langston's lingering smile.

His eyes shot to hers, annoyed, as if he had hoped to be able to ignore her entirely. "Your boyfriend doesn't have a hope now, no matter what voodoo thing you have going with him." Excitement spread across his face and widened the smile. "The hate is so thick Theseus couldn't cut it with his sword. Ares won't pull away now. He loves it too much."

Ruby's heart raced.

Sage stood too, so that the three of them made a loose triangle. "What did you do?" she asked.

"It didn't take much," he said. "A few whispers in the right ear. That Allied soldier wasn't exactly stable to begin with."

"What?" Ruby asked. Her eyes darted from Langston to Sage and back.

"You made the bomber kill all those people?" Sage said, putting the pieces together. "You knew Ares wouldn't be able to resist."

"Wrong!" Langston shouted as he turned on Sage. "I can't *make* anyone do anything. You know that. Gods can suggest. We can hint. We can whisper in the ear of a crazy man." He looked Ruby in the eye and added, "Or end up in a silly girl's dream. What he or she chooses to do with that, well, that's up to them." He smirked at her. "Turns out some people can't take a hint."

Sage glanced at Ruby, a flicker so quick Ruby couldn't read her emotions.

Langston's eyes were bright with satisfaction. "Ares brought this down on himself. He needed to be distracted. He thinks the rules don't apply to him? He thinks he can challenge Zeus? He thinks he can march some human slut up to Olympus, despite the visions of an oracle? Despite the consequences?"

"We could have found another way." Sage's voice was low. "This ... This is too much. People will die. People *have* died."

"We are *saved*," Langton shouted. "If Ares wants to self-destruct on a war binge, I say let him, but guaranteed he's already forgotten about her." He pointed in Ruby's general direction. "I'm going back. Today. Come with me."

"I won't let you and Ares bring down the human race to save my own skin," Sage said. "Or yours."

Langston huffed and turned away.

Ruby felt a scream rising in her. She wanted to lunge and tear at him. She wanted to run out the door and not stop until she found Ash. She wanted to sit on the floor and cry. A choked sound escaped her.

Langston laughed, a short harsh laugh, that ended abruptly as he disappeared into thin air.

☙৪৶

The silence in the coffeehouse was all-encompassing with no espresso machine running, no milk foaming, no customers chatting. A refrigerator in the back clicked on and Ruby started. Her eyes moved over the dim room and to the dark windows, but there was nothing.

Almost a week had gone by since Ash left. Langston hadn't been back either. The war raged on. Casualties mounted and talk of peace faded.

It was after midnight and Ruby was tired, but she knew that if she went home she wouldn't be able to sleep. The nightmares had stopped but she would lie awake and listen for little noises, hoping that each rattle of the old furnace or creek of the settling timbers meant that Ash had come home.

She looked down at her history text again, Prussia and the Austrians. She had been reading for hours but little had sunk in. What was the point anyway? Even if she got into medical school, even if she earned a double residency, even if Medics for Mercy wanted her, what would any of it matter without Ash?

Most days she stayed at Athenaeum and read the yellow myth book that Sage lent her instead of going to class. Sage gave her a key to Athenaeum and she came and went as she pleased.

Ash—Ares—had not been back to Olympus, Sage—Athena—had told her. Sage always used their Greek names now, but Ruby still had a hard time thinking of Ares as anything but Ash.

Zeus and Hera weren't suspicious, Athena said, but others were talking. They wondered if Ares knew what he was doing. Langston—Apollo—had kept quiet. If he gave Ares away he would be giving himself and Athena away too. So far his plan was working. Ares was still off fighting, and he and Ruby were apart.

With each passing day Ruby felt more and more desperate. She longed to know that Ash was well, and whole, and uninjured. Why had he stayed away? What was he was thinking about? And then the most painful question, did he love war more than he loved her?

She looked at the chess board at the back table. She had practiced a few of the problems Ash had taught her, end games, where only a few pieces remained on the board and the goal was to finish the game in a set number of moves; mate in two or mate in four. But playing only made her miss Ash more and she quickly gave it up.

She took a deep breath and closed her eyes. She pictured him in as much detail as she could. She saw him happy and excited, his eyes luminous and his face serene. She imagined him unhurt and healthy. She tried to feel his arms around her, and their energy flowing together. Her breath slowed at the thought but she jumped when she heard a sharp tap, tap, tap on glass.

Her head snapped around to the front window. The shadow of a tall figure stood in the drizzle outside. A moment of fear washed over her. Then her heart began to thud in earnest, her body knowing, even before her mind, the exact height, the outline of the curly hair, the length of the leg.

She stood, her own legs shaking. Why was he out there? Why not appear here, in front of her? Her emotions swung from relief, to anger, to joy, and back through them all. She had wished and hoped for this moment, but now that he was here she didn't know what to feel. What should she say? What had he come to say to her?

She tried to gauge his health as she approached the locked door. A streetlight behind him lit up a slanted cone of drizzle. It gave her enough light to see that his limbs were straight and that there was no blood on the jeans or the black leather jacket he wore.

His eyes followed her movements.

She opened the door and stepped back, making room for him to enter. He walked past her, close enough for her to smell ozone and send a charge across her skin.

She scanned his back. No blood there either. Anger seeped in with her relief and she crossed her arms over her chest. He turned to look at her. His eyes were dark, rimmed in red, and sunk deep in dark sockets.

"Where have you been?" she asked. She tried to keep her nerves steady.

"Lots of places." His voice was husky and low, as though it had been worn out.

The roughness of his voice softened her anger. "Ares ..." she whispered and her crossed arms dropped to her sides.

A small smiled touched his lips when she said his true name, but he turned away before she could see if the smile held. He walked to her table and pulled the history text toward him.

"The Battle of Leuthen," he said. "Frederick II and Charles of Lorraine. Old Fritz used the Oblique Order against the Austrians." His eyes flicked in her direction. "Worked like a charm."

"Ares, where have you been? I've been so worried."

He smiled again, but it didn't touch the pain in his eyes. He shook his head. "I'm sorry. I couldn't resist it." His two hands came together; the fingers on the right twisted the dark ring on the left.

She moved to him and placed her hands over his. He grabbed at her and held her hands tight, as though he would not have dared to make the first move.

She felt the buzzing, the sting, the burn; strong and constant. The energy of war flowed from Ares into her. It nearly rattled her bones. She held on despite the pain. She hoped to see his eyes clear, but he shut them. She felt the energy ebb and fade, though it didn't disappear completely.

"What can I do?" she asked.

He shook his head. "There's nothing. I can't fight it. You can't help me." He opened his eyes, still dark and shadowed. "It's out of my control. All I can do is ride it."

"I don't understand." She squeezed his hands tighter. "Why isn't it working?"

"The hate is too strong." He shook his head and raised their joined hands. He scoffed. "We don't make a big enough difference."

"Ares, it's you." The thought surprised her, but it felt true. "Stop fighting."

He shook his head. "I can't—"

"Hate is about fear and suspicion," She spoke over his doubts. "Love is about trust. And I trust this." She shook their held hands. "If you want it, you have to be brave. If you want it, you have to jump."

He swallowed and looked at her. "How?"

She shrugged, and from somewhere deep and unscripted she said, "Lay down your weapons."

"Surrender?" His brow creased in disbelief. "I don't give up. I don't lose."

"Then change your mind."

His head tilted to the side. His lips parted and his eyes searched for something around her.

"Then we can go to Olympus," she said. She now knew there was nothing in life for her without him. "We'll do whatever it takes to be together."

He gently pulled his hands away from hers and reached into his jacket. He pulled out a sleek black gun, square around the edges and modern looking. He held it between them.

She licked her dry lips. "Why do you have that?"

"I was going to a war," he laughed. "It helps to have a gun. And usually a bigger one." He looked down at the pistol. "I didn't use it, though. I went so that I could be a part of it, so that I could feel the rush of it." He inhaled and half-closed his eyes. When he opened them he looked at her. "I missed you."

He bent down on one knee and laid the gun at her feet. "I love you, Ruby. You are where I want to begin."

She touched his lowered head and slid her fingers through his silky hair. The electric feeling of him calmed to a smooth stream.

His fingers worked at something in his hands. He looked up and held it out to her.

His ring.

"Ruby," he whispered. "Be my beginning."

She blinked. "Ares—"

"The thing is," he interrupted. "Even on Olympus you'll still be human. We'll only be together for a little while. I need you to be with me for forever."

She shook her head, not entirely sure what he was saying.

"*Hieros gamos*," he said. "The marriage of two gods. Only Zeus can perform it and only Hera can bless it. I can make you a goddess." He smiled and this time his eyes brightened. "Ruby, marry me."

A *goddess*? Immortal? She couldn't imagine any of it.

She took the black ring from him. It was heavier than she expected. The surface was rough and pitted. *Old*, she had thought once, but she had no idea then.

It was thousands of years old, he told her: iron, and made for him by his brother, Hephaestus, the god of forge and fire. "To remind me of my weaknesses."

"Who would make a ring like that?" she asked. She thought she saw a darkness pass over his features but it was hard to tell in the dim light of the empty coffeehouse.

"It's a long story," he said. "For another time. I want you to wear it now. It will remind me of our strength. The war is already slipping away. I can feel it. The pain and the suffering are nearly gone. We are *meant* to be together, Ruby."

She felt the weight of it all, the ring, the power he had—the power *they* had—the fact that she was tied to him in a way she never knew one person could be tied to another.

"Our love is your future," he said. "When you're a goddess the energy that is attuned to you will become your influence. You *will* help people. That will be *your* legacy."

She had already promised to do whatever it took to be with him, and in truth she knew that he was right. She did belong with him. This was her moment to trust her instincts, her moment to be afraid and do it anyway. This was her moment to jump.

She thought of the prophecy, but there was no way she could know the future, even if Apollo thought he had a pretty good idea. And the past was full of loneliness and isolation.

She looked at the ring again and back to him. "Yes, Ares, I will mar—"

But his lips were already on hers.

ELEVEN

ATHENA'S LIVING ROOM walls were lined with white shelves of books. Ruby could smell the old paper and linen. Interspersed among the books were earthen statues, rough-hewn bowls, and weather-worn glass vessels. *Museum* was the word that came to Ruby's mind.

"You're being reckless," Sage said. She leaned in the doorway that led to her kitchen in a plush white robe. "I'm willing to support you, but not this way. It's not just you who'll pay."

"I'm willing to risk it," Ares said. They had come straight from Athenaeum. Now that their plan was set, now that they were going to Olympus to face Zeus and ask him to marry them, Ares wasted no time.

"Do you think he'll hesitate to send you to Tartarus? Or worse?" Sage asked. "Do you think he'll let her live for more than a minute?" She only glanced at Ruby.

A shock of fear ran through Ruby to hear her possible fate stated so plainly. She glanced at the reflection in the sliding glass doors on the far side of the living room. She and Ares stood across from Athena. She didn't want them to fight. What might happen on Earth if gods decided to fight? She realized that if Langston's prophecy came true she might find out before too long.

"Turn on the radio," Ares said. "I'm sure the news is everywhere."

Sage stared at him a moment and then reached into the kitchen. The sound of a tired announcer filled the room. "...odd and amazing. Events that we will surely tell our grand-children about."

"What is this?" Sage said. "Another cease-fire?"

Instead of answering her he looked at Ruby.

"It's three-thirty a.m., folks," the announcer said. "If you're just tuning in, breaking news this morning: neither the Rogues nor the Allies, nor any country in Africa or Asia, not even the long-standing armies in the Middle East can rally their troops to war today. Soldiers across the world have laid their weapons down at their feet and have refused to fight."

"You wanted world peace," he said to Ruby.

She took in a sharp breath and felt the newness of his ring on her finger. Somehow it fit her perfectly despite the fact that Ares had worn it on his larger hand for thousands of years. "A trick of the metal," he had said when she slipped it on.

"Ares, are you sure you want to bring this down on your-self?" Sage said. Now she did look at Ruby. "On her?" Her tone was serious, not angry. "I see the value. There's no denying that, but do you want to become Zeus's next great example of why he should not be crossed?"

Ruby felt lightheaded at the thought of Zeus and eternal punishment. She glanced at the sliding glass doors again. "I need some fresh air."

"Are you okay?" Ares asked her.

She nodded, but looked away quickly. She didn't want him to see that she was afraid, that she might lose her nerve if she heard what Athena had to say.

Cold misty air met her when she slid the door open. The large balcony, complete with barbeque and cushioned patio set, seemed so human. It reassured her.

She rested her elbows on the waist-high railing and looked down into the courtyard garden below. There was a large statue of a man holding a huge orb on his back with spotlights around him; Atlas.

She felt a little like that now. Like the weight of the world was on her shoulders.

Tall trees jutted almost leafless black branches into a dark indigo sky. Autumn was wearing on. Was she on the threshold of a new life, a completely different life than she ever imagined, or was she on the precipice of her death? And if it was the latter, what would it mean for Ares, who would live no matter what? What kind of punishment might he suffer?

She didn't want to think of those things. She couldn't. Not now. If all she accomplished in her life was to love Ares, her contribution to humanity would be a time of peace. "At least for a little while," she said out loud and at the same time she felt, more than saw, Ares standing next to her.

"What's for a little while?" he asked, leaning close.

"Atlas, right?" She asked before he could claim an answer.

He looked from her face to the garden. "Yes, Atlas. Holding up the heavens." .

"I thought he held up the Earth."

"He keeps the heavens separate from the Earth. Compliments of Zeus after the Great War."

The weight of the heavens was on her, she corrected her earlier thought, and realized that the analogy was more accurate.

"Why didn't Zeus send him to Tartarus with Kronos and the rest of the Titans?" She thought of the vision Athena shared with her. Which punishment would be worse?

Ares gave her a sidelong glance as if he were surprised she knew so much about it.

"It's in a lot of books," she said, repeating what he told her about the Battle of Hastings, what seemed like years ago.

"I don't know why. You can ask him yourself."

Her skin prickled at the thought of meeting Zeus.

"Athena said she'd help us," he said.

Ruby exhaled and leaned in against the cold metal rail of the balcony. At least she would have one friend besides Ares in all of this.

"She's taking a great risk for us," he said. "If it doesn't work out like I think it will, if I can't get him to accept you, he'll leave none of our allies unpunished."

Ruby shivered at his wording. Their allies. The war had started when the Rogues broke a decades-old peace treaty with the Allies. So, weren't she and Ares the Rogues? Weren't they the ones breaking the rules?

"I need to go," he said. "I need to find a way to get you to Olympus." He kissed her on the forehead and stepped away.

"Now?" she asked. He had just come back and she didn't want to be without him again.

"Try to rest," he said.

She turned to the garden. "Will I ever get to come back?"

He didn't answer.

He was already gone.

ঞ৩৻

The familiar smell of home hit Ruby when she walked through the front door. She had been afraid that she would second-guess her decision to go to Olympus if she came back to the old house, but she could not leave without saying good-bye. Memories flooded her; birthday parties, Christmases with her father, long months with the nannies and au pairs who raised her.

She glanced to the rose-colored chair in the front room and to the couch across from it. She pictured herself and her father, talking and laughing with the chess board between them. The chair was the same one Ares had eaten Ambrosia Bars in after he healed from the bullet wound in his chest. Despite her worry for him at the time, and Athena and Apollo's anger, even that memory felt sweet.

She tried to conjure something of her mother, but she had been a baby when her mother died in the car accident and there was no memory to summon. Furniture and pictures were the only connection Ruby had to her.

Her parents' faces smiled from the photos that ran up the staircase. What would they think of her now? She realized that in truth she didn't really know what they would have wanted for her. She had barely known either of them.

She wasn't giving up her dreams, she reminded herself. She was owning them. She might get to see history in the making and the next chapters in the story of humankind. She would understand the hows and the whys of the things that happened. If Zeus accepted her.

If she lived.

She took a picture of her parents from the wall. The paint underneath was brighter than the faded green around it. In the picture her parents stood on a beach with a vast blue ocean behind them. She didn't know where or when the picture was taken, but they were together and they looked happy.

Silent tears slipped down her face, a strange mixture of regret and hope.

She thought of going upstairs, to the TV room, or to the kitchen, but she didn't know when Ares would return from Olympus. She had slept through the morning and it was already late afternoon. She was eager to get back.

She closed the front door, placed her palm flat on its smooth wooden surface, and said a silent good-bye. She turned to walk back to Athena's, and almost dropped the picture when she ran into Mark coming up the porch steps.

He caught the frame by its edge before it landed on the hard wooden boards. "You're here," he said, as though he was surprised to actually find her. He looked at her face and hesitated. "Are you crying?"

"No." She wiped the tears away. "I'm fine." She took the picture from his loose hands and held it close to the front of her rain jacket as she went down the porch steps and into the chilly Northwest drizzle.

"Ruby?" He stopped on the path and touched her lightly on the elbow. "You haven't been in class all week. What's going on?" His brow was furrowed with concern.

"Nothing. I'm fine," she repeated.

He glanced again at the photo in her hands. Was it so odd to be holding a five-by-ten picture of your parents and nothing else? If it was, he decided to ignore it.

"The final's in three weeks," he said. "I'm sure I could talk the study group into letting you back in if you wanted me to."

"My chemistry grade isn't a measure of my overall well-being, you know?" She glanced to the peeling red paint of her house behind him and shrugged. "I might drop organic, anyway."

He looked to the side and exhaled. His head whipped back around to her as if he needed to say something quickly, before he lost his nerve. "Does this have anything to do with the guy who was here the morning after the exam? You've been acting weird ever since then. Is he hurting you?"

She swallowed. Was Mark Harris the only person on Earth who noticed that something had changed for her? Was there no one else who cared?

She thought of Zeus and Apollo. Even the threat of two powerful gods seemed like a better choice than living in a world where almost no one cared about her at all.

Something inside her hardened. She had bigger fish to fry.

"You know, Mark—" She looked him in the eye. "—it's really none of your business."

She saw his fair skin turn the color of boiled lobsters before she turned and walked away.

"I've read about this, Ruby," he said in a loud voice that followed her down the street. "First he'll control where you go and what you do, then the emotional abuse will start. One day he'll snap and hit you. It's a classic abuse pattern. You don't have to ..."

She let his words trail off behind her. Let him think whatever he wanted.

ఎఏ౬

Athena pulled dress after dress out of her immense walk-in closet. Each one covered in a thin plastic film. Her high-ceilinged bedroom was painted ivory and trimmed with gold. The bed was large, but the wooden headboard, carved with pictures of people wearing long robes and examining scrolls, was massive.

"You and Ares can still surprise Zeus and Hera," she said. "If you don't act quickly they might realize that something is going on. The energy of the Earth is calm. Too calm. Most gods block it, but a shift like this could draw attention."

"How will Ares get me there?" Ruby tried to sit up straight in the oversized chair but the pillows were too soft and she kept sinking back down.

"I'm not sure how Ares will do it," Athena said as she shook out a dress and laid it flat. "Apollo's influence might have helped. He has more friends than Ares. In any scenario he'll have to ask for favors and secrecy from other gods.

Olympians love to gossip. The clock may already be ticking for both of you."

"I thought gods would be more, I don't know, cultured," Ruby said. "More interested in knowledge, or ethics, or something." She turned Ares's ring on her finger and wondered if Apollo was telling Zeus about her at that moment.

Athena took several pairs of sandals from her closet and lined them up at the foot of the bed. "Imagine spending a few thousand years in the same small town with the same handful of people. It gets dull." She removed the thin plastic film from the dresses strewn across the ivory bedding.

The bright colors were at odds with Ruby's mood. "How can he make me a goddess?"

"I wouldn't worry about that yet." Sage had a dress half unwrapped. "Focus on Zeus and Hera. I'll be honest with you." She glanced up. "Your chances aren't very good."

A nauseous wave of fear traveled through Ruby's middle. "Still," she swallowed. "I want to know."

"Ambrosia," Sage said. "And nectar."

"But I've already eaten ambrosia in your bars at Athenaeum."

"The small amounts I put in the bars won't do it. Not on Earth. At best my customers will find that they outlive most of their friends. To become a god you must eat pure ambrosia and drink unadulterated nectar on the hallowed grounds of Olympus; the true food and drink of the gods in their true home.

"The ambrosia will fortify your molecules and strengthen their bonds. The nectar will develop your will. Together they'll bring out the energies that are most attuned within you. Your presence on Olympus will galvanize their force."

"What do you think I'll become the goddess of?" This was at the crux of her fears. Even more than facing Zeus. What would the wife of the god of war become?

Athena looked at her, her grey eyes softening for the first time. "I can't know that, Ruby. No one can."

"Has anyone else ever done it? A human, I mean?"

"A few. Ares's son's wife, Psyche, was human once. She's the goddess of the soul."

Ruby's eyes shot to Athena. "Ares's son?"

"Eros, the god of love. Cupid is what the Romans called him."

She knew that Ares had been deeply in love before, but she hadn't known there was a son. An anvil of dread lifted from her chest. Ares's son! He wasn't the god of pain or the god of misery, or any of the other horrible things she had imagined. He was the god of *love*.

Athena fluffed out the fabric of a turquoise dress. Silver decorations flashed in the light from the ornate overhead light.

"Why all the dresses?" Ruby asked, feeling a little better.

"Not dresses. Peploses." Sage held up the hanger. The fabric was attached at each shoulder with an intricate silver pin. "It's what we wear on Olympus. Which do you like?" She picked up one of the shapeless pieces of fabric lying on the bed. "Maybe the pink. It will look nice with your brown hair and brown eyes." She took it off the hanger, but then stopped and threw it back down with the others.

"No. This one." Athena smiled. "It's perfect." She held up a floor-length silky white peplos with golden leaves resting at the waist. "For purity. Hera's the goddess of marriage. She'll love it." Athena shrugged. "Or else Zeus will. Either way, it can't hurt."

"Huh?" Ruby asked, nervous at the gleam in Athena's eyes.

"The alternative to Zeus striking you dead on sight is that he *likes* you. He does have an affinity for humans."

A chill went through Ruby, though she wasn't sure if it was at the thought of being struck down by the king of the gods or of being desired by him.

Athena seemed unbothered by the possibilities. "If Hera likes you …" She arched an eyebrow at Ruby. "… if she thinks you're pure enough for her favorite son, well, then she can save you."

Sage looked back at the white peplos. "She'll be able to tell how virginal you are, one way or the other. She'll feel it on you. But a little strategic marketing can't hurt either."

⁂

The white peplos was two long pieces of fabric sewn shut at the right shoulder. The left shoulder was made by bringing the front and back pieces together and attaching them with an intricate butterfly pin. The butterfly's wings were made of spiderweb-thin strands of gold that attached to a delicate outer edge. Its long body was a line of red gems.

"Rubies," Athena said with a smile, as she finished knotting a gold braided belt around Ruby's waist and stepped behind her. They both looked in the full-length mirror. The white silk fabric fell gracefully on Ruby's curves. The golden sash was the only thing that held the peplos together. She turned to the side. The ruby pin glinted red in the light and the movement opened the peplos slightly, revealing the bare swell of her hip and the beginning of the curve of her breast.

"You'll fit right in," Athena said.

Ruby shivered with so little between her and the world. She didn't see how this outfit would express the purity Hera would want her to possess, but Ruby knew she wanted Ares to see her in this.

Athena gave her a pair of sandals with flat bottoms and gold cords that wound up her calf and tied at the top. She brought a black velvet tray of jewelry to Ruby.

"Hera and Dionysus are famous for their dinner parties," Athena said. "All twelve Olympians, and most of the lesser gods, will be there tonight."

Ruby's eyes went quickly from the elaborate necklaces and bracelets to Athena's heart-shaped face. She began to sweat despite the thin peplos and the cold rain outside.

"I'm going to a party?" All she could think was that if Zeus decided to strike her down with his famous bolt of lightning she would be killed in front of a crowd and that somehow seemed more awful.

"Safety in numbers," Athena said. "Ares thinks Zeus will react better if all of Olympus is watching." She turned Ruby's numb body toward the mirror again. She piled her hair on top of her head and stuck a gold comb with small ruby butterflies along its upper edge into the middle. A few straggling hairs fell down to frame Ruby's oval face.

Ares walked in through the open door behind them. He stopped short. A large canvas bag dangled from one of his hands. His wide eyes roamed over Ruby. She saw him swallow.

"You look—"

"She's ready," Athena said before he could finish.

Ruby breathed in and nodded. "How do we do this?"

"Yes, Ares. How will you do it?" Athena mocked.

Ruby glanced at Athena and wondered how much confidence she had in Ares. Apollo thought it was crazy to openly defy Zeus, crazy to ignore an oracle's vision. So crazy that he had killed people over it.

Instead of answering, Ares bent to the canvas bag and pulled out a pair of gold sandals covered in feathers. They gave a little shake and a pair of large golden wings fluttered out of the back of each one.

"The Talaria?" Sage gasped. "You can't trust Hermes! It will be all over Olympus by now."

"Relax," he said. "I told him things were about to get lively. That was enough for him." He turned to Ruby. "Getting a human to Olympus is no easy thing. But the winged sandals will get the job done."

Ruby stared as he bent to put the sandals on his feet. He carefully wound the intricate ties around his ankles and lower legs. When he stood she could see the wings of the sandals beating back and forth in a steady rhythm beneath the hem of his jeans. They seemed too amazing to wear.

He rummaged through the large bag again and pulled out a curly golden fur. It shone bright in the light. "You'll want to wear this," he said.

She reached out hesitantly to touch it.

"It's the Golden Fleece," he said. "From the only twenty-four carat sheep that ever lived. It will protect you from the weather."

Ruby expected the fleece to be heavy, but when he handed it to her she found that it was as light as silk. She draped it over her shoulders. It covered her completely.

Ares put the picture of Ruby's parents in the canvas bag. He walked to the window and motioned for her to follow. A cold gust of air touched her cheeks as he opened the window but her body, covered by the Golden Fleece, remained warm. She peered down onto the street and sidewalk below. Both were dim and empty. Behind the grey clouds the sun would soon be setting.

He gently scooped her up in his arms. He looked into her eyes and kissed her, his lips soft and warm against hers. "This is going to work," he said.

She nodded and pulled the fleece tight around her. She snuggled down into his strong embrace. If this was to be her last day to live, her last moments even, then she was glad they were with Ares.

"Thank you," Ruby said to Athena over Ares's shoulder.

Athena pressed her lips together in a thin line and nodded.

Ruby braced herself as Ares stepped off the window ledge, but she felt nothing; no change in how he held her, no dip down as he made that incredible step out into nothing. The rain and cold did not reach her wrapped in the Golden Fleece and Ares's strength did not falter.

TWELVE

THEY ROSE HIGH INTO THE AIR. Lights marched down the roads to make bright boxes with cross streets until the city was reduced to a simple pattern of lights and darks.

The wide grey river traversed it all at an irregular slant, not conforming to the manmade city's lines and angles, but snaking and twisting through on its own terms. Ruby closed her eyes and made a silent wish that she and Ares would survive the night.

The winged sandals flew them northward. The lights became scattered and more spread out. A thicker grey swath of river, the Columbia, passed beneath them. Smaller cities and towns appeared below, a smattering of lights nestled into the great deep forests of the Pacific Northwest.

Ruby let her head fall against Ares's chest and concentrated on his heartbeat, strong and sure, and endless. Nothing but calm energy flowed off of him. She breathed in his scent.

The cold drizzle fell on her face, but she was amazed at how comfortable she was beneath the soft Golden Fleece. Ares was only partially covered by it. He wore jeans and a t-shirt but she felt no shiver from him.

They flew on, silent. Ruby tried not to think about what they were doing, but found it impossible. Would Zeus kill her instantly? Would he send Ares away to Tartarus? The memory of it filled her; cold and damp, dark and desolate. Ruby shivered.

Ares held her tighter. "We're getting near."

Already?

She looked down. There were no lights here, only the black-green forest occasionally interrupted by lighter patches of grey at the peaks; early snow. It was the Olympic range. And somewhere here was Mount Olympus. And above that was the real Olympus, the home of the gods.

Ares rose higher into the swath of charcoal sky. She began to see a glow in the distance before them as it broke through the dark. The light was faint at first but it broadened quickly. It felt warm on her cheeks and it soon filled the sky. Sunshine? Were they above the clouds?

She wondered about altitude sickness and at what point her oxygen might run out, but except for the butterflies that battered themselves against the walls of her stomach, she felt fine.

She saw a bank of white clouds before them. They looked like a solid mass that filled the sky as far as she could see above, below, and to either side. Four women appeared in front of the clouds. They seemed to be standing on solid ground, though Ruby saw nothing but white puffs beneath their bare feet. The women were young and crowned with wildflowers.

One had hair the color of wheat and wore a crown of pinks and yellows. Another wore purple and blues. Her hair was a brighter blond. The redhead was crowned in orange and golds. The last was raven-haired, with flowers of white and red. Their peploses matched their crowns.

Ares did not slow at the sight of them. Instead the four figures moved, two to a side, and created a space between them. They bowed low and the wall of clouds separated to let Ruby and Ares pass through.

Ruby looked over Ares's shoulder and saw the women peek through the clouds at them. They were huddled together, whispering and giggling, as the white mass closed.

"Who are they?" she asked.

"The Seasons," he said. And then, as if to relieve her worry, added, "Only minor gods."

"We're on Olympus?" she whispered. She looked back at the bank of clouds. "Could they have stopped us?"

"No. They can't stop me. They will talk, though. All of Olympus will know we've arrived soon."

"*All* of Olympus? Even your father?" She was suddenly terrified to be on Zeus's turf. All her happiness in the world relied on his approval.

"He'll be too absorbed in his garden to notice. But he's the only one. The Seasons will tell anyone who'll listen, and everyone will want to hear. Even Hera."

Ruby wondered if the goddess of marriage would be glad to see her most beloved son happy. Or would she be furious that he had been to Earth, and worse, that he had fallen in love with a mortal?

She tried to concentrate on what was around her. This might be her only chance to see Olympus. The sun was low and bright on the horizon. The Golden Fleece kept her body at a comfortable temperature, cool now instead of warm.

A few clouds, white and puffy, cast shadows down on the green trees below. Scattered in and among the tress were the buildings of Olympus. Each one was unique. And huge.

A pink alabaster building passed beneath them. It was covered in blooming red rose vines. Close by it was a black building made of a rough metal. Sculptures stood around the open green space surrounding it and covered its walls.

They passed over a building that was pure white, also covered in vines, but with no flowers that Ruby could see. Another, far in the distance, was silver, and still another seemed to be made of a deep purple stone. Amethyst?

In the middle of everything was one building that stood out from the rest by its sheer enormity and its unlikely color. The center piece of Olympus was solid gold and two or three times bigger than any other. Immense columns rose at least five or six stories from floor to ceiling on all sides. The walls were carved with scenes of battles and feasts, but she and Ares were moving too fast and Ruby couldn't make out the details.

She counted eleven large buildings surrounding the massive golden one. Smaller buildings followed out in a ring from there. A hierarchy. The one in the middle, the golden one, belonged to Zeus, she was sure.

A wide river encircled the buildings and surrounding forest. Snowcapped mountains lay beyond the river to the East. To the north green forests rolled on and on, past the serpentine water. To the south and west the river opened up to a large bay.

The jade green water curved on the horizon like any large body of water would do on Earth. Was it an entire ocean? What could hold up such a mass of water so high above the world? The bay was dotted with islands that scattered out from the shore. The yellow Olympic sun dipped its edge into the water as it began to set.

She wanted to ask Ares about what she was seeing. But his focus was still firmly in front of them, his eyes locked on the horizon, determination set in his jaw.

She felt them descend. Beneath them was a white marble building with red-streaked veins running through the stone. Windows marched along at intervals, like soldiers in ranks. Marble steps led up to a large double door entrance of hard oak.

Ares set them down onto the grass, springy under Ruby's sandaled feet. The air was fragrant with subtle sweetness: honeysuckle, jasmine, magnolias, and other scents she couldn't name. The smells mixed and separated and then mixed again on a gentle breeze.

Ares took the Golden Fleece from her. She felt the setting Olympic sun on her bare arms and shoulders. It sent a pleasant quiver across her skin beneath the thin peplos.

"My abode," he said and looked from the marble edifice to her. "Home."

On either side of the building was a baffling assortment of trees and plants. Palms grew next to firs and blue spruce and what she thought might be a Joshua tree. An impressive-looking saguaro cactus stood off to one side. An orchid held tight to the high branches of an oak. Its stiff leaves jutted up and its delicate flowers ruffled forth from woody stems.

She wanted to be happy at the thought of spending time in this lush place, with Ares. Instead her nerves tensed.

He took her hand. She relaxed, a little.

"When do we go to talk to Zeus?" she asked, forcing herself to face the reality of why they were there.

"Not yet," he said. "I want Hera's party to be in full swing." He motioned to the building. "In the meantime I can show you around."

His abode was plain in comparison to the greenery around it. She found that it reminded her of him, solid and handsome, but not likely to give away what was on the inside.

A pair of owls perched high on either side of the massive double doors. They seemed to look down on her. Their orange eyes gleamed.

She felt like she had when she first met Ares, when he was still Ash, always wanting to be with her, and always ignoring everyone else. It simply wasn't possible. It simply wouldn't work. What was she doing here, with *him*, on *Olympus*? What was she doing preparing to face the king of the gods, asking to *marry* his son?

"What's wrong?" he asked.

Her eyes darted to the owls, the flora that made no sense, to Ares, his hand fitting so perfectly in hers. His strong energy soothed over her doubt. It was too late to go back. The Seasons would be spreading the rumor of a mortal's arrival by now.

Ares pulled her close. She glanced around, worried that they were being watched, that Zeus would come from the darkening sky above them and strike her down with a bolt of lightning. But Ares's eyes were placid and serene. They did not waver from hers. "You have to trust this," he said.

She closed her eyes and took a deep breath. She allowed him to lead her to his abode. When she opened her eyes she concentrated on the wooden entrance they were approaching and didn't look at the owls.

A scene was carved into the oak doors. The left panel showed a soldier dressed in ancient garb. He was caught mid-fall, with an arrow through his chest. The right door showed an opposite picture; a tall man, curly hair and intense eyes, standing on a hill above a battle. His arms were stretched out to the sky, commanding, reveling in the glory of it. The two sides of Ares. One part felt the sting of the arrow, the other felt triumph in the victory.

Ares reached for the iron handle and swung the door wide. He stepped back and made room for her to enter before him.

The entrance hall was a large round room. The curving walls were the same red-streaked white marble as the outside. At the back of the room was a double staircase. Each set of stairs hugged the bowed walls and met at a balcony at the top. An upstairs hallway followed back from there and went toward the rear of the building.

Ruby looked up to the high ceiling. It was painted with scenes of battles. Alcoves in the walls housed statues of men in military dress. They wore short peplos, medieval armor, and modern uniforms. There was a statue of a small man with a bicorne hat that she thought might be Napoleon.

Lower, along the floor and on the walls, the room was ringed with statues, vases, sculptures, and tapestries. The floor itself was a mosaic of the Earth with each of its landmasses outlined in red marble.

There was a set of double doors on her right and another set on her left. Their dark wooden surfaces were smooth and perhaps the only unadorned things in the room. Both sets of doors were closed.

Ruby's hand came up to touch her throat, overwhelmed at the history, the detail, and the beauty of it all. "It's incredible," she whispered.

Ares stood next to her and smiled.

Beneath the balcony, standing directly across from them, was a statue of an owl, similar to the two that overlooked the entranceway. But this one was the size of a man. Its feathers were metal in varying shades of browns. The eyes were large, bright orange, and seemed to stare into her. Above each eye were feathers that jutted up like horns.

"What's with the owls?" she asked.

"Horned Owls. They're fierce fighters," he said. "Hephaestus made them."

"Hephaestus? The brother who made your ring?" She touched the iron band on her finger with her thumb.

"Yes. My only true brother. And he made *your* ring," Ares corrected her.

A smiled flitted across her lips. "My ring," she agreed and then his words sunk in. "You're not half-siblings? Hera *and* Zeus are his parents?"

He nodded. "We're the only sons from their marriage."

Ruby flinched. Athena said that Ares was Hera's favorite son. What kind of mother would choose?

She motioned to the room. "It's big."

"We have all the space and materials we want." He held his hands out, palms up. "The sky's the limit."

"I thought we were above the sky," she said with a wry smile.

"Like I said. No limits."

"What's upstairs?"

"Rooms." His eyes widened. "Lots of rooms."

"I want to see it." She looked at him from the corner of her eye and broke away into a run for the left staircase. Ares ran to the right. Ruby had started ahead of him, but Ares was faster and they reached the balcony at the same time. He picked her up by the waist and spun her in a tight circle, as if it were planned, something choreographed, as if everything had been prearranged.

They kissed and she let her anxiety fall away. She was glad to be there with him, if only for a little while.

He put her down. She trailed her hand along his arm and down to his hand. He let her lead him down the long hall.

Statues stood in nooks, again wearing armor or battle clothes from different eras. She stopped at an Asian warrior about her height. He wore what would have been soft flowing robes if they weren't made of metal.

It was not his outfit or the menacing sword he held that caught her attention. Whatever this warrior had fought for was dear to him. Whoever had made the statue had captured it in the wrinkles around his eyes, the set of his jaw, and his broad stance.

"Hephaestus?" she asked, marveling at the craftsmanship, at the incredible talent.

Ares nodded.

She tried to reconcile the beauty and depth of Hephaestus's work with the cruelty of the ring he had made for Ares and found she couldn't.

Gold-trimmed doors lined the passage. Ruby opened every one. Each housed a large bed, or a desk, or paintings, or statues, or books, or large musical instruments, but none of the rooms had any real feeling.

"I don't see you here," she said after closing the door on the ninth or tenth room. "I can't sense you."

"I don't spend too much time up here," he said. "What am I going to do in all these rooms anyway?"

"Why do you have them?"

He looked surprised. "Why not?"

She felt her face screw up in disapproval. "Isn't that a waste?"

"Nothing's wasted," he said. "If I tire of this statue," He pointed to a foot-tall jade soldier on a pedestal in the hallway. "I can send the molecules back into the universe. Everything can be disbanded, moved, begun again."

"It would take all twelve of you?" She asked and looked at the statue, remembering what he had said about the Olympians moving Olympus.

"Something small like this could be pulled together by two or three of us. Only Zeus could manage it alone. Either way, it might not be pretty unless Hephaestus was involved."

"Zeus could do it alone?" she asked and touched the little soldier. She ran her finger along the edge of his coat. It, like the floor beneath her, felt real enough.

"He's the king of the gods," Ares said. "He has the most power, the greatest will. My uncles, Hades and Poseidon, are next in line. They each control their own realms."

"Poseidon is the god of the sea?" Ruby said. "And Hades rules the Underworld?"

Ares nodded.

As they continued through the upstairs Ruby felt more and more like they were walking through an upscale model home. She recognized Athena in a painting. The goddess wore a full set of armor. There was a fierce look in her grey eyes.

She saw Apollo, too, many times. He usually had a pear-shaped guitar with a bent neck in one hand and a cup in the other. He was often alone, though, and that surprised Ruby. She thought of him in Athenaeum where he always seemed to have a woman nearby.

Soon the rooms and their extravagant furnishings ran together in Ruby's mind. It wasn't until the last room in the corridor that she found something worth noting.

The woman in the tapestry was life-size. She had thick strawberry-blond hair that fell in a cascade of waves around her shoulders. Her skin was flawless, a blush of pink over fresh cream. Her bright green eyes seemed to dance and sparkle from the very fibers of the embroidery. She wasn't smiling. Instead full red lips parted to reveal perfect white teeth. Her sheer flowing robes hid little of her voluptuous body.

Ruby's breath caught in her throat. Could it be a real woman? A goddess? Who was she? She turned to ask Ares but he looked away into the hall behind them.

Ruby tried to focus on the next painting, the next statue, anything, but all she could see were empty possessions. Ares remained quiet. She tried to concentrate on her real worries: Zeus, Hera, and imminent death. But her fear only intensified the gap between her and Ares.

"Are you hungry?" he finally asked, when they had visited all the upstairs rooms.

She nodded, though she wasn't sure she could really eat. They went down the curved staircase toward one set of the double doors in the main entrance hall.

"Wait," Ruby said. "What's in that room?" She pointed to the double doors opposite the pair he was leading her toward.

"Nothing really."

She stopped. "I want to see it all."

He shook his head. "It's a mess in there. It's not decorated or anything."

She walked to the doors. She felt on edge about the woman in the tapestry. She was willing to push him a little. "I don't mind."

"It's no big deal. It's just ..." he stammered.

She opened the doors.

The room was larger than any of the others they had seen. It was nearly as big as the entrance hall itself. And Ares was right. It was a mess.

A heavy wooden table stood in the middle of the room covered with oversized papers. An equally substantial desk stood in the corner. It too was covered. Books were open everywhere in haphazard piles and mounds on the floor. Maps hung along each wall. They showed the Earth in strikingly rich detail. There was not just one map of each continent, island, and land mass, but many: physical maps, population maps, political maps.

One showed religious factions by density. Another showed natural resources by region. Some were like the ones she had always seen, with countries, provinces, and states.

One map was covered in wavy lines and imperfect concentric circles with small numbers next to each one. It was purely topographical, no countries were named. It represented the Earth without borders, boundaries, or politics. It was the Earth without humans. The only thing that would change this map would be an earthquake, a volcano, or some other—*act of god*. She shivered.

She looked around again and saw that the large sheets of paper on the tables and desks were also maps, but in much greater detail. The one on top was of the Rogue Nations. It was of their cities and the rural areas in the hills.

She saw one of the Allied Countries and others of Africa and Asia. There were globes and instruments too. She recognized some as oddly shaped rulers. Others were compasses for drawing circles. Still others she had never seen before.

This was it. *This* was where he lived.

She thought that she might feel angry over such a place, but she only felt sad. Sad for the Earth and sad for Ares. She pictured him here over the years, the decades, the centuries, poring over these maps, planning and plotting, his body wracked with the pain of it, his mind overloaded with the desire for more.

With a pang in her chest she envisioned the moment when he could no longer stand to be apart from it. The moment he would leave this room and go to war.

She touched the maps and ran her finger over slick globes and sharp instruments. She followed the mechanics of war around the room until she got back to him, still standing in the doorway, watching her.

She looked into his guarded eyes. "*Now* I can feel you." she said. "*Now* I'm glad I came."

A smile touched his lips and then faded as his brow pinched together. "I love you," he said, his expression more pain than joy.

She felt that too. It hurt her to see this room and to feel Ares in this way, but it was part of him.

She placed her palm flat against his chest and felt the steady rhythm of his heart. "I love you too."

The room across the entrance way from the war room was its opposite in almost every way. It was furnished with tapestries of fruits and animals, dogs especially. Couches and overstuffed chairs were spaced around ornate rugs in clusters for conversation. This room, like most of the abode, held little of the real Ares.

In one corner stood an ornamented table. Its top was a chess board; the squares and the pieces were polished glass, red and clear instead of black and white. The table had carved gilt legs that ended in claws on the marble floor. The chairs looked like thrones with matching legs and arms, tall padded backs, and seats covered in red or white velvet.

Light glinted off the crystalline queen, and as Ruby got closer she could see that the pieces were faceted like gems. She touched the cold cut surface of the closest red pawn and turned to Ares. "It's beautiful."

"Diamonds vs. rubies," he said.

She drew back her hand, an old impulse impressed on her as a child to not break something expensive. The chess set would be worth millions on Earth.

A heavy stone settled in her stomach. What could the gods do if they turned their attentions back to the Earth, not for their own pleasure, like Apollo; not for their own interests, like Athena; and not for relief from their own suffering, like Ares, but for the good of humanity?

They could change everything.

She glanced around the opulent room and saw all the empty possessions for what they truly were: an opportunity.

Ares led her to an intimate table set for dinner that stood in the middle of the room. Next to the table was a cart with several covered dishes. The scene reminded her of room service in a fancy hotel, something she'd never experienced, but had seen in movies. It wasn't Thai takeout, but it would do.

Dinner included several cuts of meat, grape leaves stuffed with fragrant spiced rice, and roasted vegetables in brilliant hues. Ruby pushed her food around with her gold fork. Her stomach was more interested in doing slow somersaults than in eating.

She waved off the wine Ares offered her. She wanted to keep her wits about her. He poured a dark red liquid from another decanter into his own silver goblet but he didn't offer her any.

If Ares was nervous about confronting Zeus with a human woman he wanted to marry it did not affect his appetite. She sneezed when a fleck of black pepper he generously applied to his meat floated her way and caught in her nose.

"Sorry," he said. "I forgot about pepper."

"Right, gods don't sneeze," she said and rubbed at her nose. She suddenly felt annoyed that their differences were so fundamental.

When Ares finished eating he lifted the lid off the last of the covered trays. There was a single glass goblet filled with a translucent golden pudding.

Ruby's eyes went wide. Her mouth began to water.

Ares shot a glance at her and quickly replaced the cover. "I'll go change," he said. He pushed his chair back and stood. "The party's probably warming up right about now."

She felt beads of sweat form on her upper lip and she swallowed the saliva that had collected in her mouth. She watched Ares leave the room and glanced at the covered dish. She pictured herself eating the cup of pure ambrosia quickly and secretively before he got back. Would he ever know? She gave her head a quick shake to chase away the ridiculous thought.

Ares returned in a few minutes wearing a white outfit similar to hers. His was made of a rougher material and was shorter. His stopped at the knees instead of the floor. "A chiton," he said. She glanced at his lean legs and at the muscles that slid over one another as he moved.

She stood and ran her hands down the silky front of her own peplos. The gold earrings Athena had chosen jingled in her ears and added to her nerves. Ruby's shaking hands went up to touch her elaborate hairdo and she felt for the ruby butterfly pin that barely seemed to hold her outfit together. "Would you normally zap over there?" she asked.

"To the Great Hall?" He raised an eyebrow at her. "No. There's no disassociating within Olympus or the other godly realms. It's forbidden."

"Right," she said with a nervous shudder. "Zeus and his rules."

THIRTEEN

OUTSIDE, THE OLYMPIC AIR WAS WARM. A gentle breeze swept Ruby's peplos softly across her skin. Torches lined the path leading away from Ares's abode. More paths branched off the main. Even in the dimness Ruby could sense the life around her, lush and verdant. The smell of evening primrose and sweet rich earth permeated the air. *Ironic*, Ruby thought, *since we're so far from Earth*.

"How should I act in front of Zeus? What should I say? What should I do?" She gripped Ares's hand. "Should I bow? Should I not turn my back on him? What's the etiquette for the king of the gods?"

"He'll want to deal with me," he said, his jaw set and his eyes a fierce blue in the light of the torches. She steeled her courage and readied herself to follow his lead.

The path widened as they walked. It opened into a large clearing. There before them was the huge golden building she had seen from the air. The soft radiant light of a thousand torches lit the structure like a glowing ember. The relief carvings that decorated almost every inch of the facade cast eerie shadows that distorted the faces of their subjects.

The structure had looked large from above, but now Ruby could see how truly massive it was. She and Ares were dwarfed by the columns that lined each side. Her neck cramped as she looked up at the ceiling.

Ares started up the stairs that led to the main entrance without looking around. Ruby stopped to stare and pulled him back by the hand without realizing it. "Whoa," she whispered.

He scanned the ceiling as though he were surprised she would find anything interesting up there. Every surface was etched, carved, or decorated in some way. And every inch was gold.

Her eyes roamed all over, and still she could not see it all. She felt a tug on her hand. Ares led her through one of the many arched entrances into the hall.

The entranceway was a vast gallery lit by candles and lamps that lined the walls and hung from the high ceiling. The carvings were so real and lifelike that it seemed their subjects might shift their positions and step out of their scenes. Color was laid over the gold in places. There was a goddess with blue robes and a creature that was half man-half lion in a red and yellow tunic.

Ares led her further into the building, past hallways that branched off into the distance and double doors two or three stories high. On the far side of the gallery Ruby saw the biggest set of doors by far. Ares's pace slowed as he reached them.

Fear coursed through her like electricity and made her fingertips numb.

The look of determination remained set on Ares's face and he stood with all the power and prowess of the god of war.

Ruby stood up as straight as she could.

He pushed on one of the great double doors. The solid gold easily swung open under his power. The room was larger than the entrance hall. Round tables were set up in front of a stage where a long rectangular table stood.

She saw Zeus right away. It was obviously him. He sat in the middle spot at the long table on the stage. He had a trim white beard and hair. He looked fit. He was tanned and she caught a glimmer of light blue eyes, not intense like Ares's, but kind. Gentle, even. She could see how women would have been attracted to him.

To Zeus's right was a beautiful goddess. She looked to be fifty or so. Her auburn hair was braided into ropes pinned to the top of her head and hanging down in graceful loops. She talked easily with a handsome black-haired god next to her. His eyes were fixed on her as her hands played in the air describing something to him.

Ruby thought the goddess must be Hera, though she wasn't sure which god the younger one was.

She looked up and down the long table. It was obviously where the Twelve Olympians sat. Two older gods were on Zeus's left side. The one closest to Zeus was clearly his brother. He had Zeus's looks, though he did not have his presence.

The other god, one seat farther down, was dressed in black with stick-straight ebony hair. He was thin and lanky. His eyes scanned the room from deep hollows. He looked at Ruby and she saw that his eyes were the color of coal. His gaze didn't linger. He continued to peruse the room, apparently unperturbed by seeing a stranger on Olympus.

The other end of the table was abuzz. Younger gods and goddesses talked over and around one another. Several were eating the same golden dessert that Ares had hidden away from her: ambrosia. Ruby swallowed at the thought, but her mouth was dry.

The gods held their cups out to a blond teenager with shaggy bangs and a slender build. He filled the golden goblets with the deep red liquid Ares had drunk with dinner: nectar.

Ruby spotted Athena and Apollo sitting next to each other. Athena's black ringlets had been straightened and were braided into one long plait. Apollo leaned back in his chair. One long leg was crossed over the other. He plucked absently at the same pear-shaped stringed instrument she saw him with in the tapestries in Ares's abode but she couldn't hear the music he was playing over the din of the crowd. He chatted with a tall blond goddess whose face was serious. She barely looked at him while he spoke.

Next to Athena, on the other side, was an empty chair: for Ares.

Ruby scanned the Olympians she couldn't name. One was young, maybe younger then Ruby. He was pretty more than handsome, like the lead singer of a boy band. Near him was a god who sat sideways with a deformed leg that jutted out from under the table. Ruby came up short when she saw the goddess sitting next to him.

It was her, the woman from the tapestry in Ares's abode. The one Ares wouldn't look at. She had the strawberry-blond hair, green eyes, and perfect skin. She was involved in the goings-on of the table. She looked away from the deformed god and said something to Apollo several seats away. She was even more beautiful there in the Great Hall, smiling, laughing, and moving, than the tapestry could capture.

A group of young goddesses stood behind the long table. There were nine or ten in all. They wore whimsical masks and had wings attached to the backs of their colorful peploses; costumes for a dance or a play.

The lesser gods sat at the tables around the room. Their peploses and chitons created a mosaic of color. Heads turned to see who had come into the Great Hall and whispers traveled along the round tables.

"He's here."

"He brought her."

"Who is she?"

Soon the murmurs reached Zeus's table. Athena was the first to look up. She gave Ruby a quick smile but then glanced down at the goblet in her hand. Ruby smiled at her one friend, besides Ares. Her smile died, though, as more gods and goddesses turned to look at them.

Most of the gods' faces were placid and unperturbed. The goddess from the tapestry smiled at Ruby. Ruby flinched at the unexpected gesture and quickly glanced to the goddess's side.

The deformed god, she noticed, hadn't bothered to look at them at all.

The whispers soon gave way to complete silence. Ruby caught one stray note from Apollo's instrument before he too stopped what he was doing to watch them.

Zeus looked up at her with those blue eyes. "Ah, here is the source of all your worry, dear," he said. He looked to the auburn-haired goddess next to him, definitely Hera. But then his eyes were back on Ruby.

She tried to remember to breathe.

"The rumors bear true after all," Zeus said. "Your son has brought a human to Olympus. Is she to dine with the gods?" He held his golden goblet out and looked straight at her. A generous smile formed on his lips.

When his eyes shifted to Ares, the smile faded and his nostrils flared. "I can think of nothing more absurd than that. Nothing more foolish than for a god to ignore the edict and bring a stranger ... a *human*—" His eyes shot to Ruby then back to Ares. "—to Olympus." He paused, but only for a moment. "Can you, Ares?"

"She has not come to dine with the gods." Ares's voice was as steady as Zeus's eyes. "At least not yet."

Ruby heard gasps. She saw mouths drop open in surprise. She glanced to Athena, who looked straight at Ares, her mouth open slightly, as though she knew nothing about this.

Ruby's eyes darted to Apollo. What could he do in this moment? Athena said that Apollo had more friends than Ares. Ruby hadn't worried about it until now. What kind of influence did he have here?

When he shifted in his seat her heart froze. She watched as the tall god straightened one leg and then the other. He stretched them both out in front of him and crossed them at the ankles. He looked as though he were bored, as if none of this concerned him. She was as angry as she was relieved. He would play it cool, apparently. He would save his own skin above everything.

"We've come for your blessing, Father. And Hera's too." Ares nodded in deference to his mother.

"A blessing?" Zeus's head cocked to the side, but his face was unsurprised. Had he been expecting them, expecting this, after all?

Ares held up their clasped hands and looked at Ruby. Her cheeks flushed hot as she felt every eye in the room on her. "I love her," he said. "We are to marry."

More clamors of disbelief ran through the room. Zeus glanced around. Ruby looked at Hera. Her brow was knit. Hera's eyes darted to the tabletop and then back to Ares.

Zeus said nothing. The room quieted. "Marry? She's *human*." His voice was deep, rich, and commanding. Ruby could feel his eyes on her. She looked to the golden floor. "You know the decree, the edict. No contact with humans. Ever!" The last word was a shout and Ruby did not doubt his anger or his power.

She felt her arms begin to shake. Ares squeezed her hand but it only helped a little.

"Marriage?" Zeus continued. His eyes widened. His muscles tensed. "It's out of the question."

"I'm lucky," Ares went on, as if Zeus had encouraged him to tell them more. "She loves me enough to give up her life as a human. She's willing to become a goddess. She will be bound to me in *hieros gamos*."

The murmurs doubled. Ruby's eyes shot around the room. Gods and goddesses turned in their golden seats to see the reactions of those around them.

Zeus spoke over everyone. "Of course she's *willing*, you fool. What human wouldn't want immortality, and worshippers, and *wealth*?" He narrowed his eyes at her.

Ares stepped forward and pulled Ruby with him. "*Listen*," he said, holding Zeus's gaze. "We're in love. We ask that you marry us in *hieros gamos* and that we have the blessing of Hera."

The room was silent now as Ares looked to his mother. "Bless us as the goddess of marriage, like you used to do for even the lowliest peasant couple, if they were truly in love and truly humble before you."

Ruby braved a glance up in Hera's direction. Her auburn hair framed her ivory face and those green eyes shone like emeralds: bold, beautiful, and cold. "I'm glad for your happiness, son." Her voice was calm and smooth. "But as you know, it is not up to—"

"You have disregarded my command, despite the consequences," Zeus broke in. "You have been to Earth. You have brought a human to Olympus. To the Great Hall!" he bellowed. "Now you ask for this? This impossible thing that will destroy Olympus and destroy our way of life?" He waved dismissively at them. "Take her back to Earth. While you still can."

"I won't take her back," Ares said. "I need her. She is the only balm to sooth my affliction. Earth only knows peace, *I* only know peace, when Ruby's with me."

"Ruby?" Zeus scoffed. "That's rich. Your jewel?" He laughed a great roar of laughter. The rest of the room erupted too. Ruby was reminded of a high school cafeteria where the biggest bully makes a joke and everyone laughs out of fear.

"I love her. Like you love Hera. I need her, like you need your goddess."

The room returned to a hush as if every breath hung on Zeus's response. Zeus looked at no one but Ares. His face gave nothing away. Gods shifted in their seats, squirming in the silence.

Ares stood straight. He was not about to bend. He gestured to the room with his free hand. "Who among you has been in love?" He waited for a response but the room was quiet. "Which of you sit here with your wives, your husbands, your lovers?" He asked this while making eye contact around the room. Some gods smiled. Others looked away.

"How many of you had to leave your loves because they were mortal?" He paused and Ruby saw gods cast their eyes down or place a hand on their chest.

"Which of you left your children? Is there one of you who can say they haven't missed the energy of mortals?" Ares's eyes shot to Apollo, but Apollo was looking down at the table before him, his arms and legs still crossed.

"Who misses the pure, fresh joy of beings bursting with the rush of life?" Ares asked.

Almost every god in the room nodded and loud approving whispers rippled through the gathering.

"Who among you is ready for the separation to be over?" He sounded like a general rallying his troops.

"I am!" one god shouted, though Ruby hadn't seen who said it. The outburst was met with increasingly louder declarations of approval and more vigorous nodding of heads.

Zeus's cheeks were a deep pink and his eyes were wide. They ranged over the crowd. "Silence!" he shouted.

The room was quiet in a second.

"You do have nerve, son. A steel nerve." Zeus's fists were balled on the table, like he was barely keeping himself under control. Ruby was shocked when he smiled, but the smile wasn't genuine. It was the smile of a small-town politician, practiced and phony-looking.

"There's no reason for everyone to get up in arms here," the king of the gods put up both hands in front of him. It was an odd gesture for an absolute ruler. It looked like surrender.

"I care little for the goings-on of Earth, you know that." He glanced around the crowd as if to gauge their reaction. The lesser gods looked at their king with their mouths hanging open.

"But I can see that you do care," Zeus said to Ares. "You. And some of the others." His eyes shot down the Table of the Twelve, and then around the room. "I know you wouldn't have gone to Earth alone, at least not to anywhere where you would have met *her*." Zeus looked at Ruby again. He held her gaze. "Your little jewel is indeed quite a treasure."

A chill ran across Ruby's skin at the compliment. She thought of all the mortal women Zeus had pursued on Earth and felt the fear of that. If she had ever thought that it would have been flattering to have the king of the gods come from Olympus to show you special attention she now realized that it must have been terrifying, especially as she saw Hera sitting there, emotionless green eyes staring down at her.

The rest of the gods exchanged knowing glances or snickered to one another. Zeus had regained control of the crowd. Now she was nothing more than a sideshow, a diversion.

"I see the girl is important to you, Ares," Zeus continued. "And I'll be relieved to see my malcontent son satisfied at last. I'll grant your wish. She'll eat the ambrosia. I will perform *hieros gamos*. I will make your human girl your wife." Zeus looked to Hera. "As far as the great mother's blessing, you'll have to ask her."

Hera looked Ruby over. Her green eyes traveled down her body. "She's unspoiled at least," Hera said.

Ruby felt her face get hot.

Hera looked at Ares. Her green eye softened. "Be sure, my son. Be sure you want *this*."

Ruby cringed at the implication.

Ares said nothing, but stared back at his mother without emotion.

Hera took up her formal tone again. "I will bless the marriage if she remains pure until the day."

Ruby stopped breathing. *Yes?* They had both said yes? But then why was Ares so serious? Why the heavy quiet in the room?

"When?" Ares demanded, apparently not ready to celebrate their engagement yet.

"Spring," Zeus answered, as if he knew the question was coming. "A few months to think on it will do you good. I needn't remind you that *hieros gamos* is forever. Once she is immortal and your wife, there will be no going back. We are not about to change *all* the rules for your whims, Ares."

"Spring." Ares nodded. He squeezed Ruby's hand until she felt it might be crushed. "But I need your word, father. Your oath."

Zeus's eyes shifted to the side but then met with Ares's again. "I swear it by the River Styx. When the first flowers bloom on Mount Olympus you shall marry your human girl. Here even," he spread his hands out before him. "In the Great Hall. A marriage truly fit for a god and goddess."

Could it be this easy? No bolt of lightning to smite her? No eternal punishment for Ares? She hadn't dared to imagine this outcome. Now a rush went through her and she felt unsteady on her feet.

Ares nodded to no one in particular. He turned and led Ruby out of the room with all the confidence he had strode in with. They walked back through the huge golden entryway and out past the columns. Now neither of them looked around.

In the dark Olympic night the stars shone a blazing swath of silver-white. Ares stopped. He picked her up in a tight hug around her waist and lifted her into the air. He laid his head on her breast and let out a long breath. She lowered her cheek onto the top of his head. His black silky hair was soft on her face. He didn't say anything.

She wanted to feel relief and excitement, but he hugged her as if she would be snatched away if he let go. When he put her back down on her feet she saw that he wasn't smiling. There were tight creases around his eyes.

"Aren't you happy? It was everything we had hoped for. He's going to do it. And Hera will bless us."

"I don't trust him," Ares said. "It was too easy."

"But he gave his oath ..." She wondered if oaths were different for gods. Maybe she had misunderstood.

"You're right. He has to marry us. He swore. An oath by the River Styx is unbreakable for any god, even Zeus." His eyes remained narrow. "It's just ... You don't know him. We can never trust him. Not really."

FOURTEEN

ATHENA'S ABODE was much like her apartment on Earth, but bigger and grander. Statues, tapestries, ancient-looking pots, and small stone figures lined every shelf and stood on pedestals in every nook and cranny. If there were velvet ropes and a crowd, Ruby thought, it really would be a museum.

The abode itself was typical in an Olympic way. The walls were polished amethyst and, like Ares's abode, Athena's was much too big for one god. Doorways led to luxuriously furnished rooms that had probably never been used. And, like Ares, Athena had taken one room for her own.

The library was two stories high and made up one entire half of the main floor. A tight metal staircase led up to a mezzanine level that housed most of the stacks; shelves of books from all eras of Earth's history.

The downstairs furnishings were rich but practical. Heavy oak tables and chairs sat around the room in convenient locations. Gold or black lettering marked the spines of many of the books on the shelves that circled the room. Ruby saw English, Spanish, French, Chinese or Japanese and what she thought were Greek, Russian, Hebrew, and Sanskrit. Others were too faded or cracked to read at all.

One wall of shelves contained not bound books but yellowing rolled scrolls stored in diamond-shaped cubbies. Some of the scroll's edges were singed black.

"Well done, Ares," Athena said from the couch across from Ruby and Ares. "You played well to his weaknesses. He hates to lose control." The blue peplos she had worn to Hera's dinner party shaded her eyes a deep grey.

Ruby looked at Ares. He nodded but his eyes still held a hint of tightness.

"You'll stay with me until the wedding," Athena said to Ruby. "Hera will appreciate the gesture."

"I can't stay with Ares?"

"It's for appearances," the goddess said. "On your wedding day Hera will know if you're still a virgin or not, no matter where you've been sleeping."

All this talk of Ruby's virginity, like it was a ribbon in her hair for everyone to comment on, was starting to wear on her. "Why does it matter so much?"

"Hera has a distinct sense of propriety," Athena said. "She wants to know that you're innocent and that your sons are Ares's sons. But more than that, it's something she can hang over him. She'll make him sacrifice because she can."

Ruby glanced again at Ares, but he had no reaction. The idea that his mother would deliberately make life uncomfortable for him didn't seem new.

Ruby looked around the room from books, to statues, to scrolls. "This is incredible," she said.

Athena followed her gaze and beamed like a mother receiving praise for a talented child.

"Where are they all from?" Ruby asked as she looked up at a shelf that reached to the top of the tall room. "How old are they?"

"Most would seem very old to you," Athena said. "I've rescued them from many places over the years."

Ruby thought of the full shelves of books at the bookstore and how no one ever bought any. Athenaeum was a clearinghouse for Athena's collection and this is where they would end up.

"These scrolls," Ruby stood and walked to the diamond-shaped cubbies. "What are they?"

"Most are from the Library of Alexandria," Athena said as she followed. "The library was destroyed in a fire."

Ruby reached her hand out to touch one and hesitated. She looked to Athena and the goddess nodded. The scroll made a crinkling sound as Ruby unrolled the stiff parchment. It was a star chart. The handwriting was tiny and perfect. Each foreign letter had been formed with an exacting hand.

The stars on the chart were represented as dots strung together into constellations by thin black lines. It was an attempt to figure things out, to take what information was available and make sense of the world. It was the same thing people still did today, thousands of years later, but with more sophisticated equipment.

She scanned the thousands of books in the library. Most would have had to have been written out longhand. The printing press wasn't invented until ... when? The fourteen hundreds? "A fire would have been devastating," she said, more to herself than to them.

"Especially one set by an invading Julius Caesar," Ares said, now standing next to her.

Ruby glanced to him and wondered whose side he had been on in that battle. Caesar's or the scrolls'.

·∞·

Ruby woke the next morning surrounded by an ocean of white sheets. Sun streamed in through the tall thin windows set into the amethyst wall of Athena's abode. She kicked off the covers and went to look outside.

Ruby had chosen this room because it overlooked a courtyard with a little gnarled tree. Although all of Olympus felt magical, this small courtyard called to her especially. She looked into the blue sky. The weather was perfect and she wondered if it ever wasn't.

Ruby dressed in the white peplos Athena had left for her. This one was less formal than the one she wore to the Great Hall. There were no gold adornments and it was made from cotton, not silk. There was a white piece of cloth to cinch around her waist and a small leather purse. Stamped into the leather was an owl sitting on a branch and under the branch was a stylized A. She braided her hair to one side in a weak attempt to copy what seemed to be in style on Olympus and pulled the braid over her shoulder.

She saw the picture of her parents she had brought from her house on the silver nightstand. Her sunny mood clouded and a pang of regret flared in her chest. She was to marry Ares, become a goddess, and live on Olympus. This place, if not this room, was her new home. She could not forget the past, but she could not dwell on it either.

Downstairs she crossed the large entryway and looked for Athena. A set of silver double doors led out to the same court-yard Ruby could see from her room.

"Good morning," Athena said and motioned for Ruby to join her at a wrought iron table where she was eating breakfast next to the ancient-looking tree.

Ruby breathed in the summer scents of Olympus and took a seat across from the goddess. She saw that Athena's hair was in a loose braid at the back of her head.

"Thanks for the peplos," she said, happy she got the hair right too.

"Much nicer than jeans. No pinching waists." Athena wrinkled up her nose. "Help yourself." She motioned to the table and raised a silver pot toward Ruby. "Coffee?"

Ruby scanned the table of beautifully arranged foods. There were grapes in a silver bowl, crusty rolls on an amber tray, brie and other cheeses on a large marble slab with a silver knife to cut them. Her eyes stopped when she reached the bronze basket in the middle of the table. "You made Ambrosia Bars!" she said as she reached for one.

Athena touched her wrist. "Not those."

"What?" Ruby's mouth had already begun to water. Her eyes were trained on the biggest one.

"Not here." The goddess shook her head.

"Why?" Ruby's stomach growled loud enough for her to hear.

"They're made with pure ambrosia. If you eat one there would be no reasoning with Zeus or any of the other gods after that. On Earth the effects and the amounts I use are inconsequential. Here it's different."

"But, I've been eating them for months. You said a little wouldn't—"

"Ruby." The pressure on her wrist increased. She pulled her attention away and looked at Athena. Her grey eyes were serious. "If you eat any amount of ambrosia or drink any amount of nectar in the godly realms it will begin the process of making you immortal. I know that's the goal, but not yet. There have been mortals who've tried to steal one or both but…" She shook her head. "It didn't end well."

Ruby took a warm roll instead and glanced to the gnarled tree, deliberately keeping her eyes from the Ambrosia Bars. She didn't recognize the tree's small pale leaves, creamy white flowers, or green berries. "This tree is beautiful. What kind is it?"

"It's The Olive Tree."

Ruby tore off a chunk of roll and took a bite, but it tasted like a mouthful of white flour compared to an Ambrosia Bar. "*The* Olive Tree?"

Athena turned her body toward the tree. Her face softened. "There once was a city in Greece that my uncle, Poseidon, and

I both loved. Poseidon was at the feast last night. Did you see him?"

Ruby shrugged. "No time for introductions."

"He looks like Zeus." Athena waved her hand dismissively. "Anyway. We each gave the city a gift. Poseidon, the god of the sea, gave them a saltwater spring," she rolled her eyes at Ruby. "Not terribly useful. *I*," she placed her hand over her chest, "gave them *this*," she flopped the hand forward and motioned to the tree.

"An olive tree?" Ruby asked. She was pretty sure that Greece already had olive trees.

"I gave them olive *trees*. Much better than a saltwater spring. It provides food, oil, shade … beauty," she looked again at the tree. "And this is the very first one."

Ruby smiled at this casual conversation about the innovation of olive trees as she sat with their creator beneath the branches of the prototype.

"What became of the city?"

"Athens?" Athena raised her eyebrows.

"Oh, of course." Ruby felt herself blush as she pulled a grape off its stem.

"The city is my child in a way."

Ruby knew Athena was one of the virgin goddesses, along with Artemis and Hestia. "Don't you *want* children?" Ruby asked, as she popped another grape in her mouth. "Is it a choice you made? Or is it another of Zeus's ideas of propriety? Or Hera's?" She bristled at the reminder that she was under their thumbs.

"It's a choice. I'm free of men and family. I'm able to keep my head clear. I make my own decisions. Love so often muddles one's clarity."

"Is that what you think?" Ruby sat back in her iron chair. "That my mind is muddled by love?"

"Love is a powerful thing." She held Ruby's gaze. "I think you have done some things for Ares that maybe you wouldn't have done if it weren't for loving him."

Ruby thought of all the good their love had done on Earth. "What about the men that would have died in the war? They will live for decades instead."

"Last night you stood in Zeus's Great Hall and told the king of the gods that you would defy all his rules. That you would make yourself a goddess and marry his son." Athena gave her a sidelong look. "If that's not muddled thinking, you tell me what is."

Ruby opened her mouth to respond, and then closed it. It *was* irrational, what she had done. "But our love may save humanity." It sounded conceited and crazy, but she had come to believe it was true.

"I didn't say that love wasn't good. I said it can cloud your judgment. I need my mind to be clear. The goddess of wisdom in *love?*" She laughed. "It's a bit of an oxymoron. Don't you think?"

"No. I think there is wisdom in love. I think maybe the answer to everything lies at the heart of love."

Athena's gaze went back up to the olive tree. After a moment she nodded, as if the tree had asked her a question and she was answering. "I want to give you an early wedding gift.

An olive branch is the symbol of peace, not wisdom, ironically." She stood and took a pair of garden sheers from a table nearby. "Peace is the result of your love with Ares." She cut off a small branch with the shears and handed it to Ruby. "Grow this branch and it will bring peace and harmony to you both."

Ruby took the slim branch. She touched the leaves. They were dark green on one side and silvery white on the other. The small flowers were cream-colored with yellow centers and mildly scented. The branch felt oddly stiff. The leaves and the petals would not yield to her touch.

"It's enchanted. I've slowed their molecules," Athena said. "It will stay as it is until you plant it. Wait until after the wedding. Plant it in your own garden."

"Thank you," Ruby said in awe, and carefully tucked the small olive branch into the leather pouch that hung from her waist.

☙❧

Ruby left Athena's after breakfast. The bare dirt path beneath her feet was well worn. She now knew that it started at Zeus's Great Hall, wound through the woods, and branched off to the other gods' abodes. She had seen many of the abodes from the air the day before, but it had been dusk then. Now she caught glimpses in the morning light. Metal or stone structures peeked over foliage in the distance.

The plants here were as incongruous as the ones that grew in front of Ares's abode. Massive evergreens stood back from the path while smaller plants lined the trim walkway and flowered in a glorious riot of every color known to nature. The air was full of their fragrances. They mingled in spicy sweet breezes beneath the china blue sky. The sun warmed her face and neck.

Ruby closed her eyes and breathed it all in. She tried to taste the beauty of it. Taste seemed to be the last of her senses that she could not enjoy on Olympus, at least not until she became a goddess and could eat ambrosia whenever she wanted. She thought of Ambrosia Bars and tried to remember their exact taste but it was more frustrating than satisfying and she gave it up quickly. She opened her eyes and saw movement ahead, tall and blond. It pulled her up short.

Apollo's long lanky strides rounded the corner and met with her quickly, too quickly to hide, which was her first instinct, and too quickly to run, which was her second. She knew she would have to face him at some point but it hadn't occurred to her that it might be alone and in the woods. The carefree feeling of being in nature left her as quickly as heat leaves a body in a gust of wind.

"Rubes!" he drawled with a wide grin.

She plucked up her courage to face him. Even if she didn't feel like she belonged here yet, she felt like she could fake it.

"Enjoying your stay on Olympus?" he asked. He tilted his head and raised his eyebrows at her.

"It's beautiful," she agreed. "I can't see why you ever left it."

His eyes darted to the side and Ruby realized that she did have power over Apollo. She wasn't completely at his mercy. Zeus knew that other gods had been to Earth, or at least he assumed it. But he didn't know which ones. Ruby did.

"The trees *are* nice." He looked directly at her. "But sometimes one longs for more … stimulation."

She ignored his lewd comment. "I'm here to stay, Apollo. You heard Zeus. Ares and I will be married. I'll become a goddess." The words, and her confidence, were new, but they felt good on her lips.

"Oh yes." He laughed. "I heard." He stared at her, as if waiting for her to laugh too. "You can't really believe it?" He scoffed. "Certainly Ares can't."

"Why do you hate me so much?" Ruby looked him in the eye, unafraid of the answer.

"This is the thing, Rubes." He leaned down toward her, uncomfortably close. "I can't stop you from being here. I can't stop Ares from his own willful desires. But I *must* stop the destruction of Olympus."

"What destruction? Your vision was wrong. There was no split among the gods. No—"

"It's not you, Rubes. It's not even that you find my creepy brother attractive that bothers me." He looked at her as if he were looking at a pest he'd found in his house. "It's what you are. What you represent." He shrugged. "It's nothing personal."

"So humans are good enough to sleep with, but not good enough to marry?"

"Yes." He looked her up and down and grinned. "You're definitely good enough to sleep with."

"What about nymphs?" she shot back. "Good enough sleep with but not marry?"

Ruby got a chill from the cold stare he gave her. "Leave Kissiae out of this. I've taken care. And that's completely different."

"Why do you sleep around on Earth if you supposedly love her so much?" She had been curious about this ever since Ares had told her that Apollo was in love.

His nostrils flared and she saw him swallow. "This is a dangerous place, Ruby. Not for me. Not for Ares. For you. The gods are dangerous. What I can't figure out is why your boyfriend and his accomplice don't tell you that. If Ares loved you, he'd try to save you."

"I think you're jealous," she said.

"You have no idea what's at stake," he countered.

"What then?"

Apollo gritted his front teeth and hissed, "Everything."

❦

The beauty of Olympus was forgotten as Apollo's dark words ran through Ruby's mind. She soon found herself standing in front of Ares's abode. He didn't answer when she knocked on the oak door and she thought of the enormity of the place. How would he ever hear her out here? The door opened easily when she turned the handle. No need for locks on Olympus, it seemed.

She entered the main hall and looked up to the soaring ceiling covered in paintings. She was about to call out for Ares when she heard muffled voices coming from the war room.

She reached for the door handle but then pulled away. Who was he talking to? Should she interrupt? Instead she followed the arc of the curved walls of the entrance hall and looked at each painting, vase, and tapestry in turn.

She was a quarter of the way through the circuit when she heard a feminine, melodic laugh come from behind the closed doors. She looked at the smooth wood door and was about to dismiss it when she heard Ares's laugh mixed in. His seemed higher than normal, nervous maybe. The laughter came again and Ruby moved closer to the door. She was about to knock when it swung open.

Her body jerked back as the goddess from the tapestry, the same one she had seen at the Table of the Twelve, walked toward her. Up close she was even more stunning. She wore an emerald green peplos that played up her reddish blond hair and her sparkling green eyes. Her complexion was luminous, perfect.

"Well, here she is now." The goddess's smile lit up her eyes.

"Ruby!" Ares moved in front of the goddess and put his arm around Ruby. "This is Aphrodite."

Ruby felt the floor shift beneath her. Aphrodite? The goddess of love and beauty? But what was the goddess of love doing laughing behind closed doors with Ares?

"Don't make my mistake." Aphrodite winked at Ares. "He's a keeper."

Ruby felt Ares's grip tighten on her shoulder.

"I've gotta run now." Her voice was smooth and velvety. She spoke with a slow, leisurely rhythm that was almost hypnotic. "Everyone's going to the river. You two should come." She looked back at Ares and playfully tugged on his arm.

Ruby didn't like to see her touch him.

The goddess turned and walked toward the front door. She moved like a silk ribbon. In the doorframe she half turned and glanced back with a sultry smile.

When the door closed Ruby looked at Ares. "What was that about?" She tried to sound casual.

"It's just Aphrodite."

"What did she mean? 'Don't make my mistake.'"

"I don't know what she meant. I mean … She doesn't always make sense."

She looked him in the eye. "I don't want to have secrets, Ares. That's no way to start a life."

"It's just … She … We …"

Ruby searched his eyes, his face. "*Her? She's* the one?"

"It was a long time ago," he said, and shook his head.

Ruby felt her eyes getting too big in their sockets. "*She's* the one you haven't been able to get over for three thousand years?" Her voice escalated with each word.

"Ruby." He looked at her with panic on his face. "It was a long time ago. I got over her. I love *you*."

Her head was still spinning. She didn't want to blow it out of proportion. They had just been talking. But what bothered Ruby was not that they had met behind closed doors, or Aphrodite's undeniable beauty. It wasn't even her walk. It was the laugh. Not Aphrodite's, teasing and playful, but Ares's, high and uneasy.

"What's going on at the river?" she asked, to change the subject.

"A bunch of gods are getting together," he said, looking relieved. "We should go. Everyone will want to meet you."

Her throat tightened at the thought of meeting *everyone*.

"Have you eaten?" he asked.

"Yes. Athena is taking very good care of me." Her mood lightened. "She gave us a wedding gift." She pulled the branch out of the purse at her waist and again marveled at its simple beauty.

Ares took the branch from her. "This is a rare gift. Athena doesn't cut up The Olive Tree for just anyone. We'll make a special garden for it."

"She said to plant it after the wedding."

He handed it back to her and slipped both his arms around her waist. His touch and energy reassured her. "After we're married then."

"I still can't believe Zeus said yes." She searched his face, looking for the doubt he had expressed the night before and thinking of what Apollo said on the path.

His eyes darted away for a split second, but then they were back on her. "I'm sure Athena and Aphrodite will want to help us plan for it. And Dionysus, of course."

"Of course," she said in a low voice. "Which one is he again?"

FIFTEEN

AS THEY WALKED TO THE RIVER Ares pointed out who lived where. The abode near Zeus's Great Hall, the one Ruby had mistaken for silver, was platinum. It was Hera's.

The white marble one belonged to Dionysus, the god of wine and fertility. His abode was almost completely covered in vines. "Every variety of grape that grows on Earth and a few that don't," Ares said.

"Aphrodite lives there." He pointed through the trees to a pink alabaster building filigreed with blooming rose vines. Ruby caught the familiar scent of the flowers on the air. Aphrodite's abode stood in contrast to a black metal one nearby. It was the one with all the sculptures that Ruby had seen from the air. She couldn't help but feel a little relieved that Ares and Aphrodite didn't live right next to each other.

She was glad to leave the buildings behind and happy that they hadn't run into the main residents of either the gold or platinum abodes. Ares assured her that only the younger generation of gods would go to the river. "Technically speaking, we'll be breaking a few rules."

She instinctively looked around but Ares didn't seem concerned as he led her down a narrow trail through the thick woods. At the end of the trail they came to the edge of a river.

"Oceanus," he said as he stretched out his arms in a grand gesture. "The great river that runs in a circle around the core of Olympus before it flows out to the sea." He pointed south.

She thought of the seemingly endless ocean she had seen as they flew in. Here it was only a few hundred feet to the far side of the clear water where the forest picked up again.

"This is our boundary." He looked down to the water. "Zeus has forbidden us to go beyond the water's edge."

"What's on the other side?"

"Maybe I'll show you sometime." He smiled at her and she saw a glimmer of the excitement she had grown accustomed to seeing on railroad bridges and at the base of sheer cliffs.

They strolled hand in hand along the river, kicking up rocks and taking their time. Soon they came to a group of gods standing on the bank up ahead. The gods were dressed in peploses or chitons of different colors. They talked in loose groups, and looked to the far side of the water as if they expected the trees to uproot themselves and walk away.

Athena spoke to a cluster of gods but stopped midsentence when she saw Ruby. All eyes turned to them. Athena walked to Ruby and put her arm around her shoulders as Ares continued to hold her other hand. Ruby stood up straight. She was glad that she had these two flanking her. The others approached in a large crowd, except for Apollo, who hung back and continued to look down into the water before him.

"Welcome," a young god said as he led the pack to meet her. His hair was the color of wheat in August. His eyes were as blue as a summer sky. He was young and cute with boyish features. Ruby recognized him from the dinner party and remembered thinking that he looked like a member of a boy band back home. He wore an off-white chiton and held a gold staff in one hand.

"Hermes," Ares said with obvious affection in his voice. "This is Ruby."

Hermes took her hand and shook it.

"You own the winged sandals, right?" she said. "Thanks for the loan."

His smile was lopsided, charming. "Ares assured me he was up to no good. I was happy to help." He winked at her. "I had no idea it would be this good."

A tall goddess with a silver bow and a quiver of silver arrows on her back stood next to Hermes. She wore the shorter chiton that the male gods wore and had long, lithe arms and legs. She had been talking with Apollo at the Table of the Twelve the night before.

"Artemis," the goddess said, not waiting for Ares to introduce them.

Ruby took her outstretched hand and shook it. The goddess had white-blond hair and familiar blue eyes. Ruby glanced past her to Apollo.

"We're twins," the goddess said.

"I see you got the looks out of the deal," Ruby said as a joke, giddy and self-conscious from all the attention.

Artemis didn't laugh.

Aphrodite pushed through the crowd. She took Ruby's hand. "Don't mind her. She has no sense of humor. Have you begun to plan the wedding? I'd love to help. And Dionysus will create you a new wine," she said. She waved to a god with short-cropped black hair standing toward the back. He smiled and waved at Ruby.

"We haven't talked about the wedding much, but I'll let you know," Ruby said.

"Yes, you must," Aphrodite said and with her next breath added, "And this is my son and his wife. They'll help too." She pulled in a matching pair of beautiful blonds. If Aphrodite hadn't said that they were husband and wife Ruby would have thought they were twins, too. They seemed as young as Hermes.

"Eros, Psyche, this is Ruby. She'll be your ..." Aphrodite looked to the forest behind Ruby, apparently searching for the right label. "Stepmother."

Ruby's eyes widened—not at meeting Ares's son or at the confirmation of what she already suspected, that Aphrodite was Ares's son's mother—but at meeting Psyche. She had been human once.

Eros stuck his hand out to her. She started when she saw Ares's turquoise eyes looking out of Eros's otherwise unfamiliar face. "Nice to have you here," he said.

Other gods were introduced. The names were familiar, though there was no time for Ruby to place name to myth before the next god was presented. After about twenty gods and goddesses, she stopped trying to keep them straight.

She shook yet another hand.

"*Pan*," Ares said, and exaggerated the name with a smile.

Ruby's smile fell when her eyes instinctively traveled down to his legs, which were furry and ended in hooves. She glanced back to his face. His eyes were pale yellow and his pupils were black horizontal slits. In the tangles of his curly brown hair she saw two little horns sticking up. "Nice to meet you," she finally managed.

"Don't let my brutish side disturb you, dear," he said. "I'm only forty-nine percent goat. Mostly god. At least where it counts." There was a definite twinkle in his golden eyes.

Ruby smiled again. She was surprised at everyone's warmth and how welcoming they all were.

Apollo, still standing by the water's edge, called out, "Pan, get your pipes."

The group walked to the water with Pan in the lead. He produced an instrument of five hollow reeds lined up in descending height order, held together with black and gold lashing. Pan brought the pipes to his mouth and blew across them as one might do with an empty wine bottle to produce a note. He began to play a light melodic tune.

The gods around Ruby looked into the river and at the trees that lined the far bank. The water was as clear as glass, like a rippling window that ran over the smooth grey and brown stones of the riverbed.

The sweet music from Pan's pipes lulled her. Her thoughts wandered. It reminded her of cycling, of that meditative state she would sometimes get to. There was no real sense of time passing or of the gods around her.

She startled back to the present when she caught a glimpse of movement across the river. Something had shifted among the brown trunks and the green leaves of the trees.

"Here they come," Apollo said. Loud. Eager.

Other gods pointed into the river. Ruby looked down. Shapes glided through the clear water, so fast she couldn't make them out. Alarmed, she backed up into Ares who was standing right behind her. He didn't budge but instead put his arms around her and whispered in her ear. "Don't be afraid."

She relaxed into his embrace and watched as figures came into focus on the far side. They were women, young and graceful. All nude. The shapes in the water slowed too. They seemed to be more a part of the clear currents of the river than something foreign in it.

The women across the water drifted above its surface and came toward them. The swimmers climbed out of the water down the bank from where the group of gods and Ruby stood. No one seemed surprised or embarrassed that the women were naked.

"Who are they?" she whispered to Ares.

"Nymphs," he said. "Nature spirits that live in the woods and the streams. They don't often leave their groves or springs but they will abandon everything when they hear Pan's pipes."

The nymphs walked toward them on the near bank. They were the height of humans or gods. They had creamy white skin and long flowing hair in rich browns and deep reds.

The gods went to greet them.

Ruby saw one god walk faster than the others. His blond head was high above anyone else's. His light blue eyes were fixed on a single point. Ruby followed Apollo's line of sight. Before she could find what he was looking at, he stopped. His face brightened.

He took the hand of a plump little nymph. She wore a crown of ivy atop her waist-long brown hair. He bent to kiss her hand, as he had done to Ruby so long ago when they had first met, but instead of a sly smile and a playful gleam in his eye, Ruby saw unrestrained adoration. She felt like she was looking at a completely different god.

The nymph was not especially beautiful but she had an open face that suggested laughter and kindness. There was not a hint of arrogance or smugness between them.

The pair walked away together toward the forest. The nymph's head was craned back to look up into Apollo's shining face and they soon disappeared into the trees.

Ruby's attention was pulled away by loud voices from the other direction. Artemis was with a group of nymphs who were all talking at once. She said something to them. They all turned in the same direction and pointed downstream. In an instant the goddess and the group were off, running down the bank of the river.

"Where are they going?" Ruby asked.

"On the hunt. There's likely an unlucky stag headed that way."

"Hunting?" The nymphs and Artemis carried one bow among them, and all but Artemis were still naked.

"Artemis is the goddess of the hunt," he said. "She's the closest of all of us with the nymphs. I think she prefers their company to any of ours."

Pan and Hermes stood near where Artemis and the nymphs had run off barefoot into the woods. The two gods were surrounded by a group of nymphs, who laughed as the pair spoke over one another, vying for their attention.

Ruby and Ares sat on a fallen log near the river's edge. "Do you do this often?" she asked as she watched Pan lean on a large rock, one goat leg crossed over the other, and blow a breath across his pipes. Music filled the air again.

"I never come. I wanted you to see them," Ares said. "It's always the same. Pan calls them. Most go off hunting with Artemis. Those that are not dedicated to her, those who have not taken a vow of chastity, meet with Pan, or Hermes, or any other god that will have them, to lie in a meadow for the afternoon."

Ruby picked up a curved stick from the ground and dug it into the soft sandy dirt. "What about Apollo?" She thought of his many conquests on Earth and glanced to the trees where he and the nymph had disappeared into the woods.

"Apollo only ever sees Kissiae."

"I saw him go off with her." Her eyes remained on the trees, but the two were nowhere in sight. "How long have they been together?"

"Hundreds of years," Ares shrugged. "I haven't kept track."

Ruby thought of the pain of being in love for hundreds of years and having to hide it. "I thought she was mortal. How can she be hundreds of years old?"

"Nymphs live for much longer than humans. When the stream or the tree they are bound to dries up or dies, they die too."

"The nymphs live across the water?" The trees on the far side of the river were the same as the ones around them, a combination of the bright green leaves of deciduous trees mixed in with the darker green of conifers. Ruby could hear distant birdsong over the gently flowing water. The ground beneath the trees was a carpet of brown leaves and needles. It was more like a forest on Earth than the unusual variety of plants that lined the pathways near the gods' abodes.

"Yes. The nymphs live in the outer realm of Olympus," he said.

Ruby tossed her stick aside. She saw Aphrodite standing between two gods. A slender teenager with shaggy bangs challenged a much bigger god to a wrestling match. The blond was the same god who served the Table of the Twelve the night before. His chest was puffed out and he was talking up into the larger god's face.

The bigger god rolled his eyes at Aphrodite as if to say, *I'll be with you in a minute, honey. I just need to beat this guy's eyes out.*

Ruby looked at Ares. He watched the exchange with a slight smile. She kept her eyes on him. "She's very beautiful."

His smile dropped and he glanced to the ground in front of him. "She *is* the goddess of beauty."

"And love," Ruby finished the moniker.

"But not hearts," he said, as he caught her eye.

"Everyone else seems quite taken with her." The smaller god was now removing his sandals in preparation to fight. The larger god remained stoic. His feet were planted in a wide stance.

"I think it's a curse to her," Ares said.

"A curse?"

"Men immediately become overcome with desire for her. Women are instantly wary, suspicious, and jealous."

That was exactly how she had reacted to Aphrodite. But she had reason, she reminded herself. Aphrodite wasn't just beautiful. She and Ares had been in love once.

"She's married to a bitter god she doesn't love," Ares said. "And everyone else loves her too much. I think she's pretty lonely."

Ruby watched Aphrodite place her hand on the chest of the smaller god in an attempt to dissuade him from the fight. Light filtered through her red-blond hair. It shone like copper.

"Who is she married to? Is he here?" The gods and nymphs talked or sat on the bank of the river. They all ignored Aphrodite and her suitors.

"Hephaestus?" Ares said. "No. He's probably in his work-shop, alone, engineering some marvel over a bed of hot coals."

Ruby's thumb played at the iron ring on her finger. She put her palm flat on the rough bark behind her and leaned back. "Why is he bitter?"

"He was born deformed. His feet are as useless as his hands are brilliant. For a long time he was shunned by the gods. He's practically a hermit."

Ruby was surprised that Aphrodite, who could have anyone, would choose an introverted, deformed god to marry. "She loved him once?"

He shook his head. "All the gods used to fight over her. Everyone but Heph. She had great fun teasing us all. She'd pretend to pick one of us and then change her mind and pick another. Zeus eventually got sick of it.

"I don't know if he did it as a punishment to Aphrodite, or as a reward for the son he had always ignored, but Zeus chose Heph to marry her. She's never loved him," Ares said quickly. "She was never faithful."

"You." Her eyes darted to Ares. "She cheated on him with you?"

"I was so in love with her. I never thought about the consequences."

Ruby glanced at Ares's son and tried not to feel jealous that Aphrodite shared a bond with Ares that she did not. "Are you close with Eros?" She sat up again and rubbed at the marks the coarse bark left on her palms.

"He's always preferred his mother's company. They both rule love. That's made them close."

"Why are there two gods for love?"

"Aphrodite is the goddess of love and beauty. Eros is the god of love and desire. There is a bit more fire to his style of love. Some say he got it from his father."

"I see." She laughed, but she thought he might be serious. The passion of war had mixed with the passion of love to produce desire. She looked to the far trees. She didn't want to picture a passionate Aphrodite and Ares together.

SIXTEEN

RUBY SAT UNDER THE OLIVE TREE in Athena's garden. The small leaves rustled in the breeze but Ruby didn't look up. The tree was still beautiful to her, and special, but it was there every morning when she woke and there every evening when she went to bed.

She thumbed through the yellow myth book Athena had shown her so many months ago in Athenaeum. She had studied most of the stories and she was even beginning to understand the complicated family connections that linked them together.

The spring equinox had come and gone. She and Ares should be married by now. She should be immortal. They should be living in their abode and thinking about their family. In short, they should be moving on with their lives, as it were.

Instead they were still waiting for the first flowers to bloom on the slopes of Mount Olympus. The weather on Earth continued on as rainy and cold as ever and Ruby was annoyed with the wait. Even Ares, used to having an eternity, began to share her impatience.

A hair fell into Ruby's face with the next breeze. She swept it behind her ear and flipped around the pages of the myth book. She passed the stories she knew so well: Pandora, Echo and Narcissus, Hercules. She stopped at the picture of Persephone being pulled into the Earth by Hades. She hadn't read that one yet. It bothered her more than the others.

Athena rushed into the garden. Her face was flushed. "Where's Ares?"

"He went with Hermes and Pan, to see if the flowers—" she paused at the look on Athena's face. "What's wrong?"

"I went to Athenaeum and then to your house. I got the things you wanted." She held up a small duffel bag. "A guy was there as I was leaving. Mark?"

"Are you kidding?" Ruby laughed. "Mark was there?" She pictured the last time she saw him. He had accused Ares of being controlling and abusive.

"He was asking all kinds of questions," Athena said. "He wanted to know who I was and if I'd seen you. If I knew anything about this tall guy with black hair that he saw you with. He wanted to know if I knew why you'd stopped coming to class and why you never seemed to be home."

Ruby was shocked that Mark cared so much or that he would pursue it so far. They had been study partners. This seemed—

"Who is he?" Athena demanded.

"He's just a guy. Someone I used to study with."

"He said he was going to call the police. He wants to file a missing persons report."

"So? It's not like they'll find anything." Ruby closed the book and put it on the table.

"They won't find *you*," Athena said, her head cocked at an angle as though Ruby were being dense.

"But they won't find *anything*. I'll just be one of those people who never turn up."

"They'll think you've been kidnapped, or worse. Ares will be the main suspect. And now I'm involved. This Mark guy saw me leaving your house with a bag of your stuff."

"So? They won't find you or Ares." Ruby shrugged. She still didn't understand why Athena was so concerned. "Mark might wonder what happened to me for a little while but he'll be in medical school soon. His brain will be so crammed with information he'll forget all about me."

Athena put the bag down on the ground and rested her hands on the back of a chair. "I know you're happy here, and Ares is. But Apollo and I still want to be able to go back. I'm not closing the store. I'm hiring management. I don't need the police looking for me."

Ruby nodded as the implications dawned on her. "Of course." Athena had done so much for her and Ares. Ruby had not thought of her at all. "What can we do? What did you tell him?"

"He caught me off guard." Athena shrugged, a motion Ruby had never seen the goddess make before. "I said you were away." She glanced at the tabletop. "On vacation."

"Vacation?" Ruby laughed. She couldn't think of anything that would seem more ridiculous to Mark.

"It was the first thing that came to my mind," Athena said without apology.

"When did you say I'd be back?"

"Next week. You have until Tuesday."

"What day is it today?" Ruby realized she had no idea.

"It's Thursday."

"We have a few days at least." She thought of Mark's tenacity with his schoolwork. "He can be so stubborn. I remember once he ..." she stopped, her eyes searched Athena's.

Ruby stood. "I know who can help."

✺

Ruby and Athena walked on the now-familiar paths of Olympus. Ruby no longer worried about whom she might meet on the trail. The factions on Olympus were as well-defined as the river Oceanus. The gods Ruby had met at the river were Ares's friends, or at least not his enemies. They were mostly the younger generation of gods. The ones who were weary of long days on Olympus with little to do and the same gods and goddesses they had always known.

Apollo ignored her most of the time and she enjoyed a polite, if distant, relationship with Hera. The goddess had sent Ruby a platinum crown of laurels. Dionysus had hand delivered it. "It's a great honor," Athena had said when she saw it. Ruby wore it to every party.

Zeus, thankfully, ignored Ruby most of the time. Occasionally she saw him look away from her, his eyes tense and his face serious. Other than that he never acknowledged her.

Ruby took a side path toward where Hephaestus and Aphrodite lived.

"Are you going to ask Heph to make something to contain Mark?" Athena asked. "Would you imprison him?" Athena's face contorted with surprise. The goddess's black curls bounced along as she tried to keep up.

"I'm not from here, Athena. I think in much less drastic terms."

The path opened into a wide clearing with the husband's and wife's abodes each to one side. Aphrodite's rose-covered abode stood in direct contrast to Hephaestus's black iron one. It was so overrun with sculptures and ornaments that the original form was obscured. Heph's abode had its own type of beauty. No one could look at the work of the god of forge and fire and not be in awe.

Heph was reclusive. Ruby had never even talked to him. Gods fell at Aphrodite's feet and tripped over themselves to impress her. Heph was only called upon when there was a need. Now Ruby needed Aphrodite. She hoped the goddess would help her.

Ruby tapped a large swan knocker against the solid gold door. There was no answer but she didn't pause before she let herself in. The knocker was a decoration. Ruby used it out of habit more than anything.

Aphrodite was in the wide hall, coming toward them. Her green eyes became wide when she saw Ruby. "Is it time? Have they bloomed?" Her smile fell. "But then you wouldn't be here. Would you? You would have sent Hermes."

Ruby's eyes darted away as her mind was unexpectedly drawn back to the wedding. The alabaster hall was carved with couples in erotic poses. There were men and women embracing, kissing, and more. She was always startled by the contradictions of Olympus. Zeus and Hera wanted it to be a pure place, a place where gods lived high above carnal urges, a place where sons married virgins. The gods played along, but only to a point.

"I have a favor to ask you," Ruby said as she walked farther into the abode. She didn't want to lose her momentum.

The goddess followed Ruby with her eyes. "Anything," she said, and Ruby believed her.

Athena had explained the basics of the wedding: the importance of the vows, the ribbon that would tie Ruby and Ares's hands together in a symbolic binding, and the crowns that would mark her and Ares as the king and queen of the ceremony. But it was Aphrodite who had filled in the details.

It was Aphrodite who had made sure the crowns were olive branches and that the ribbon was white, as it had always been in ancient times. It was Aphrodite who'd insisted that Pan play his pipes at the reception and that a silver pair of scissors be on the altar. "Never mind why," she had said to Ruby with a playful grin.

Unlike Athena, Aphrodite knew what love was and believed in it as a force for good. And she, of all the Olympians, understood Ares the best. When Ruby told Aphrodite that Ares borrowed Hermes's winged sandals and took her to the mountains on the far side of Oceanus, Aphrodite didn't shake her head in disdain, as others had done. Instead she smiled a soft wistful smile that made Ruby feel sad.

They never spoke of Aphrodite's affair with Ares, and Ruby tried not to think about it. She saw how Ares looked at the goddess sometimes. It was no different than the way other gods looked at her, but their shared history made it hard for Ruby to dismiss.

Sun filtered in from a dome of windows above the massive sitting room of Aphrodite's abode. The middle of the smooth alabaster floor was sunken and rimmed with a couch that could easily seat thirty. Deep reds in the sofa played up the soft pinks of everything else. Cut red roses stood in waist-high vases. Their fragrance filled the room.

"What are you thinking?" Athena asked.

"There's this guy," Ruby said to Aphrodite. "I think maybe he wanted to go out with me."

Aphrodite leaned in. "Did you?"

"No." Ruby laughed at the idea. "I met Ares at about the same time. Anyway, he's been hanging around my house looking for me."

"He was asking a lot of questions," Athena said. "I managed to stall him for the time being, but he threatened to call the police. I said she'd be back in a few days."

"Why did you tell him she would be back?" Aphrodite gave the goddess of knowledge a quizzical look. "She'll be married to Ares any time. This is her home now."

"*I* know that, and *you* know that, but Mark *can't* know that. This is a modern human we're talking about," Athena said. "He has to be told something logical and normal."

"So," Ruby said. "I was hoping you could … *distract* him."

"Distract him?" Aphrodite pulled her head back in surprise. "How?"

"You could go to Earth, and you know … do your thing." Athena said, catching on.

"My *thing*?" Aphrodite said, annoyed.

"You know, that thing where men completely forget about everything they ever cared about, when you walk into a room," Ruby said.

Aphrodite looked from one to the other of them. "I don't actually do anything, you know. I just walk into the room."

"I know," Ruby said, hoping to lessen the insult, if that's what it was. "I know it's not something you try to do, but it *is* what happens. I'm not asking you to date him or anything. Just distract him."

"No," Aphrodite said, without hesitation. "I can't risk getting caught going to Earth. Have Ares take care of it."

Ruby was shocked by her callous response. "Take care of it?" she said. "You mean … kill him?" She felt like she was in a gangster movie.

"I don't know," Aphrodite said. "Ares will think of something."

Ruby looked at Athena but her face was impassive. She seemed to be fine with the idea. Ruby realized how much like them she had become in these months on Olympus. She wasn't ready to kill Mark for her own gain, but she would easily send the goddess of love to manipulate him.

"That's not an option. I don't want to get Ares involved. I'll figure something out," Ruby said. She didn't know how Ares might react to Mark poking around.

"Maybe Apollo will have an idea," Athena said.

"Not Apollo." Ruby stared at Athena in horror. "He reignited a war the last time a human got in his way."

"Well, what can *you* possibly do?" Athena asked. "You can't travel to Earth. You have no power."

Athena was right. Ruby was completely reliant on the gods around her.

Ruby sat in the large leather armchair across from Ares. He moved a black bishop on the old marble chess board that sat between them. The ruby and diamond board sat in the corner of the room, but Ares never used it. He said he preferred this one and had asked Athena to bring it back from Athenaeum.

His reputation for being unbeatable was as present on Olympus as it had been on Earth and Ruby loved to tell Pan or Hermes how she had beaten him. Ares would listen to the story and smile, either proud that Ruby was smart enough to match his wits or lost in the memory of when they had met.

Ares taught Ruby tactics and theories. Her game improved greatly, but tonight she felt distracted by her problem with Mark and by Athena and Aphrodite's reaction. She was worried that Athena would tell Apollo. If he found out, he might hurt Mark to spite Ruby as much as to solve the problem.

Ares stared at her.

She smiled quickly when she realized that it was her move. She had been attacking with her king, rook, and bishop. She thought she was getting herself into a good position, but Ares had built a fortress around his king and Ruby could not see how to get through.

She moved her pawn into the path of one of his. Sacrificing it was the only option she could see.

He half smiled and glanced up at her from under his black lashes. Her breath caught at that look. It was a good move.

He accepted the sacrifice, but she immediately saw her mistake. It had been a good move, but not a winning move. Ares was now in a position to advance his own pawn to the end of the board and promote it to queen, and that would win him the game. Ruby's only hope was to checkmate him before he could do it.

She breathed in the smell of the rich leather in the room and felt the cold marble of the king between her fingers as she moved the piece.

Ash shifted forward, toward her. His chiton moved to rest below the olive skin of his collar bones. He looked straight at her as he moved his bishop. "Check," he challenged.

She licked her parted lips and tried to steady her breathing. The game now looked similar to a practice problem she had worked recently. It gave her an idea. She moved her king to the right.

Ares nodded and tried not to smile, but failed. He moved his pawn closer to promotion.

Ruby moved her rook within striking distance of his king. She could checkmate in four moves, but Ares could promote his pawn in three. He would have to decide, defend his king or continue to move his pawn toward promotion and winning the game. If he went for the promotion and had missed anything in his strategy he would lose.

He moved the pawn.

Ruby met his eyes, blue, bold, and confident. A deep and carnal shiver ran through her. Only Ares would dare to leave his king open like that.

She closed in with her bishop. "Check," she said with a heavy breath. Now he had no choice. He had to defend.

He moved his king to the corner. His cheeks were flushed. He licked his lips and let the flesh scrape between his teeth.

Ruby smiled at having his king on the run. She bit at her own lip and moved her rook to push his king into the path of her bishop.

He touched his chin and drew his finger across his jaw, thinking.

Ruby imagined her own hand there, and her lips. She swallowed and tried to concentrate on the game.

Instead of moving his king to a safer position he advanced the pawn again.

She saw her mistake, she could have checkmated him on the next move but only if he had defended his king. She didn't care. Her hands were shaking with the desire to touch him. Her jaw clenched in a weak attempt to hold her body still.

Her next move was blind. She didn't know what piece she moved or where. It didn't matter, he had already won.

Ares knocked the chessmen to the floor in a single swipe of his hand. The pieces fell to the carpet in a quick succession of dull thuds.

He picked her up from her leather chair in one swift motion. Her burning lips met his. She wrapped her legs around him, each leg free from her peplos on the sides. The thin fabric between them did little to hide his rising excitement and the feel of him only increased the heat that threatened to overtake her.

He laid her on something soft and smooth, a couch maybe, but to Ruby there was nothing in the world but Ares. She thought of their virginal promise and moaned in frustration. They could only ever take it so far. *Why won't spring come?* a voice inside her head wailed.

"I love you," he whispered as she kissed the vibrating ridges of his throat. "I will always protect you. You can always come to me. You can always tell me."

She stopped and looked into his face. "Come to you about what?" She swallowed and felt the heat of her desire vanish.

"About the human," he said and kissed her. She pulled away and tried to sit up but they were too tangled and she couldn't move. "Athena told you?"

"No. Aphrodite." He ran his finger between her partially exposed breasts. "Don't worry, she'll take care of it."

She broke away from him and sat up. "Aphrodite said she wouldn't go."

"I liked your plan," he said. "It's simple and it will work."

"What changed her mind?" Ruby asked, suspicion fighting with relief that Mark would no longer be a problem. Of all her options seduction was the least severe.

His brow wrinkled. "I don't know. Something about human clothes and new shoes."

"So she won't do it for me, but she'll do it for you?" Ruby couldn't help but state the obvious.

⁂

Ruby sat at a round table in the Great Hall. The platinum crown of laurels Hera had given her dug into her scalp. The Seasons sat across from her in their multicolored peploses and crowns of wildflowers. The four goddesses twittered and giggled at everything Ruby said and she found it difficult to have a conversation with them.

Ares sat at the raised table at the front of the room, at the Table of the Twelve. He rested back in his gold chair and joked with Hermes and Athena.

Aphrodite leaned over and motioned something to Zeus.

Apollo talked with Artemis, but the huntress always seemed uncomfortable in the Great Hall. She scanned the room as if she expected a deer to be flushed out from under one of the tables at any moment.

Ganymede, the teen with the shaggy bangs, was cupbearer of the gods. He filled Hephaestus's goblet of nectar and glanced often at Aphrodite with nothing short of lust in his eyes.

Hephaestus drank the dark red nectar in two short swallows. He stood and hobbled on one crutch behind Aphrodite's chair, but his wife didn't look up at him. He continued to the edge of the dais and lumbered down the golden steps to the main floor.

Ruby wondered if he was coming to talk to the Seasons. He headed right in their direction. The girls took no notice of him. They were busy tittering as they watched Pan play his pipes for the Muses, who were dressed in almost nothing in an attempt to look like nymphs.

Hephaestus did not even glance at the Seasons, though. Instead he limped over to Ruby and lowered himself into the empty chair next to her. His disfigured foot jutted out from under the white tablecloth.

"You should be careful," he said without preamble. They were the first words he had ever said to her.

Ruby's eyes met his. They were deep brown and soulful. Was this warning more of what she had already gotten from Apollo? *We don't want you here.*

"Why?" she said, as if she were completely uninterested. She had started to feel like she belonged on Olympus.

"Ares had no regard for the sanctity of *my* marriage. I doubt he'll have any regard for the sanctity of *yours.*"

Ruby's head tilted. The laurel crown shifted. This was not what she had expected.

"I think he's changed," she said.

"Oh, I doubt it."

Ruby didn't respond.

Ares looked over and scowled. The god of war stood and the god of forge and fire shambled away.

෨෧෧

The next morning a black bicycle appeared at Athena's door. The frame fit Ruby perfectly. It was so light she could pick it up by the crossbar with one finger. On its stem was Heph's symbol, two crossed hammers over an anvil. She had no idea how Heph knew she liked cycling.

The bike pedaled almost effortlessly in the clear morning. It had rained overnight and the air smelled fresh and clean.

The paths of Olympus were endless and they constantly changed. She would sometimes start out on a familiar path only to find that the scenery was now different and that there were new wonders around each bend. Occasionally she would see some of the gods out, strolling or picking flowers, but often it was as if she had Olympus to herself.

She rounded a corner that normally brought her to the edge of the river Oceanus, but today there was a sea of lavender instead. The fragrance hit her senses almost as strongly as the intense purple color. She stopped her bike in wonder and let it gently rest on the ground.

The plants were still wet from the rain, but she walked into the field of knee-high lavender anyway. She closed her eyes and breathed in the slightly woodsy-camphor smell. She smiled to herself. Not much happened on Olympus. The gods kept themselves busy with games, and nymphs, and gossip, but she thought that the natural splendor alone could sustain her for an eternity.

"Beautiful," a man's voice said close to her.

Her heart thudded like a herd of cattle running through her chest. She opened her eyes. Zeus stood no more than three feet in front of her.

The king of the gods smiled and reached out to touch her cheek. His fingers were smooth on her face. A chill went through her.

"Don't be afraid," he said. "I could never bring pain to such beauty."

Ruby doubted if Zeus's idea of pain was anything like a human's.

"The bike is a gift from Hephaestus, unless I miss my mark," he said. "You've caught the interest of more than a few gods, I see."

She shook her head, wanting to deny such a thing, but no words would come out of her mouth.

Zeus chuckled from deep within his chest. His fingers trailed down her neck.

She swallowed reflexively and he smiled.

"You even feel different," he whispered. "Your energy ..." He inhaled deeply but didn't finish the thought. His azure eyes glazed over and his widened lids relaxed.

A cold sweat chilled her as she realized that she hadn't told anyone where she was going. She often spent hours riding her bike on the paths of Olympus. Ares would think nothing of it if she were gone for the entire morning.

A high pitched noise grew in her head, stress, or fear, or ... No, it was a distant whistle, she realized, from somewhere up the path behind her. Random notes turned into a tune. She froze.

Zeus looked at her. His jaw tensed. "Who is that?"

She looked all around, hoping that it wasn't Hestia, or Apollo, or any of the other gods who would take one look at Ares's fiancée standing alone with Zeus and turn away without a glance backward. A terrifying thought came to her. She hoped it wasn't Hera.

Zeus grabbed her arm and pulled her deeper into the lavender, toward the forest. The whistling got louder. Zeus pulled her more forcefully. Ruby tried to yank away, but his grip was too strong.

They were twenty feet from the woods when Aphrodite came around the bend. Ruby's breath left her in a rush of relief and surprise. She thought the goddess had gone to Earth to deal with Mark. Was it Tuesday yet? She had no idea, but the goddess of beauty had never been a more lovely sight. Surely she would not leave Ruby to deal with Zeus on her own.

Aphrodite stopped short when she saw them. The empty basket she carried swung loosely on her arm.

Zeus stopped. "The morning continues to brighten," he said with a smile, still half-turned toward the forest and still holding Ruby by the arm.

"Save your flattery," Aphrodite countered. She held her hand out and motioned for Ruby to come to her.

Ruby did not hesitate to move away from Zeus. His fingers trailed down her arm and through her hand as she left. Ruby went to her bike. She picked it up but she didn't know if her shaking legs would be able to pedal.

Aphrodite put her arm protectively around her shoulders. "I think I hear Hera calling," she said to Zeus.

Zeus held the goddess's stare for a moment and then tramped out of the wet lavender.

They watched him walk away. When he was gone Ruby finally felt like she could breathe. She wanted to thank Aphrodite. She wanted to tell her that she had no idea what she would have done if she hadn't come by. Instead she said, "Please don't tell Ares. I don't want to start a war."

"I just came to pick some flowers before I go to Earth. Their lavender isn't quite up to par," Aphrodite said. She didn't questioning Ruby's request for secrecy. Lies and intrigue were part of life on Olympus and Ruby couldn't help but think that whether she was a goddess or not, she was more like them every day.

⁊৹৻৾

Ruby pulled up in front of the Great Hall and propped her bike against the golden building. Ares leaned on one of the giant columns, waiting for her. She rushed up to him, though she still felt weak and scared from her encounter with Zeus.

"Hi," he said with a smile that reached up to his eyes. She stood on tiptoe to peck him on the lips. He followed her back down to flat feet and kissed her more deeply. Ruby's eyelids flashed open. She scanned the large hall of Zeus's abode and pulled away.

"How was your ride?" he asked, searching her eyes.

"I found a new meadow," she managed to say. She took a purple sprig from the purse at her waist and gave it to him. "Lavender."

He twirled the flower between his thumb and forefinger and took her other hand. His energy flowed into her and her fear melted away. They walked to the middle of the Great Hall and stood under the willow branch altar Ares had built for their wedding. Everything was ready. There was no more planning to do.

"What's the news from Earth?" she asked, feeling better and hoping for good news.

"The peace is intact," he said.

She smiled, but it made her nervous that he had started with that. "How's the weather?" she prompted.

"Rainy. Cold."

Her stomach tightened. She touched a willow branch on the wedding altar as it wound in with the others, its cool surface smooth beneath her hand. "What's going on, Ares? Do you have any ideas?"

"I'm not sure." He looked away from her. "It's late for spring to come but …"

She looked at him not looking at her. The incident with Zeus paled in her mind. "It's *too* late, isn't it?"

"Something's wrong," he said. "Persephone should be back by now. Demeter should have let spring come."

"What do you mean?"

"Haven't you read about Persephone yet?"

She thought of the picture of Hades pulling Persephone into the ground. She shuddered.

Ares held up the lavender sprig. "Hades saw Persephone picking flowers in a field and he fell in love with her."

Her heart nearly stopped as she recalled the memory of Zeus in the lavender. "Why did he steal her then, if he loved her so much?" she said with more anger than was probably appropriate.

"You *have* heard it." Ares cocked his head at her.

"No. That's all I know." That had been enough.

"Hades isn't good with people. He's arrogant." Ares paused, and then smiled. "Maybe he didn't know enough to take her bungee jumping."

Ruby laughed a pitiful little laugh.

Ares looked at her. "You okay?"

"Yeah." She forced a smiled.

"When Persephone's mother, Demeter, found out that she had been kidnapped, nothing on Earth would grow. The goddess of the harvest was in mourning."

"What does it have to do with us?" She was anxious to get to the heart of the matter.

"Demeter's energy is tied to the Earth's." He held her gaze. "Without Demeter, spring will never come."

"Why can't someone else help? Helios could bring the sun a little longer each day, or—"

Ares shook his head. "It's not just the temperature or the amount of sunshine. It's a shift in the energy of the Earth."

"I don't understand. Obviously there have been many springs since Hades kidnapped Persephone."

"Hades and Demeter shared her."

Ruby flinched.

"After Hades abducted Persephone, when the Earth began to die, Zeus had to intervene. He told Hades to release Persephone. Hades said he would, but he insisted on holding her to the rules of the Underworld. Including that she not eat the food there."

"Food? In Hades?"

"Only inhabitants of the Underworld can eat the food there. Anyone else who eats it will be trapped. Persephone had been there for days by then. Hades gave her a handful of pomegranate seeds and she ate them."

"He tricked her." She looked around the great hall at all the golden gods staring down on them.

"Hades had Zeus by his own rules, but Zeus often finds a way to move things to his own advantage. Persephone had only eaten six seeds before she realized her mistake. Zeus decreed that Persephone would spend six months, half of every year, as the queen of the Underworld with Hades. One month for each of the seeds she had eaten."

"Fall and winter," Ruby said.

"When Persephone returns to Olympus, Demeter's sadness lightens. The Earth awakens. Spring comes. Then summer."

"Well, where is she? Where is Demeter? Where does she go when she's in mourning?" Ruby had never met the goddess of the harvest. She had never even heard her spoken of.

"I asked the Seasons if they've seen her. If anyone would know, it would be them." He didn't say anything else. He just shook his head.

"Where's Persephone then?" Ruby looked around the empty Great Hall. "Why isn't she coming back?"

Ares shrugged. "No one knows."

SEVENTEEN

RUBY RAN INTO THE MAIN ENTRANCE of The Great Hall. Why would Zeus want to see her? Alone? She kept on moving. She saw nothing but a blur of color as she sprinted by.

Through the entrance hall, past the willow altar, she headed to the right. The note said he would be in the garden.

She went through the curved archway at the back of the chamber. Looking down from above were two commanding eagles, each with a lightning bolt in its talons. Next to them was a carved oak and then two golden bulls. Silver steam pushed forward from their flared nostrils. She glanced up and felt the weight of it all above her, but she didn't slow.

On the garden path she passed his many sculpted trees. Huge maples and oaks that were planted close together with their branches trained and the thing is into twisted shapes.

She glanced at one with a straight trunk at the bottom. Its early branches had been trained into an elaborate knot. The branches met again above the knot and continued straight up and leafed out as normal. Beyond the knot tree were three small trees growing close together. Their trunks were trained into a bench sturdy enough for a group to sit on.

She walked quickly. Her eyes darted around at everything. She saw it all and she barely saw any of it.

In the note he told her to meet him at the fountain in the middle. Hermes delivered it to her while she read in Athena's garden, but he seemed as confused as she was. He shrugged when he handed it to her.

He waited as she read it and looked at her all the while. The note said to come alone. She simply said "Thank you," and tucked the note in the purse at her waist.

As she rounded the bend into the large central part of the garden, Zeus was there, tall and imposing, especially without Ares at her side. She thought of meeting him in the lavender days before, and shuddered.

He didn't look up. He was intent on pruning a small bonsai. Several were lined up on a potting bench in front of him. Racks and racks of these smaller versions of his tree sculptures lined the edges of the space.

A large gold fountain with an eagle holding a lightning bolt in its talons dominated the area. Water issued from below the eagle and collected in a large basin.

Ruby looked at his hunched back. She willed herself to say something, but her voice would not work.

He didn't turn, but spoke before she could muster her courage. "Ruby. So quick. What a good girl." He clipped at tiny branches.

Her heart raced at being alone with him. She didn't think Aphrodite would show up here to save her.

Zeus looked at her, low and from the side. "I have something to show you," he said, and stretched out his hand.

A cold heat ran through her, like when she held snow for too long. She shivered in the warm air of Olympus. She moved closer but she didn't touch him. "Zeus …" She started and then stopped. "I was surprised to get your note." She hoped ordinary words would make her feel more normal.

He smiled, but it did not warm his cool blue eyes. "Come sit by the fountain."

The fountain was at least two stories high, the eagle and lightning bolt towered above Zeus's head. He did not look up at it, though. Instead he looked down, into the pool of water that was at waist level. She looked too and saw a perfectly mirrored reflection of the blue sky above.

She didn't sit. Neither did he.

"You, no doubt, have enjoyed your time here," he said. "Bike riding and such."

She nodded slowly.

"And Ares does seem to … enjoy you." He looked at her again. His eyes flashed down her body. She felt uncomfortably warm. She wanted to move from him, but she held her ground.

"The thing is, Ruby …" He let her name hang in the air and looked away. "Having you here doesn't work."

The hot feeling in her body amplified. "I don't understand. The wedding …" She trailed off. Her mind touched on Ares and her thoughts froze. Her pulse throbbed in her head. She thought instead of her friends: Athena, Aphrodite, Pan, and Hermes.

"Ruby …" He sounded as if he were letting a child in on a secret everyone else already knew. "There won't be a wedding."

"But, everything's ready," she said with a dry mouth. "The altar. The crowns. Everything." Her eyes searched the ground. Then she looked at him, square on. "You swore."

"I swore?" He gripped the edge of the fountain. "I swore that I would marry Ares when, and only when, the first flower blooms on Mount Olympus." He smiled. "But nothing *will* bloom, my sweet. Not as long as you're here. As long as you're here, nothing will ever bloom on Earth again."

She jerked back. "What?"

"Ares thought he could just go to Earth, pick up a juicy little thing, and bring her to *my home*." His knuckles turned white on the rim of the fountain. "It will not stand." He looked down into the water again. Ruby followed his gaze.

Images began to develop on the surface of the water. She saw fields covered in snow beneath steel grey skies, bare vines that were brown and twisted, orchards filled with scraggly leafless trees with their thin branches shivering in the wind.

"It's May on Earth already," Zeus said. "There's no war. Ares would know if there was. But there is fear, Ruby. It's almost too late to save this year's crops." He looked at her. "Almost."

Ruby's heart beat hard and loud. "I don't understand. Where's Demeter? Where's Persephone? When will spring come?" She forced the words out of her constricting throat.

"Only when you are gone from here will I suggest to Hades that he set Persephone free," he said.

"He's keeping Persephone?" she said, her voice a croak.

"Hades just needed to be reminded that *he* is the god of the Underworld. *And* his wife's master." Zeus stood straight and reached his full height before her. "And I believe I'm the only one who can bring him back to his senses. I'm the only one who can remind him of the ancient agreement to share Persephone with her mother. Then, and only then, will Demeter feel relief from her long suffering." He laughed at his own cruel joke. "Then spring, life, and food will be brought back to the people of Earth." He paused and looked into her eyes. "And you, Ruby dear, in turn, are the only one who can convince me to want to have such a conversation."

"By leaving?" Tears pricked at her eyes. "I can't. I love him too much," she whispered.

"You can certainly stay here, where it's always warm, and there's always food. You can have your way. But will you be able to forget what you sacrificed? The millions, no, the *billions* who will starve for your love?"

Ruby looked to the grey gravel path, then back to the images still clear in the water. "No. No. Of course not. I thought being with Ares would be good for the Earth." A tear rolled down her cheek. She hated that she was crying in front of him.

"I can't go back," she realized. A sob came halfway up her throat but she somehow managed to hold it in. "The Great

Peace will end. The wars will start all over." These were her excuses, but her reason was only one. Ares.

"Don't worry. I'll deal with Ares," he said and added quickly, "I have arranged for Helios to take you back to Earth. He's at the edge of the garden. Come this way."

Zeus turned and headed down the path that led away from the Great Hall. Ruby began to follow in the direction where Helios waited to take her from Olympus, from all her friends, from Ares.

Her mind raced. Her eyes scanned the garden. She saw nothing. She could think of nothing. Then she was speaking, with no sense of what she was saying. "No. No. I … I have to … I have to go get something at Athena's." Her voice cracked. Her eyes were obscured with tears. She needed to have something of this place to take with her.

"No, you must go now." He grabbed her arm. "It's now or never."

She pulled back and wrenched free from Zeus's tight grip. He stared at her. His icy blue eyes pierced her fear. She let it flow in and over her. She let it move past her. Her tears slowed. "I have to get something. I won't see Ares. I won't tell anyone."

"I must insist," he said.

"No. I insist. I will come back. Alone. I won't let Earth perish for my own selfish desires. *I* am not like that," she said, stressing the difference between them.

His face changed. His smile turned up in one corner and the tiny lines around his eyes relaxed. He walked toward her. Soon she could feel the heat of his body. She could smell the fresh Olympic dirt that was on his hands. She was barely breathing when his face came down to hers.

He put his mouth next to her ear and whispered, "You are so beautiful when you're frightened." She could hear the smile in his voice. "I should take you for my own."

Shivers ran through her. His hand came up and pushed the hair away from her neck. She felt his hot breath on her skin.

"I need clothes. I can't go to Earth in this," she said softly, trying to think, trying to keep to the point at hand, terrified of what Zeus might do. "I won't talk to anyone."

His soft beard grazed her cheek. The muscles in her throat contracted. Then she heard his teeth come together with a loud click and a single word.

"Run."

EIGHTEEN

RUBY RAN. Away from the fountain, past the sculpted trees, through the Great Hall, and back toward Athena's. Was this really happening? Was she really leaving? She looked around and tried to savor her last minutes on Olympus, but her head ached and her body throbbed. Ares's face flashed in her mind. She shut it out. Not now.

She ran the entire way. Her sides ached and her breath burned in her lungs. She stopped before Athena's abode. She tried to relax and seem casual. She didn't expect anyone to be there. Athena was on Earth with Aphrodite and Ares had gone off with Pan that morning.

She opened the door and listened for sounds from inside. There were none. She ran up the stairs, down the hall, and into her room. *Her room.* She knew it had been temporary, but she thought she would be leaving this room happy and excited to move into Ares's abode as his wife. The thought was too painful. She focused instead on why she had come.

There on the dresser, next to the picture of her parents, was the olive branch Athena had given to her and Ares. She touched it carefully, even though nothing could hurt it in its enchanted state. She fingered the small leaves and delicate white flowers with her trembling hands. Would the enchantment endure on Earth? She'd plant it right away. She'd grow something beautiful from this ugliness that was happening to her.

She put the branch in the leather pouch she wore around her waist. *I'll even miss these clothes.* She had gotten used to the freedom of her peplos. She pulled on an old pair of jeans and a T-shirt, clothes Athena had brought her from Earth, and tried to distance herself from Olympus. She wrapped the leather pouch, with the olive branch in it, around the waist of her jeans and covered it with her rain jacket. She slipped on her sneakers and laced them.

She looked around the room. Her resolve to leave faltered. The worst part was that she knew no one here would judge her if she chose to stay. Most gods felt that their desires trumped thousands or even millions of human lives. She may have found herself more and more comfortable on Olympus with each passing day, but she could never let herself become that much like them.

She walked to the window. It groaned as she lifted the sash. She closed her eyes and stuck her head out into the fragrant Olympic air. She breathed in, hoping to imprint the smell on her brain forever. There was laughter from below. Startled, she opened her eyes.

Athena and Ares were both staring up at her. "What are you doing?" Ares called with a smile.

Ruby panicked and pulled her head back in. "Nothing." Her eyes were wide. She didn't think she could hold it together in front of him. He would sense that something was wrong.

She ran down the hall, down the steps, into the large foyer, and headed for the front door. But it was too late. Ares met her there with Athena close behind. He was serious. "What's going on?"

"Nothing," she exhaled. "I thought I'd go for a walk. I need some air." She hoped her face wasn't red from crying.

"In that?" Athena looked over her outfit.

"I … I got homesick for regular clothes," she stammered. "I need to go for a walk. Alone," she said a little too quickly. "To clear my thoughts."

"To clear your thoughts about what?" Ares stepped toward her.

"It's—it's the wedding," she said. "I feel like it's never going to happen. That's all. It's making me sad, and that's making me homesick." She wondered if those dots connected.

"Can I come? I want to be with you if you're unhappy." Ares touched her arm.

Later she would never know how she had held it together at that moment. Was it to protect the Earth? To protect Ares? Whatever it was she heard herself say, "No. Thank you. I'd like to be alone." She kissed him, a moment longer then she might have otherwise, and walked out the door.

Ruby ran again as soon as she was clear of Athena's abode. What would Zeus do if she wasn't there soon enough? She was lost in thought when Hermes came running down the path toward her.

"Ruby," he gasped. He doubled over with a hand on each knee. "You—" he gulped for air. "—can't go."

Ruby stopped. Hermes was the messenger of the gods. He ran all over Olympus, day and night. She had never seen him out of breath before.

"Are you all right?" She put a hand on his bent shoulder. He was hot from running.

"You can't go," he panted. "You have to hide. He'll kill you." He stopped for a breath again. His sand-colored hair was disheveled and hung in his face.

"I don't understand …"

"Zeus," he snapped and stood up. "He's going to kill you."

"Kill me? No. But he's making me leave."

"No, Ruby." His breath was returning to normal.

"He's sending Helios to take me back to Earth."

"Do you know who Helios is?" He looked at her.

"I've read about him, yeah. He guides the sun through the sky. So what?"

"The sun never touches the Earth. Does it?"

She shook her head, confused. "I guess not, but…"

"I was suspicious that Zeus would send you a message. Your reaction when you read it alarmed me even more. I followed you to his abode and into the garden. I overheard everything he said to you. When you left I stayed. Zeus told Helios to throw you into the ocean from the sun's highest point."

Ruby flinched. "He's going to kill me?" she whispered. She searched Hermes's sweaty face.

"You have to hide. I'll get Ares. We'll figure something out. We have to be quick." Hermes took her by the arm and led her off the path into the woods.

Ruby trusted him. If anyone knew the back ways of Olympus it was Hermes. But she pulled away and stopped him in his tracks. "No. The Earth will die. He'll kill it if I stay. I don't want to leave. It might kill *me*. But I can't be happy knowing the rest of humanity suffered."

"He can't do this," Hermes said. "Ares won't let him. *I* won't." His eyes glanced to the ground, then back to her. "Zeus's cruel games have gone on for too long. We'll find a way to keep you here and help the Earth." He held out his hand.

Ruby wanted to believe. More than anything, she wanted to believe. She looked around the woods and up the path toward the Great Hall where Zeus waited. She looked in the opposite direction, to Athena's, where she felt the pull of Ares. She slapped her hand down into Hermes's palm. He did not hesitate, but turned and pulled her into the shadowy woods.

⁋

Ruby tripped over another root. Hermes pulled her up by the hand. "We're almost there," he said.

"Where exactly is *there*?" Small branches scraped at her face. She pushed them away, but more crowded in.

"I'll know it when I see it." He looked around, peering through the trees.

"I thought you knew every place on Olympus."

"I do." He glanced back at her and then to the forest again. "I'm not looking for a where. I'm looking for a who."

"Who then?" She stumbled again, but recovered without Hermes noticing.

"I think they're this way. We'll have to cross Oceanus." He picked up the pace again. Ruby lurched forward.

They came to the edge of the river but Hermes didn't stop. He ran straight into the water. Ruby followed in behind him. The river was only about forty feet across. The water came up to her knees. It was cool, but not cold. The water sloshed in and around her sneakers and her wet jeans were plastered to her legs. They were out of the water, and back into more dense forest, almost as quickly as they went in to it.

Hermes grabbed for her hand again and she took it. She realized that they were breaking the edict by crossing the river, but in the next second she would have laughed if she had any extra breath in her lungs. Zeus already wanted to kill her.

They came into a small clearing not far from the river. Sun streamed down in shafts from above. "Come out," Hermes said in a loud deep voice as Ruby panted next to him. She scanned the trees where he was looking. But she didn't see anything.

"We request your assistance in the name of Artemis." His voice boomed. Ruby was startled that Hermes, ever happy and agreeable, could be so commanding.

"I don't think anyone's here." Ruby looked around the clearing at the silent trees on the edges.

"They're here all right. This is one of their groves." The two of them stood still and silent. Ruby waited for something to happen.

Soon ethereal figures appeared among the trunks. Ruby recognized their floating movements before her mind could separate out an individual. Nymphs. They glided inward but stopped short of the clearing.

"We need your help," Hermes demanded. "Ares's bride is in danger from Zeus. You must keep her here. Guard her, until I can return with the Goddess. Zeus will kill her if he finds her."

A tall nymph floated out from behind an oak and began to walk on two feet. Her chestnut hair hung down below her bare breasts. Her fair skin glowed faintly in the sunlight. Her dark eyes met with Ruby's.

"We will keep her," she agreed.

"I'll return as soon as I can," he said to Ruby. He turned and ran back into the woods.

Ruby smiled at the nymph, but the nymph remained stone-faced. Ruby looked beyond her and saw more shapes moving among the trees. Some came into the clearing right away, others hung back. She had seen nymphs several times, when Pan would play his pipes and call them. Most ran off with Artemis to hunt. Some stayed to be charmed, wooed, and bedded by the gods, but they were never interested in her.

"Thank you." Ruby addressed the dark-eyed nymph who seemed to be in charge.

"It's nothing to us," the nymph said without emotion. "If the Goddess wishes us to keep you, we shall. If not, we won't. We answer to her."

"*The* Goddess?" Ruby never heard anyone refer to just one goddess before Hermes said it moments ago. "Artemis?" She pictured her, aloof and cold.

"The Goddess of the Hunt. We answer to her. And her alone."

⌒⊙⌒

Ares, Athena, and Hermes rushed into the clearing. The nymphs startled into defensive poses around Ruby. Ares walked past them as if they weren't there and took her into his arms.

"I'll kill him," he said into her hair, her neck, her cheek, kissing her everywhere.

Ruby stifled the sob that had crept up when she saw him. She laughed instead. "He's immortal."

"I'll find a way."

She held him tight. She had thought she might never get to see him again. "Why does he hate me so much?"

He looked into her eyes and then rested his chin on the top of her head. "He hates himself," he said. "Don't worry. You're safe now."

"Safe? Is there a place on Olympus where Zeus can't find me? Is there a way for me to save the Earth *and* stay here? Zeus said he could convince Hades to release Persephone, but only if I leave."

Ares was silent.

"Come with me," she said in a rush. "Come back to Earth with me. The wars won't start again. We can live there and be happy. At least for a while." She pictured a life where she grew old and died, and Ares didn't.

He shook his head. "No. I won't. I will marry you *here*. We will be together forever."

"I don't see how," she whispered.

Hermes and Athena stood at the edge of the clearing, giving them space. Ares spoke louder, inviting them to come near. "I'm going to the Underworld to find Persephone," he said. "I'll bring her back myself."

"All right!" Hermes shouted. His fists were balled up at his sides as though he expected a fight to break out in front of him.

Ruby's eyes shot to Ares's. "You can't! You can't challenge Hades in the Underworld. He'll ..." She wasn't sure what Hades would do, but she knew that in his own realm Hades would have free rein. Zeus only got involved in the rarest of cases. And in this case, she imagined, he would gladly sit back and let Hades do what he willed.

"I'll find a way." Ares's turquoise eyes blazed with determination.

"How?" Athena asked, with only logic in her voice. "How will you find an entrance? How will you find Persephone once you're there? How will you bring her back?"

"I know of an entrance," Hermes, who sometimes shepherded the dead to the Underworld, broke in. "I can show you. I'll come and help you to cross the river and get you past that infernal dog."

"No. I need you here." Ares glanced to Hermes. "Take care of Ruby for me."

Ruby looked at him, but he was staring into the trees beyond Hermes, plotting already. She thought of Ares leaving and fresh tears threatened.

"She can't stay here," Athena said. "Zeus will kill her."

Ares nodded and spoke to Hermes. "Take her back to Earth."

"I'm not going back to Earth," Ruby said. "I belong with you." She paused at her next thought, and then rushed on. "I'll come with you."

"It's too dangerous." He shook his head. "Even for a god."

"I can't wait on Earth wondering if you're ever coming back or if Zeus is lurking around every corner." She pulled on his elbow. The soft skin there reminded her how vulnerable his flesh was, even if once torn and broken it would knit back together.

"The Underworld has its own rules," he said. "They can be tricky. I may be able to get you in, but I don't know whether I'll be able to get you out again."

"But she's right, Ares," Athena said. "There's nowhere for her to go that Zeus can't find her. She'll have less protection on Earth than she would have here and it won't be easy either way. Hades isn't going to just let you walk out of the Underworld with Persephone, even if you can find her. Imagine how happy he must have been when Zeus suggested this plan. He won't let her go easily."

"A human will slow me down," he said with all the reasonable sense of a tactician.

"I'm not just *some* human," Ruby broke in.

"No, I know." Ares blinked. "It's not that I don't want you with me—"

Apollo strode into the clearing then. "Well, Rubes, looks like the jig is up." He scanned the solemn faces around the grove. "Or have you heard?"

Ares shot him a cold look, but he did not respond.

"It's begun then." Apollo looked to Ares and Athena in quick succession. "Should I say, 'I told you so?'"

"I don't believe that. This is just Zeus being Zeus," Ares said.

"That's all it takes. All it takes is Zeus being Zeus, and the rest of us getting sucked in." Apollo held Ares's gaze. "The question is, what will you do now? Are you ready to drop this charade? Ready to let Zeus have her? Ready to move on?" He didn't look at Ruby.

Ares's nostrils flared. Ruby put her hand on his arm again. She felt a hot current run through him as he stared at Apollo. His energy had been so calm for so long that the feeling shocked her and she sucked in a breath.

Apollo sneered. "A tour of the Underworld it is, then," he said. "Persephone won't be easy to find. And frankly, I don't envy you and Rubes the trip."

"Ruby is not coming," Ares said. His eyes bored into the taller god. Apollo's endorsement of the idea seemed to solidify Ares's opinion against it.

"Well, why not? She's the reason this is coming down on us," he said without apology.

"She's my wife—"

"Not yet," Apollo cut him off. "And maybe not ever."

Ares searched the faces in the clearing for some support. Athena spoke up. "Things may get ugly up here. Zeus will know some of us helped you. Apollo's early vision may yet come to pass. We can't protect her."

Could this really be happening? Could her love for Ares tear apart Olympus?

"Apollo's visions don't always come true," Ares reminded the group.

"I'm not willing to stake Olympus on a chance," Apollo said. "And frankly, Ares, you've always been a dark horse."

Ares clenched his fists. He looked to Ruby. "We leave right away."

⚬⚭⚬

"Dionysus won't get involved," Hermes said as Artemis and Pan followed him into the clearing. It didn't surprise Ruby. Dionysus and Hera were close. He had always been cordial and accepting of Ruby, but he wasn't about to go out on limb for her.

Artemis spoke in low whispers with the nymphs at the edge of the clearing. Ruby could tell by their tone that the nature spirits were not happy about this invasion of their grove.

Pan came to Ruby and took both of her hands in his. "Take my pipes. When you meet Cerberus, don't be afraid. Play him a tune. 'Music hath charms to soothe a savage beast,'" he quoted. She didn't ask who Cerberus was, she had decided it was best to not think too far into the future, but the loan touched her deeply. She couldn't remember a time that

Pan was without his pipes. She hugged him and breathed in his slight animal smell.

Eros handed Ares a bronze torch. "It will never run out of oil. There's a fire striker here." He opened a latched door at the base of the torch to reveal a piece of dark metal that was shaped like a fat bobby pin and a long piece of white quartz with one bowed edge. Ruby's father had taught her to light a fire with a flint and steel on a camping trip once. This looked like the ancient equivalent.

Hermes lent them his winged sandals for the third time. Athena, ever practical, gave them each a leather backpack, a bag of dry-looking biscuits she called hardtack for Ruby to eat, and Ambrosia Bars for Ares and Persephone. She handed Ares another small sack that jingled softly. "Obolus," she said. "To pay Charon."

Ruby loaded her leather backpack with the hardtack, the sack of coins, the Ambrosia Bars, and Pan's Pipes. She slung the pack onto her shoulders.

"Remember, only eat the hardtack I gave you and drink the water you're bringing," Athena cautioned. "If you eat or drink anything from the Underworld, you will be trapped there. There will be nothing any of us can do to help you."

Ruby nodded. These words should have shaken her, but her fears were set aside by this show of support from their friends. Friends she was determined to make her family.

Hermes took Ares aside to tell him where to find the entrance to the Underworld. Ruby heard a rustle in the woods behind where the two gods stood. All the gods that she and Ares could count as friends were already in the clearing, even

Apollo. Ruby's heart rate doubled in an instant. Had they waited too long? Was Zeus coming?

But it was Aphrodite who stepped out of the woods and into their midst. She had been on Earth dealing with Mark. Ruby hadn't thought she'd get to see her before they left.

Aphrodite wore jeans tucked into knee-high black boots and a tight pink sweater. She held a sword in one hand and a leather scabbard in the other. It was an incongruous picture of the prettiest girl on campus mixed up with a warrior princess. The goddess walked to Ruby and smiled as if she didn't have a sword held out between them.

"Dionysus told me where to find you. Don't worry." The goddess paused and Ruby wondered if she had good news. Zeus had changed his mind, maybe. Or perhaps Persephone had returned on her own. Somehow they were going to be all right. But instead she said, "I'm taking good care of your friend."

"Oh," Ruby said, deflated. Mark hardly seemed to matter now.

"We need to go." Ares walked to Ruby. He wore jeans, a flannel shirt, and Hermes's magic sandals, with the wings tucked up against his ankles. He held a pack similar to Ruby's. It held skins of water and hiking boots for later.

"I'm ready," she said. She felt for the pouch around her waist and readjusted the leather pack. Her jeans had dried substantially, but her shoes were still soaked from running through the river.

Ares glanced at Aphrodite and stopped short. She looked gorgeous in modern clothes. Ruby felt a pang of envy. But it was the sword and scabbard he reached out for.

He sheathed the sword, but he didn't buckle the straps around his waist as Ruby expected. Instead he secured it across his chest, with the scabbard at an angle on his back. The hilt of the sword stuck up, within easy reach, over his right shoulder. He slung the leather pack over the sword.

He made eye contact with Aphrodite. Ruby saw something old and deep pass between them. He nodded at the goddess of beauty, but neither said a word. Ruby's envy threatened to become jealousy.

Artemis stepped close to Ruby. "Take my bow and my arrows."

"I ... I can't," she stammered.

"Release your energy into the bow. If you give yourself over to it the arrows will shoot true. You will need that."

The goddess was right. Ruby had never used a weapon before in her life.

Ruby took the silver bow and the arrows in their quiver. She felt a slight tingle run up her arm as her hand wrapped around the cool metal. The bow weighed less than she expected. The arrows were fletched with the grey and white striped feathers of a falcon.

"But ..." She hesitated. "... what if I don't bring them back? I mean, what if I don't come back at all?"

"You will," Artemis said with confidence.

Ruby smiled at the show of faith.

"Ares is too great a warrior to let Hades best him," the goddess said, without smiling back.

Ruby nodded.

Artemis tied the quiver onto Ruby's pack and hung the bow over it. She showed Ruby how to reach the bow and then the arrows in quick succession by pulling them forward from behind her.

Ruby tried it but she fumbled the job badly and dropped the silver arrow before she could nock it. She looked at Artemis, who wore a tight expression.

"I'll practice on the way," Ruby said.

"Yes. You should."

"Time," Ares said.

"Be careful," Athena's heart-shaped face was tense with worry.

Ares took Ruby's hand and looked around the group again. "We won't forget your help."

"You've known the risks all along. And you've taken them." Apollo said. He and Ares locked eyes. "Now it falls to us."

NINETEEN

THE WINGS OF HERMES'S SHOES beat against Ares's ankles. The soft grass in the clearing fluttered with the movement. Ares took Ruby in his arms and they rose gently off the ground. The gods below waved and then looked to one another. Ruby wished them well in her mind, hoping she would see them again.

They lifted above the green treetops. She hadn't seen Olympus from this vantage since Ares had brought her to meet his family months ago. What was foreign then was now familiar. Athena's amethyst abode, and Ares's red-veined marble one. Aphrodite's pink alabaster, covered in red roses, stood in contrast to Hephaestus's dark iron.

Past those were the abodes of lesser gods, Eros and Psyche, and Pan. They looked like mere cottages compared to the impressive homes of the Olympians, but Ruby had been inside many of them and knew that they were as big and as well-appointed as any of the finest homes on Earth. In the middle of it all was the golden Great Hall, the abode of Zeus, and off to the side was Hera's platinum one.

Ruby took it all in, trying to see the beauty of it, and not the politics and gossip that she now knew ran deep through the heart of Olympus, as entrenched as Oceanus itself.

From the corner of her eye she saw a group of gods entering the Great Hall. Hera's auburn hair shone in the sunlight. Her long yellow peplos flowed out behind her. She was followed by Poseidon, whom, like Hades, Ruby hardly ever saw on Olympus. She had the impression that Zeus's brothers didn't like to leave their realms. Hephaestus was a short distance behind Poseidon. His lopsided gait was unmistakable, even from this height.

Trailing Heph were three hulking creatures Ruby had never seen before. They were taller than the other gods, and there was something strange about their faces. She squinted to make out their features. They—she jerked back—they had only one eye in the center of their foreheads. "Cyclopes."

"Huh?" Ares was concentrating on moving forward, not saying good-bye. Now he looked down too.

"Damn oracles," he said quietly, more a rumble in his chest than anything.

She searched the ground below them. Other gods moved toward the Great Hall but she and Ares were too high for her to make out faces or details.

They approached the entrance to Olympus. Ruby saw the Seasons, with their youthful faces and long flowing hair. They waved in recognition.

Ruby ignored them.

Ares didn't say more about the Cyclopes, but she knew. Zeus was gathering his forces, as Ares had informally done in the grove before they left for Hades. Her throat started to close with tension. "It's me," she said. "I'm the cause of all of this."

The weather changed as they passed through the gate of clouds. Cold mist collected on her rain jacket and dampened her jeans. She shivered.

"The balance of power on Olympus has been shifting for a long time," Ares said. "You and me, our love, it's brought the tensions that were already on Olympus to a head. The gods are beginning to see through Zeus's flimsy excuses to the real reason we are forbidden from mortal realms: he can't control himself.

"I've never been a favorite on Olympus," he said. "I don't have Hermes's charm, Pan's talent, or Dionysus's ability to command a room, but the gods are coming to my defense. To *our* defense. They want to feel that if they fell in love they wouldn't be denied because of Zeus's lust, the way others already have been."

"Like Apollo and Kissiae," she said. They flew over the tree covered mountains of Washington and Oregon; the coast to their right, wide dormant valleys to their left.

"I'm not sorry," he said. "I'm willing to fight for you." He kissed the top of her head.

His words rang in her ears. He *was* about to fight for her. She was about to fight for him. She thought of the silver bow and quiver of arrows hanging over her pack. She wasn't a fighter. She wasn't brave. Who was she kidding?

⚬ᘰ⚬

The sun came out in patches as they left the Northwest behind and headed into California. Even as it became warm, the ground below remained brown and barren. She knew that there was more to spring arriving than just temperature and sun. It had to do with an awakening in the Earth, and the energy Demeter worked to bring the seasons about.

Soon the full strength of the sun blazed down on her, hot enough to make her want to pull away from Ares. She lifted her head from his chest and tried to get air between their sweating bodies. She felt Ares and the winged sandals slow.

"Where are we?" She wiped at her sweaty face.

"Badwater Basin in Death Valley. Hermes says there's an entrance here below a peak called Dante's View. We need to look for a crevice in the rock at the peak's base."

The flat land was desolate, dry, and cracked. Despite the brutal heat, the ground appeared to be covered in drifts of snow. Beyond the close hills were mountains thousands of feet high. It was as stunning as it was bleak.

"That's Dante's View." Ares pointed to the highest peak among the hills.

Ruby scanned the foot of the rocks and looked for a crevice or opening of some kind. Ares descended. The white earth crunched under their feet as he set them down about twenty yards from the side of the hill. Not snow, she realized: salt.

The flat basin was silent, with no birds or insects to lend their sounds. The brittle salt under their feet gave way in places to a murky brine beneath. Ares's foot broke through. When he pulled it out Hermes winged sandals were covered in a light brown sludge. The wings gave a little shake like a dog.

They walked across the unstable ground in the overwhelming heat. Walking drained their energy and the hot air felt heavy in Ruby's throat and lungs. The ground was more solid near the hillside where they continued along the edge, scanning for an opening.

"This must be it." Ares stopped.

It was a small gap, low to the ground. They would have to crawl. Ruby hoped the ground would hold.

She peered into the cave, into complete blackness. They would not be able to light Eros's torch until they got to a place where they could stand. If they could stand at all. How far was it to Hades? How long would it take to get there if they had to crawl?

"I'll go first," Ares said. "You carry the torch so I can use my hands to feel the way." He unslung his pack and traded the winged sandals for boots.

The coolness of the cave was a relief after the brutal heat of Death Valley. They had a few moments of light before their bodies blotted out the sun from the entrance. There was a harsh metallic smell. It made Ruby's stomach clench. The hard earth beneath them made her hands and knees ache.

Soon she sensed space around her. The tunnel felt like it was wider. The smell was no longer as strong. She reached up into the darkness and felt for a ceiling but found none. She pushed up off the ground.

"I can stand," she said.

"Hand me the torch." Ares voice was distant.

"Here, can you feel it?" She swung it away from her in a wide arc. He took hold and they pulled each other in toward the center.

She heard him release the door at the base of the torch. Sparks broke into the darkness as he struck the quartz along the iron of the fire starter.

A wavering flame lit up the space as the wick caught. Harsh shadows danced on Ares's face. It felt better to see him, but the deep cavern beyond was at least three stories high and it felt oppressive to be surrounded by so much dark space.

A passage continued ahead on the far side of the cavern. The path started to pitch downward almost immediately. The grey, water-streaked walls were wide enough for Ruby to put both hands out and barely touch the sides. The briny smell of wet rocks persisted.

To pass the time Ruby would pick an outcropping as a goal, but once achieved there was always another for them to reach. Ares walked in silence before her. The torch made their shadows flicker on the walls.

"How much farther do you think it is?" she asked after a while.

"They say that Hades is as far below the Earth as Olympus is above it," he said. "But that's just an old expression. They're separated by mystical boundaries, not physical ones."

"What will it be like?"

"It's not Hell," he said, guessing at her fears. "All souls, or shades, go to Hades and most are judged there. The righteous are sent to the Elysian Plains. Ordinary shades stay in the

Fields of Asphodel. Evil shades are sent to Tartarus, far below Hades."

The vision of Tartarus Athena had given her months ago in Athenaeum rushed into Ruby's mind. She felt the memory of the suffocating depression, the gnawing hunger, the desperate thirst. Above all there was the profound loneliness which was quickly followed by a deep desire for revenge. It took her breath away.

She cleared her throat in an attempt to rid the feeling from her chest. "*Most* shades are judged there? Who isn't judged?"

"The ones that will reincarnate."

"Reincarnation?" She stopped walking, happy that her favorite idea of the afterlife was true.

"It's rare. But some shades return to the mortal world."

"Which shades?" She followed Ares as he continued down the tunnel again. "Who decides?"

"No one decides. At least not directly. Only shades whose lives were stolen from them can choose to return. Only shades who were murdered."

Ruby started, stunned by the justice of it. "Do they remember their old lives?" She knew some people believed they could.

"No. Shades reincarnate by eating the fruit of the Tree of Life. The Tree of Life resides on an island in the middle of the Lethe, the river of forgetfulness. The river washes their memory away."

Her heart constricted at the thought of not having her memories anymore. Her home on Earth, her father, Ares!

"Do they get to choose? Do they know that they'll forget?" She was afraid that this would turn out to be another cruelty of Ares's world. Maybe Zeus decided, haphazardly, without regard for anyone but himself. Or maybe Hades chose, and if you were pretty it wouldn't matter what you wanted.

"They know," he said tenderly, aware of how precious her memories were to her.

The cave grew colder with each step. What was initially a relief from the heat of Death Valley was now a bone-deep chill. Ruby shivered. Her sneakers were still damp from stumbling behind Hermes through the river Oceanus and her feet were numb.

"Are you cold?" Ares asked, as if he felt her shudder.

"Only a little," she lied.

"Here, take this." He took off his flannel shirt and slung it over her shoulders, pack and all.

"I'm fine," she insisted. "You should keep it."

"I don't need it." He smiled at her in the cold dimness, now wearing only a T-shirt and jeans.

Even in this abysmal place he was gorgeous.

ॐ

Ruby's back ached from the weight of her leather pack as they walked. The water that had been seeping out of the rocks now began to collect in a trench to the right of them. The flow of water increased and babbled melodically as it became a creek.

The path began to level out. The rocks above and around them were shot through with veins of minerals. She thought of the rock collection she had as a kid. "Quartz?" she asked, pointing to a series of clear crystals.

"Diamonds," Ares corrected.

Her mouth dropped open as her eyes followed the trail of diamonds all the way up the wall and saw it curve into the ceiling. Some would be too big for her to get her arms around. "Hades, the god of death and *wealth*," she said, remembering reading that somewhere.

"The most valuable things on Earth are found beneath it," he agreed.

The passage opened up. The creek was now a rushing river. It veered off to the right.

Ares stopped suddenly in front of her and she nearly ran into him.

"What is it?" She craned her neck to look around him.

"Steps," he said and started down a narrow set of stairs carved into the rock.

The stairs curved into a spiral and went down for several stories. The light of the torch intensified as its flame reflected off the close rocks around them. The sound of rushing water was a constant, though there was no water in the stairwell. At the bottom they passed through a stone archway.

Ruby wondered who had carved it all but her thoughts were pulled away by the massive waterfall that now stood across from them, on the far side of a narrow dirt path.

"The headwater of the Styx," Ares said without taking his eyes away from the rushing water.

"Welcome to the Underworld."

TWENTY

THE LIGHT OF RUBY AND ARES'S TORCH was doubled by another one attached to the rocky wall of the Underworld. The Styx ran parallel to the trail and both curved out of sight not far ahead. The water itself had changed, she noticed. It was thicker, more viscous. She shuddered.

Ares snuffed out Eros's torch and stuck the handle end in his pack. "We'll have to cross the Styx to get to Hades proper." He looked down at the dark water. "But not here. We need to find Charon."

A subtle wave of nausea rolled through her stomach at the thought of actually reaching Hades, but her anxiety was replaced with a shock of fear and alertness when Ares turned to her in a sudden move she didn't expect, his head cocked to one side, listening.

The first time Ruby heard the groan it seemed like a trick of the rushing water next to them. Probably just her imagination. But when she heard it again, it was too loud to mistake.

Ares moved in front of her, his elbow bent, his hand ready to reach behind him for the hilt of his sword.

Ruby looked in every direction, but between the echoing cavern and the rushing water, the sound was hard to localize. Her instincts told her to run. Ares held his ground. It gave her courage.

She peeked out from a gap between his arm and his torso. All she saw was the thick water of the Styx and the empty path before them. She looked behind them, at the stairs they had descended into the Underworld, but there was nothing that way either.

The sound came again: a cross between a growl and a moan. It didn't sound like an animal. There was something pitiful, even desperate, in it. Something human.

Ares moved forward. His head was still bent to listen. Ruby followed. Was someone there, beyond the outcropping of rocks where the path bent to the left?

This time the sound was louder, with the resonance of language mixed in. Not words, but drawn out a's and deep m's. She saw Ares's muscles flex as he quietly drew out his sword and held it in front of him.

She suddenly wondered if they had brought enough weapons. Shouldn't Ares have more than one sword? What about a gun?

She thought of Artemis's silver bow and arrows. She imagined reaching behind her, freeing the bow, grabbing an arrow, and firing. She saw it all in her mind in four quick movements.

She drew her right hand back over her head but found nothing but soft cotton cloth against her fingers. Ares's shirt. He had draped it over her for warmth, but now she was unable to reach the bow in a hurry.

Ares stopped before rounding the outcrop. His stance was wide. He put up one finger, telling her to stay put.

He rounded the corner with the quick and sure reflexes of a fighter. In one motion he was facing whatever was beyond the rock, his sword held high, ready to strike. Ruby couldn't tell what he saw. She only heard the shriek.

"Ares!" She raced around the corner, but as she moved she realized that it wasn't Ares who had cried out. It wasn't a battle cry, or even a cry of pain. It was a cry of surprise and fear.

She stood next to Ares but all she saw was another torch in the wall. She followed his line of sight to the ground. Tucked into the base of an outcropping of rock sat an almost skeletal man in tattered clothes. His hands were crossed in front of his face, warding off Ares's attack.

Ares lowered the sword and relaxed his position. The man on the ground let his arms fall away to reveal a grimy face and sunken eyes. He smelled as if he hadn't bathed in a long time.

"Who are you?" Ares demanded with all the authority of a general.

Ruby had already relaxed. This man was not a threat. If anything he needed their help.

"Don't hurt me," the man said in a weak voice. He had a thick English accent.

"Are you okay?" Ruby bent down.

Ares pulled her back. "Don't touch him."

"He's hurt, and probably hungry. We should help him."

Ares didn't respond to her. Instead he said again, "Who are you? Why are you here?"

"I'm going." The man scrambled up on skinny legs.

Ares towered over him. "Sit."

The man sat.

"Who are you?" Ares demanded.

"It does not matter who I was. I am nothing now. Stuck wandering here …" He trailed off as if he didn't have the energy to continue.

Ares bent and picked the man up by the collar of his tattered clothes. "Who are you?" he screamed in his face.

Ruby flinched.

"John," the man said, stiff with fear. "John Wright."

"Why are you here?" Ares snarled in his face.

"Why?" he said, as if he was asking himself the same question. "I have not the fare."

"The fare?" Ares's brow knit. Then his face relaxed. He let go his grip on John and looked down the path. "Are we near?"

"No. Not near. We are safe here. Safe for now." John's pale blue eyes danced in their sockets, looking all around.

"Near?" Ruby looked around for whatever it was they were talking about.

"Charon. The Crossing," Ares said to her. He grabbed John by the shirt again. "Show us."

"I'm not going back there. I have not the fare. There is no food. They ran me out. I will spend my eternity right here."

"What is he talking about?" Ruby asked.

"He has no money to pay the ferryman. He can't pass over into Hades."

"You mean?" She stared at the man in horror. "You mean, he's dead?"

Ares nodded, but he was looking down the path. "He's a shade."

Ruby looked ahead too. All she saw was another bend in the flickering torchlight.

"What happens if he can't pay?" Ruby glanced to the ragged man, and it was he who answered.

"Nothing. That's what happens. Nothing. No food on this side. Bullies and thieves everywhere. The Brigand." His eyes were wide.

Food? She thought of Persephone and the pomegranate seeds she had eaten after Hades had abducted her. The man was so skinny. Could he starve, and die again? "You have to eat when you're dead?" she asked.

"No, of course not," Ares answered her.

"But it is good," John whispered, "tastes so good." He licked his grimy lips. "And I am hungry."

She glanced up the path again. "What about the thieves? The Brigand?" she asked.

"Take us to the crossing." Ares insisted.

"I will not," said John. Determination was set in his bony jaw.

"Do you know who I am?" Ares's eyes narrowed.

Ruby glanced at him in surprise.

"I don't care who you are," John Wright said.

"I am Ares," Ares said it as if the man were already impressed.

Ruby saw a smile form on the ragged man's lips. "Ares? Hera's favored son? The god of war? That Ares?"

"That Ares," Ares hissed.

The shade burst into peals of raspy laughter.

Ares's face went slack.

"Ares? Right. And she … she's Aphrodite." He was holding his stomach as he looked at Ruby and laughed.

Ruby tried not to be offended. She never expected to pass for Aphrodite anyway.

Ares lifted the man again. "I am Ares!" he bellowed into his face.

The man became silent. His face turned ashen. Ruby didn't know whether he believed Ares or simply realized he was outmuscled either way. His response was a quick and supplicating, "Ares. Yes."

"You will lead us to the ferryman," Ares said.

John stumbled up the path when Ares released him, toward the place he had said he would not go back to again.

They soon ran across more shades on the path. Many were as desperate-looking as John. They sat on the edge of the trail, begging.

"What do they want? Why are they here?" Ruby asked Ares in a low voice.

"An obol." He matched her low tone. "Payment for the ferryman. These people were either too poor or too friendless to have been buried with the fare."

"But people aren't buried with an obol anymore. How can they pay?" She pictured her father's funeral. It had been a closed casket. There wasn't enough of him left after the bomb to try to piece him back together. Would she see him here, or in Hades? Would he be whole again?

"Charon will take anything of value," Ares said. "Anything he finds appealing."

John led them on, muttering his displeasure and ignoring the line of beggars that became thicker along the path, even as the path became wider as they went.

The trio pushed their way through, until, all of a sudden, the beggars turned toward them and rushed in the opposite direction in one great wave.

Ruby, Ares, and John were now alone in an open area large enough for five or six men to stand abreast.

John stopped. His back stiffened.

"What is it, man?" Ares's voice rose in anger.

"It's them," John whispered. "The Brigand." He tried to back up on the trail, but he ran into Ares, who stood like a brick wall in the path. The shade was trapped between the threat of thieves in front and the god of war behind.

Ares said nothing, but looked ahead. Resolve settled into his features.

Ruby heard them before she could see them; a rowdy crowd after the bars have closed, when no one's ready to go home and the cops are scarce. She stood close to Ares.

She remembered her bow and had enough time to free it from the tangle of shirt on her back. The metal thrummed in her hand, more intense than when she had touched the bow before. She nocked a silver arrow on the string and tried to squelch her feelings of inadequacy.

Artemis's words came back to her, *release your energy into the bow ... the arrows will shoot true.* She breathed out and relaxed her tense shoulders. She imaged her hand melding with the metal of the bow and her energy flowing into it. The thrumming melted into a pleasant warmth.

Ares leaned toward her. "Hold the bow low. Don't let them see it at first. We're not enemies yet." His bright blue eyes caught hers. "Trust your instincts."

She nodded and held the bow and arrow in separate hands at her sides, loose, but ready.

The leader of the group was obvious by the way he came into the light of the torch first, loud and giving orders. He stopped short when he saw Ares and Ruby standing in his way.

"What do we have here? Newcomers? And a couple at that." His tone was one of mocking sweetness. "What was it? Car crash? Tragic accident? You're both *so* young." He was tall—as tall as Ares—and burly.

Ruby could see why he was so confident. He led a small but well-equipped group of four men and three women. Most were larger than any of the other shades she had seen so far. They wore warm clothes and jewelry, as well as an assortment of other Earthly items. One had on a Yankees cap. Another wore green and white wing-tip shoes. The tallest woman was draped in a soldier's dress jacket with a military insignia Ruby didn't recognize. The leader had a gold ring on every finger.

"Let us pass," Ares said in a clear deep voice.

The leader laughed. So did everyone else in his group. Even John, who had stepped to the side, giggled. This made Ruby more nervous than anything else. She tightened her grip on the silver bow.

"You may pass." The leader smiled. "There's just the matter of a small fee. Say, that bow your girlfriend's carrying."

Ruby pulled the bow and arrow behind her.

"Now, now," the Brigand leader said, "hand it here and you'll be on your way. No fuss, no muss."

"I don't think so." Ares looked him straight in the eye. "Move aside and we won't hurt you."

Again the group laughed. They pulled weapons out from beneath their clothes. One man held a long, curved sword. Another had a hatchet. The leader drew out a sword with a gold hilt encrusted with jewels. The grandeur of it seemed ridiculous in the dimness and squalor of the Underworld.

Ruby sucked in a breath as she saw the taller of the women pull out a pistol. She found her voice with that breath.

"Your weapons won't do you much good. We're already dead, right?" Ruby asked, wondering if they could tell she was mortal.

"Newbies, through and through," the leader said. The rest of his gang chuckled. "You are most rightly dead if you're here. But the knife still cuts. The bullet still shreds. And believe me, the flesh still feels." He turned his head. Ruby flinched at the sight of an angry red scar that ran from above his ear to below his jaw. "You won't die. But, oh, you'll suffer. And in the end we'll have that bow."

"This is your last chance to lower your weapons and move aside," Ares said.

The Brigand leader smiled a large grin of rotted teeth. He nodded and the band came at them; eight on two.

Ares reach behind him, drew out his sword, and stepped forward to meet them.

The bow shook in Ruby's hand as she nocked the silver arrow, looked in the general direction of the woman with the gun, and let fly. The arrow wobbled, then straightened. Ruby stood slack-jawed as it found its mark and stuck. A red flower bloomed on the woman's chest as the force knocked her flat.

Ares's sword flashed repeatedly in the torchlight. He turned this way and that, deflecting blows. The attackers stumbled over each other's bodies as they fell under Ares's power.

The man in the Yankees cap saw an opening. He rushed at Ruby with a rusty dagger in one hand and a shiny hunting knife in the other.

She raised the bow, this time giving all of her energy over to it. The arrow zinged and hit the man square in the throat. He fell backward as though someone had kicked his legs out from under him.

Her heart pumped fast and hard with adrenaline. Cold rushed through her center. Heat shivered across her skin. The bow felt like an extension of her own arm, like it was a part of her. She held it up, looking for another villainous character to dispatch. Instead she found Ares, sword in hand, with six bloody and broken victims at his feet. His blue eyes nearly pulsed in the dim light.

Ruby felt her smile fade. She had shot two people. They were already dead, but she had *shot* them. She looked at Ares again, at the bodies around him. Now she knew why he only brought one sword into the Underworld. One was all he needed. His victims were not just unconscious, not just cut, they were in pieces.

Her heart, already pumping like crazy, sped even faster at the thought that Ares—*her* Ares—was capable of such destruction.

She watched him scan the bodies for movement. Satisfied they weren't going to paste themselves back together anytime soon, he looked around for John, who had hidden when the fighting started. The shade was with a group of others, cowering under a rocky overhang. Ares pointed to the bodies. "Take what you want."

All at once the beggars were on them, going through packs and pockets, and picking up scattered weapons. Ares stopped them with his commanding voice, and pointed to John. "He picks first. Then he comes with us."

John beamed, "Yes, sir, Ares." He picked up the hunting knife the Yankees fan had dropped and crammed the cap on his own head. He took a package of fruits and breads from one of the women, and a gold ring from the leader's motionless hand. "Like some? Ares? Aphrodite?" He held out an apple to each of them.

Ruby's stomach was already churning from fighting, from seeing what Ares could do, from seeing what she could do.

She reached for the fruit with a numb hand, her mind still reeling. "Thanks …"

Ares grabbed her arm. "No." He gave her a stern look.

Like jumping into a cold river, she came to her senses. The Brigand could have killed her or hurt Ares, but the fruit could condemn her to an undead eternity in the Underworld.

John put the apple in his ragged coat pocket and bit into a pear he held in his other hand. Juice dripped down his chin. Ruby looked away, feeling as if she were intruding on a private, almost intimate, moment.

Ares walked to Ruby's two victims, pulled the silver arrows from their bodies, and wiped the blood on their clothes. The woman moaned. Ruby recoiled.

He brought the arrows to her. The falcon feathers were straight and unruffled. She watched, still dazed, as he tucked the arrows back into her quiver.

John slipped a mango in with the apple. "My favorite," he said with a grin. "For later."

"Ready?" Ares asked Ruby.

"Yes, sir, Ares," John responded just short of a salute. He bowed his head and looked at Ruby. "Aphrodite."

Ruby took Ares's lead and nodded at the man. She glanced at Ares.

He winked at her.

John continued, eager now, on the path. The number of shades languishing there multiplied. People were dressed in styles from throughout time. Women wore long dresses with their hems sweeping the dirty ground. There were men in knee length pants and long socks, and children in grey-brown gowns. A few shades were naked and Ruby realized they must have been so poor their families didn't have the money to dress their dearly departed.

It was a sad, dismal place, and they hadn't even crossed the Styx yet. The lost souls held out their hands, hoping someone would take pity on them and spare them a trinket valuable enough to buy their passage across the river. Ruby wished she had something to give them.

Soon the crowd thickened even more. People here were better dressed. They weren't begging. They were waiting. The rock walls were full of markings: *Cecil, 1456*; *Henry, 1873*; *Suzan, 1989*. There were countless languages and symbols, many she didn't recognize.

John led them through the crowd, pushing and demanding his way through. "Make way for the gods." The shades around them didn't seem to hear, or maybe they didn't care.

The crowd stopped of its own accord about fifty feet from the water's edge, as if there were a glass wall holding them back. Ruby, Ares, and John pushed through and stepped into the empty space between the crowd and a feeble wooden dock. At the end of the dock was a single lantern casting a small circle of yellow light into the yawning cavern.

The crowd, which had been loud and jeering with people vying to be next on the ferry, was abruptly quiet when they saw the three of them. John scurried back into the crowd, leaving Ruby and Ares alone in the open.

Ruby scanned the area, searching for what danger might lie here. Ares only looked ahead, across the river. The far side was shrouded in mist and darkness. There was little movement on the river's surface. Fat, lazy ripples reflected the lamplight in slow motion. Not like water. Like something thicker. Like liquid night.

They had not stood there long when a wooden skiff, traveling in its own circle of lamplight, came into view. A tall hooded figure stood at the helm. His body bent and then straightened as he used a gnarled wooden pole to push off the bottom of the river.

Charon.

What little heat Ruby still had drained out of her. She would have rather faced the Brigand again, stayed with the destitute dead forever, or walked all the way back to the barren wastelands of Death Valley, than get in that boat and be in the middle of that water.

Ares strode to the dock as the ferryman glided in closer. Ruby watched as the boat's black hull cut silently through the heavy water.

Charon tied the ferry to the lone post at the end of the mooring. Ares met him there. Ruby pulled her feet from the sticky pools of fear that held them and followed.

"Charon, old friend," Ares said in a voice that was genial, light even.

The ferryman started at the sound of Ares's voice. He threw back his cowl and turned toward them.

Her stomach lurched.

His eyes were red. They glowed; faint, like some deep-sea fish that had evolved over the millennia to survive beyond the reach of light. The red eyes slipped past Ares and landed on Ruby. He frowned.

Though his eyes were unnerving, Ruby found that his face was not unkind, not skeletal or malicious, as she had expected. He looked haggard, tired, worn out. His beard was twisted into knots and his cheeks were sunken.

Ares stepped closer to the ferryman and spoke in a low whisper. Ruby crossed her arms over herself as she stood outside their conversation. The onlookers were silent, watching too.

"Ruby." Ares motioned for her to come closer. The ferryman looked her way again, but she could not read his expression.

"This is Charon," Ares said when Ruby reached the end of the unsteady dock. "He has agreed to ferry us across."

She forced herself to smile at the red-eyed creature, though she wanted nothing more than to look away.

"You have the fare," Charon said without emotion. His voice was rough and thick, as if it hadn't been used in some time. "It's Hades you'll have to contend with, on the other side." He turned to ready the boat for the trip across the water.

Ares took three of the bronze coins from the leather pouch Athena had given them and tucked the purse back into Ruby's pack. Each coin had a woman's face in relief on one side and an owl on the other. Ruby thought that the woman must be Athena, though it didn't look much like her.

Ares walked up the dock toward shore. The wood creaked as he went. "John Wright," he bellowed.

There was no immediate answer.

"Ares calls you," he said louder. A ripple of surprise ran through the onlookers. A group of shades parted to reveal John crouching low among them.

"You've earned your fare," Ares said. "You're coming with us."

The thin man's dull eyes brightened. A wide smile nearly split his face in two. He raced down to the dock. It swayed and complained under his slight weight and Ruby worried that the whole thing might collapse under them.

Charon reached out to help her into the wobbly little boat. His hand was cold and clammy. She had to stop herself from wiping her own hand on her jeans when he let go.

Ares jumped in behind John and handed Charon the three coins. Ruby saw the ferryman tuck them into his dark robes before he pushed away from the dock. As if on cue, the crowd at the edge of the water began clamoring for their turn again.

Ruby looked around. The small lantern, hanging from a pole in the middle of the boat, only revealed more of the black and viscous water. John's eyes were wide. His foot tapped. Ruby took his hand. He was dead, she remembered as her fingers wrapped around his bony hand, but it felt normal and she was glad she did it.

"Thank you, Goddess," he whispered.

She felt like an imposter. She looked at Ares on her other side. His attention was focused at the front of the ferry, into the mist before them and the blackness surrounding them.

"Is it water?" she asked him, trying to keep her lips from pulling up in a disgusted sneer. It smelled faintly of metal.

"The Styx is the River of Hate. A burden for anyone," he said, and then added as an afterthought, "Don't touch it."

She wasn't about to.

The wall of mist closed in on them. As they entered its cold shroud she thought of the clamoring souls, the desperate pleas, the anxious dead. She shivered as she imagined going in and out of this suffocating mist and traveling across the River of Hate so many times a day.

In the next moment her dark thoughts were surrounded by light. She could see the far shore. There was a cave made from the same grey rocks they had left behind on the bank behind them. The air was warmer here, though there was no source of heat or light that Ruby could see.

She looked to Ares.

He nodded.

They were in Hades.

TWENTY·ONE

CHARON'S FERRY SLID ONTO THE FAR BANK.
Ares made his way to the bow and turned to help Ruby. When
she was on the shore he stuck out his hand to Charon. "Thank
you, old friend."

The ferryman shook his hand and nodded. "Find Persephone and get out as quick as you can," he said, looking Ares in
the eye. When he let go of Ares's hand, he looked at Ruby.

She smiled at him, her good manners temporarily overcom-
ing her fear, but the ferryman of the dead didn't smile back.
He turned back to the skiff, the river, and the other side without further comment.

The river's edge ran as far as Ruby could see in either direction. Behind them was a large open tunnel lit by torches.

Ares hitched his pack up onto his shoulders. "Charon's
right. Let's not waste time."

Ruby slung her own pack up onto her back. The silver bow and arrows hung off, now easily accessible. It was warm here and she no longer needed the flannel shirt.

They walked up the torchlit tunnel. Along the walls were small alcoves carved into the rock. A statue stood in each. Ruby slowed to look. The one she stopped at was silver, a tall goddess standing in a wood, a sliver of a moon over her and a familiar-looking bow resting against her leg. Small trinkets lay at the goddess's feet, offerings left by souls that had passed through.

The statue was so lifelike Ruby could almost see the ice-blue of Artemis's eyes. She smiled. Only Hephaestus could have created it.

Many gods were artists. Apollo wrote poetry and songs. The muses entertained all of Olympus with their plays and stories. Many other gods and goddesses dabbled here and there with painting or weaving, but no other god was as prolific or as singularly talented as Hephaestus was with metal. None seemed to leave their signature on everything they touched like Heph did.

Ares and John walked ahead. Ruby scanned the alcoves. There was Hera, with a pomegranate in one hand and a peacock standing at her feet; Apollo, with his lute, the guitar-like instrument he always played; Aphrodite, made of ivory, was rendered perfectly with all her beauty intact.

Around the base of Aphrodite's statue were piles of jewelry. Cufflinks, thick rope necklaces, even wedding rings. Wealthy souls had left piles of prized possessions for their idols, while legions of others languished on the far side of the

Styx waiting for a single valuable thing to buy their way into the afterlife. She wanted to scoop it all up and run back to give it to Charon. It would get hundreds of souls across.

She looked down the tunnel, the way they had come. The river was lost behind a bend. Ares, trailed by John, was far ahead in the other direction. There was no time.

She walked up the tunnel, faster than before, but still looking for one statue in particular. Then, near the end, she saw him, tall and proud, and as handsome as ever; Ares chiseled from stone.

Around Ares's feet were military decorations, paper poppies, and sets of dog tags. There were some weapons, but Ruby was stunned to see that what predominated the shrine were symbols of peace. There was a ceramic dove with an olive branch in its mouth, plastic buttons with peace signs, faded poems and songs written on yellowing sheets of paper. The tokens reminded her of what her love for Ares meant, not just for them, not just for her, but for the world.

She looked up the tunnel again. The real Ares had stopped. He was looking at her, patient, while John wandered here and there, nearly bouncing off the walls, eager to get on with the afterlife.

She turned back to the statue Ares, kissed her fingers and put them to his stone lips. She ran and grabbed Ares's hand as she reached him. His energy flowed into her. She felt like she could sit on the stone floor of the Underworld and weep for an eternity over that feeling. He looked into her eyes and she saw a flash of Ares, *her* Ares. Not the god of war on a mission to the Underworld, but the god she loved.

She lifted up on her toes and kissed him on the cheek. He smiled, his expression curious. She shook her head—*don't ask, just be*—and drew him up the tunnel toward Hades.

⚬⚬⚬

The passage became wider as they walked. The statues of the Twelve Olympians were behind them now. "Soon we'll be at the Adamantine Gate," Ares said. "It's guarded by Cerberus. He'll be our first real problem in Underworld."

Ruby's mind leaped from Death Valley, to Charon, to the Brigand, in three quick steps. She wondered what qualified as a "real problem" to Ares.

"Cerberus's job is to keep unwanted visitors out of the Underworld. Especially mortals," he said with the voice of a tactician. No fear, just facts. "He's a giant three-headed dog with a mane of asps and a cobra for a tail. A bite from the snakes will kill a person in minutes. There's nothing to counteract it."

She nodded and felt the blood slipping away from the top of her scalp.

"Cerberus hungers for human flesh. He lets shades pass unharmed, and he won't bother me, but he'll want you."

She swallowed. "How do we … How do *I* get past him?"

"Luckily, he's easy to distract. Do you have Pan's pipes?"

"Yes! 'Play the pipes for Cerberus.'" She repeated Pan's words and retrieved the pipes from her bag. Her heart ached at the sight of them, the five hollow reeds lashed together with black and gold ties. She thought of Pan and his lilting songs, of the nymphs by the river, and dancing in the Great Hall.

"I'll play," Ares said. "You stick with John and stay calm."

Ruby nodded, trying to imagine the creature he had described, trying to envision herself being calm when he came for her.

"At the far side of Cerberus's lair is the Adamantine Gate. It's cut out of a single diamond. Once we're through the gate we'll be safe and he won't be able to follow, but if anything happens to Cerberus the gate will close and we'll be locked out of Hades. We can't use our weapons."

Ruby barely had time to take this all in before Ares called John back from his eager strides ahead. "When we get to the gate, I need you to watch over ..." he hesitated for a moment, "Aphrodite. Cerberus is angry at her. If he attacks you'll have to help her run."

The skinny shade nodded and stood closer to Ruby, who was nearly as tall as he was. "I will guard her," he said.

The tunnel continued to widen until they came into a large cavern. Lit torches lined the walls. At the far end was the gate. It was at least three stories high. A single diamond. Its clear surface was carved with images of gods and goddesses. How could a diamond be carved?

The Adamantine Gate was wide open, ready to welcome the newly dead. To the right and left of the gate were two tunnels branching off. Both of these were dark and did not hint at what might lie inside.

"All we need to do is cross," Ares reminded her as they walked into the cavern. In his hand he held Pan's Pipes, ready to play.

Part of the way through, with no sign of the big dog, Ruby's spirits lifted. Maybe they had lucked out. Maybe Cerberus wasn't on duty. Her impulse was to pick up the pace, but Ares held her back by her hand. "Keep it cool."

She tried to control her breathing, tried to focus on her footsteps, tried to stop herself from running. The far side of the cavern, and its promise of safety, was so far away.

Then she heard it. Not a bark. Not a growl. A sniff.

A loud and definite sniff. It came from the tunnel on their left. Ruby glanced in that direction, but she saw nothing in the gaping darkness. "Ares?" she whispered with a reedy breath.

He kept his focus on the gate. They were halfway there.

"Keep heading toward—" But Ares didn't get to finish.

Cerberus was there, in front of them, before Ruby could register that he was coming at all. He was enormous, black as pitch, and with orange- and brown-striped snakes curling and twisting around his heads. A massive cobra came around him from behind—the tail. The cobra's hood was splayed and it hissed at them. Cerberus's three giant heads reached halfway up the height of the cavern. Their muzzles dripped with heavy ropes of saliva.

Ares began to blow across the top of the pipes. But instead of the beautiful music that called Nymphs from their wood and entertained rooms full of gods, thin feeble notes came from the pipes. What Pan made look effortless, Ares tried in vain.

Cerberus bent his awful heads down toward Ruby and sniffed again.

She began to shake, but she was unable to move forward as the dog smelled her.

John stood motionless on the other side of Ruby.

Ares's presence of mind remained. As he continued to coax a tune from the pipes, he kicked John into action.

The dead man moved. He grabbed Ruby's hand and pulled her along past two enormous paws and toward the gate.

Cerberus was agile for such a large creature and he turned in one quick motion. Snakes darted out at them, hissing and snapping. There was no way they could get to the gate before he swallowed Ruby whole.

One of the dog's heads bent close from behind and sniffed again. Why hadn't that awful cobra-tail come to bite her yet? Why wasn't she dead yet?

She felt a tug at her back. She half turned and saw a giant black eye over her shoulder.

It was happening. Here it was. Colossal teeth would be ripping her open any second. She waited for it. Her eyes squeezed closed.

Instead the monster tore loose her pack, pulling it free, and headed off toward the dark cave he had come from.

Ruby's eyelids flew open wide. Her fear was replaced with anger. *The bow!* She changed direction. "Give me back Artemis's bow," she screamed.

"Ruby! Forget it," Ares called out as he put the pipes back in his pocket and ran to her. He grabbed her hand and pulled her toward the gate.

"No." Ruby tried to pull away from him. It wasn't Artemis's wrath she feared, or anything else. She wanted that bow.

The giant dog slowed then. He stopped when he reached the entrance to his cave. All three heads bent to the pack. He tore open the top flap with his middle head. He pulled out one of the smaller sacks with the left head, and another with the right. Then he hurried away into the darkness, leaving behind the torn pack with the silver bow still attached.

Ruby wasted no time. She pulled free of Ares and ran to the pack. She fumbled with it, trying to hold the torn leather together, and ran.

Then, from behind her, she heard Cerberus's nails clink against the stone floor of the cavern. She didn't look back, but the expression on Ares's face told her everything she needed to know. The giant dog was right behind her.

Ares drew his sword, wanting to save Ruby more than he wanted to get into Hades.

Ruby reached for his sleeve and pulled him along as she ran past. "Let's go."

Cerberus's panting was loud in her ears as she ran. He was close, but she thought that the gate might be closer. Her legs ached and her lungs burned. When she passed beneath the diamond arch she felt as though her heart would explode, it was beating so fast. She turned back toward the dog, wanting to see how close she had been to death.

Cerberus stood on the other side of the gate, right behind them.

Ruby blinked as familiar dark brown crumbs slid down his foamy saliva, but her thoughts were blasted out of her head in the next moment as Cerberus barked his disappointment, with all three heads, loud enough to make her ears ring.

TWENTY·TWO

"CERBERUS MUST HAVE SMELLED the ambrosia in Athena's bars. Few beings can resist the food of the gods. He ate the hardtack too. And this pack is useless." Ares threw the shredded leather to the side.

"Lucky for us he has a good nose," she laughed, still giddy from adrenaline and from not being dead. "You might want to brush up on your piping skills."

Ares smirked. "I've never been musical. Who would have thought it was that hard?"

They could joke, but only because Athena had, either through foresight or luck, managed to distract Cerberus with her baking. They would miss the food, but Ruby had Artemis's bow and Ares had his sword. They still had several skins of water, Eros's torch, the winged sandals, and Pan's pipes. The coins were gone, either eaten by the giant dog or lost, but she and Ares were already across the river. They had already paid Charon.

Ares handed her one of the skins of water. "Don't drink too much. We need to ration it."

She took small sips of the water and looked around Hades proper. They were in a space so large she couldn't call it a cavern. The ambient light was brighter here and it was a little warmer, almost sunny feeling. The dark grey walls were far away from the gate, she could barely make them out. One wall, opposite the Adamantine Gate, was darker than the others.

"Hades's Palace," Ares explained when she asked.

In the massive space between the gate and the palace, shades wandered around, standing and talking, or sitting on stone benches. Many held small plates piled with food. It reminded Ruby of a garden party, but with millions of guests. Ares was right. It wasn't scary. The dead seemed to be enjoying themselves.

Ares put the water skin in his pack and slung it on his back.

Ruby did the same with her quiver of arrows and her bow.

As they walked into the crowd she saw shades playing lawn games and heard groups of people laughing. The shades were dressed in clothes from throughout time. She wished there was time to sit with some of these people and ask them about their lives. She caught snippets of conversation, but Ares was moving too fast for her to catch more than a few words.

"How can I understand what everyone is saying?" she asked.

"There's only one language in the immortal realms. It sounds like the language you already know, or the one you prefer the most. Even on Olympus the gods can choose to hear a different language than the one you're speaking."

Ruby was stunned. She had never heard that before. "What language do you hear?"

"English," he said. "Well, at least since I've known you."

She smiled, though Ares was ahead of her and couldn't see. She scanned the nearby crowds. "Where's John?"

"He stopped at the first buffet table we passed."

She glanced to where a group of shades was huddled around a long table of food. She didn't see him there, but buffet tables in Hades were like raindrops in Portland—there were plenty.

"What now?" she asked, focusing again on their task.

"We find Persephone," he said, as though it were the easiest thing in the world.

Beyond the large swaths of shades milling about, Ruby saw green fields covered in yellow and white flowers, and farther on there were trees. The air wasn't as sweet-smelling as on Olympus, but it was pleasant, like grass and late-afternoon rain.

Ares moved into the crowd. Many shades had special items from the upper world: ceremonial weaponry, fishing rods, musical instruments. One woman cradled a ceramic pig in her arms. Ruby's bow and arrows and Ares's sword did not stand out.

"Is this it?" she asked. "Is this all of Hades?"

"We're in the Fields of Asphodel, where most shades spend their eternity."

"The righteous go to The Elysian Plains and the evil shades go to Tartarus," she said, to remind herself of what Ares had told her as they walked down to the Underworld.

"Will I see my father or my mother?" she asked, at the same moment she thought it. Fear gripped her, followed by a deep longing to see them. She could meet her mother!

Ares turned to face her. He was silent and looked from her to the crowd and back again. "They're here," he finally said. "But they won't know that you are. Shades sense when a family member dies, they feel it. But you haven't died, so they won't know."

She tensed and scanned the crowd. They could be right in front of her.

"Your father was a war hero. He undoubtedly went on to the Elysian Plains. He would have had the option of taking your mother with him. If he didn't, and she's here, you will need to avoid her. If she sees you, she'll know you're mortal."

To her surprise Ruby felt relief. She missed her father, and she wanted to know her mother, but not like this. Not here. Not now.

They passed small gardens as they walked, filled with daffodils, fragrant lilies. She looked to the far wall again, now closer. Unlike the three dark grey walls of Hades that she thought were granite, the far wall was black and shiny, like cut glass. Two huge flags hung off the top, near the rocky ceiling. One was black and fully raised. The other was white and stood at half-staff. Both hung limp in the windless air.

"Why the flags?" she asked.

"Black for Hades. White for Persephone," he said over his shoulder. "Persephone's flag stays at half-staff for the part of the year that she is on Olympus."

"Do the shades think she's gone to Olympus?" Ruby asked and glanced again at the half-lowered flag.

"Let's find out." He approached a large group of men sitting in faded recliners arranged in a loose semi-circle around a man and a boy throwing a football between them. The man throwing looked like he was in his late sixties or early seventies. The boy had close-cropped blond hair and was about ten or twelve. They both wore blue football jerseys with a horseshoe on the front. They were the same number, nineteen.

The men in recliners watched and talked. The youngest looked like he might be forty. The oldest was at least in his eighties. They were all eating chips and drinking beer. *Guy heaven.*

"... Sully tackled the wrong guy," one of the men said. The group erupted in laughter.

Ares smiled, as though he was part of the joke. There was a pause when the laughter died down. "Where's Persephone?" he casually asked. "I just got here and I want to see a real goddess."

All heads swung his way and the football landed in the tall man's hands with a thwack. A brawny man dressed in a kilt, with a soccer ball in his lap, spoke up. "She's gone, man," he said in a thick Scottish accent. "Disappeared. No one knows."

Ruby heard the blood rush loud in her ears. Had Hades hidden her somewhere else? Had they spent all this time getting here only to find out that she wasn't even in the Underworld?

"Hades is holed up in his palace, heartsick," the big football thrower said. Ruby looked from one number nineteen to the other, the little boy. His eyes were downcast, as though he felt pity for the god of the underworld.

"Oh," Ares said in a disappointed tone. "Well, thanks."

He walked away and Ruby followed behind. "She's not here?"

"I'm surprised they know she's gone. I don't think they could tell if she's still in the Underworld or not. They only know what Hades tells them."

"So, how do we find her?" Ruby scanned the crowd.

"We ask him," Ares said, his voice stony.

"Who?" she asked tentatively, afraid she already knew the answer.

"Hades. He knows where she is."

Ruby recognized that hard look of determination in his eyes. He was heading to that place where there was no stopping him. In this context it scared her. He turned from her and headed in a straight line toward Hades's palace.

As they got closer Ruby could make out the features of the palace: spires, balconies, and parapets. It looked like the front of a medieval castle, but instead of layered bricks it was carved glass. There was one wide arched entrance in the face of the enormous black building.

She heard the murmur of moving water mix with the chatter of the shades around them. A river came into view. The river was not wide like the Styx. She could throw a stone across it. The water seemed normal. It was clear and not thick. There was a footbridge up the bank that led to the palace entrance. Ares headed for it.

"Wait."

"What?" He blinked when he looked at her, as if just now remembering that she was with him.

"What are we going to do once we cross over that bridge? What are we going to do when we see Hades? What is our *plan*?"

"I don't know." He looked around. "We get him to hand over Persephone."

"I know that sort of thing works for you," she said. "But I need to know why we're crossing this bridge. What's over there? What's inside the palace? Cerberus's puppies? Or worse?"

"I don't know what's in the palace." He took her hand. His strength and courage flowed into her. "I trust my instincts."

She nodded.

The palace was no more than twenty feet before them. Ruby looked up, but from this perspective the top of the palace was lost to infinity. She could barely see the two flags jutting out, black and white.

Shades crossed over the short bridge with them. They didn't mill around, like in the garden party, but went right into the palace with determination in their serious eyes. She was heartened by their lack of fear, but then she remembered that the dead had much less to worry about in this place than she did.

As if to punctuate the thought a scream came from beyond the arched entrance. Ruby's eyes flew to Ares. He scanned the area, his hand halfway to his sword. Ruby's heart beat wildly and her stomach tensed. She thought of the Brigand, and her bow. She reached for it, but Ares put a hand out to stop her.

He relaxed his stance and nodded to the shades around them. None of them had so much as looked up at the sound.

"What was it?" she asked.

He shook his head. "I don't know."

They walked toward the entrance behind a line of shades. Ruby stopped at the black wall of the palace and touched its cool surface. Now that she was closer she could see that it was slightly rippled. Not glass. Obsidian.

She pictured Hades, thin and gaunt, his black hair greasy. He was the guy you didn't want to share a seat with on the bus, the one that made you want to cross the street when you saw him coming. She felt sorry for Persephone, living in a black palace against her will with Hades for a husband and screams of terror ringing in the air. If they didn't have to save Persephone for the world and for themselves, surely they had to save her for her own sake.

Ares and Ruby passed through the archway and found themselves in a courtyard. In the middle sat three men on a dais, each in an ornate golden chair. A long line of shades stood before them, waiting.

Ruby was confused. Where were the torture devices, the monsters? Where was the source of the screams? *Where was Hades?*

She looked at the three men on their stage. The one in the middle sat in a chair raised higher above the others. He was older too, with gray hair, and deep lines drawn down with the loose skin of his face. He wore a large gold crown on his head.

The man to his right was handsome and vibrant-looking with black hair and a trimmed beard. He too wore a crown, an unadorned thin circlet of gold.

The last man's crown was platinum, like his hair. His was ornate, etched with scrolls and vines. His elbows rested on the arms of his chair. It was a throne, Ruby realized.

"Didn't I tell you I'd go to the gates of hell for you?" Ares said. It sounded like a joke, but his tone was grim.

"Didn't we pass the gate to hell a while back?" Her retort was hollow in her ears. Whatever this place was, it was serious.

"That's it." He nodded beyond the men. "That's the gate to Tartarus."

A black iron door was set into the obsidian at the back of the courtyard. There was a gruesome sculpture of a hanged man on its front. The man's head was nearly detached from his body by the noose he dangled from. The pain was evident on his face even from this distance. Iron crows pecked at his body from all directions. Metal rats chewed at his metal toes.

Ruby could now easily tell Hephaestus's work. She was fascinated by his ability to turn iron into something so grisly it made you feel sorry for the metal itself.

On the right side of the same wall was a gate opposite the entrance to Tartarus in every way. This one was golden, carved with a man in armor, a shield in one hand and a sword in the other. Rays of light emanated from him, golden threads stretching to the edges of the door. The soldier looked as though he might jump from the gate and rush into battle in all his golden glory.

There was an open corridor in the middle, between the two gates. Through it Ruby saw the same light that permeated all of Hades and more of the black palace walls.

"Where are we?" she whispered to Ares.

"This is where shades are judged. The three kings decide. The golden gate leads to the Elysian Plains. The black gate leads to Tartarus."

Now she understood the screams. They weren't the sounds of people being tortured or threatened. They were the sounds of people hearing their own eternal fate. The sound of souls being condemned to hell.

"The kings were alive once," Ares said. "The sons of Zeus and mortal women. Rulers of ancient cities long ago destroyed." He nodded at the black-haired king on the left, "Rhadamanthus." He motioned to the blond king on the right, "Aeacus." Lastly he pointed to the king in the middle. "Minos, though I've heard that most shades call him St. Peter; a reference from newer times."

Ruby smiled at the joke. "They're your brothers?" she asked, surprised to find yet another branch in his gnarled family tree.

"Yeah." He shrugged. "I guess."

A black man wearing a dark suit and holding a bible stood before the three kings. He looked back and forth between them. This obviously wasn't what he had expected. The kings looked at him for a quiet minute. The man stood straight and tall.

First the dark-haired king, Rhadamanthus, spoke in a voice that didn't carry beyond the group of waiting shades. "A good man. A shepherd of the people. A fighter for rights."

Aeacus nodded in agreement. His decorative crown dipped with the movement. "True to his convictions. Fearless."

Minos, the raised king in the middle, St. Peter, spoke last. "Elysian Plains."

The man nodded and walked to the golden gate as it swung open to let him pass. He disappeared into the golden light beyond.

The next soul walked forward. New shades came into the courtyard and joined the end of the line. Ruby scanned the faces. "John," she whispered to Ares.

"I see him, but we need to go beyond here." Ares pointed to the open archway between the two gates. "Behind the dais is the rest of Hades's palace. That's where we'll find Hades."

"Wait," she said as he started to pull her beyond the three kings. "I want to watch."

"Watch what? They'll be doing this all day, and tonight, and tomorrow."

"I want to see how John does." She didn't look at Ares, but watched the next shade being judged. He was sent back to the Fields of Asphodel.

After him was a man in his fifties or sixties, dressed in a light blue seersucker suit and white dress shoes.

Rhadamanthus pronounced him, "A man of the community. A healer. But a darkness lurks."

"He takes advantage." Aeacus added. "I hear children. They beg him to stop."

Ruby's eyes darted to St. Peter.

The grey-haired king looked at the man for a long time. The shade stood with his hands clasped behind him. The only movement was his middle finger tapping fast against his thumb.

Finally St. Peter spoke. "Tartarus," he said in a loud voice.

The man started to shake his head and mutter, "I didn't want to do it. I couldn't help myself." Soon he was shouting. "No. No. No!" His head quaked back and forth in fast little movements, as if he were trying to shake it free. His feet were rooted to the ground.

His sobs made Ruby feel sorry for him. She tried to think of what the kings had seen—the two sides of him—the doctor and the child molester. How could she pity him?

The gate to Tartarus swung open. The man's screams increased into unintelligible begging. He remained frozen to the spot in front of the kings.

Two shadows appeared out of the darkness and entered the courtyard. They surged toward the man and swirled around him like a rushing tornado. A low hum filled the courtyard. The man looked at the cloud in all directions, his face a mask of terror. He screamed and tried to ward the clouds off with his hands.

The shadows thickened and darkened until the man was cloaked in the blackness. It lifted him off the ground, swirled back through the gate, and was gone in the next instant.

Utter quiet replaced the howling winds and the screaming man. The shades waiting to be judged bounced nervously from one foot to the other. Their eyes shifted from face to face. The kings sat with blank looks and waited for the next in line.

It was John's turn. He stepped forward. Ruby held her breath. Rhadamanthus looked him over. "I see much suffering. For him and for those he loved."

"A man of poor means, but with an honorable heart," Aeacus said.

St. Peter made the final pronouncement. "The Fields of Asphodel."

John turned away from the kings with a big smile on his face. He caught Ruby's eye as he passed them. "Thank you, goddess."

Ruby tipped her head at him.

Aeacus spoke to the next shade in line, "Envy, and jealousy …"

"Okay, let's go," she said to Ares, who was only waiting for her cue.

They walked past the line of shades. No one looked in their direction as they moved beyond the kings' thrones and deeper into the courtyard. Ares made for the middle passageway, the Elysian Plains to the right, Tartarus to the left.

They passed through, into yet another open space. This second courtyard was long and narrow and more like a proper garden with trees and raised beds. It was quieter as well. A few shades walked around, but this seemed like a place of solitude.

A wide set of obsidian steps led up to the right. Ares climbed them without hesitation. The now-familiar begging, followed by a terrified scream trailed them up the stairs, but neither one looked back.

The stairs wound up and around to the second floor of Hades's Palace. It reminded Ruby of an abode on Olympus. The requisite precious metal statues stood in every corner, under exquisite paintings and finely woven tapestries. Open doorways led off the main hall all along its length. In one room Ruby saw a dining table, another was full of shelves of books, and still another housed a giant harp.

The hallway ended in more winding steps. Ares strode to them without looking around.

"Where are we going?" she asked.

"Up," he said. "The largest balcony is on the ninth level. The throne room will be there."

The palace zigzagged up and up. Every level consisted of a flight of stairs, a long hallway lined with rooms, and the next set of stairs. Gold filigreed windows were cut into the obsidian. They looked out over the Fields of Asphodel. The crowds below receded as Ruby and Ares climbed. At the higher windows Ruby saw the flowers and trees beyond the edge of the party. Only a few shades milled there.

By the time they reached the throne room Ruby's legs felt wooden. This level was not a long hallway like the others, but one great open room. At the far end, instead of another stairway, the large balcony looked out over the fields below.

Ruby and Ares stood next to a golden fireplace embossed with animals. A small replica of Cerberus stood on the mantel next to a plain metal helmet. Ruby jerked when she saw the tiny three-headed dog. More of Heph's work. How much could one artist produce if he had forever?

Two thrones sat in the middle of the room. They were carved from stone, one black, the other white. They reminded Ruby of chess pieces, the king and the queen. The white throne, which looked to be made of quartz, was empty. The black one held the king of the Underworld.

Hades sat motionless with a two-pronged spear lying across his knees. Ruby had not let herself think of what would happen if they actually found Hades. Now that she was looking at him, picking at the loose threads of his black robes, she felt pity for him.

"So you've come." He didn't look up. "I didn't know if you'd be brave enough." His dark eyes rose and fixed on Ruby. "Or dumb enough."

Ruby shivered under his dark gaze, the fear returning.

"A mortal, Ares? Really?"

"I'm not here to discuss my personal life with you," Ares said. Then, with all the authority of Olympus behind him, he added, "I'm here to bring Persephone back, in accordance with the ancient agreement struck between you and Demeter, under Zeus's great and wise guidance."

Hades let out a cold and humorless laugh. "There's been a new agreement. Also come down from on high, also under Zeus's *great* and *wise* guidance." The sarcasm was clear in his voice. "The new agreement, the new order, the new way—" His voice became louder with each phrase. "—is that she's *mine*. Always."

"Even Zeus doesn't have that authority." Ares said. "Especially when only one party was present. You can't seriously think he does."

"He's the king of the gods," Hades bellowed. "Absolute. All-powerful." His voice fell. "He does what he pleases." Hades returned to picking at his threads.

"What about Earth?" Ruby's voice sounded strangely calm to her. "What about the millions of people on Earth who'll starve if Demeter doesn't restore the seasons?"

"What do I care of the Earth?" He only glanced up for a moment. "Sure, we'll get busier here, I suppose." His eyes darted to the balcony that overlooked the Fields of Asphodel. "As for the seasons, that's not really my thing. Ask Demeter what her problem is. Ask her how *she* could let the Earth starve."

"Where's Persephone?" Ares demanded.

"You'll never find her." He didn't look up. "She's hidden. Deep and well."

"Aren't you afraid she'll hate you for doing this to her?" Ruby asked. "She must have come around to accepting her time here with you. You realize that you've probably ruined even that much now."

Hades's fingers stopped picking. He didn't look up or move. "I'll tell you what. I'll give you an hour."

Ruby's heart stopped. Was he going to help them?

"One hour," he repeated. "I assume it was your love, Ares, that made you do such a stupid thing as coming into *my* realm to steal *my* wife. I'll give you one hour to right this wrong and erase the insult. One hour to make it as if this never happened. Go back the way you came or go some other way. I don't care. Leave now, or I'll send every beast of the Underworld after you." He looked at them with these last words: "Leave now, or you never will."

Ruby felt the hate coming off of him. She wanted to take his advice. She wanted to turn and run back to Death Valley. She wanted to run and never stop.

"We'll find her, Hades," Ares said, his voice steady. "We'll find her, and we'll free her, one way or the other. You can choose to lose whatever love or kindness she may have for you." He paused. "Or you can help us. Let us tell her that you wanted to make this right."

"One hour," was Hades's only response. He reached to a stone table between the two thrones and flipped over an hourglass filled with red sand. The thin red line fell from the full end of the glass to the empty one.

Two creatures appeared by the door behind them. They had men's bodies, but lion's heads. They held long, iron-tipped spears and wore red and yellow tunics. They moved into the room toward Ruby and Ares.

Ruby screamed, but her shriek was interrupted by an evil chuckle. "Yes, you'd better leave, Ares, and soon," Hades said. "I don't think your girlfriend will like it here much longer."

Ruby's only focus now was on the lion men. Their golden manes shook slightly as they came toward them. Their six-inch canines were bared in dual snarls. The sound threatened to turn Ruby's legs to water.

Ares pulled his sword from its scabbard. Ruby grabbed clumsily for her bow.

The lion men circled, but kept their distance. Their intention was not to attack, but to get Ares and Ruby moving. It worked.

Ruby and Ares turned, keeping the lion men in front of them, and backed down the stairs. Ruby looked to Hades one last time before he was out of sight. He sat in his throne and picked at the threads of his robes as if none of this was happening. The red line of sand in the hourglass streamed down next to him.

The lion men didn't follow them down the stairs. When Ruby and Ares reached the next level Ruby began to run, half-blind with fear.

Ares grabbed her and held her back. "Don't panic," he said with that now familiar warrior look in his eyes. "It's time to dig deep. It's time to gather our courage and do what we came here to do."

She pictured the lion men waiting at the top of the stairs above them. They could walk down here and kill her in an instant if Hades told them to. She began to shake.

A tear rolled down her cheek, not because she was afraid of death, or even of an eternity as an undead captive here. Her tears were for being weak and scared when Ares was strong and brave.

He cupped her face and wiped her tears. His energy soothed her.

"I'm not going to live without you." He kissed her, as if to seal the deal, as if their love could make it true.

TWENTY·THREE

"HERE," A VOICE WHISPERED from a room near them. "I'm in here."

Ruby's and Ares's eyes met. They were on the bottom floor of the palace, near the entrance. Ruby's mind flashed to the horrible lion-men a few floors above them. Chimeras, Ares called them, immortal beings that were a combination of man and any manner of beasts.

Ares pulled Ruby behind him as he drew out his sword, but once in the room he lowered it and relaxed his shoulders. He looked back to Ruby and motioned her closer.

It was a dining room. The board was laid with silver bowls of fruit, platters of whole chickens, ducks, and roasts. There were bread boards with crusty loaves half-sliced and flagons of wine. Each of the twelve places was set for a multicourse meal.

Ruby's stomach growled. Cerberus had scarfed down the hardtack, the only thing Ruby could eat, with the Ambrosia

Bars and the coins for Charon. How many hours had it been since she had eaten?

A man sat alone near the head of the table. He was brawny with red hair and a red beard. He looked young and strong, but he sat motionless, as if he were stuck there. "I know where the queen is," he whispered.

Ares approached him, then stopped. "Pirithous?"

"I know where he's hidden her. You must find her. Bring her back to me." A tear stood in the corner of his eye.

"Where is she?" Ares demanded.

"*Tartarus.*" It came out as a moan. "Beautiful Persephone, imprisoned with those monsters." His jaw clenched. Ruby saw anger overtake his sadness. His eyes met Ares's. "You have to help her," he demanded.

Ruby stepped closer to the man and saw that he was lashed to the chair, not with ropes, but with snakes. Their scales were light brown with darker brown splotches running up their backs. They wound their way up and down his arms and legs. One of the snakes reared its head in her direction. She could see a horn on each side of its head, like a devil. The snake flicked its long tongue out at her. She recoiled.

"What happened to you?" she asked the man.

"Save her. Bring her back to me," was his only response. Ruby turned to Ares.

"It's Pirithous." There was little emotion in his voice. "A king foolish enough to fall in love with Hades's wife."

"She's my only joy in this place," he said. "And now she's gone."

"How do you know she's in Tartarus?" Ares asked.

"Hades told his guards to take her there. He said that Zeus commanded it. I think he forgets that I sit here, day and night. I may not be able to move my body, eat when I'm starving, or fight for the woman I love, but I can hear. Information is the only thing I can offer her."

"Does she love you?" Ruby asked, unable to stop her curiosity.

His face changed. "She might. She could have. She can never tell me if she does. *He* is with us all the time. They come to eat their supper while I starve, and then they leave. She can't look at me. He's too jealous."

"If you want to help her, come with us. Ares, cut him loose." She looked down at the snakes and wondered if Ares could kill them without cutting Pirithous.

Ares positioned his sword to saw at one of the snakes. "It won't work," Pirithous said. "Heracles himself tried to free me."

"I'm not Heracles." Ares bristled at the comparison to a mortal hero. He began to slice at the snake around Pirithous's arm. The serpent reared up its horned head and hissed. Ares's sword slid back and forth against the brown scales, but the snake remained uncut, even as the ground of Hades shook. Ares stopped cutting at the snakes. The tremor stopped too.

"He'll know you're here with me," Pirithous said. "You need to go. Hades told the guards to take her deep. You must find her."

Ares resheathed his sword.

"How can we leave him here like this?" Ruby asked.

"You have no choice," the former king commanded. "Save her for me. If I can at least see her. If only once a day. If only for part of the year. It's more than I have now. She's everything to me."

⁖⊙⊙⁖

"How will we get into Tartarus?" Ruby asked Ares as they came out into the open area of the garden courtyard. Ares didn't respond, but walked faster. She reached out and grabbed for his hand. "How can we get in?" she repeated. Anxiety had replaced the determination she was used to seeing on his face. "What's wrong?"

"I can't take you there," he said and headed in the direction of the Fields of Asphodel.

The vision of Tartarus returned to her. She swallowed the harsh memories down and focused on Ares. "You have to. *We* have to. There's no choice." She managed to pull hard enough on his arm so that he stopped walking.

"I can keep you safe *here*." He pointed down to the grassy floor of Hades. "Maybe." He paused. "I can fight off Chimeras, and even the god of the dead. But I can't say the same in Tartarus. We'll have to find another way."

"What other way? I can't go back to Olympus, Zeus will destroy me. We can't live on Earth. The planet and everyone there is dying. We can't stay here. Hades will send his guards after us." She tried to look into his eyes, but they searched around her, not making contact.

"What lies in Tartarus is worse than all of those things," he said. "I can't risk it."

"*I'll* risk it!" She almost yelled. "I absolve you of your responsibility for me. *I* assume the risk."

"I can't lose you." He shook his head.

"You want us to settle? Now?" A shot of fear went through her. It didn't seem like Ares. She caught her breath before it ran away from her.

"What happened to it being time to dig deep, to gather our courage and do what we came here to do?"

Ares didn't answer.

"If we stop now, I'll have to go back to Earth. You'll have to go back to Olympus. We'll be apart." She paused, but he said nothing. "I'd rather try and fail. I can live with that."

Again there was silence from him.

"I won't surrender," she said.

Ares flinched at the implication that he would.

Three guards came into the courtyard. Ares took Ruby's hand and led her toward the line of souls to be judged. They stood near the crowd. "Don't look at the guards," he said in a low voice.

She tried to look anywhere else, but the lion-men were magnets to her eyes.

Ares's focus was on the bald head of the shade in front of him. "We'll need Hades's helmet in Tartarus."

Ruby's pulse sped up. No, Ares wouldn't surrender either.

"The Helm of Darkness. I saw it on the mantle in the throne room. It makes the wearer invisible."

"How can we get it? Those guards ..." she glanced at the golden haired lion-men scanning the crowd and tried to control her rapid breathing.

"I'll go. You stay here."

"Wait—," she started to say, but he was already walking away.

෨ඔඬ

Ruby stood at the end of the line of shades and watched the judging. The souls were silent as the kings looked at them before their fates were pronounced. She wondered if there was a telepathic connection between them. The kings somehow saw deep inside each of them, to where their darkest secrets dwelt.

Sometimes the shades that passed her on the way back to the Fields of Asphodel had tears in their eyes. *Tears of relief?* Good and evil can be so hard to dissect. She wondered how she would fare when—no, if—she was ever in this line for real.

She thought she was good. She tried to be. There were times when she had struggled to do the right thing. Would raising money for the American Lung Association in tenth grade cancel out the time she had had a little too much to drink at a party and drove her dad's truck home anyway? She remembered waking up that next morning horrified by what she had done. She could have killed someone. But she hadn't, and no one would ever know.

The kings would know.

Every second Ruby waited she expected to hear a struggle from the palace, feel the floor of Hades shake, or see Ares in the custody of the Chimeras.

But it was just a normal day here in the Underworld. The only screams were from the occasional shade being carried off by the black cloud into Tartarus. Otherwise the show moved on with its play of judging, while Ruby waited to find out her own fate. The longer she waited, the worse the pronouncement seemed to be. What would she do if Ares didn't come back? How long should she wait before she went in after him?

She watched more guards move through the courtyard, scanning the line of souls. Was their time up already? Had the red sands slipped through the hourglass? It was impossible to tell if time were passing at all here. The shades ignored the guards. Ruby tried to do the same.

Most souls were sent back to the Fields of Asphodel. Not evil, not virtuous. Every time a soul was sent to Tartarus, Ruby looked on with new interest. She'd watch the swirling blackness envelop them with keener eyes. She tried to look past the open gate to get a glimpse of what lay beyond. Only dark.

A little girl of about six was being judged when something firm slid down Ruby's arm. Strong fingers entwined with hers. A warm body leaned in against her own and she could smell Ares's masculine scent.

Ares spoke into her ear, "Hey, beautiful."

She blinked as she looked at the empty space next to her.

"Neat trick, huh?" She could hear the smile in his voice and wished she could see it. "You're invisible now too. I made sure no one was looking when you disappeared."

She looked down. She could feel her feet standing on the ground but she couldn't see them.

An Asian man stood in front of them, waiting to be judged. She reached out and touched his back. He turned to look at what had poked him, but his eyes looked through her and then all around. He gave up and turned his attention toward the front of the line.

"Did you see Hades?" she whispered to Ares. "Did you run into any guards?" She was concerned that she couldn't *see* that he was alright.

"I had to dodge a few guards. Hades doesn't seem to be around."

She nodded, but stopped when she remembered that he couldn't see her. "How do we get in?" she asked.

"We wait near the gate. When it opens next time we'll go in before it can close again."

"Is there a guard? Will it, or they, or whatever it is, let us in?" *What kind of creature would guard the gate to Tartarus?*

"There's no guard," he said. "No one wants in."

They walked hand in hand, unseen, past the three kings, to the awful black gate. The sculpted hanged-man was twice the size of a person. Metal tendons stretched from his body to his nearly-severed head. She could almost hear the crows cawing as they pecked at his eyes. She felt sick and looked away.

They watched as soul after soul was turned back to the Fields of Asphodel. A nun made it into the Elysian Plains, then more average shades were judged.

"Where's an evil shade when you need one?" she whispered to Ares.

"One will come." He was serious.

Ruby looked down the line of souls. She tried to pick out which one it might be. The sixty-something guy wearing a motorcycle jacket? The young skinny kid with oddly few teeth? Or the old lady in a pink wool suit and pearls? If Ruby had learned anything from spending time in the courtyard, it was that you never really could tell.

The kings looked upon a youngish skinhead. Tattoos ran up his neck, and he had several piercings in his face. It didn't surprise her when they said in turn: "Bigotry." "Intolerance." "Hate." The final pronouncement: "Tartarus."

Ruby watched as the now familiar swirl of blackness came to claim his soul. The man stood still, without emotion. The usual screams and apologies were held deep within him, if they were there at all.

Ruby had no more time to wonder about him, though, as Ares moved them through the black gate to Tartarus. Panic rose in her chest, her breath stopped in her throat. She squeezed Ares's arm, still entwined with hers. He squeezed back.

The black cloud, with the man inside, swept past them. A cold wind chilled Ruby through. The gate to Tartarus swung shut behind them with a loud clang.

TWENTY·FOUR

ONLY A LITTLE LIGHT filtered in from the gate. It found its way in through cracks between the hanged man's feet and among the iron feathers of the crows.

The wind carrying the skinhead to his fate in Tartarus echoed down the long corridor in front of them. When the sound faded, the silence left a vacuum that was filled by darkness so complete it seemed like a being of its own.

Ruby didn't feel the hate and crushing depression she expected from the vision Athena had given her of Tartarus—maybe those feelings were specific to Kronos. She only felt Ares's arm entwined with hers, warm, solid, and real. He soon pulled away, though. She clutched at his hand, afraid to let him go.

"I'm not going anywhere," he said.

A soft yellow light bloomed around them as he lit the bronze torch. He took off the Helm of Darkness. She let out a sigh of relief. She had known he was there of course, had felt him and heard him, but she was glad to see him again.

"We should drink some water," she said.

He handed her one of the skins and she drank greedily. She was thirstier than she realized. The water filled her empty stomach, making her remember that she was hungry. She stopped drinking before her thirst was slaked and handed the skin back to Ares. He took a short drink and stuffed the skin down into his pack.

"Now we find her and get out of here as quickly as we can," he said.

"What do you know about this place?" Ruby asked. "Where do we go? How do we find her?"

"I don't know much. Tartarus is a place even the gods don't venture. As far as which way? It seems like down is our only choice."

She looked around in the dim light. They stood in a narrow passage cut out of the black rock. It was large enough for them to stand upright, but no more. There was only one passage and it led sharply down. *How much further down could there possibly be?*

Weakness washed over her. The water had only awakened her hunger. She knew Ares was hungry too, but he would not die from it. Even if he never ate again he would live on and on. At some point her body would begin to fail without food and rest. *What would be the first signs? Lightheadedness? Stumbling over her own feet?*

She concentrated on walking, each step moving them closer to whatever lay below. She tried not to think of her gnawing insides but there was little else to occupy her. She could have talked to Ares, distracted them both, but in Tartarus it seemed that silence ruled. She let it.

They continued down for what seemed like hours. Ruby felt a blister forming on her big toe from the constant downward pressure. Her eyes adjusted to the light, or lack of it, but there was nothing to look at but black rock. She was sure they had overstayed their welcome in Hades by now. They would be in danger whether they went up or down.

Ruby heard the faint sound of flowing water. The path leveled out and she could see better. An indistinct glow emanated from the right. She saw a river flowing beside the path. Dancing atop the water were orange and yellow flames.

"What is it?" she whispered.

"The Phlegethon. The River of Fire."

She turned her attention back to the trail, not wanting to think about why a river would be on fire. She let it flow into the background of her mind.

Instead she thought about when she and Ares would leave this place and go back home. *Home.* Her house on Earth. Ares's abode on Olympus. It all felt so far away, like a dream.

Ares stopped in front of her.

"What is it?" she asked.

"Time to choose," he said.

The path forked. One trail was larger and more worn than the other. Ares peered into the dimness down each. "We should take the larger one. We'll have better luck finding someone to ask about Persephone."

Ruby nodded but she thought that she'd rather take the path where there was no chance of meeting anyone down here.

They walked a few feet before they heard the first moans. Ares reached for his sword but by the time he had drawn it the passageway was silent again. They stood still with their ears bent toward where the sound had come from. They heard it again: distant, one voice, and then another, then many.

Ruby withdrew her silver bow, now steady in her hand, and nocked an arrow. They continued on, cautiously, their weapons at the ready.

The unrelenting cries came and went like waves in the ocean, steadily getting louder, getting closer.

Ruby scanned the uniformly dark walls in the dim light.

Ares stopped short. He wobbled and stuck his hands out to the sides to steady himself. He had stopped with his toes over the edge of a round hole in the floor. He lowered the torch and they peered inside, into the darkness, into the silence.

Ruby squinted, trying to make out any features. Nothing. Then the familiar cries rose from below. Ares moved the torch lower, the flames dangerously close to his forearm.

Ruby pulled back in surprise and horror. It was a deep pit, an oubliette, full of shades. They were so crowded together they had to stand with their arms packed tightly against one another. The shades stood in knee-deep water, but they were wet from head to toe. The water level began to rise, and the shouts started.

Ruby gasped.

A soul looked up and saw her. The rest looked too.

Ruby could see the desperation in their half-crazed eyes. They were shouting up at her and Ares.

"Help me!"

"God no."

"I can't breathe."

The oubliette continued to fill with water and as the water rose, the shouts rose too. Then silence. Ruby's hand came up over her mouth. She could see the faces, now covered by water, their eyes wide with panic. "Oh my god, we have to help them."

She looked at Ares, but he didn't respond. "We have to help them," she repeated. Her fingers trembled against her lips. Her bow was limp at her side.

The water receded again. As the souls' heads cleared the water line she heard frantic gasps, followed once more by sobs and pleas for help. She turned back to Ares, looking for an answer. But he only shook his head.

"We can't help them," he said. "This is their fate. Whatever their crimes were in life, this is their punishment now."

"To be drowned again and again? What could their crimes have been?"

"I don't know." He looked at her again and something in his eyes made her feel that maybe he did know. He shrugged. "Torture?"

"Torturers?" She looked into the oubliette, at the screaming souls. The water rose again. "Like, medieval torture?" It occurred to her that these souls could have been here drowning in this pit for hundreds, even thousands of years.

"There are ways to torture people without using thumb-screws," he said. "Their real punishment is the same as any-one's in Tartarus. Knowing that their suffering will never end, and worse, that they have no one to blame but themselves."

Ares stood and walked around the pit to continue on the path.

Ruby followed.

They walked slower, now aware there were dangers in the floor.

Ruby's thoughts turned to dark matters—life, death, wick-edness, and punishment. She was lost in these contemplations when Ares put his hand on her arm to stop her. It wasn't until she looked up at him that she saw a brighter light burning be-yond the flaming river, on the far side.

A large alcove had been carved into the rock across the burning river. In the alcove was a long steep hill that rose par-allel to the water. About halfway up was a man in dirty rags that might have once been white. The man's shoulder was pressed against a round rock the size of a Volkswagen Beetle. He grunted and pushed at the rock with his full weight behind him. His face glistened in the light of the torches set in sconc-es along the alcove as the rock scraped up the hill.

When the boulder finally rested at the small flat space at the top of the ramp the man straightened himself. His hand pressed into his lower back. He leaned against the wall and wiped his brow with the back of his arm.

The boulder teetered on the edge of the landing, and then began to roll back to the bottom. The man made no move to stop it. The stone hit the far side of the ramp with a deep, heavy boom.

Ares cupped his hands around his mouth. "Sisyphus," he shouted across the wide, slow moving water and its flames.

The man turned in tired surprise. "Ares," he said. His inflection was flat as he walked down the hill toward the gigantic boulder.

Ruby knew who Sisyphus was. She hadn't read the story on Olympus, or even learned about it in her myth class. She remembered it from childhood: the man condemned to roll a rock up a hill only to have it slide back down again, on and on into eternity.

She wasn't surprised Ares knew him, but she was surprised that Sisyphus would so easily dismiss the god of war.

She watched as Sisyphus walked around the boulder, got close to it, touched it, and then stepped away again. He clenched and unclenched his hands. A moment later his shoulder was pressed to the great stone again with his body driving it forward.

"Sisyphus," Ares shouted again.

The man looked in their direction but continued with his task. "I'm busy," he yelled.

"We're looking for Persephone. Have you seen her?"

"I don't look around much, warlord. The view has always been the same. If you don't mind, I have work to do."

"Zeus commands that you tell me. Your punishment can still be improved."

Ruby stared at him, shocked by his bold-faced lie, but Ares kept continual eye contact with Sisyphus.

"I told you. I don't see anything." Sisyphus paused halfway up the hill. He stood straight and let the boulder slam against the far wall again. "But I do see you have a lovely young shade there with you." He looked at Ruby. His eyes lingered.

His hair was a filthy tangle and he had a long scraggly beard, but he walked toward the edge of the river with the swagger of the hottest stud in the bar.

"How about this—you send the pretty little shade across to me, and I'll tell you what, if anything, I know about a certain fair goddess being led away into the dark pit of Tartarus."

Ruby saw the tendons and muscles in Ares neck strain. "You don't want her," he said without a glance at Ruby.

"Oh, but I do." The king in tattered robes leered at Ruby.

"She would be … *missed*," Ares said. "If you get my meaning."

Sisyphus turned back to his rock. His hand reached out to touch it. He looked at Ares again. "Well, I need a trade. Few people of means come by this way. I have seen Persephone, but what can you offer me to tell you which way she went— and with *whom*? You'll want to know with whom, trust me there." He smiled a brown-gray smile that made Ruby's empty stomach pitch.

"We have water. From Olympus." Ares said it with the crafty voice of a street hawker.

"Good. Very good." Sisyphus turned back toward them. "What else?"

Ares's breathed out in frustration. They couldn't afford to give Sisyphus anything. They barely had what they needed for themselves.

"An olive branch," Ruby said before the thought was fully formed in her mind. Both men looked at her, surprised.

"An olive branch?" Sisyphus repeated as if he were dealing with a demented child.

"From Athena's garden. From *The* Olive Tree. Grown from the will of a goddess and raised in the sun and rain of Olympus. It's enchanted. It will never die." She had no idea why an arrogant king from two millennia ago would want such a thing, but it was all they had.

Sisyphus's gaze fell to the endless black water of the fiery river. Ruby took the branch out of the leather purse that hung from her waist. She had put it there when she thought she was going back to Earth with Helios. It was still as perfect as the day Athena had cut it from her olive tree. Its silvery green leaves were lush. Its flawless white flowers were still delicate and slightly fragrant.

Sisyphus's face went slack. He looked across, not to Ruby, but to the branch she held out in her palm. She bent toward the water. A smiled curved at the edge of Sisyphus's mouth.

"Where'd they take her?" Ruby's voice was soft as she leaned forward, poised to send this precious gift across the black water to this king she did not like. "Who was she with?"

"That way." He tilted his head in the direction they had been headed. "She's hidden deep. Aegaeon was with her."

"How was she?" Ruby asked.

He took his eyes from the olive branch and looked at her. "The queen of the Underworld commands a certain level of respect, even from the foulest monster of Tartarus. Whoever's hiding her must care for her, even if they would condemn her to this place, or else they would have sent her with Cottus."

"How long ago?" Ares asked.

"I can't say. I may have rolled the boulder ten times or a thousand since then. No one will ever know."

Ruby dropped the branch into the black, slow-moving water. Sisyphus watched it as it floated to him, untouched by the flames. He picked it out of the water and held it in his cupped hands. He turned from them as if they no longer existed.

Ares started up the path again, untouched by the humanness of wanting to see something beautiful, to hold it, to own it.

Ruby allowed herself a glance back. Sisyphus placed the olive branch on the ground where he could see it. His shoulder once again pressed to his labor. The boulder rolled and scraped its way up the slope. Not one thing had changed since they came upon him, except for the faraway look in Sisyphus's eyes.

"We have to put on the helmet," Ares said, as soon as they had gone around the next bend.

"It'll slow us down," Ruby said.

"Aegaeon is no one we want to meet without at least the element of surprise." He pulled the dark metal helmet from his pack while Ruby held the torch.

"Who are they? Aegaeon and Cottus?"

"They're more whats than whos." He shrugged the pack into position on his back.

She swallowed. "Okay, *what* are they, then?"

"Hecatonchires. Giants with fifty heads and one hundred arms."

"Huh? What does that even look like?"

"I hope you'll never have to find out. If we do run into them, hiding is our best option, though it's almost impossible to escape their fifty sets of eyes. They have immense strength, they could easily crush both of us, and they can wield a weapon in each of their one hundred hands."

Ruby felt the blood drain from her already nutrient-starved brain. She felt faint. The creatures themselves sounded horrible, but it was Ares's wanting to hide instead of fight that really frightened her.

"And there are two of them?" she managed to ask.

"Three." His blue eyes were dark in the dimness of Tartarus. "Aegaeon, Cottus, and Gyges. We need to be under the Helm of Darkness. We need to put out the torch. There's enough light from the river to see if we're careful."

"Why did Sisyphus say Persephone was lucky they didn't send Cottus?" Her head was pounding.

"He has the worst temper. Cottus the Furious they call him."

"And Aegaeon?" Somehow she knew it wouldn't be Aegaeon the Amiable.

"Aegaeon the Vigorous. The third brother is Gyges the Big Limbed. They have no quarrel with me or any other gods. We fought together in the Great War to overthrow the Titans, but if Hades has commanded them to guard Persephone, they won't back down from their task.

Ares put on Hades's helmet and disappeared. Even though she knew he was still standing there, the thought of being in that place without him scared her. The torch winked out and she jumped.

ॐ

Dim light came from branching paths along the way, but Ruby and Ares stuck to the main. A wet dankness permeated the air and occasional screams or moans came down the passageways to them. Mostly they ignored them, arm in arm, invisible.

More shades, enduring their eternal punishments, were stationed along the path. Some were alone, others were in groups or pairs. One pair was in the middle of the path. The first shade stood on the head and shoulders of the other and reached for a golden ring. The shade beneath then threw off the first. The shade lay on the rocky ground, bleeding and bruised. He got up, and was climbed on by the shade that had thrown him off. The second shade then reached in vain for that same elusive treasure.

Ruby and Ares skirted around them. Ruby's foot hit a stone that thudded against the side wall of the passage, but neither shade looked up. They only wanted the treasure.

Later, Ruby was lost in thought when movement on the river caught her eye. She turned to see a man chained to an island of rock in the middle of the flames. Ares slowed and removed the Helm of Darkness, making them visible again.

The man on the rock took no notice. His attention was focused on a cluster of grapes above him. He reached up, straining his body as far as he could, and almost touched them. He couldn't reach though, and he fell away from the effort.

He gave up trying to reach the grapes and instead bent to drink from the river. As he stretched down with his cupped hands the water receded out of his grasp. He soon gave up and returned to reaching for the grapes above.

Ruby could relate to this torture more than the others. Touching Ares gave her strength and dulled her hunger. But now she looked to the juicy red grapes hanging from the large leafed vines above, and her stomach growled. She wished again for the hardtack Cerberus had eaten. She looked away from the grapes and caught sight of the water. She imagined drinking the whole river.

"Tantalus," Ares yelled.

The man looked up and then stood. He peered across the river.

"Where is Persephone?" Ares shouted.

"Oh! Ares!" Tantalus was unsteady on his feet. His voice shook with relief. "Can you help me?" He pointed to the grapes. "I just need a boost. Then I'll be able to reach them."

"Persephone," Ares repeated. "Have you seen her?"

"I think if you lace your hands together I can stand in them to reach. I only need an inch or two."

"Did you see Aegaeon?" Ares tried a different tack.

"And the water," Tantalus kneeled down, also approaching the conversation anew. "Do you have a cup?"

Ares looked at the half-crazed man for a long minute. His knees were scraped and bloody from reaching for water he could never get.

"Let's go," Ares said, as he replaced Hades's helmet on his head. His bodiless voice finished his thought, "He can't help us."

Ruby glanced back to the starving man. She locked her arm with Ares's and disappeared.

"No! Help me!" Tantalus screamed. "They're right *there*. I can get them."

But they were already gone.

෧ඛඔ

The occupants of Tartarus were clustered closer together now. The river flowed away behind the rocks. It was darker and the going was slower.

Soon after leaving Tantalus, Ruby and Ares came upon a row of shadowy cells carved into the rock. Black metal bars made up the front of each cell. There were no doors. Ruby shivered when she saw them. It was colder here and something, maybe the darkness, or the foul smell, made her want to pass by quickly.

Ares quickened their pace, as if he had read her mind.

Her heart beat faster with each step. Her breath came quicker. The passage narrowed where the rocks jutted out. There was a cell on each side of the constricted path. Ruby's head pounded. She wanted, she *needed*, to be past this place.

Ruby thought they were through the narrow spot when a hand shot out from between the bars and grabbed her invisible arm, jerking her back. Pain and surprise made her yelp. Ares pulled her toward him, away from the bars of the cell. The attacker's grip did not give and she felt like she was being ripped apart.

"A human," a husky voice said, like a starved man who'd stumbled into a feast.

She continued to fight, trying to pull away, but his grip was too strong. Ares held her with one hand as he reached for his sword with the other. Before he could get it, the voice, now full of command and authority, said, "Don't try it, *boy.*"

Ruby was shocked and twice as frightened. Even people who didn't know Ares as the god of war would never speak to him that way. His sheer physical presence forbade that.

Ares pulled away. He let go of Ruby's arm. She was visible again. "And a pretty one," the voice sneered.

Ares took off Hades's helmet and drew his sword. "Who are you?" he demanded. His blade was poised above the wrinkled and gnarled arm that held Ruby.

"Come closer. Bring your light." Ruby could hear the sounds of other shades, if that's what they were, moving in their cells to have a look.

Ares lit the torch and moved in closer.

In slow motion Ruby saw the flame cast its light one inch at a time: black bars with flaking patches of rust, broken sandals and dirty feet, skinny white legs, then the hem of dirty and tattered golden robes. A filthy belt was tied at the waist and hung down to the man's knees. He was dressed like an Olympian, but dirty and ragged. When the light reached his face Ruby saw that his features were strong; commanding, even. He looked to be sixty or so. Sky blue eyes, dirty gray hair and beard.

In the dim light she saw Ares's jaw tighten. "Kronos."

"Grandson," Kronos said with feigned emotion.

Ruby began to shake, but neither Ares nor Kronos noticed.

This place *was* familiar, from the vision Athena had given her. The rank smell, the cold, and the darkness mixed with the flickering light from the fiery river Phlegethon in the distance. And she knew how Kronos felt. She had felt the consuming hate, and the bottomless despair. The desire for revenge.

Zeus had indeed sunk the Titans deep in Tartarus: the only prison strong enough, and cruel enough, for his greatest enemies. And now the king of the Titans held Ruby's arm painfully against the bars of that prison.

"We have no quarrel with you, Kronos. Or any of you." Ares eyes glanced to the other Titans, now looking through the bars of their own cells that lined the narrow passageway. "Let her go and we'll move on."

"You may have no quarrel with us, but we have not forgotten your deeds, Ares. In fact we've had quite a lot of time to think on them." The oiliness of his voice, mixed with the authority it assumed, made Ruby's legs shake. Even with him on one side of the bars and her on the other, she felt like he had all the power.

"I have no quarrel," Ares repeated.

Kronos laughed a cold, hearty laugh. "Ares, you've changed," he said. "You used to have nothing but quarrels. Has the god of war become a sap? A sucker?"

Ares didn't take the bait.

"And why would you bring such a lovely treasure to such an abysmal place? It's not the way to win a girl's heart, Ares. Surely your father taught you something about winning with the girls."

"Zeus and Hades have taken Persephone. We've come to rescue her. My father's overstepped his bounds."

Yes, Ruby thought. *Get him to be on our side, against his old enemies: his children, Zeus and Hades.*

Kronos perked up. "Trouble topside, eh?"

"You know how Zeus is." Ares left it at that.

"Yes." Kronos's grip on Ruby's arm slackened, just a bit. She felt the blood returning to her skin. She didn't breathe and hoped he might forget about her altogether.

"Have you seen her?" Ares asked.

"Oh, yes. I saw her. Beautiful girl. Just lovely." Ruby wondered if Zeus had inherited his wandering eye from dear old dad. "Aegaeon was with her. No time to talk, though. All business."

"Did they go this way?" Ares asked.

"Yes," he hissed. "Follow them. Rescue the girl and show Zeus he's not all-powerful. He's king in name only, sitting on a stolen throne." Kronos's blue eyes shone bright in the torch light.

"Let's go," Ares said to Ruby, now pulling her away.

Ruby, to her great relief, felt Kronos's grip continue to loosen. Her arm slipped through his grasp until her small hand was in his larger one. Then he tightened his fist and pulled her close again. She saw him glance at something on her hand. Ares's ring.

Kronos sneered.

Ruby's heart, already pounding, quickened to a dangerous pace. Panic engulfed her throat.

Kronos's blue eyes blazed. He held her tight and began to chant, "Bazagra berebescu bescu gen paid areo peira part apat alg anade tropa aiti neo basil bescu berebescu bazagra."

She stared at Kronos, unable to look away.

Ares pulled Ruby from the other side, but it was useless, Kronos's power was too great.

She couldn't tell how long he held her that way, when he suddenly let go. She and Ares tumbled across the passage and into the hard iron bars on the far side. They both grunted from the force.

A hand came out and stroked Ruby's cheek. Her voice, which had been frozen in her throat, broke free and she screamed. Her heart pulsed through her body, beating like a jackhammer. Her shaking muscles nearly convulsed in panic.

Ares grabbed for her. He pulled her up in a run. Hands reached out from the bars of the cells as they passed. Voices repeated the same strange chant Kronos had said.

Kronos called out after them, "A human girl who wears Ares's ring. The downfall of the Olympians is close."

They ran on and on, long after the dim lights next to the cells had faded.

Ruby could not stop shuddering.

Ares pulled her close, holding her together with the strength of his body. His energy soothed her.

When the tremors abated, he looked at her. She burst into tears. He pulled her in again. "My love. My love," he said over and over, holding her, his hands in her hair, his cheek resting on her head, as she cried and cried.

When she found her voice again it was thin and choked. "What was it?"

Ares didn't answer, but continued to hold her. His silence scared her more.

"What did he do to me?" She felt no different, but she knew Kronos's chants meant something.

Ares let out a slow breath. She pulled away and looked up at him. "What?"

He shook his head. "Nothing. He has no power."

But it had felt powerful, and Ruby wasn't so sure. "What did he *try* to do to me?" Her voice shook.

"It's not important." He looked into her eyes. "Let's go. The Titans are held deep in Tartarus. I'm sure we'll find Persephone soon."

"You have to tell me." She found her courage. "What was that chant about? Did he curse me or something?" She sputtered out a laugh, high in her throat, nervous.

He looked at her for a long time, concern in his blue eyes "He ... *suggested,*" Ares started and then stopped. He took a deep breath. "He said that you would bear a son." He hesitated. "*My* son. A son to overthrow the gods, and rule over them."

"Like his son did," she said. Kronos had overthrown his father, and Kronos's son, Zeus, had overthrown him. "He cursed me to bear the son of a god, who would someday overthrow the gods?" It wasn't really a question.

"It means nothing. Kronos swallowed his children whole to prevent them from overthrowing him. We'll be better parents than that. I promise." He smiled, but Ruby couldn't smile back.

"Can we remove it, somehow?"

"Ruby. *Please* don't worry about this. We have to concentrate on Persephone and on getting ourselves out of here."

He was right, and the reminder of why they were here, what they were doing, and the danger they were in brought her up to the present moment.

Kronos's curse would have to wait.

TWENTY•FIVE

FEW PATHS BRANCHED OFF of the main one now. It was narrower here, with more twists and turns, and darker too. The fiery river had not come back into view.

She and Ares stayed beneath the Helm of Darkness, invisible. They did not dare light Eros's torch. The light might draw the Hecatonchires. The dark and the curves in the path made the going slower. Ares stopped often to peer around a corner. Their stealth would be pointless if a fifty-headed monster came barreling around the bend.

They rounded a turn and saw light ahead. It made Ruby nervous. She had begun to equate light with the punishments of the Underworld. There was no hiding in the dark. Not in Tartarus. Only the Titans were kept in the shadows.

The passageway opened up ahead. She held fast to Ares's arm and tried to pique her wounded courage.

They approached at a measured pace and maneuvered into a small recess in the rock where they could stay at a distance and still see into the cavern to assess what lay ahead. Torches illuminated the space. There was a lone cell door in the far wall. It was open. A brown-haired goddess in a pink peplos sat outside the cell at a small table. Persephone.

Ruby's heart stopped cold when she saw the implausible creature that sat opposite the queen of the Underworld. He was enormous. A true giant. His broad shoulders sported a thick, muscular neck the size of a tree trunk, which in turn supported smaller branching necks leading to the creature's many, many heads. Ares had said fifty and Ruby didn't need to count them to believe it. *How can we get past a creature with one hundred eyes, one hundred ears, and fifty noses? Are all his senses multiplied by fifty?*

He wore a metal breastplate over rustic brown clothes. There were an unknown number of swords, knives, and other weapons hanging from a leather belt around his generous middle, an easy reach for any of his one hundred hands.

Persephone's face was serene. Her hands were behind her back. One set of the giant's hands was also hidden behind his massive back. Persephone looked at the monster and smiled.

Ruby flinched. *How can she smile?*

"Go!" the goddess said, as if to start a race.

Both the Hecatonchire and Persephone threw their two hands around to the front of them. They each spread out a different number of fingers on their hands. Persephone looked up at the giant as he looked down to their splayed out fingers.

"Seven," the giant boomed. "I win!"

"Are you sure?" the goddess's voice was playful.

"I'm sure. See." The giant stuck out the pointer finger from another of his one hundred hands and began to count his fingers. "One, two, three…"

When he got to seven Persephone laughed. "You got me again."

"Let's play more," the giant said and they each drew their hands behind their backs again.

Ruby and Ares backed up the small passageway and out of sight. Ares removed Hades's helmet and held it in his hands.

"How can we fight him?" Ruby whispered. Even Ares could not battle such a creature with only one sword, and all six of her arrows would not be enough to stop him.

"That's Aegaeon. He's the slowest of the three brothers. They aren't terribly bright in general, even with all those heads. Some are just tangles of neuron bundles, not even brains. The heads that do have brains tend to confuse each other. Hecatonchires take orders well, but they can't think clearly on their own."

Ruby tried to make sense of all those heads and all those brains, but her fear was clouding her own. Animalistic grunts and heavy footfalls echoed toward them from up the passageway, a loud thudding that reminded her of a locomotive's massive pistons hitting down and down.

Ares shoved the helmet on his head and pulled Ruby close on top of him, flat against the rock. As he did, two more of the giant beasts came into view. The ground shook beneath them as they ran right for Ares and Ruby.

First one, and then another of the huge creatures passed by, almost crushing them against the wall. Their unwashed scent caught up in the air drafts created by their movement.

Ruby choked and felt a tickle rise into her throat. She stifled it as best she could, but it remained on the edge. She gripped Ares's hand.

He took it as fear and squeezed back.

The Hecatonchires reached the cavern where their brother and Persephone sat, both with their hands behind their backs.

"Put her in the cell," their many voices yelled in unison.

"But we're playing Morra. And I'm winning," Aegaeon complained.

"You fool, she's letting you win."

"She wouldn't trick me." For all his height and brutish looks, he sounded like a wounded five-year-old.

"Put her back. Hades has summoned us to the Fields of Asphodel. Ares is here." Ruby's heart jumped into her throat, bumping the cough that still sat there. "And he's brought a *human* with him."

The second brother laughed; fifty laughs at once. "Hades promised her body to whoever finds and kills her."

Ruby shuddered. Ares tightened his grip on her. She had known she was in danger coming here, but she never imagined that she would be a prize for the monsters of the Underworld.

"We're going. Stay here," a chorus of heads said. "Guard the queen. Ares might even be in Tartarus."

"But I want the human, too," Aegaeon protested.

"We'll split her with you," the other brothers said as a compromise.

Ruby heard the metal clang of a cell door shutting closed. If the queen of the Underworld said anything Ruby couldn't make it out. The two Hecatonchire brothers passed by Ares and Ruby again, almost running them over in the small recess. Their stench revived the cough that persisted in Ruby's throat.

Ares lifted off the helmet. He drew her in and whispered, "I'm so sorry. I should never have brought you here."

She shook her head and pulled away. She felt the cough rising into her throat and tried to swallow it down.

"Now that Persephone's in her cell, I have to reassess," he said. The calculating warrior look returned to his eyes.

"There must be a key," Ruby croaked and fought her working throat. The cough was closer to the surface with each word. She tried to remember back to the cells that held the Titans, but they didn't even have doors, let alone keys. Her eyes filled with tears as she fought against her body, but in the next moment the cough overtook her in a loud fit.

A memory flashed into her mind at the sound, random and important at the same time. Ares telling her about gods, and immortality, and strong chemical bonds: *It's how I can heal from a mortal wound in a one night. It's why immortals never get sick, or cough, or even sneeze.*

The only being in the Underworld who would cough was a human.

Her eyes went wide. She heard the pounding boots of Aegaeon coming their way. Ares shoved Hades's helmet on her head.

He drew his sword and ran up the passageway. "I'll find you," he yelled as the giant sped past her, close on Ares's heels. Her heart almost burst with fear and love at the same time.

Ruby sat in the quiet they left behind, still stunned. Then her wits came back to her. *Persephone!* She was no longer guarded.

Ruby ran into the cavern. The goddess stood near the bars of her cell. She stared at where the Hecatonchire had run out. Ruby remembered that she was invisible and removed the Helm of Darkness.

Persephone's hazel eyes bulged, then darkened with fear. "Are you Ares's human? You have to get out of here. The Hecatonchires are after you. Everyone is. Hades has …"

"I know. We have to hurry. Where's the key?" She scanned the door for a keyhole but she didn't see one.

"The key?"

"Yes. The key. To open the door."

"There's no key. Ask to free me."

"Ask who?" Ruby said. Why was Persephone being vague? She thought of those old movies where the big metal key hung on a hook right next to the cell door. Why couldn't it be like that?

"Just ask," Persephone insisted.

"Release Persephone," Ruby said, absently, as she continued to scan the grey walls for some help.

"You have to mean it."

Ruby couldn't squelch her irritation any longer. "Open the damn door!" she yelled.

A creature appeared between her and the cell. Another Chimera. Ruby stepped back in surprise. The creature had a woman's face, a lion's body, and the wings of a bird. She sat with a serene expression as a scorpion's stinger waved behind her at the end of her tail.

"Don't worry. She's a Sphinx," Persephone said. "Solve her riddle and the door will open."

"The riddle of the Sphinx?" Ruby knew that one. Everyone did.

"One of them," Persephone said. "It changes every time. You only get one chance to answer."

"What if I get it wrong?"

Persephone didn't hesitate. "She'll eat you."

"Great." Ruby let out a pent up breath she hadn't realized she'd been holding. "Can I worry now?"

"What?" Persephone cocked her head at Ruby.

"Never mind."

The Sphinx had long black hair. Her black eyes shone like marbles. Her skin was a rich dark brown that became covered with fine golden fur just past her collarbones. Her lion body was sleek and powerful looking with huge golden wings that attached near her ribs. Even the scorpion tail moved gracefully. Ruby didn't doubt that it would find its mark if the time came. She swallowed the thought and remembered Ares running away, drawing the danger toward himself to save her.

She had to be brave.

"What's your riddle?" she asked. Her voice sounded far away, like her ears had already distanced themselves from all of this.

To Ruby's shock, a chess board appeared in front of her. It hovered in the air about four feet off the floor. It was made of light grey and brown stone. It was obviously old, much older that Ares's marble set. The chessmen were only vague forms of modern chess pieces. The stone wasn't polished except in the spots where fingers had held the pieces over the millennia and had worn the rough stone smooth.

The board was not set up for a new game. It was already in play. Grey only had five pieces left: a couple of pawns, a bishop, the queen, and the king. Brown was only slightly better off with seven, less valuable, pieces: five pawns, a rook, and the king.

This was the riddle? It was the Sphynx chess problem? It was known as one of the most difficult endgames in the world.

"Grey plays first," the Sphinx said. "Mate in eleven or less."

Ruby breathed in a shuddering breath and slowly exhaled. *Checkmate in eleven moves or less? The Sphynx? The hardest chess problem in the world? "Trust your instincts,"* she heard Ares's voice in her mind.

She looked at the board and tried to see what her best move was in this endgame of life and death. She had fewer pieces than the Sphinx. Her first instinct was to protect her material and see if she could wait the Sphinx out. Maybe the Sphinx would sense Ruby's fear and make bold, stupid moves. Ruby could take advantage of her confidence. But the Sphinx would only see Ruby's fear if she allowed her to see it. Yes, Ruby had fewer pieces, but they were more valuable. They could move more freely. Ruby could be offensive.

Ruby moved her grey queen to the left side of the board and immediately put the Sphinx's king in check.

The Chimera's face remained serene. The Sphinx had lion paws, not hands. Ruby wondered how the Sphinx would move her piece when she saw the brown rook, the only valuable piece the Sphinx had besides her king, move of its own accord to block the check.

Ruby swallowed. It seemed the Sphinx wouldn't be intimidated.

Ruby could feel beads of sweat forming on her forehead. If she ever needed Ares, it was now. Not for his strength, or his sword, or his thousands of years of experience on the battlefield. His formidable knowledge of chess would have been nice, but what she really needed was his unwavering belief in her.

Ruby licked her dry lips and tried not to think of the scorpion tail that waved lazily in the air behind the Sphinx. She moved her bishop close to the Sphinx's king, but out of reach of being taken.

The brown lump that served as the Sphinx's pawn moved into position to take Ruby's rook. Ruby couldn't afford to lose the rook, but she couldn't let the Sphinx bully her either. She ignored the threat and moved her bishop again.

Instead of taking the rook the Sphinx moved her pawn to put Ruby's king in check.

Ruby inhaled sharply. She had been worrying about the rook and hadn't seen the threat coming. She wasn't in any real danger, she simply took the pawn with her king, but it was a stupid oversight that could have cost her everything.

The Sphinx moved a different pawn that was outside of the main action of the game. It was a throwaway move. A move made to get a sense of your opponent's strategy.

Ruby scanned the board and wondered if she had missed something else. Her eyes stopped short on the Sphinx's brown rook. Ruby had been trying to win in eleven moves or less, now she could see a way to win in the next two. She didn't want to be overconfident. She couldn't afford to be wrong.

Ruby moved her queen to the eighth rank, the last row, and put the Sphinx in check again.

The Sphinx's rook began to move to protect the king. Ruby's heart leapt in her chest. She might have made a sound; blood was rushing in her ears and she couldn't tell, but something had caused the Sphinx to look up at her suddenly.

The rook stopped halfway to the eighth rank.

Was the Sphinx trying to change her move? Once a chess piece was touched the player had to move it. Did that extend to telepathic chess too?

The stalled rook moved toward the last row again.

Ruby moved her queen to take the rook. A small dry sob of relief escaped her.

"Checkmate."

TWENTY•SIX

THE SPHINX VANISHED like vapor. The cell door swung opened and Persephone rushed out.

Ruby's sense of relief at freeing Persephone vanished as she looked around them. The cavern was a dead end. The only way to go was the way Ruby and Ares had come. But what lay back that way? Ares, yes, but also the Hecatonchires and whatever else Hades may have sent down here to find them.

"I'm Ruby. Take my hand," she said to Persephone. "The Helm of Darkness will work for both of us if we're touching." Ruby held out her free hand, but Persephone just looked at her with her deep amber eyes.

"Where did you get Hades's helmet?" the goddess asked, a touch of possessiveness in her voice.

"Uh ..." Ruby hesitated. "We had to borrow it."

"I see," Persephone said with a scowl. She looked away, down the tunnel. "It was Ares that Aegaeon chased?"

"Yes."

"Where are we going? Where are you to meet him?"

"There was no time to decide on a place," Ruby's hand was still outstretched to the goddess. "He said he'd find me."

Persephone nodded and put her hand in Ruby's at last.

They had to work harder at walking together in the passageways. She and Persephone weren't as in sync as she and Ares had been. And Persephone didn't seem to be concerned with being quiet either.

"Why did you come?" the goddess asked.

"Why?" Ruby was surprised. There was no thank you, no relief in her voice. "To save you. And … Demeter won't let spring come without you."

"Your wedding to Ares. It's in the spring?"

Ruby was surprised Persephone knew anything about it. She didn't have a sense of what news from Olympus reached the Underworld.

"Zeus tricked us," Ruby said. "He tricked everyone. He's the one who told Hades to keep you in the Underworld. He did it so that spring, and the wedding, would never come."

"Zeus." Persephone *tsk*ed. "He does hold a lot of sway over Hades. Hades told me of Zeus's new plan, for me to stay in the Underworld all year. But what about Mother? At first Hades seemed to understand my other obligations, but I wasn't surprised when he asked Aegaeon to accompany me to the Styx and we ended up at the gate to Tartarus instead. Hades had never let me go that easily before." Persephone sounded like she was retelling a story that was stressful in the moment but had become funny over a length of time.

"Aren't you mad?" Ruby asked.

"At Hades?" Persephone laughed. "No. Not really. He means well. And there's no point in being mad at Zeus. He's just—Zeus."

Ruby looked at Persephone's invisible form, as one would in any conversation with a person who isn't making any sense. "Weren't you afraid down here?" she asked.

"No," Persephone said, like it was a ridiculous idea. "Aegaeon is kind enough. Every creature in the Underworld, and below, knows they would face Hades's wrath if they were to hurt me. And I know Hades wouldn't be without me, not for long. He would have come to get me sooner rather than later. Everything will get back to normal now. Mother will be so glad to see me. And you'll be dancing at your wedding."

Ruby tried to imagine her and Ares surviving this, facing down Zeus, and enjoying their wedding, but the gloom of the Underworld had a dampening effect.

They walked on in silence. Ruby tried to wrap her head around Persephone's apathy. The goddess stopped and pulled her hand free of Ruby's. She became visible again.

"This way." Persephone motioned to what appeared to be a dark line in the rock, but as Ruby got closer she saw a crack large enough for a person to fit into. She took off the helmet and turned sideways to enter.

The passage was tight; big enough for a person, but not a fifty headed giant. "I can't," she said. "Ares won't know if I've rescued you or if we're still down here somewhere."

"We have to go on," Persephone said with little patience in her voice. "Ares will meet us. He's a warrior, Ruby. He may be full of passion and lover's whispers in the bedroom. But right now he'll be practical."

Ruby felt her face get warm at the implication, but she knew Persephone was right. She had seen it in Ares's eyes.

Persephone led the way through the dark passage. This was less like walking and more like climbing. They scrambled over large boulders that filled the space. It was so narrow in spots Ruby had to turn sideways. Her jeans and shirt scraped against the rock as she went.

The helmet, which had saved her life in Tartarus, now became her main hindrance. She passed it from one hand to the other as she climbed. She put it on her head when she needed both hands free, and took it off if she needed to fit through a tight space. If Persephone looked back Ruby would appear as badly timed animation, first here on this rock, then ten feet farther up on that one.

Persephone made it look easy as she scrambled over rocks and slipped through tight spots in her pink silk peplos, with no helmet in her hands or bow and quiver on her back to slow her down.

Ruby saw a diffuse light up ahead. They must be getting close. She had been feeling hopeful about reaching Hades, but now doubts crowded in. She was with Persephone, but would that make her any safer?

She looked up to see the goddess standing erect, shafts of light all around her. Ruby concentrated on getting past the boulder before her and then she too was standing in the ubiquitous light of Hades. She blinked. Her eyes watered from such a long stretch in the dark.

They had come out on the edge of the Fields of Asphodel. Not many souls were here in the forested part. Persephone reached for Ruby's hand and nodded at the Helm of Darkness. Ruby put Hades's helmet on and the two disappeared.

They walked to the edge of the crowd where there was a loud commotion. Ruby stood on her invisible tiptoes, straining to see over the heads of the shades that milled around. She glimpsed the three Hecatonchire brothers running through the crowd of shades. They lumbered on ungracefully with a fair amount of speed. They were in hot pursuit of something.

Joy and terror leaped into her heart at the same moment. *Ares!* She started to run, pulling Persephone behind her, but the goddess was slower.

Ruby tried to wrench her hand free. Persephone held tight. "I have to help him," she cried and with a jerk she did pull free. She reached behind her for Artemis's bow.

The queen of Hades, no longer under the power of the Helm of Darkness, appeared among a group of souls engaged in a round of bocce. The players dropped their colored globes and bowed, welcoming her as she stumbled into their midst.

Ruby ran on, toward where she thought Ares would be in the next few seconds, which was several feet in front of the giant's many heads bobbing above the crowd. She wanted to scream out and let Ares know she was there, but she held back in a lucid moment of self-preservation.

The crowd got thicker. People pushed in toward her to make room for Ares and the giants. Her bow and arrows were useless pinned against her sides. She knocked into shades who looked around for someone to blame, but found no one.

She sidled through one group of shades and pushed through another until, at last, she was near where the giants were running. She scanned over heads, desperate to see Ares, desperate to see that he was all right. She had no way of knowing what other creatures he had faced on his way out of Tartarus.

The hugeness of the Hecatonchires, the stench of them, and the gasps of the crowd all pulled at her mind. Then her eye caught him. He was taller than most of the shades and she saw his dark curly head moving above theirs. Relief flooded her, but it was fleeting. The giants were too close. Much too close. Almost on top of him.

She saw Ares go down, but it was the sound of clashing metal weapons and armor followed by the dull wet sound of breaking bones that tightened a vice around her chest. She heard an undertone too, maybe only audible to her, of the air being forced out of Ares's lungs as one of the brothers fell on him, so much larger and heavier than he was.

The two other giants were running fast. Their mass was too great to stop in time. They buckled in quick succession, increasing the pile of oversized bodies, too many heads, and too many limbs that lay on top of Ares.

Ruby stifled a scream. She listened for any sign of life but heard nothing over the din of the excited crowd. She couldn't tell if they were rooting for Ares or the monsters, but the break in the garden party seemed a welcome change of pace to the onlookers.

She saw other creatures of Hades coming onto the scene. There were more Chimeras, different mixtures of human, animal, and bird. Had they been chasing Ares too? Ruby shrank from them despite her invisibility.

The Hecatonchires tripped and lurched as they pulled themselves off of one another. Ruby's hands clenched and unclenched as she peered through the crowd and waited to see what remained of Ares lying at the bottom of all that flesh. One of the giants pulled him up by the arm.

He stood loosely, like his joints had been unhinged. His head lolled on an unsupportive neck. A trickle of blood came from the corner of his mouth. She let out a small squeak that went unnoticed by the crowd. But he's alive, she thought. A light of relief swept across her mind.

The vice that squeezed her ribs loosened enough so that she could breathe again. She laughed with that breath, almost hysterically. Of course he was alive. He *couldn't* die. They could just hurt him, over and over.

Two giants supported Ares, one on each side. The third Hecatonchire brought up the rear. They walked back through the opening in the crowd to where the other creatures of Hades waited. They would have to pass right by where she stood. She willed Ares to see her. She wanted to look into his eyes.

He lifted his head and scanned the edge of the crowd. One of his eyes was already black and blue. Her mind shouted for him and he jerked his eyes toward her.

Her heart jumped into her throat at the fierce god who looked back at her through swollen lids. She saw the bloodied corner of his mouth move. He was saying something, talking to her. She tore her eyes away from his and looked to his bat-tered lips.

"Go," he mouthed.

She searched his face; sure she had gotten it wrong.

The giants turned him away from her as they headed to-ward the palace. Before she lost eye contact with him he said it again, as clear as if he had whispered it in her ear, "Go."

No. She shook her head. She couldn't go. She wouldn't. Not without him.

The horde was breaking up. Persephone was somewhere behind her in the massive crowd of twittering, wandering souls. Ruby looked in every direction, turning this way and that, hoping for a glimpse of the brown-haired goddess.

The shades around Ruby seemed happy for the brief dis-traction of Ares's capture but they were equally happy to get back to their dull afterlives. She pushed through them, making herself go away from Hades's palace, tearing herself from her need to find him. To help him.

She needed Persephone.

∾◦◦

A shade backed up into Ruby, accidentally knocking Hades's helmet off her head. The man turned and started to apologize, but his mouth froze midsentence. He looked her up and down.

She looked down too and saw how out of place she was with her filthy clothes and her silver bow and arrows. Many souls carried souvenirs from their former lives, and some were ragged and dirty, but none were both. She would draw attention. Would she draw Persephone? Or would she draw the guards?

A small boy hit a croquet ball with a mallet much too big for him and looked up at Ruby. "Why is she so dirty, Mama?" he said.

His mother, a woman who looked to be eighty, might have hushed him, but all Ruby heard was silence as every soul within earshot turned to look at her. She wanted to jam Hades's helmet back on her head and forget Persephone. But she knew if anyone could help her, it was the queen of the Underworld.

She looked among the shades staring at her. One held a huge plate of food. Her stomach growled loud enough for anyone to hear. Did shades' stomachs growl? Would someone call her out as being alive? She tried to swallow, but there was nothing.

With that she realized that Ares had their water, Pan's pipes, the winged sandals, everything. All she had was Artemis's bow. Panic threatened. It was a desperate feeling in her chest. Dizziness washed over her and she worried she might faint. She was pretty sure souls did not faint.

She forced a smile and willed her muscles to keep her standing. She gave the boy a gentle look that said *Aw, isn't he cute*, even though she wanted to clamp her hand over his mouth.

Whispers spread through the crowd around them. "Is it? It can't be," she heard someone say near her.

"If Ares is here ..." Her ears pricked up at his name.

"Are there more Olympians?" She heard from another quarter and saw an old stooped woman looking at her.

Ruby realized that though the boy had seen her as dirty and ragged, the crowd saw her as something else. She held Hades's helmet and Artemis's silver bow rested on her back. John Wright had thought she was Aphrodite.

"Persephone?" Ruby called, in her most regal, most goddess-like voice.

She heard more whispers. "Is the queen here?"

"Yes, the queen is here, I saw her," a tall shade said. "Over there, by the shuttlecock courts." Ruby strolled as casually as she thought an Olympian might, in that direction. Groups of shades stopped their conversations as she passed.

She finally saw Persephone. The goddess had a large crowd of children sitting in a semicircle around her. "Narcissus would not move from the small pond, for he had fallen in love with his own reflection," Persephone said to the slack-jawed youth.

Ruby cleared her throat.

The goddess looked up at her. "I'll have to finish the tale another time, children. Hades will be looking for me and I must go to him." The children recoiled at the sound of Hades's name. It seemed they feared him as much as they loved his sweet and beautiful wife. Ruby realized that Hades was smart to bring Persephone here. He needed better PR and she was it.

"Where have you been?" Ruby asked Persephone when they were again side by side.

"Where have I been? You're the one who ran and left me to appear in a crowd of shades."

"But, telling stories?"

"Ruby, this is what I do when I'm among my subjects. I tell them about who they used to be. I compliment them on their children, even though two are infants, one is a teenager, and the rest are older than their parents. I soothe them. That is what a queen does."

"They took Ares away," Ruby said, her voice insistent. "Where would Hades keep him? Where would he hold a prisoner? Does he have a place other than just throwing people into Tartarus?" She really hoped that Persephone would have a better option than going back there.

An image came to her then: Kronos's blue eyes, inches from her own, his corrupt breath, and his curse. She pushed it aside.

Focus.

"We don't get a lot of prisoners here." Persephone said. "Souls come, they're judged, and that's it. It's been that way for thousands of years."

"No accidents for a million days?" Ruby said, but the bitter joke was lost on Persephone. "Where can we go?" Ruby tried again. "Hades gave Ares and me one hour to leave the Underworld and that was …" She shook her head. "I have no idea when that was. Are you in danger? Do you think Hades will send you back to Tartarus?"

"No." Persephone shook her head. "I'm sure that's over."

Ruby thought of Hades, slumped in his black throne and picking at the loose threads of his robes. He was clearly miserable without her.

A crowd gathered near the palace again. Ruby looked up to see a detail of eight guards questioning souls who were pointing in their direction.

Such an exciting day in Hades.

"I guess we're about to find out what Hades's plans are," Ruby said, trembling when she saw the lion-men coming closer. She thought to reach for her bow but the math was easy: six arrows, eight guards; and plenty more where they came from.

Ruby turned her head to look for an escape but the souls behind them were gathering at this new excitement. The group was too thick to run through. She felt like a trapped rabbit. Her only comfort was knowing that anywhere the guards took her would be closer to Ares.

The guards stood before Persephone, so close Ruby could see their whiskers twitch. They did not seize her and Persephone; instead, the guards kneeled down before the goddess.

"Your Majesty," one said, his voice a near growl. "Hades has sent us to check on your welfare and escort you back to the palace. Are you well?"

"Yes. I'm fine. Thank you, Jemet. I'm ready to go home."

With that the guards stood and readied themselves to follow their queen to her palace. Ruby followed too, but a guard stopped her with his long iron-tipped spear. Persephone intervened. "She's with me."

The lion-headed guard let her pass. Ruby looked for some sign from the beast—embarrassment, hate, confusion even—but she could read nothing in his animal features. She only saw the slightest flare of his nostrils. He was sniffing her. Restraining himself. *They're more beast than man,* she thought. They don't need a command to attack. They need to be told to hold back.

Persephone's subjects made an easy path before her, bowing and speaking soft words of love and adoration. It wasn't until they saw Ruby coming up behind, carrying her pack, her weapon, and Hades's helmet that the whispers spread like a wave across water.

Yes. It was a very exciting day in Hades.

❦

The palace, big even from a distance, loomed over them as they approached. Souls were newer here, still finding their way, still marveling at the full schedule of daily activities, the sunny forecast, and the mountains of calorie-free food.

Oh, food!

The entrance of the courtyard was as busy as always with the kings pronouncing their judgments and St. Peter with the last word.

Ruby's head ached from stress, hunger, and thirst. What judgments lay within the palace for her? What eternal punishments were in store for Ares?

Persephone greeted souls as they walked. Everyone—frail grannies, beefy middle-aged men, and children—received her with wide dewy eyes and open arms.

They reached the first courtyard of the palace, with the golden gate to the Elysian Plains on one side and the black gate to Tartarus on the other. Ruby's feet stopped even though her mind willed her to be strong, to move forward, to help Ares. A guard pushed her from behind and she staggered on.

They walked into the second courtyard and up the obsidian steps to the first level. Hades stood in the main hall waiting for them. He had deep dark circles under his eyes. Ruby took a breath, ready to face whatever he planned to do to her.

But Hades only had eyes for Persephone. Deep lines in his forehead relaxed. His smile became wide. It made him look like a different person, not the god of the dead, but a god in love. Ruby wondered if he remembered that he was the one who imprisoned her in the first place.

"Hades," Persephone seemed to caress his name as she said it and walked into his open arms.

"Forgive me, my love," Hades spoke into her lustrous brown hair.

She pulled away and looked into his pale face. "Don't think of it. I'm well. It's behind us."

Ruby wanted to scream. How could she forgive him?

Hades put his arm around Persephone's shoulders and led her up the staircase. His hand stroked her back and settled on her behind.

The guards, still standing on either side of Ruby, said, "Your Majesty. What should we do with her?"

"Who?" Hades half turned but kept his bright black eyes on his wife.

"The girl."

Hades turned toward Ruby, as if just now realizing she was standing there. "I should send every beast of the Underworld after you. That was my promise." He looked back to Persephone. His pale pink tongue darted out between his partially opened lips. "But seeing as how you were helpful to me, I can show you mercy." He looked to the guards. "To the Fields of Asphodel," he said, mimicking St. Peter passing his final judgment on her.

He turned Persephone back toward the steps and they began their ascent again. Ruby tried to make eye contact with Persephone, but the goddess didn't look back. She was climbing the stairs, abandoning Ruby.

Hate bloomed in Ruby's chest like a poison flower. So kind and mild, so willing to put up with anything. All of Ruby's compassion left her.

The guards took Ruby by the arms and escorted her out of the palace and shoved her into the courtyard with the three kings. As a last thought one of the guards plucked Hades's helmet from her arms. She had forgotten about it until that moment. Now another loss struck her.

She stood alone as new souls fidgeted in line. She wandered out of the courtyard and into the Field of Asphodel proper. More new shades were here, reuniting with family and friends.

Her stomach growled painfully, as if to add another tick to the list of her problems. She looked at the plates of food on long tables. A dark whisper of a thought filled her mind: *just eat something.*

The thought horrified her, but her eyes darted to more plates of food. How would she do it? How would she seal her fate of being trapped in Hades forever? With one of the bacon wrapped meaty things, a wedge of brie, a slice of cake?

The whisper returned: *eat one, and you can eat it all.* She pictured Ares bloodied and bruised, being carried away by the beasts of Tartarus.

No, she wouldn't give up. She was not like Persephone, willing to forgive every transgression. She wouldn't stop fighting for her own life. Thoughts of Ares, and love, and friends, and honest-to-goodness sunshine filled her mind.

She imagined Ares holding her. She felt his energy flow into her, giving her strength and dulling her hunger. Her pain faded, as though thoughts could be sustenance.

She nodded at no one, her focus renewed. She had to find Ares.

She had to save him.

TWENTY·SEVEN

PERSEPHONE WOULDN'T stay in the Underworld for long. She had been happy to reunite with Hades, but she had told Ruby things would be back to normal soon and she would be going to her mother. Ruby didn't think the desolate Hades she had seen in the throne room, picking at the loose threads of his robes, would have fortitude to imprison his wife again.

At least she and Ares had done what they came to do. The Earth would be saved from eternal winter. Now the flowers would bloom on far away Mount Olympus. Ruby and Ares's wedding plans would finally be falling into place, minus the bride and groom.

Without Persephone, Hades would have more time to attend to his prisoner. Ruby stood outside the palace and looked up to the ceiling of the Fields of Asphodel. Both flags, black and white, hung there, Persephone's no longer at half-staff. She hadn't left for Olympus yet.

Ruby thought of the way Hades had looked at his wife, the way he touched her, with one thing on his mind. She grimaced at the thought of them being romantic, but then she brightened.

This was her window to save Ares.

She walked in a slow zigzag through the courtyard with the three kings, and into the quieter second garden space. She wandered toward the palace steps and wondered where Hades would keep Ares. Was he still inside the palace?

She jolted when she saw two guards at the base of the stairs. Chimeras. One was a lion-man, the other had the body of a man but the head of an eagle.

The eagle lifted his yellow beak and made a high-pitched noise when he saw her. The lion-man's shaggy head jerked to look her way. His expressive nose twitched, smelling her. He took a step forward, his iron-tipped spear in his hand, but eagle-man held him back by the arm.

Hades had dismissed her, but what did that mean for the Chimeras who, like their larger cousin Cerberus, desired human flesh? Was she a target for these creatures? Or was Hades's declaration that she be sent to the Fields of Asphodel also protection? Was she to stay there unharmed?

Ruby walked away from them, deeper into the garden courtyard and watched from a distance. Her horror at the lion-man's sniffing ebbed into hope. There hadn't been guards outside the palace before she and Ares showed up. If there were guards outside, Ares was still inside.

⁂

Ruby sat in a small grove of apple trees in the garden courtyard outside Hades's palace. She thought she had been watching the palace for hours, but it could have easily been days. The only thing that marked time was her hunger which, she realized, was now fading. Did that mean that she was closer to starvation? People who froze to death stopped feeling cold just before hypothermia overtook them. Was it the same with hunger?

She looked to the palace entrance for the millionth time and again she saw the lion-man and the eagle-man standing there, one on each side of the closest entrance. Her eyes scanned the length of the building. The long obsidian wall stretched on until it met the solid rock of the Underworld. There were only a few windows on this side and three narrow entrances. Each entrance had a set of mixed-up animals guarding it. As far as Ruby could tell no one had come in or out.

The Chimeras' eyes scanned the courtyard in tireless sweeps. They responded to slight sounds with a twitching golden ear or a raised head. A lizard man stood at the last entrance, his forked tongue lashing out at intervals.

Shades wandered about. Ruby scanned them. She watched as they lolled in the grass and picked ripe fruit from the trees. One woman walked toward the back of the palace with a determined expression on her face.

Ruby sat upright. Her eyes shifted back to the guards but they weren't paying attention to the woman. Ruby refocused on her. She was in her mid-forties. Her black hair sat on the top of her head in an elaborate bun with two braids hanging down in loops on either side, and she wore a simple white peplos. She looked like she had just arrived from Olympus.

Ruby stood and walked toward her.

The woman didn't glance at the garden. She kept her eyes forward. Not a new shade, Ruby decided. This woman knew where she was going. But where was she headed? There was only the black wall of the palace and the rough gray rock of Hades. Then, abruptly, the woman was gone.

It took Ruby a minute to realize what had happened. The move the woman had made was subtle. And where had she done it? Near the end of the wall? Ruby followed, staying as far from the guards as she could.

She scanned the smooth black surface of the palace and looked for a doorway or a set of stairs. She didn't want to miss the place where the woman had disappeared. Even more she didn't want to miss the woman coming back out. A shade who had been in Hades a long time, and knew its secrets, was a shade she needed to meet.

Ruby neared the end of the obsidian, but still there was no sign of the woman. She backtracked, thinking she must have missed something.

When Ruby reached the end of the palace she saw that the two walls didn't actually meet. It was like the fissure through which she and Persephone had come up out of Tartarus. From a distance the rocks appeared to be a solid jagged face but there was a narrow opening between them.

The gap was as tall as the palace, as tall as Hades itself. A small river ran there, not black like the Styx, or fiery like the Phlegethon, but crystal clear, like a glass ribbon, like Oceanus.

The water didn't babble or make any sound at all. It was completely silent.

Ruby took a tentative step behind the palace. Her foot gave way on the loose soil and she nearly fell into the stream. She grabbed for the smooth wall out of instinct and righted herself after a few panic-stricken, wobbly seconds.

"Careful," a quiet female voice said. "Don't want to end up in the Lethe before it's time."

Ruby looked up to see the woman in the peplos standing ten feet in front of her. She faced the river, which widened as it went along into a basin. There was an island in the middle of the basin and on the island stood a lone tree. The tree was old and twisted. Large deep-red fruit grew in clusters like giant raspberries. The air smelled clean, like fresh grass and new leaves. The smell reminded her of early spring.

Ruby looked back to the water, still dangerously close to the edge. The Lethe. The River of Forgetfulness. It was the river shades waded through to reach the Tree of Life, to forget their former selves, to reincarnate.

"Are you making a journey back?" the woman asked Ruby.

Somewhere between seeing the laugh lines around her mouth and her bright violet eyes Ruby decided that this woman would help her. "No," Ruby said.

"I've been thinking about it for a while." The woman looked to the island and at the tree. "It's probably time to go." She said it to herself as much as to Ruby.

"Do you just walk across?" Ruby didn't think she'd get very far pretending she knew more than she did.

The woman laughed. Her eyes sparkled. "I figured you were a new shade. Barely dead at all. You still have the whiff of life about you."

Ruby ignored the comment. "I saw you come this way. I was curious."

She thought of the other thing Ares told her about reincarnating; your life had to have been stolen from you. This woman had been murdered. Ruby scanned her up and down for some obvious injury but the woman looked the same as any other shade.

"This isn't for you." The woman glanced at her. "You should go back."

Desperation tightened around Ruby. "I need your help," she blurted.

"Go back to the party," the woman nodded her head toward the Fields of Asphodel. "This spot is the only thing that could be trouble for you."

"I need help finding a way into the palace." What would she do if this woman wouldn't help her? Where would she go? "I *need* to get inside, but I can't go past the guards."

The woman looked at her for a long second with narrowed purple eyes. "Child, why do you want to get into the palace? Everything you need is in the garden."

Ruby's shoulders dropped, as the weight of everything settled on her.

The woman looked back at the river. "What you need is to leave this place. If a drop of the Lethe falls on you, you'll forget everything you've ever known." There was fear and desire mixed in her voice. "The only other way in is not an easy way for a young shade to go, or an old shade either." The woman shrugged. "It only goes to the dungeon, anyway."

Ruby brightened. "A dungeon?"

ఴ

The woman wasn't from Olympus, of course, she was from the ancient world itself. Adelpha was her name. She'd been killed during one of the many Roman-Persian wars near the height of the Roman Empire. Ruby had not seen shades as old as her before.

"Hades is infinite," Adelpha explained. "The walls and size are an illusion. If you kept walking you'd find that you could walk forever. Every rock face would open somewhere new and Hades would continue."

Ruby explained about her love for Ares and the wedding, and Zeus and Persephone. "Zeus hates me," she said. "Hades doesn't care about me, and Persephone, who *could* help me, won't."

"I see," Adelpha said with less sarcasm than she was entitled to.

Ruby thought that she might even believe her.

"Then you're on your own, I suppose," the shade said.

"Unless you'll help me."

"I can show you the way. It's not hard to find." Adelpha turned in the opposite direction Ruby expected her to, away from the courtyard, and farther down behind the palace.

Ruby followed her. Her left foot skirted the unstable banks of the Lethe and her right shoulder scraped along the black obsidian of Hades's palace. The bank widened and soon Ruby could walk with no fear of falling in. The walls of the palace and the Underworld towered high above. They seemed to curve inward and join together at the top.

"It's right around here somewhere," Adelpha said. She looked at the ground beneath her sandaled feet. Ruby looked too but all she saw was soft, grassy riverbank.

"You've been here before?" Ruby asked.

"Not in a long time."

Ruby felt a stone of desperation form in her stomach. This couldn't be it. There was no sign of life. No footprints in the soft dirt at the river's edge. *No one* had been here in a long time.

Fear and hunger worked at her mind. Had Adelpha made up the dungeon? Was she stalling? Did she work for Hades?

Adelpha pounded on the ground with her foot. It produced a dull thud, like something hollow. "Yes. Here it is," she said. "Looks like they stopped using it."

At the bottom of the wall, very close to where the palace met the grass, Ruby saw that the dirt was concave. Adelpha stooped and began pulling the grass and soil away with her hands.

Ruby joined her. She put her hand into the empty space between the wall and the ground and pulled away handfuls of dirt. The stone of desperation in Ruby's stomach lifted high up in her chest and began to feel like hope.

They dug for several inches, until they hit upon something solid. "The door is in the ground. It lifts up like a root cellar," Adelpha said.

The edge of the wooden door was rotted. It was easy to break it up and make the hole bigger. Adelpha saw what Ruby was doing and moved to the other side of the opening to help.

When the hole was big enough Ruby lay on the ground and reached into it with her dirt-covered hands. A musty, closed-in smell came out of the hole and she yelled in surprise when her knuckles hit something hard and rough. Steps, she realized as she touched one and then another further down. Stone steps.

Ruby looked at Adelpha. "Are you sure this leads to the dungeon?"

"This is the main entrance." Adelpha looked around. "Well, it used to be."

Ruby looked into the hole and then back to Adelpha. Her eagerness to find Ares was matched only by her fear of what lay at the bottom of those steps. But there was nothing to do and nowhere to go but down.

"Thank you," Ruby said and looked into Adelpha's eyes once more. "Do you know anything else about the dungeon? Anything that can help me find Ares?"

"I only know about the entrance because I've spent so much time on the banks of the Lethe." She glanced at the ground where the door was now covered with dirt. "I think Persephone stored things in it mostly. Tributes and gifts may-be."

Ruby blinked. Hades was imprisoning Ares in the queen of the Underworld's extra storage? She didn't want to worry about the foolishness of Hades and Persephone. But the thought reminded her that she didn't have much time. Per-sephone would be heading back to Olympus soon, leaving

Hades six months to deal with Ares before she returned to distract him again.

If Ruby didn't pluck up her courage now, she would have an eternity to stare at that hole.

∽◦◎◦∾

Ruby eased her legs into the fathomless darkness of Hades's dungeon and felt for the stone steps. She found them with a sharp kick. She got her footing and backed down into the abyss.

She looked up at Adelpha. "You won't come?" she asked again, though the shade had already refused once.

Adelpha shook her head, her two black braids swinging with the motion. "I'm determined to go back, to reincarnate and start over."

Ruby nodded and lowered herself further into the ground. Adelpha handed her the silver bow and the quiver of arrows. Ruby slung them over her back in the limited space.

The steps were uneven and littered with large chunks of broken rock. Going down was slow and unsteady work made worse by less and less light as the hole above her got smaller and smaller.

She made a vain wish for Eros's torch, or even a less significant one, but Ares had all their supplies: the torch, the winged sandals, Pan's pipes, and the water. Ruby couldn't bring herself to think about the water. How long since she drank from the skins in Ares's bag? Before Sisyphus or after?

Her stomach growled and she thought of what they had sacrificed to Cerberus, all their food and even the obolus, eaten by the giant dog, though she doubted he'd even noticed.

The stairs seemed to go on forever and she had a flash of fear that she might be headed back down to Tartarus. She strained to listen in the black muffled space, wondering if she would hear the fiery river Phlegethon, but there was nothing except her own small scraping sounds and the labored breathing in her dry throat.

What if this abandoned stairway led nowhere? Time meant nothing here and now she had been robbed of the one sense that could give her the most information, her sight. It was in the midst of these unnerving thoughts that Ruby heard the first rattle of pebbles hitting stone.

She stopped dead and listened with every cell in her body. The noise was hard to localize. Above? Below? Near? Far? Her fear told her to run. Her mind told her to hold still. She didn't want to meet anything that would make this place its home.

Her heart was loud in hear ears until a voice broke through. A whisper in the dark. "Ruby?"

Her heart beat faster, almost stopped, and then leapt. "Adelpha?"

"Ruby?" The whisper came again, now with recognition. "Wait. I'm not going back to yet. I'm coming with you."

Thank you, thank you! Relief flooded her. She swallowed what little moisture she had in her mouth. "What changed your mind?"

Adelpha was close to her now. Ruby could feel skittering sprays of dirt on her skin. "I've been in Hades for two millennia," she said. "And on the day I decide to return to the mortal realms, a human girl asks me to help her save the god of war. What would you do?"

Ruby laughed. It was a strange sound in the dark pit. "Do you think this is right? Do you think we're headed to the dungeon?"

"I know we are," Adelpha said, next to her. Ruby felt Adelpha's arm brush hers as the shade passed her on the stairs.

They continued down. A damp chill crept into Ruby's bones. Her knees ached. She thought of standing, but the loose rocks would surely trip her. She almost set her hand on a jagged rock, but pulled it away before the rock cut her. She jerked. "Adelpha?" she asked in a whisper. "Can you see?"

"Maybe." Then a pause. "I think so."

Ruby slowed, trying to avoid knocking loose stones or creating more noise than she had to. If they were near a light, they might be near shades, or guards, or who knew what. *Ares?*

The distinction between grays became more pronounced. Ruby's hands became dark lumps. Adelpha's dim shape stopped below her. "There's a wall," the shade said.

Ruby heard a dull thud and then a sharper crack. Muted, dancing light flooded into the stairway, making Ruby squint.

They were at the bottom of the old broken stairs. Adelpha had pushed through a thin screen of rotting boards that blocked it off from use. Ice picks stabbed at Ruby's contracted muscles as she rose from all fours. They were in a short stone hallway that turned to the right or left at the end.

They peered around the corner in turns and found yet another corridor. The gray rock walls were cylindrical, made by tunneling through the rock with some large boring instrument. The second passage ran in both directions and was brighter. Lit torches in sconces ran the length in each direction.

The sconces made Ruby flinch. It was the Sphinx, shrunk down to the size of something a celebrity might stick in her purse back on Earth. Her black eyes and pointed scorpion's tail looked like the real thing.

"Heph," Ruby said under her breath. Homesickness replaced her fear. She thought of her friends on Olympus and wondered what they were going through. Was a war that she had ignited tearing apart the gods at that very moment?

Adelpha turned right again and they were soon peering around another corner similar to the last. They followed it to the next, and the next. They were in a network of corridors that led on and on with no doors or rooms. A maze.

Ruby was so turned around she didn't think she could find her way back to the stone steps, and there was nothing of promise before them. Her head ached. Her throat was dry.

Adelpha peered around the next corner. Ruby set to follow when the shade's head snapped back, almost hitting Ruby in the nose. Adelpha turned. Her eyes were wide with panic. She shook her head and motioned back to the last corridor that they had come out of.

"A guard. A Chimera." She breathed into Ruby's ear. "Lion's head, lizard body, and a snake for a tail. It's not just a hallway, though. He's guarding a room."

The blood rushed into Ruby's head. "Good. We're getting close."

꧁꧂

Ruby's plan was dangerous. Not for her, but for Adelpha. Chimeras tolerated shades, but neither she nor Adelpha knew what their reaction would be to a shade in Hades's dungeon.

"I'll do it," Adelpha said with a curt nod.

Ruby fought back tears and hugged her new friend. Adelpha pulled away and looked her in the eye. "Find Ares," she said with a smile. "Marry him and be happy."

Ruby nodded and Adelpha walked, without ceremony, into the corridor with the Chimeras. Ruby hadn't known Adelpha for long, but she felt a strong connection to this woman from another time. A time that felt closer to Ares.

Ruby leaned her back against the rough rock wall. She closed her eyes and waited to hear what would happen.

"What are you doing here?" A slow guttural roar came from the Chimera.

Adelpha, who might have been an actress in her former life, said, "Where am I? I was in the garden. I came inside for just a moment."

"You have to leave. Go now," the Chimera roared.

"I don't know the way," Adelpha answered and Ruby pictured her dark braids swinging as she looked in all directions. "Do you have any of those little quiches? I love the spinach ones."

"Leave!" the guard roared.

Ruby held her breath but Adelpha answered in a calm voice, "So many rights and lefts. How can I possibly choose?"

"Just choose a wall. Follow it to the end," the Chimera said, with obvious annoyance at this distraction. "You'll eventually get out."

"That sounds silly," Adelpha laughed like a tipsy twenty-year-old.

There was silence from around the bend and Ruby almost ventured a look, but if the guard saw Ruby, or worse, smelled her, her quest for Ares would be over.

Finally Ruby heard the guard speak. The venom was barely contained in his voice. "This way." Then she heard the lizard's tail scrape against the stone floor of the passage. She shuddered when she realized that the sound was coming closer to her.

"That can't be the way," Adelpha said. "I've just come from there."

"It's all the same," the guard grunted. "This is the center of the maze."

"Let's go another way. I've seen all that already." Ruby smiled at how incompetent Adelpha sounded. "How do you know how to get out if it's all the same?" the shade asked.

Ruby heard the scraping head in the opposite direction. She stole a brave look around the corner and saw Adelpha, the Chimera, and a large archway behind them.

"Follow me." The Chimera pointed to the right with a spear held loosely in his lizard claw. Ruby ducked back before the snake tail whipped around to face her.

When they were gone Ruby stepped into the corridor and walked to the edge of the archway the Chimera had been guarding. She hesitated before entering the room. What might she find? Disturbing images flashed through her mind; Ares tied up, Ares being tortured, Ares unconscious, Hecatonchires, some crazy cousin of Cerberus, or even Hades himself with his full attention aimed at Ares.

She knew she didn't have much time before the guard came back or another one replaced him. She closed her eyes and pictured Ares happy and whole. She held the image close. She pulled Artemis's bow off her back and peered around the corner.

Inside the room were none of the horrors she had imagined. There was only a giant spherical rock, the size of a large house. The huge rock sat in an enormous stone basin of water. The room was round too and just bigger than the stone itself, massive. The room had several other arched entrances like the one she was peering in from.

From her vantage point she could see three guards, one at each of the entrances adjacent to hers. They stood like statues and stared out into the hallways before them. She knew there must be more archways and more guards on the other side of the stone.

She looked at the smooth rock and wondered what it was. With all these guards it had to have something to do with Ares.

She nocked an arrow and took her aim at the first guard to the left, a lion-man in a yellow and red tunic. A soft *thunk* was the only sound as she let go the string and the arrow found its mark. The Chimera crumpled in a heap but Ruby barely saw. She had already nocked the next arrow, had already aimed at her next target.

In quick succession she dispatched the first two guards. The third turned to her and she shot him as he realized what was happening.

Two guards came around from the far side of the stone. One was a lizard-man. The other had a bird's body and a man's head. The bird-man lifted off the ground to come at her. His wild half-human eyes stared at her. The lizard-man ran at her with a spear. She reached for another arrow, nocked it, shot, and repeated. *Thunk, thunk.* Both guards dropped in quick succession.

Ruby's blood ran hot in her body. Her mind was crystal clear, hunger, thirst, and fatigue were forgotten in the pure rush of adrenaline.

The Chimeras weren't mortal. Ruby knew they would rouse themselves soon. She needed to be gone by then.

Her bow was nocked with her last arrow as she checked the entrances for more guards and found none. She retrieved her arrows from the limp bodies of the Chimeras and wiped the blood on their clothes as she had seen Ares do.

She looked to the massive stone.

It was dark granite, at least thirty feet high and perched on a basin of water twenty feet in diameter. The stone tickled something in the back of her mind. She had seen something like it before. But where? When?

She focused on the details and tried to drag the memory in. The stone she was thinking of was smaller, still big, but Ruby had been little herself at the time. Yes! That was it. A school trip to the science center. There had been a stone like this.

She remembered touching the cool wet surface with her small hands and pushing. After she got some momentum going the giant rock had rolled in its stone base. The thousands of pounds of granite had been *floating* in the water and even a little girl could move it. But this stone was so much bigger than that one, bigger than her house on Earth. There was no way she could move this one.

Still, she put both hands on the cold wet stone and pushed up with all her might. Nothing. She tried again. And again.

Her shoulders slumped in frustration. It had to be something else. But this stone was the key. Why else would the Chimeras be guarding it?

She got lower and braced her feet against the floor. She placed her hands beneath the fine sheet of water. Her palms found more purchase at this new angle then they had before. She heaved up with every fiber of her being. Her legs tensed, then her abs, then her shoulders.

Her body lengthened forward. Had it moved? She repositioned her hands lower, regained good contact with the rock, and pushed again. Yes. It was moving. Not much, but a little.

When her strength gave out she stepped back to look at the stone again. She walked the perimeter, hoping that something about the rock had changed.

The bird-man that had flown at her rolled over and let out a groan. She looked at him then turned back to the stone, unwilling to give up a second of her precious time.

Then she saw it.

A black square in the rock. A cutout. She could only see the corner of it. She put her bow down, curled her fingers around the edge, and pulled up with all her might. This time the stone moved more easily with her better grip. She pulled and strained, alternating between pushing on the outside of the rock and pulling up on the edge of the cut out.

Soon the black square was at thigh level. She peered inside. Toward the back of the cut out, to the left, was another space. She peered in and tried to see around the bend.

The bird-man grunted. A lion-man was getting to his knees. He was facing away from her, but he would turn around in the next second.

Panicked, she grabbed Artemis's bow from the rocky ground and scrambled into the small space of the stone.

TWENTY•EIGHT

RUBY CROUCHED in the small space and felt the stone slide beneath her weight. The cutout in the rock now faced the bottom of the basin, out of the sight of the guards. She was hidden and she felt safe until the true nature of her situation dawned on her. She was trapped.

She would rather face the guards and Hades than die in the suffocating closeness of the sphere. She pushed on the wall of the cramped space and tried to get the rock to move, but it wouldn't budge.

She focused on her breathing and tried to calm down.

It should have been dark, she realized, but she could see. The light was dim and diffuse. It came from above her. She looked up and saw a shelf. It was the corner she had seen when she first looked inside the cutout of the rock. She put her hands on the ledge, pushed off the bottom of the basin with her feet, and worked herself into the new space of the shelf.

This space was about as big as the first one, and also had a corner, this time to her right. She followed it around on her hands and knees. This new space was even bigger. She could stand upright. She looked for the next corner, but there were only solid walls around her. She was stuck. There was nowhere to go but back, and back led to nothing.

The panic returned. She felt like she couldn't breathe. She tried to open her throat by tilting her head back and letting it rest on the rock wall behind her. There, near the top of the ceiling, was another shelf. She reached up and put her hands on the edge, ready to pull up again, but this shelf was higher. She didn't think she could pull herself up that high.

She bent her knees in the cramped space and jumped up as best she could. The awkward maneuver tipped her off balance and instead of jumping straight up she fell forward onto the hard wall before her.

She lay on the rock and laughed, partly at her lack of grace but mostly out of frustration and fear. She tried to stand again but found she couldn't. The rock she now lay on had been straight up and down before, but it had tilted when she jumped. She had moved the rock from the inside.

It was another maze she realized, a maze in three dimensions. Instead of hallways branching right and left, this one branched right and left; up and down; backward and forward.

Would the guards notice the stone moving? She didn't think so. The only distinguishing mark was the cutout, and it was just a small spot on the huge sphere.

She inched forward on her belly and looked down into the small space that had been above her before the stone moved. She spun her body around and lowered herself into it.

There was now an opening near the floor. She crawled through it. The low passage soon became larger. As she went along the floor began to narrow. The sides dropped away from her. Soon she was crawling along a granite platform, like a wide balance beam, that ran through a huge stone room.

She glanced down. What she saw made her knees weak. The floor of the sphere was at least twenty feet below. The open space around her was crisscrossed with dozens of narrow granite beams like the one she was on now. She winced at the thought of falling onto those hard crosspieces.

On one side the sphere was built up. It wasn't concave, but flat. In the middle was a hole just big enough for a person to wiggle through. It glowed a faint red. Ruby's heart quickened. She thought of the maze that led to this room and the guards posted outside. Ares was in that hole. She could feel it.

She looked at the network of granite beams around her and wondered how she could get from here to there. She walked further along the crossbar but it dropped off into nothing two feet in front of her.

She looked in every direction. There had to be a way to use her weight to make the stone move again. The nearest beam was to the right and down, at a ninety degree angle to where she was now. She might be able to reach it. She held her breath and hiked out over the hazardous space with her arms outstretched. Her body tipped, her weight landed on the beam and the stone moved on its wet perch. The beam that had been below her was now before her, flat, and right where she needed it to be.

She pulled her legs up onto the stone beam. This one was wider. She stood and walked its length. She looked for the next beam and wondered in what plane she would find it. The next beam led straight to the smooth rock wall, but the glowing hole was across the giant room from her.

She stood with her back against the cold stone and looked for her next move. The only possibility was directly above her. She stretched up and grabbed the beam. She could barely lift her weight with her arms. As she pulled, the stone moved again. The beam she had intended to walk on was now more like a smooth pole in front of her, with no way to climb it, but there was a beam in front of her she had not considered before.

One beam after another, she moved around the stone room.

∽◉౬

Ruby pulled herself up to the next beam and wiped the sweat out of her eyes. She was disoriented. She looked again for the red glowing light where she thought Ares was. It was now above her and to the left. She wondered if these beams actually led there.

Beneath her she saw a crosspiece four feet below she thought she could safely jump to. If she missed she would hit five or six stone crosspieces on her way down to the hard floor below.

With no other options she decided to risk it. Again the sphere shifted under her weight and the new beam in front of her was now an uphill walk on a thin strip of rock. She put her foot down heavily with each step and soon the sphere shifted in her favor again.

She followed the beam across to the far side of the stone. Now the red glow was above her, maybe fifteen feet away. "Ares?" Her voice echoed in the large space, but there was no response.

She saw no beams that could get her closer. In front of her, along the wall of the sphere, ran a deep groove. It traveled up above her head. She ran her fingers along the trench. The beginning of it was notched. *For traction.*

She put her foot in the furrows cut into the rock. She leaned forward with all her weight and pressed down. She grunted with the effort and licked a salty drop of sweat from her lips.

The sphere moved. Just a little.

She repositioned higher and tried again. The stone moved more and more, until what had been a wall in front of her became the floor beneath her. The red glow was now mere feet away. She ran along the groove with the web-like rock beams hanging in the air above her.

As she approached the hole in the floor she could see the red glow flicker and dance. Winter nights in front of a fire came to mind. She began to shiver. What had she come all this way to find? She looked tentatively into the pit. Her shivers multiplied, threatening to shake her apart.

Ares was there, lying on his side. He faced away from her, motionless, at the bottom of a clear bubble. The bubble was engulfed in flames.

She squeezed her eyes shut, too late to stop the tears, and willed for her mind to hold together. Her body had already passed out of the realm of feeling as her knees smacked against hard granite next to the hole. She tried to blink the tears away so she could see. She had to think.

The odorless flames flared up to the top of the pit. If she went into the cell she would burn. All she had with her was Artemis's bow and arrows. She had nothing she could lower to him even if he was conscious.

Maybe she could break the bubble. But would that burn him? Or put the flames out?

If he caught fire there would be no way for her to help him. She would have to stand there and watch him burn. Not dying, just burning. But if breaking the bubble put the flames out, she could get to him.

With trembling hands she reached back for the bow. She nocked a shaky arrow, still wet with Chimera blood, and took cautious aim for the far edge of the clear bubble. She let her energy flow into the weapon. The arrow steadied. She pulled back, the muscles in her forearm tensing. She kept her sights on the exact furthest spot of the bubble from Ares and hoped the bow would be true to form and not miss its target.

She let her fingers go. The arrow seemed to leave the bow in slow motion, reflecting the red fire on its silver surface as it flew. At the same time Ares's body shifted beneath the flames. He rolled and looked up at her. His face was covered in yellowing bruises, but his eyes were wide and obviously lucid.

Her smile was instant. Relief flooded through her in a warm wave. His look matched hers but was quickly replaced by wide eyes and a gasp she could see but not hear. His hands shot up in a defensive position, as if to ward off a demon.

Her eyes widened with fear as she saw his reaction. She had chosen wrong. The fire would continue to burn. *He* would burn.

The arrow struck. Hit its mark square. The bubble shattered and disappeared. She waited to hear him scream. But there was no sound at all. The fire had gone out. Thick tendrils of acrid black smoke wafted up out of the cell past her and into the large sphere above.

She felt the rumble at the same instant she heard Ares yell for her. "Ruby!" He looked beyond her, to the top of the sphere. She turned.

The dark tendrils of smoke gathered against the ceiling, so many stories above, coalescing into a dark form. She felt a chill and looked back to Ares.

He held out his hand. "Jump."

She did it before she could think. And then she was on the shaking cell floor with him.

Her attention was drawn back up to the top of the sphere with her next heartbeat. The black smoke-shape was still forming. She could make out a long neck, a large body, and a massive head. A dragon.

The rumbling continued, like an earthquake. Horny protrusions grew like storm clouds on the dragon's head. It grinned at them with pointed, razor-sharp teeth.

Ruby swallowed dry, gulping down fear.

Ares grabbed her arm. His energy flowed into her.

"Get ready to run," he said.

Where? She tore her eyes away from the increasingly hideous smoke dragon above them. The stone cell was cracking and breaking. The dragon was now too large for the sphere. It reared up and exploded out of the granite above its head. She felt a pull on her arm as Ares dragged her through a growing crack in the wall of the cell.

They were in the large room again. Chimeras were everywhere. Ruby held the bow and reached for her arrows, but the guards took no notice of her and Ares. They watched in stunned silence as the black smoke dragon drifted up to touch the ceiling of the room.

Ares pulled on her. As they crossed under one of the massive stone archways, Ruby looked back and wished she hadn't. The dragon reared up, sucked in what might have been its first breath, and let loose a long, stretching fireball directed right at them. She turned her head, not wanting to see, and ran level with Ares.

Ares turned to look at her. She saw fear light in his eyes.

He swung her close and slammed her into him with enough force to knock the wind from her lungs.

She looked at him, dazed.

He pulled her along at a breakneck pace.

Her mind was a confused mix of pain, where Ares had thrown her against his body, and raw terror.

୭ଇୡ

Ruby and Ares ran along the many branching corridors, rounding corners close and fast. All Ruby could hear was her own heartbeat and the thud of their shoes on the stone floor of Hades's dungeon maze. She dared not look back to see if the dragon or the Chimeras were following. She simply held Ares's hand and tried to keep up.

Ares glanced back, his eyes tight and searching. What he saw, or didn't see, gave him hope and he slowed enough for her to gulp in a swallow of air.

A few turns later he stopped and scanned the right side of her body; the side that still ached from where he had crashed into her.

Her lungs recovered quickly thanks to so many hours of biking, but now she felt something new. Her right lower back and hip felt cold and hot at the same time. A moment later true pain set in.

Ares looked at her face. "You're burned pretty badly." His voice was husky and deep.

She tried to look, but he put his hand on her face and pulled her focus back to him. "We have to get out of here. How did you get in?"

"I ..." she stammered. His T-shirt was ripped and dirty, his hands rough and scabbed. She looked from his hands to his bruised face. He shook his head in a way that meant, *don't worry*. He kissed her and whispered, "Ruby, think."

"I came down some abandoned steps," she said in a rush. "That was so long ago, or so far away, or just too many turns past." She glanced around, but all the gray-walled corridors looked the same. "I don't know. I don't even know which way we left the big room with the stone sphere."

She thought back; the sphere; the Chimeras; Adelpha and how she drew the lizard-guard away. Her eyes widened. "We have to pick a wall and stick to it."

The Chimera had said that to Adelpha, and she had heard the same thing once long ago. The way to solve a maze was to follow one wall to the end. "If we always keep a hand on the right wall we'll eventually get out."

The pain in Ruby's hip throbbed as they walked. It blotted out the nagging ache of thirst and hunger that had returned as the adrenaline of their escape drew off.

Ares didn't have his pack anymore. Hades had taken it. Their water was gone. So were Ares's sword, Pan's pipes, Eros's torch, and Hermes's winged sandals. She winced at the thought of losing the gods' most prized possessions. Her dry lips cracked with the movement.

Ares stopped in front of her, head cocked, listening. Then she heard it too. A distant grunt followed by a closer growl. Chimeras. They were on the move, and moving fast. It was only moments between hearing the first distant shuffles of paw or claw and the immediate sounds of bodies around the bend.

Ruby and Ares backed away down the passage, tripping over themselves. Ruby's hand lost contact with the right wall as she turned to run. The animal noises of the Chimeras kept coming. She and Ares made random turn after random turn.

He pulled her around the next bend and brought them both up flush with the wall of a short corridor. They pressed their backs against the cool rock. The Chimeras came into sight in the next moment. Ten or twelve in all.

They didn't look down the hall where Ares and Ruby stood, but rounded the next corner and were soon out of sight. Ares moved to peer around the bend, but came up short. His eyes darted to Ruby's and he shook his head.

She listened, hoping for a clue of whatever it was he saw. She heard nothing, saw nothing, but then … a scurrying, *quiet as a …*

She didn't get to finish the thought before she saw it. Not a mouse, but a rat: a rat with the large glowing eyes of a cat. Fangs poked out from the sides of its mouth, and its tail bent up and ended in a curved scorpion's stinger.

This Chimera was small, comical even, but Ruby knew it was no joke. She reached behind her, heedless of the noise she might make, and pulled the bow forward. The Chimera looked up at her and smiled a fangy rat smile as it darted away after its brothers, eager to report her and Ares.

Ruby nocked her arrow and let it fly. She skewered the creature and it let out a high-pitched squeal.

Ares's head jerked. He looked at her with wide eyes that settled into one raised eyebrow.

She bent to pick up her arrow with the Chimera still attached and scraped the length of it across the edge of the wall. The little beast dropped to the ground with a dull thud.

"I think we're clear."

◌◌

"Careful now," Ares whispered in her ear. "This is the most dangerous part."

What stood out the most about the end of the maze was how ordinary it was. Just another corridor among the hundreds they had walked through, but instead of another hallway there was a long staircase carved out of the same gray stone as everything else in the dungeon.

In the maze they could, and had, backtracked if they heard the Chimeras approaching. Once they started up the stairs they would be in the open with nowhere to go in a hurry.

They took the stairs two at a time. Near the top the steps beneath Ruby's feet were no longer dark-grey, but black and shiny. Obsidian. She kept her excitement in check.

In the first hallway at the top of the stairs her hope faltered. They were in a long obsidian corridor, similar to the seemingly endless granite ones they had left behind. Did the maze have more than one level?

She looked both ways down the hall, but neither view gave away anything about where it led. For no good reason she turned to the right, a habit now, and Ares followed.

They passed a window. Ruby saw a grassy area. It was the garden courtyard. They were in the palace, but still at the far end, near where she had met Adelpha. They neared an exit and snuck past a pair of guards looking out into the apple orchard.

Recessed doors marched down the hall on their left. Ares stopped to check one, to see where it led. The heavy wooden door opened with a low groan. It was dark inside, but Ruby could make out bulky shapes covered with cloth. She thought of what Adelpha said about Persephone needing storage. It amazed her how human gods could be.

They moved on, looking for stairs going up, looking for Hades or his guards, looking for Persephone.

A low rumble, feet marching, came from ahead of them. Ruby froze. Ares grabbed her arm and pulled her to the side against one of the recessed doors. She heard the quiet click of the door's latch and felt herself moving with Ares as the door swung open behind them.

The army rumbled closer. The ground shook. She saw a flash of red and gold as the mass swung around the corner, but what made her breath catch in her throat was the black robed figure leading them with his two-pronged fork in one hand. Hades.

Ruby and Ares fell back into darkness. Ruby's hip flared. She squelched a cry. Ares closed the door as the thunder of Hades's army was upon them.

Had they seen them? Would the door burst open with some crazy mixed-up beast pointing a spear at them? Would Hades take Ares away again?

The sound moved away. They were heading for the long flight of stairs Ruby and Ares had just come up. Ruby smiled, despite the agony in her hip. "He still thinks we're down there," she whispered.

TWENTY•NINE

RUBY AND ARES walked out the main entrance of the palace and looked up. Two flags hung at full-staff, one white, one black.

"She's here," Ruby said.

Ares nodded, his bruised face almost healed now.

They rushed back inside, trading stealth for speed. Hades and his army had gone to the dungeon looking for them. Time was of the essence.

They climbed the obsidian stairs up and up, to the next level and the next, until they were outside the throne room. Ruby went in first with their only weapon, Artemis's bow and arrow, nocked and ready to go. Ruby scanned the room and checked the corners and the walls behind her like Ares had told her to.

Persephone was there. She sat, not on her quartz throne, but at an ornate vanity that stood in the corner. She wore a flowing white nightgown and ran a silver brush through her long brown hair. She hummed softly. The room smelled sweet and flowery.

Persephone saw Ruby reflected in the mirror of the vanity. The brush and the humming stopped midstroke, midtune.

Ruby exhaled in frustration. While she and Ares had been running from a deadly smoke dragon and avoiding Hades's army of Chimeras, Persephone sat here in a dreamy state of post-coital bliss and brushed her hair. She was lucky they needed her so badly.

Ares strode to the goddess's cushioned stool and grabbed her by the arm. "Let's go."

Persephone's eyes darted to the two thrones. On the table was Hades's hourglass. The red sand had long since collected in the bottom. On the floor were Ares's sword and his pack. Next to the pack were Hermes's winged sandals, Pan's pipes, Eros's torch, and a full skin of water.

Ruby's throat contracted. The muscles in her neck tensed.

Ares picked up his weapon and attached the scabbard across his back while Ruby held her arrow trained on Persephone. When he finished he handed the water skin to Ruby and kept his eyes on the queen of the Underworld.

She ripped out the cork stopper and drank the sweet clean Olympic water down in gulps. Her stomach tightened. She tried to slow down, caught between her clenching throat, desperately dry, and her shriveled stomach that rolled with the shock of it.

Hades would soon realize she and Ares had escaped the dungeon. She took one final sip and handed the skin to Ares.

He emptied it in a few gulps, packed up the bag, and threw the pack over his shoulder.

"Come on." He reached for Persephone's arm again.

She looked at him but she didn't move. "Just give me a minute. I can't go like this."

"You'll have to," he said as he pulled the goddess to her feet and toward the door with Ruby close behind.

The Fields of Asphodel were as they always were: pleasant. Shades played croquet, ate hors d'oeuvres, and mingled. A ripple of murmurs and whispers started as Ruby, Ares, and Persephone made their way through the crowd. The queen of the Underworld didn't go anywhere in Hades without being noticed. Soon the whole party was abuzz.

"So much for any stealth we may have had," Ruby said to Ares.

"We have to move her along," he agreed.

Ares had been behind Persephone, making sure she didn't fall back. Now he moved to the front and pushed through the crowd. Persephone stopped walking and Ruby found herself in the position of having to motivate the goddess herself.

"Keep walking," she whispered close to Persephone's ear. She didn't want to let the shades around them know that Persephone was not leaving Hades entirely of her own free will. Ruby didn't know if shades would rise up and be violent, but if there was ever a cause they would fight for, Ruby knew Persephone was it, and a lot of them were armed.

Persephone walked faster. Ruby's singed hip flared with each step. Shades on both sides of the procession leaned in, trying to get a look at the queen. A few shades had tears in their eyes. Ruby wondered if this was the Underworld's winter, the rainy season, so to speak. Did they miss Persephone as much as Demeter and Hades did?

Ares stopped when they reached the Adamantine Gate. Cerberus would be on the other side with his three giant heads, snake mane, and cobra tail. Ruby trembled and wondered if he was as strict about who left Hades as he was about who came in. Either way he'd still want human flesh. They couldn't use their weapons against him or else—

"What if we fight him?" she asked. "Then the gate will close behind us."

Ares shook his head. "Hades can open it again."

"But it might slow him down, even for just a few minutes." Ruby reasoned.

"No," Persephone said. "Don't hurt Cerberus."

There was a loud uproar on the far side of the Fields of Asphodel. Iron tipped spears jostled along, pointing at the ceiling of Hades, as an army of Chimeras headed toward them.

Persephone didn't look at Ruby or Ares before she strolled out through the gate. The huge black dog came loping like a puppy out of his cave to meet her. Drool hung from all three sets of his massive jowls. The snakes on his mane moved excitedly from side to side. His cobra tail whipped around, eager to see the goddess.

He rolled onto his back and exposed his enormous belly to the queen of the Underworld. She petted his three giant heads in turn and scratched under each of his chins. With her other hand she waved Ruby and Ares through.

They entered Cerberus's lair at a near run. Ares's arm was locked around Ruby's. He was on the side nearest the big dog, ready to shield her if he could. There were few sounds here, just Persephone talking softly and the dog's contented, even breathing.

Ruby remembered the feeling of seeing Cerberus's huge black eye over her shoulder coming for her. She gripped Ares's arm and kept her eyes forward. She told herself that it would be better to be eaten, everything over in a minute, than to face Hades and his Chimeras for an eternity.

When they reached the far side of the cavern Ruby realized that Persephone had no reason to follow them. If she turned back to the Fields of Asphodel, Ares would have to follow her. What would the shades there do? The Chimeras? Hades?

But the goddess only glanced that way. She kissed Cerberus on one of his giant heads, stood, and walked to Ruby and Ares at a leisurely pace. Thankfully the goddess had a sense of duty.

Ruby's relief was cut short by the sounds of Hades's army drawing through the Fields of Asphodel. The trio walked quickly past the statues of the gods in their alcoves and down the stone tunnel that led to the bank of the Styx.

The river, with its thick, inky water, came into view. Ruby had pictured Charon waiting there on the shore, as if he would somehow know they needed to get back across the water quickly, but the shore of the Styx was empty. The ferryman of the dead was nowhere in sight.

Ares's eyes were focused on the thick bank of mist across the water. He smiled.

Ruby looked there too. Lantern light cut through the vapor, and then a faint red glow. Charon's red eyes coming to save them.

"Charon," Ares yelled. "We're in a hurry."

The ferryman slowed his pole pushing and peered at the shore where they stood. The red of his eyes intensified and then softened. He began talking, but not to Ares.

"Persephone? Is that you?" the ferryman's dark shape stood taller. His long pole reached for the bottom of the Styx with renewed vigor. "I thought it was getting late," he said in a rush. "I longed to see you."

Persephone smiled, as if she had come to the water's edge for a visit.

Ruby exhaled an annoyed breath. Was there one being in Hades who *wasn't* in love with Persephone?

Her annoyance was cut short by the echoing footfalls of Chimeras as they crossed through the large cavern of Cerberus's lair.

Charon's skiff seemed to move in slow motion, even as Charon's arms pistoned down more quickly.

The sound of marching came up the passage behind them. Ruby heard Hades's voice, mixed with the huffing and snorting sound of his beasts coming for them. "Ready your spears," he cried.

When the skiff, full of new shades, finally slid onto shore, Ares hurried forward. He picked up a young girl, set her on the ground, and turned to help the other new shades off the boat.

When the boat was empty Ruby jumped. *Let's go. Let's go.*

Charon was not in a hurry, though. He put out his bony hand to Persephone. She took it and smiled, shy and innocent.

"We've outstayed our welcome," Ares said. "Old friend, get us out of here."

The shuffling sound of animal hooves drew closer.

"I'll need your fare," Charon said, distracted. His eyes did not leave Persephone as she sat in the boat next to where he stood.

A shiver of panic ran through Ruby. The obolus. They had been in her pack with the Ambrosia Bars and the hardtack, eaten by Cerberus. She could now see Chimeras rounding the last bend of the hall to Hades. The king of the Underworld led them.

"Could we pay you next time?" Persephone asked, as calm as the Lethe. "I'd like to get back to my mother. She misses me so."

Charon's red eyes flicked to the passage where Hades's army was barreling down on them and then back to Persephone. He smiled. His hand reached up the push-pole for leverage. "Of course."

Ruby swayed as the boat slipped away into the water.

"Persephone!" Hades cried as he reached the shore with his army.

The goddess's face remained calm as she sang out, "My love! Wait for me. Don't choose another."

Ruby rolled her eyes.

"I'll be back soon," the goddess called. "Visit me at my mother's."

"Perseph—" Hades repeated his cry, but his voice was swallowed up by the heavy mists that hung over the Styx. The air was cold in an instant and the only light came from Charon's small lantern.

A pit rose in Ruby's stomach as the skiff approached the far side of the river. This, of all the things she had seen in Hades and even Tartarus, was the saddest of all; shades waiting listlessly on the shore of the Styx with no obol to pay Charon's fare, and no Persephone to beg mercy for them.

When the ferry docked Persephone lingered. Ruby watched as the queen of the Underworld let the ferryman of the dead kiss her hand.

A quiver of disgust ran through Ruby.

When Persephone joined Ruby and Ares on the path, she walked in the opposite direction Ruby expected her to.

"Where are you going?" Ares asked. "We can't disassociate with Ruby. And I'm not letting you out of my sight until we're on Olympus."

Persephone gave them an annoyed look that seemed to be reserved for the few people who weren't in love with her. "*You* can go that way if you want it to take all day. I'll meet you."

Ares gave her a hard stare. "Don't be cryptic."

"I mean, if you want to walk forever and still be thousands of miles from Olympus, then go that way."

"We have—" Ruby started, thinking of the winged sandals that would fly them to Olympus in an hour or so, but Ares stopped her.

"Show us your way," he said, though he did not relax his tense stance.

"Of course," the goddess said with a smile, her charms returning. She walked along the bank, with the Styx on her right, until they were out of sight of the waiting souls. She took a sharp left into a cave that was rocky and shadowed and began to climb up.

Ruby scanned the sheer face. "Rock climbing?" She looked at Ares. "Without ropes?"

"We'll do it together," he said.

She took hold of the rock and Ares stepped behind her. He pressed his warm body flat against her back. They climbed as one person with her tucked into the frame of his body, one tentative hold at a time. Her hip burned. She willed herself not to look down.

The rock topped out in a small cave not ten feet from a craggy opening. Ruby smelled grass, fresh air, and flowers. Earth.

Outside of the cave the bright light stabbed at her eyes. She shielded her face with her hands. On the ground before her was soft brown dirt, green grass, and in the small depressions of Persephone's footprints there were new spring flowers.

Tears filled her eyes without warning. Through her blurred vision she saw that they were on the side of a mountain, a mountain that looked out over more mountains to the east and the ocean to the west.

"The Olympics," she whispered. Her voice was choked. "We did it!"

A smile flickered across Ares lips but then died.

"Not yet."

THIRTY

RUBY WINCED at the pain in her hip as she and Ares ascended the golden steps of the Great Hall of Olympus. Persephone had gone off to see Demeter. Ruby and Ares were happy to let her go.

A large group of gods came down the main path toward them. Ruby had known the Seasons would spread the word of their arrival as soon as she, Ares, and Persephone had flown through the gates of Olympus.

The gods' faces were stoic. Ruby looked them over anxiously. She was eager for news of what had happened while they were away. She remembered the feel in the grove before she and Ares had left, like tightening guitar strings. She pictured the Cyclopes, and the gods that would side with Zeus, all gathering at the Great Hall.

But if a war had transpired on Olympus while they were gone, Ruby couldn't tell. The trees and plants were as pristine and as fragrant as ever. The abodes were intact, huge and imposing on the Olympic landscape.

The group of gods got closer to the Great Hall. Athena was there and Aphrodite. Ruby saw Hermes, Eros and Psyche, and Pan. These were the gods loyal to Ares. Behind them came a separate group: Hephaestus, Hestia, and Dionysus, the gods that would support Zeus and Hera.

Ares didn't look at the gods. He strode into the Great Hall.

Ruby hurried to keep up.

Ares passed the willow altar he had made for their wedding without a glance, and went through the archway with the two eagles holding lightning bolts in their talons.

Once they were in the garden Zeus was easy to find. He held a menacing-looking pair of pruning shears and clipped at a six-foot evergreen before him. If he knew they were there, he ignored them.

"It's time," Ares said.

"Yes," Zeus said without looking at them. "Spring has sprung, as they say." He continued to clip the tree. A large limb fell at his feet. "I'll alert your mother. She'll want to begin her preparations. She'll need a month, or…"

"Now," Ares commanded the king of the gods.

Ruby's throat was dry despite the water she had drunk in Hades's throne room. Her stomach growled.

Zeus glanced at her when he heard the sound and looked her up and down.

She knew she was filthy and that her clothes were singed. Ares's T-shirt was ragged, ripped, and dirty. She'd wanted to go to Athena's to clean up, but Ares had insisted that they not give Zeus any more time to plot against them.

"I'm afraid that's not possible," Zeus said. "We need time for—"

"Ganymede," Ares cut his father off with a shout that carried over the gathering Olympians in the garden around them.

Zeus's eyes shot to Ares's.

Ganymede came into the center of the garden and swept his shaggy blond hair out of his eyes.

"Bring us ambrosia and nectar," Ares said. His eyes did not leave Zeus's.

Ganymede looked to Zeus, but Zeus didn't break from Ares's gaze. The cupbearer scanned the group of gods. They remained silent. He left to do Ares's bidding.

Hera walked into the garden and pushed through the crowd. She looked at her husband and her son locked in a silent battle. She stood by Zeus's side. "Ares," she said. "Where have you been?"

Ruby wondered what Hera knew. Had she been in on the plan to stop the wedding?

Ares didn't answer his mother.

Ganymede walked into the garden with a tray. On it were a golden chalice and a silver bowl.

Ares's eyes broke away from Zeus to look at Ruby. He took a deep breath and smiled. Despite the pain in her hip, her hunger and thirst, Ruby smiled too.

"This is it," he said, serious now. "Your last moment to be human."

She had not thought of it like that. She had always thought of the future, of being a goddess, of being Ares's wife.

"It's a lot to ask," he said. "Maybe it's too much." He shrugged and shook his head. "I'm asking you to do it anyway."

"I'd do anything for you, Ares. I thought that was pretty clear by now," she said with raised eyebrows.

He gave her a sly smile, like he was trying not to laugh. She wished he had laughed, though. She wanted to be happy.

Ares took the gold chalice from Ganymede and handed it to her. "Nectar," he said. "The drink of the gods."

Ruby took the cup. The metal was surprisingly warm against her hand. She looked in at the red liquid. It smelled vaguely like cinnamon and cloves. Her throat convulsed, eager for any moisture.

She put her lips to the warm metal and drank. Subtle spicy warmth spread into her mouth. Her thirst was slaked with a single sip. A hot, uncomfortable tingle traveled through her entire body, from her scalp to her toes. The heat took her breath away and she gasped.

Ares's eyes were wide and eager as he took the goblet from her. "Now the food of the gods."

Her body still felt hot as he brought a spoon of the pearlescent golden ambrosia to her lips. It was cool, sweet like honey, rich like wine, and oddly light.

The coolness from the ambrosia mixed with warmth from the nectar. The two mingled, filling her cells, awakening her flesh, and galvanizing her will. Her hip no longer throbbed. Her hunger dulled.

Images and voices came to her. She didn't know if her eyes were open or closed, but she saw people. They chattered over one another in her head. Dark became light. Babies were born. Girls became women. Boys became men. Virgins became lovers. Women became mothers. Men became fathers. War passed to peace. Hate passed to love. People grew old. People died.

She felt people's dreams and their hopes and their desires. She felt their fears and their doubts. She saw people change their lives and she saw people living in the pain of fear and stagnation.

The images came faster and faster until they were a blur. Spirals danced in her vision. The images changed from people to caterpillars forming cocoons and releasing as butterflies. Over and over. She felt pulled in opposite directions. Her emotions ran like a rollercoaster; from the highest high of hope to the lowest low of fear.

Her body shook, slowly at first, then violently, in fits. Her legs gave way. Someone caught her. She opened her eyes, as if from a dream, but she felt awake and energetic. Ares was there, as she knew he would be, holding her and smiling.

He pulled her up to her feet. She was only vaguely aware that all of Olympus was watching.

"It's done," he said. His eyes searched hers and she could see his rapid breathing. "What did you see?"

"I saw everything," she whispered. Then stronger, "Life and death, love and hate, innocence and passion." Her eyes narrowed. "Spirals." She laughed. "And butterflies."

It all clicked into place.

"I saw the boundaries that hold people in and the possibilities when they break free. I heard people. I *felt* them. *Millions* of people, *changing*. Some were excited. Some were afraid. I can still feel them." She narrowed her eyes. "But it's distant."

"Ruby," he held her gaze and raised his voice so that everyone could here. "The goddess of boundaries. The goddess of transformation. The goddess of dreams and aspirations."

Yes. That felt right.

Ares's smile faded and he turned to Zeus and Hera. "We're ready," he said.

Zeus looked like he might say something, but Ares didn't give him a chance.

"You swore it," he said.

Hera looked at her son and then at Ruby. The corners of her mouth turned up ever so slightly and her green eyes softened around the edges.

Ruby smiled back.

Aphrodite pushed her way through the crowd with the wedding tray she, Athena, and Ruby had made up so long ago. She took the olive branch crowns and placed one on each of their heads. Ruby smiled at Ares with cream-colored olive blossoms nestled in his black curls.

Aphrodite handed Zeus the white silk ribbon of *hieros gamos*.

"Sacred Marriage," Zeus said, reluctantly, as he held up the wide ribbon. "The union of gods. The binding of two souls."

Ares took Ruby's hands in his and she felt what he must have always felt when they touched. The rest of Olympus faded into the background and the subtle feeling of humans on Earth lessened. She felt their energy meet and flow together in a circuit they completed with their hands.

She fixed her eyes on Ares's as Zeus wrapped their clasped hands with the ribbon that would bind their bodies, their vows, and their souls.

Zeus gave Ares a curt nod when it was done.

She expected the simple rote words of *hieros gamos* they had each memorized, but instead Ares said, "Ruby, my love. We have been separate streams." His voice was soft and quiet, as though he was speaking only to her. "From this day on our lives will flow out together as one great river. I promise to love you, Ruby, every day, for all eternity. I promise to move in your currents and bask in your eddies, and to float with you forever."

Ruby blinked back tears.

He took up a more formal tone and continued with the words of *hieros gamos*. "In the name of the Great God Zeus and the Great Goddess Hera I welcome you Ruby, the goddess of transformation, as my eternal wife."

She bit her lip to control her overwhelming emotions. It was her turn to say the vows. She closed her eyes. A tear slipped down her cheek. She felt the solidity of Ares's hands in hers. She looked at him again and took a deep breath.

"I, Ruby, take you Ares, the god of war, for my husband, to have and to hold from this day forward, for better or for worse, though there will be no sickness, only health, and there will be no poorer, only wealth; from this day forward and for all eternity."

Ares smiled, though there was a bewildered look on his face. She realized he had never heard modern wedding vows.

"In the name of the Great God Zeus and the Great Goddess Hera," she continued. "I welcome you Ares, the god of war, as my eternal husband."

A plain iron band that matched Ruby's lay on the silver tray. Hephaestus had made it for her months ago.

Ares mouth went slack when he saw it. He followed her hands with his eyes as she put the ring on his finger above the ribbon that bound them. "Let this ring be a symbol of our love, and our strength."

"Your souls are now bound by your promise," Zeus said. "But *hieros gamos* only begins with a vow. It is completed with a physical act. When male and female become one, then the two will be linked forever."

Aphrodite came forward. "We mark Ruby's moving from human to goddess and from maiden to wife in the old way." She held up the silver scissors from the tray. "She is made anew."

Ruby tensed when she felt the goddess take her long hair in her hands. Her eyes widened as she heard, more than felt, the shears snip the hair in a few jagged cuts at the nape of her neck. She reached up and touched the frayed ends that now skimmed the line of her jaw. She glanced at Ares. He smiled and she saw that he had known, of course.

Hera placed her hand over Ruby's and Ares's bound ones and said, "I bless this couple. As I have blessed all those who are truly in love and truly dedicated to one another." She looked at Ares and then to Ruby. She smiled a genuine smile. "May you bring forth many sons."

Ruby's smile fell, not at Hera's old-fashioned desire for boys, but at the reminder of the curse Kronos put on her and Ares's sons.

Ares's face was serene and content. He was not worried.

Hera's gaze held no malice. It was meant as a blessing. A gift.

Ares kissed her in front of all the gods of Olympus. Ruby let herself relax.

☙❧

"The party will go on for days," Athena said to Ruby as Pan played his pipes across the Great Hall while the muses sang and danced. Ruby was happy they had recovered all the gods' belongings from Hades's throne room.

Ruby dug her spoon along the bottom of her goblet of ambrosia. It was no longer cool to her now immortal tongue, but it was still sweet, and rich, and light. She put the empty cup on the table next to the wedding crowns and took a sip of the full-bodied wine Dionysus had created in honor of her and Ares's marriage.

Ruby's hip was completely healed. She and Ares had danced until her feet were blistered, which was much longer than she could have danced on Earth, and the blisters had already mended.

Ares sat next to her. His arm was draped over her shoulders. He wore a clean white chiton. She wore a white silk peplos with silver trim and a silver band of butterflies in her now much shorter hair. Once she learned to control her molecules she would be able to grow her hair out in a moment. For now she liked the look. She was different and it showed.

The voices and energy she felt from Earth chattered in the background of her mind. Occasionally they broke into her consciousness and sent a jolt of excitement or fear through her. Athena assured her that she would learn to block it. She hadn't gained Ares's level of connection to humans, luckily.

Ruby looked around the room and thought of her father. She had always assumed he would be at her wedding. He would give her away and they would dance together. Instead she and Ares sat at a table with Aphrodite, Athena, Eros, and Psyche. Hermes and Pan joined them as the Muses collapsed into their chairs at the table next to them.

Ares finished the story he was telling, "… Cerberus couldn't care less that I was trying to get a tune out of those blasted pipes. It was the ambrosia in Ruby's pack he wanted." The table erupted in laughter.

Ruby smiled and shifted the silver bow that leaned against her chair. Artemis had given the bow to her as a present, not for the wedding—the goddess of the hunt was not that sentimental—but after hearing from Ares about Ruby's abilities with it.

Ares took his arm from around Ruby. He became serious and leaned in toward the center of the table. "What happened after we left? There is peace among the gods, obviously, but how?"

To Ruby it was as if nothing had happened at all. Olympus was as serene as ever.

"Zeus called those who would support him against you: Poseidon, the Cyclopes, Hephaestus, and the others," Athena said. "But if they were going after you, we were ready to stop them."

Fierce loyalty jumped into Ruby's heart.

"Zeus had been expecting a fight," Aphrodite said. "He didn't get as much support as he wanted, but he was willing to take us on. It was Apollo who ended it before it started."

Ruby's eyes shot across the room to Apollo. Zeus, Hera, and most of the older generation of Olympians had left the party early. Apollo sat alone at the Table of the Twelve. His eyes were fixed on the white tablecloth before him.

"Apollo told Zeus we should have never gone to Earth," Athena said. "He said it was all a mistake. He said he would never return. He swore it by the Styx."

What? Ruby was stunned Apollo would do that. "What about you?" she asked Athena.

"Me too," Athena said with a downward nod. "I swore too. We all did."

"It was a long time coming, Ruby," Aphrodite said, heading off any blame. "It couldn't last forever. No one wants war among the gods. Zeus is king." The green-eyed goddess smiled, and then glanced at Athena so quickly Ruby almost missed it.

"What else?" Ruby asked, feeling like there was more they weren't saying.

Aphrodite shook her head. "We got you in the bargain, anyway."

Ruby's forehead pinched together. She hoped they hadn't paid too high a price.

∽ଉ୧ଡ଼

Ruby looked around the room in Ares's abode, *their* abode. It was the room she had come to think of as the front room, the room where she and Ares had eaten dinner her first night on Olympus, the room with the dog tapestries, and the ruby and diamond chess table.

She had gotten everything she truly wanted: she had Ares. Her heart tightened when she thought about what Apollo and Athena, and everyone else, had given up for them.

Ares poured two goblets of nectar and handed one to her. It was their wedding night. She decided to save her regrets for tomorrow.

He raised his goblet. "To the goddess of boundaries. The goddess of transformation. The goddess of dreams and aspiration." He paused. "To the goddess Ruby."

She smirked. It was going to take a while to get used to that one.

"To us," she agreed with a smile, and clinked her golden goblet with his.

She took a sip of the spicy liquid. Ares reached for her cup, put it on the table, and took her face in both his hands. His eager kisses took her breath away.

He pulled at her peplos and she at his chiton as he picked her up and carried her out of the room and across the huge entranceway. She was lost in his kisses when he hurried up the curving stairs and into the bedroom she had chosen for them.

He laid her on the crisp cool bedspread and hovered over her with all the gravity of the god of war in his eyes; blue, bold, luminescent. His olive skin was flushed around his bare neck and chest.

"I love you," he whispered over and over; across her hot skin, into her short hair, between their parted lips.

When his hard body met with hers she felt the binding of *hieros gamos* as the wholeness they had always shared annealed and deepened. Their passion swelled, and broke, and swallowed them whole.

And Ruby, the goddess of boundaries, crossed over.

END OF BOOK ONE

Thank you for reading *The Immortal Game*. Please consider writing a review on Amazon, Good Reads, Barnes and Noble, or your favorite book buying website.

I love to connect with readers. You can find me at:

joannahmiley.com

And on these social media sites:

Facebook.com/joannahmileyauthor
Twitter.com/joannahmiley
Google Plus
Pinterest.com/joannahmiley
(where you can see pins that inspired some of the people and places in this story)

MOST IMPORTANTLY, please share this book with a friend. Because we could all use a good story!

Acknowledgements

Special thanks to my husband Fran and to our children Olivia and Corbin, for their constant love and encouragement; to my sister Hope Corbin, for showing me every day what it means to never give up on your dreams; to my brother-in-law and developmental editor Drew Cherry, who makes me laugh at the same time he tells me to write that part again; and to my parents Suzan Kohn, and Will and Rori Corbin, for teaching me I could grow up to be anything I wanted.

Thanks to my dear friend Melissa Fenn, who patiently listened to me talk about Ruby and Ash since the very beginning, and to all my other first-readers: Dayl Phillip, Debbie Ritter, Sabine Sloley, Selah Tay-Song, Wanda George, Betsy Oppelt, Mary Melloh, Stacey Killian, Laura Osterloh (and a good portion of her book club).

Thanks to The Private Writer's Group, for their incredible talent with story; and to the Upstart Crows Writer's Association, for their expertise in everything about books that *isn't* writing the story.

Thanks also, to the histology crew at NWP for listening to me talk books in the wee hours of the morning, and to Tom Klein—AKA: Super Geek—who saved Ash and Ruby in their darkest hour, yes, when the computer crashed.

And thanks to everyone who reads this book! You are as much a part of the tale as the writer and the characters. The story lives in all of us.

ABOUT THE AUTHOR

Joannah lives in northwest Washington State with her husband, two awesome teenagers, and a black dog that sheds relentlessly on her white furniture.

When not writing, Joannah likes to read, spend time with her family, and take long walks in nature.